THE SALVATION OF INNOCENCE

THE SALVATION OF INNOCENCE

A BRIDGE OF MAGIC NOVEL

Robert E. Balsley Jr.

Illustrations in Collaboration with Jim and Shelley Charles

Copyright © 2015 Robert E. Balsley Jr.
Illustrated by Jim Charles
Illustrated by Shelley Charles
All rights reserved.

ISBN: 1512240141
ISBN 13: 9781512240146
Library of Congress Control Number: 2015908130
CreateSpace Independent Publishing Platform
North Charleston, South Carolina

THE BRIDGE OF MAGIC

The Salvation of Innocence

The Struggle for Innocence (Forthcoming)

DEDICATION

I've chosen to dedicate this book to three people. First and foremost this book is dedicated to my wife, Rhonda. Her never-ending strength of conviction in my abilities as a writer always lifted me up during the times I was ready to stop. That we are our own worst critics is a universal truth. There were many times when I would think about all the books I have read over the years and wonder how I could ever expect my book to grace the same bookshelf as Terry Goodkind, David Eddings, Stephen King, Dean Koontz, and all the other authors I've so frequently read. Her steadfast insistence, however, gave me the will to continue when I thought I was doomed to embarrassment and failure. In many respects this book is a tribute to her belief in me.

Secondly I dedicate this book to Shelley and Jim Charles, two very good friends and the inspiration, the role-model, for the principle characters of Kristen and Tangus. Whenever we are together I see their mutual interaction and love for each other. I also see their ability to extend beyond their interpersonal world of two and easily move into a world where they affect other people's lives - family, friends, co-workers, even strangers - in such a tremendous way. They too have been very instrumental in the completion of the story I have told. I hope I have been able to aptly emulate and capture their character in words.

SPECIAL ACKNOWLEDGEMENT

I'd like to thank a dear friend, Mark White, for all the effort he put into editing my book. The things he knows about grammar and the written word amazes me. Writing this book was as much a learning experience for me as it was a platform to tell a story. My next book will be easier to write because I've gained so much knowledge with this one. For that I have Mark to thank.

ACKNOWLEDGEMENT

I've been playing Dungeons and Dragons for a quarter century. The current group I play in, of which Shelley, Jim, and Mark are part of, numbers eight, including myself. It was not always that way, however. The core group consisted of Jim Charles, Ken Oakley, David Deal, and Toby Briles. It was Ken and David who first introduced me to the magic of the game. Through the years, we have had many adventures together, killed many monsters, but mostly had fun. Nothing beats the camaraderie of goods friends laughing and enjoying each other's company. It was a storyline I developed for a game I created as Dungeon Master that is the basis for *The Salvation of Innocence*. Many of the characters in the book are based upon their personalities in the game. So here's to my D&D group of Ken Oakley, David Deal, Jim Charles, Shelley Charles,

Mark White, Annette Potter, and Brian Potter. Toby Briles has relocated, but will always have a place at our table. Salute!

IN MEMORIAM

Brooke Annessa Achemire (nee Oakley)

We lost Ken's youngest daughter, Brooke, in 2004. From a very early age Brooke watched as we played Dungeons and Dragons until her father had judged her old enough to participate. From that point forward, she never missed a session, never failed to impress me with her quick wit, her ready smile, and her intelligent approach to the game. As she grew into a beautiful, young lady, it didn't take me long to understand that this wasn't just a kid who's player character would quickly die by my hand as the Dungeon Master. All of us who knew Brooke love and miss her. I hope she finds this book to be a good read.

TABLE OF CONTENTS

Forward	xiii
Prologue	xix
Chapter 1	1
Chapter 2	13
Chapter 3	53
Chapter 4	76
Chapter 5	108
Chapter 6	126
Chapter 7	148
Chapter 8	166
Chapter 9	187
Chapter 10	205
Chapter 11	222
Chapter 12	241
Chapter 13	258
Chapter 14	276
Chapter 15	287
Chapter 16	303
Chapter 17	320
Epilogue	347

FORWARD

From the Book of the Unveiled:

Empath: An extraordinary group of healers unique to the elven controlled city of Elanesse and believed to have the power to control the thoughts of another mortal being. As the empaths grew in prominence, fear of their rumored mind control abilities gave rise to suspicion and civil unrest. The elven lords of the city finally declared empaths outlaw and issued orders for their systematic capture and execution. Because the accepted truth was no magical spell could guard against the empath ability to control thoughts, the clerics of Elanesse devised powerful magic to ward against this ability. This magic also gave those who sought the empath the means by which the empath could be tracked. This magic, known as the Purge, was designed to be wielded by all willing rangers in Elanesse and the surrounding Forest of the Fey, for it was the rangers who were the enforcers of the law, and as such legal executioners. All empaths discovered within city limits were put to the sword. No quarter was given. Any empaths who escaped this slaughter were methodically hunted down by elven rangers and destroyed.

The goddess Aurora, to whom many rangers owed allegiance, did not favor her followers being used as executioners. Aurora, however, could not force her rangers to ignore the law of their mortal masters, nor could she stop the magic that allowed her rangers to be the instruments of this horrific slaughter. Other than making participating rangers outcast, there was little she could do to prevent the carnage. Mortals had a right to govern their own affairs. Althaya, the goddess of healing and the immortal champion of the empath, was just as helpless. She could only provide succor whenever possible and ensure the souls of the doomed empaths found eternal rest.

Unknown to the elven overlords of Elanesse, the empath ability often skipped multiple generations. Thus, while all known active empaths were murdered, the bloodline of the empath may not have been completely exterminated. This has never been proven, however, since there have been no reports of the existence of empaths for over three thousand years. The level of involvement, if any, played by the higher powers in this mystery is unknown.

The true power of an empath: The empath does not control thoughts. The empath is attuned to what people feel emotionally, love and hate being the two strongest. Hate can kill an empath. It was reported that many of the empaths killed in the Purge were so overwhelmed by the feeling of hatred emanating from their ranger executioners they died before suffering physical harm. While hate can kill, love can serve to protect the empath. For this reason, empaths were never alone during their childhood. To be so in the world would mean death. Their protection came from a bond that was forged with another who has a strong emotional attachment to the empath. This was usually the mother. It was only after the empath matured into an adult were they be able to thrive on their own, having by then developed sufficient internal coping mechanisms against pure emotions.

Empaths can also sense the state of the soul. They can feel good as well as evil. No evil deed or intent can escape the detection of the empath. But this ability made them a target of unnatural evil such as the undead and demonic forces.

The empaths greatest ability, however, is their natural aptitude for healing. They do this by taking the injury or disease upon themselves and allowing the empath power within to heal their own mortal body. Empaths freely sacrifice themselves for others if the need is great. This healing ability has one significant benefit for the empath. It gives them an unusually long life span. It has been rumored that the empath and an elf age at the same pace.

Author Unknown

ROBERT E. BALSLEY JR.

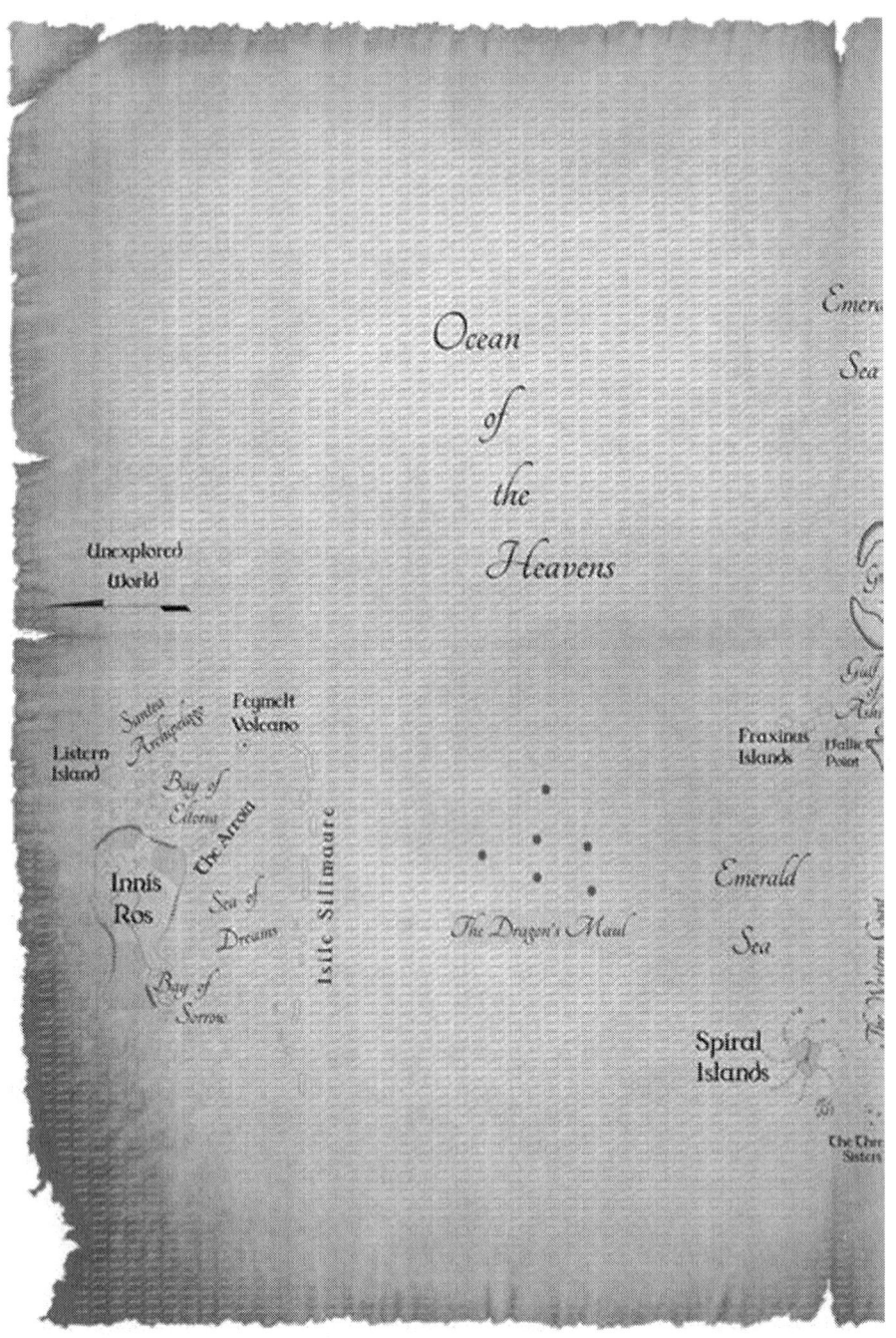

THE SALVATION OF INNOCENCE

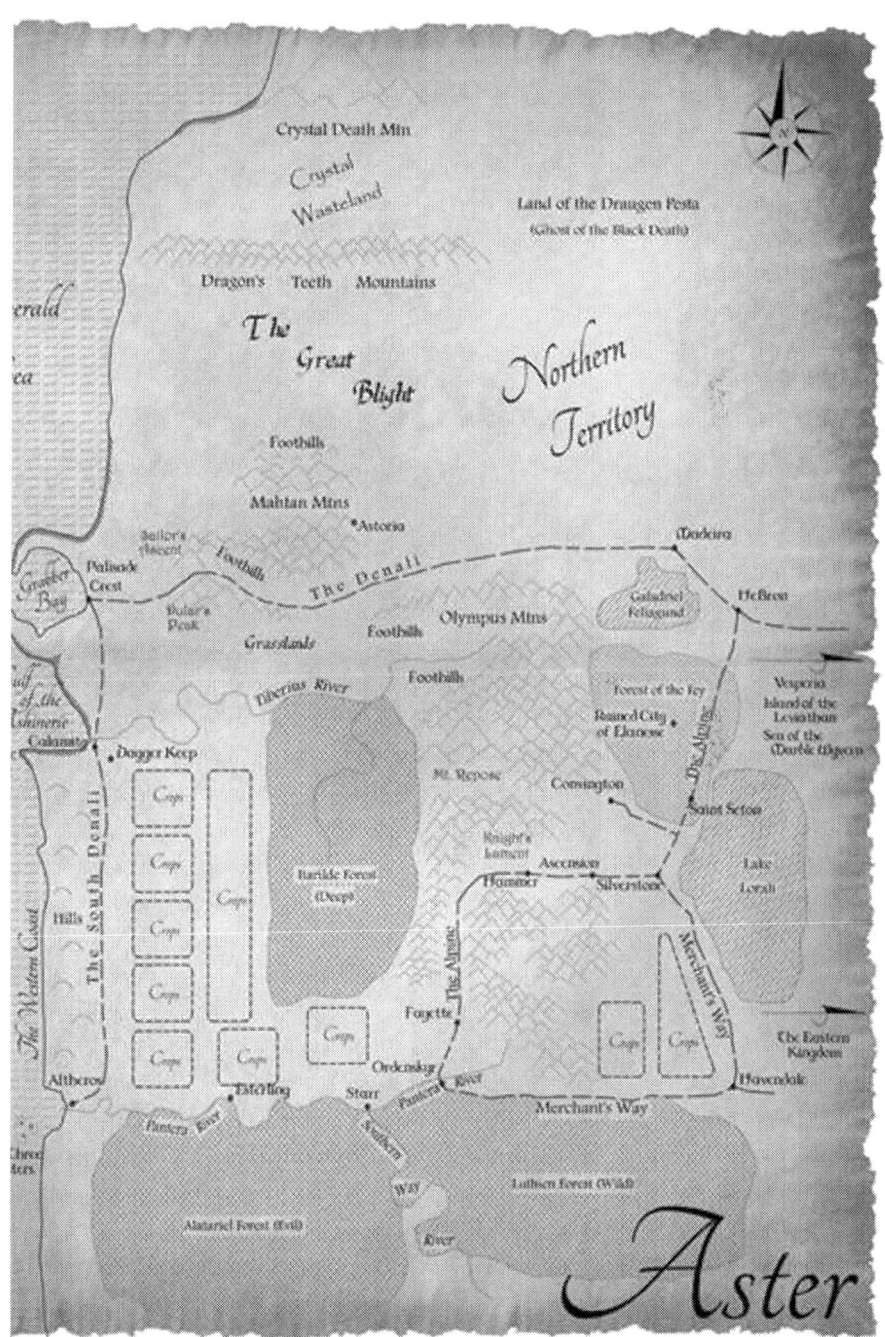

PROLOGUE

Elanesse

(3,127 Years Ago)

Good shall never perish as long as the light of innocence illuminates the way.

— *Book of the Unveiled*

The old lady patiently sat at a table in her small herbal shop smoking a pipe of tobacco and waiting for a customer, a young woman. It was very late in the evening, so much so that the other gypsy shops around hers had closed hours ago. This was by necessity, for in the Gypsy Quarter of Elanesse there was no sheriff, no ranger, to protect its citizens. Law was oftentimes served by the revenge of individual families for deeds already done rather than any attempt to stop crime before it actually occurred. The elves of Elanesse, while suffering humans within their midst, never made any serious attempt to establish or maintain law amongst the humans. They were left on their own, with stern warnings that if they ever got out of control they would be swiftly evicted from the city. So went elven justice. As a result of this inattention, however, evil thrived in the back alleys and the other dark places that frequent the Gypsy Quarter. Despite the dangers, however, the old lady's shop was only open during the night.

The customer she was expecting had a great need for the healing concoction the old lady mixed and now held in her hands. It would bring a small fortune in silver from the right buyer, but the payment that would be made tonight for this remedy would be worth far more than a few silver pieces. A slight smile escaped the old lady's face, revealing teeth as sharp as daggers, revealing the vampyre she was. She had been looking for an opportunity like this for a long time. True innocence in the gypsy ghetto is rare. The old lady couldn't help but to cackle in anticipation.

Immediately before her customer entered the small shop, the old lady could smell blood, young, vital, intoxicating. Pretending nonchalance, the old lady rose from her table and turned her back to the door as a young woman entered, pretending indifference lest she give away her craving to devour.

"Please forgive my tardiness, Madam Polina. I…I could not find someone to watch over my Emmy."

Emmy! The innocence Polina so desired, her blood would be like nectar. Composing herself, Polina turned and looked intently into the other woman's eyes. "You left your child alone?"

"I had no choice. As you already know, she is very sick and only the medicine we talked about will save her. It will save her, won't it?" the woman replied.

The old lady nodded and held up the medicine packet. "Yes Angela. From the description of the symptoms you gave me, I believe this will work. Do you have the payment we agreed upon?"

Angela Clearwater turned away from Polina's stare. "I could not come up with all of it," she said as she set a bag filled with coins down on the table.

"We agreed on thirty pieces of silver. Surely you believe your daughter is worth that."

"What? Of course I do." Angela said. "Emmy is everything to me. Please, I have twenty-five silver pieces. I'll do anything you want to work off the remainder. Clean your store, mend your clothes, or cook your food. Anything! Would you deny my Emmy her life for five silver pieces?"

Polina shook her head. "No dear, of course I don't wish to see harm come to her. We'll decide how you will make up the difference at another time. First you must see to the health of your precious daughter."

Angela sighed in relief. "Thank you so much, Madam Polina. I will repay your trust, I promise."

"Of course you will. Now here, take the medicine and run home. It's late and your daughter should not be left alone any longer than necessary," Polina said as she handed Angela the packet of medicine.

As Angela took the packet, she suddenly grabbed Polina's hand and kissed it before Polina could snatch it away. The hand was cold and lifeless, but Angela, in her relief, did not notice. "I am in your debt. I will come back in a few days and we can discuss how the final payment is to be made."

As Angela rushed out the door, Polina, momentarily stunned, sat down at the table and considered what was revealed in that simple kiss. Of course Polina sensed the blood running through Angela's veins, blood that she very much wanted to consume. But there was also something else, something sublime, hidden, in Angela's touch. At that moment Polina made a decision. She whispered, "You will reward me handsomely."

It was to be a course of action that would affect destinies across millennia.

A young man exited from a back room in the herb shop just as Angela was leaving. He was an albino. He had no color pigmentation in his hair or skin and his eyes were deep pink with black irises which matched the malignancy of his soul. With impossible speed he glided over to the door just vacated by Angela, stopping to carefully draw back a tattered curtain covering the small window in the door and watching Angela's fast-retreating back. Soon the night would swallow her, but that made no difference. He had caught her scent.

Looking to Polina, he nodded and said, "I will be able to track her to the innocent. She is mine now. After I am done, I will bring the innocent to you as we have planned."

Polina held up her hand. "Wait, Lukas. I have changed my mind."

"I need to feed! Her scent is intoxicating!" Lukas said as he continued to stare into the darkness that had swallowed up Angela.

"You will do as I say." Polina replied calmly but with her complete authority emanating from those simple words. She knew that if she did not bring Lukas back from his craving, she might miss a golden opportunity to add to the coven. The girl, Angela, was strong. Polina sensed that strength when the girl foolishly kissed her hand. But there was more. Polina's greatest wish, the one thing she would move heaven and earth to attain, the one thing left to her that was still mortal, was to have a daughter. In Angela, Polina saw that possibility. "You will have your meal, Lukas, but it will not be the woman."

"Then who will it be, Polina? Tell me, for no other will taste as sweet, as delicious as Angela. You promised her to me!" Lukas heatedly repeated his appeal to his mistress as he turned to angrily stare at her.

"I will give you the innocent," Polina responded, knowing that would get his full attention.

That threw Lukas off-balance. "But I thought the innocent was yours to use, that she was your fountain of youth? Her blood will make you young again," he said.

"My dear Lukas, wherever did you ever get such an idea?" Polina asked.

"I hear things, in the taverns and on the streets," Lukas said. "Bards tell great stories about the vampyre, stories to terrify their patrons. I get more information from them than I have ever received from you. I listen because I want to know what I am and what I have become since you changed me. You never explain things!"

"The parasite you host knows all these things, Lukas. In time, it will share with you what you are so curious about. In time, all your questions will be answered. For now, however, just let the parasite guide you. But YOU WILL follow my orders. Is that clearly understood?"

THE SALVATION OF INNOCENCE

"Yes mistress, please forgive me. But the innocent…?"

Polina frowned. "You would do well not to listen so much to mortal tales of the vampyre, Lukas," she said. "Any talk about the blood of an innocent making the vampyre young again is legend. It is a legend perpetuated by narrow minded people to explain what they don't understand. We live thousands of years…the parasite within us makes it so at the cost of our soul. But our physical bodies still age, albeit much slower. I am three thousand years old, but there is no elixir of beauty for me."

Polina walked the short distance to the door and stood in front of Lukas, allowing the strength of her power to wash over him. "Now listen to me, dear Lukas. Take Angela with a simple bite. That will spread the parasite into her. Once done, she will not be able to resist your command. Have her take you to her daughter. When you have the innocent and have given her the medicine to heal her of her affliction, take both to the vault and return to me. We will wait until tomorrow evening. Twenty four hours should be time enough for the parasite to gain complete control. Be sure to chain them, though. It is best to take no chances."

"And then?" Lukas asked.

"I must establish my dominion over Angela and her parasite before I trust her to be part of our coven. Once I have accomplished that, you may have the innocent. But not until then, do you hear me! When you die, you soul is eternally damned. But if you move to eat before I command, you will face that damnation much sooner than expected. Understand!" Polina warned.

Lukas understood that he really had no choice. He knew the threat against his life could easily be carried out by Polina. The parasite within him knew it would be many years before he was strong enough to wrest control of the coven away from her. Besides, he was satisfied he would eat soon.

Lukas bowed his head slightly in supplication. "It will be as you command, Polina."

Polina nodded and smiled. "Good. After the parasite within Angela changes her, I want Angela to watch as the life blood of her daughter is drained away. It will be the final test of her loyalty."

"The parasite within cares nothing for loyalty so why would you bother?" Lukas asked.

"You would be surprised, child, at what the parasite cares about. The parasite within you, like you yourself, is still very young and inexperienced. There is much you have to learn. And Lukas, you will never gain supremacy over me."

Lukas, surprised, stammered indignantly, "I would never seek to do such a thing!"

"Oh please. Don't deny it. You would not be a vampyre if you did not. We must get this done before the sun comes up. That part of vampyre legend is very true! Now go," Polina said, dismissing Lukas.

Lukas nodded and slipped out the door into the night, thinking about what Polina just said and wondering how she knew his innermost thoughts. No matter. He would do as she asked for now, but one day he would be powerful enough to dominate Polina. Then he'd be giving the orders!

Zindelo was drunk.

In Elanesse, strong gypsy males logged wood from the deep forests surrounding the city, and Zindelo was very strong. The pay Zindelo received from his elven employers was enough to keep him fed and housed in special barracks created for that purpose, however there was little left over for nonessential items such as drinking, gambling, or visiting one of the several brothels in the gypsy quarter.

The problem, as Zindelo saw it, was any leftover pay after mandatory expenses was not enough for all three. If you drank, you were not going to have enough left over for gambling or the brothels. If you gambled, you would probably lose more often than you would win, again leaving little funding for other pleasures. And with the prices the brothels charged, he was lucky if he could visit once a month. It was a never-ending problem that Zindelo thought about constantly, but one that he could never solve. Zindelo did reason, however, that if he drank enough, he would either forget or not care about the other two.

Hunched over in a deserted alley, Zindelo was throwing up once again. As he did so, he felt his bladder release and warm liquid run down his leg. The bottle he had bought was almost gone, but there was enough remaining for a couple of good long swallows. Soon he would return to the barracks for some sleep. He knew he would not feel very good in the morning, but once the axe was in his hands, he would soon forget about the aimless direction his life was taking. Work was exhilarating.

Staring at the blood in his latest bout of sickness and wondering what significance that might have, he heard someone pass close by. Looking up, he saw a shape hurrying down the alleyway. Even though the figure was wearing a cloak because of the night chill, Zindelo could see that it was a woman. She looked to be a very comely woman, but in Zindelo's current state, that did not matter. He started to think he would not have to pay for a trip to the brothel this month after all as he unsteadily moved to follow.

Zindelo never felt the cold hands frame both sides of his head. He never felt the wintry breath on the back of his neck. He never felt the unbelievable pressure as his head was abruptly turned, snapping his spine like kindling. Zindelo was dead before his fogged brain could register what was happening. The one who killed Zindelo, ending his lifelong quest to discover how drink, gambling and whoring could be attained at the same time on his meager salary, sprinted past Zindelo's body and was down the alleyway before it hit the ground. Later that night another logger in a drunken stupor tripped over Zindelo's still form. Grabbing the nearly empty bottle of alcohol lying close by, an unexpected treasure, he eagerly finished it and continued his blind stumble into the night.

What was left of Zindelo was picked up in the morning by garbage collectors. The body would be burned if no one claimed it within five days. Of course no one ever would. A report would be made to the elven authorities, but the single piece of parchment outlining the death of Zindelo was quickly filed away and never looked at again. And so goes life in the Gypsy Quarter of Elanesse.

Angela decided to run through the alleys that led to her home. She knew it was very dangerous, alleys shaded in night were never to be traveled lightly, but it was the quickest way. She must get the medicine to Emmy, for it was her only chance to break the hold the sickness had on her. As she ran, she angrily thought, "By the gods, why has her power not presented itself? Why is it still dormant? How simple it would be for Emmy to heal herself with her empath abilities!" Angela's mother had come into her heritage by the time she was five, and Emmy had just turned seven. When Angela thought of her mother, her breath caught, temporarily taken away as the feeling of loss threatened to overcome her. Angela's mother had not survived the Purge. She was ruthlessly hunted by one of Elanesse's many elven rangers and put to the sword. The elven city rulers, in their arrogance, refused to contemplate the good an empath could do. This conceit, in some respects, made them even more narrow-minded than humans. As Angela was running, she made the decision to leave Elanesse regardless of the cost. She would take Emmy northwest, to the hills which lie before the Mahtan Mountains. She had heard other bands of gypsy families roamed those fertile hills, raising cattle and horses. Perhaps Emmy and she could find succor in the arms of these people. Maybe an empath would be welcomed, not murdered to satisfy superstition…or fear.

Angela turned a corner and nearly stumbled into a figure bent over a pool of reddish vomit. Nimbly side-stepping the obviously drunken man, Angela did not feel he was a threat. She had dealt with his kind on numerous occasions. She could easily outrun a single inebriated man. A group of them, however, would be a different story. Even drunk, their lust made them dangerous opponents. Looking quickly over her shoulder, Angela saw the man slowly look up at her. In that moment she could almost see the hunger move from his loins to his brain. Angela was well away before he even had the presence of mind to begin his pursuit. Angela did not know his attempt to follow her was stopped before it ever began.

After having swiftly dealt with the drunken man, Lukas quickly moved to catch Angela. As a creature with supernatural abilities he knew he would have no trouble. His only concern was being seen as he approached and took her. But she ran into the alleys. No one went into the alleys at night, at least no one sober and law abiding. Anyone he met would be quickly and silently dispatched without notice. Lukas smiled as he effortlessly glided closer to Angela. She was making his mission easier. It was as if destiny were smiling down at him. He could not possibly have known the course he was traveling would lead to his own destruction several thousand years hence. Fate may indeed have been smiling down at him, but not kindly as he envisioned.

Angela did not hear or see the vampyre, and Lukas was upon her before she had a chance to react. In truth she was doomed from the moment Lukas began his pursuit. Mortals had few defenses against the undead vampyre. Superstitious folklore and stories about vampyre weaknesses had led many mortals along the path to destruction. This did not mean vampyres were impossible to kill, however. The true ways are known to specialized hunters and warriors of experience. Vampyres understood this reality. They understood they were few, and that mortals were many. They understood if attention is drawn to them, those who sought to outlaw evil, or those who sought to display or prove their prowess, would flock together and find them. Many a vampyre with no regard for discretion had ended up with a stake through the heart or a head removed from their shoulders. Vampyres who knew how to survive hunted the dredges of mortal society, the loners, the drunks, the outlaws, the poor. In a society divided into classes, such as Elanesse, these people were seldom missed. Rarely did the authorities wish to get involved, preferring instead to turn a blind eye while the vampyre preformed what the upper classes arrogantly considered to be necessary waste removal.

Angela struggled to no avail against Lukas' embrace. She was helpless as the blood was being drained out of her. But as darkness closed in on Angela and her struggling started to subside, Lukas removed his fangs from her neck, leaving Angela in a semi-conscious state. Holding her up as if she weighed nothing at all, the vampyre turned her around so that he could gaze into her eyes. Few could resist the direct gaze of a vampyre, but this was made even more impossible since he had bitten her. At this moment, while she was still in a stupor from the original contact, she was his in both mind and body.

"Soon the parasite within you will grow and you will become one of us. Resistance is impossible. I am your new master," Lukas said.

In a daze, Angela nodded. She did not have the mental strength to fight…At least not right away.

"What do you carry so carefully in your hand?" Lukas asked, knowing exactly what it was. He was testing her strength, her ability to defy his command and resist his gaze.

Angela tried to keep her mouth closed. She tried to keep the importance of her errand secret and her daughter protected. Ultimately, however, there was no recourse. She was compelled to answer.

"It is medicine…Medicine for my daughter," Angela reluctantly replied.

Lukas viciously slapped Angela across the mouth. The strength of a vampyre is equal to the strength of ten mortal men. She went flying backwards and landed awkwardly against a wall, her left leg bent terribly upon impact, her knee badly dislocated. The back of her skull scraped the wall as she slid down it, leaving hair, skin and blood. The mind control the vampyre held over her could not keep away the terrible pain Angela felt as she lay at the base of the wall, slumped over. The shock to her system caused her to vomit, the effect of which caused her to cry out in agony. If not for the parasite so recently introduced and now coursing through her veins, she would have been dead the moment she struck the wall.

The vampyre glided over and stood next to her crumpled body, arms crossed at his chest. He looked disdainfully down as Angela writhed on the cold stone surface of the alley. Shoving her with a booted foot, he said, "You look like you are in a lot of pain. When you come into your full power, that pain will be absorbed and hidden away by the parasite. When you come into your full power, you will be able to quickly heal yourself. Imagine the possibilities! But as of now the parasite is still much too young to help you."

As much as she hated giving him satisfaction as she moaned, Angela could not help herself. The pain was too severe.

"She is weak," Lukas thought to himself. He was tempted to walk away, but remembered Polina's words. She was wrong, however. This animal will not make a good addition to the coven. But he was not yet strong enough to disobey.

Smiling at the pain he was about to inflict, he readied himself for the rush of adrenaline he received whenever he had the opportunity to be cruel. Lukas reached down and grabbed Angela's mangled leg. "I am going to heal you, but it will hurt. You will wish you were dead!"

He roughly set the bones back in place, awash in the torture it was causing and relishing Angela's screams. He then magically healed both the leg and the back of Angela's head.

"Let this be your first lesson. From now on you will call me Master. Do you understand?" Lukas asked.

"Yes, Master," Angela whispered.

Lukas nodded. "Good! Now let's go visit your daughter," he ordered.

"As you wish, Master," Angela replied with wooden sounding words.

Angela and Emmy shared a small, one room apartment. Emmy was in a semi-conscious state, lying in bed, sweat soaking her pillow and sheets. The smell of sickness permeated throughout. Emmy's face was discolored and open sores covered her exposed arms. Magical healing would normally serve to easily banish the pestilence and heal anyone infected. Not all, however, had access to such luxuries. This was especially true for those in the gypsy quarter of Elanesse. Only during full outbreaks would the authorities get involved and provide clerics for healing of the effected masses. Unfortunately, official involvement also meant the destruction of whole city blocks with cleansing fires which left many people homeless.

Lukas wrinkled his nose at the destruction that ravaged Emmy's body. He found it distasteful and unclean. He did not wish to drink tainted blood, regardless of its innocence. Turning to Angela, he said, "Give her the medicine Polina concocted."

Angela moved to do Lukas' bidding, but suddenly stopped. Lukas, having walked over to open the one window in the room to let in fresh air, felt an unnatural chill coming from behind him. It was a feeling he had never before experienced. It was a feeling that said his existence was threatened. The child!

Turning to look upon Emmy, he saw that she had, within a few moments, been healed. Angela, standing at the foot of the bed, had yet to give her the medicine. "She is an empath!" Lukas hissed.

"Yes Master, blessed by the gods." Angela replied with pride. "It would appear she has finally come into her birthright. She will sleep for some time. She is very weak."

"How do you know this?" Lukas asked.

"Master, my mother was an empath. She was slaughtered in the purge, but she knew since the power was not in me, it could be in my offspring. She taught me many things. Things that would help me raise Emmy and protect her until she matured."

THE SALVATION OF INNOCENCE

Controlling his hate, his fear, for this young creature, Lukas moved to the foot of the bed to stand next to Angela. "She will not live long enough to mature, but this could prove interesting. I would never drink from such a disgusting animal, but I will have you drink in my stead. How ironic that you will be responsible for the death of your own child. Polina will be impressed." Smiling, Lukas gave Angela a little shove. "Collect your daughter and follow me. We dare not keep Polina waiting."

Angela's heart was breaking. She could not control what she had now become, nor could she refuse Lukas. She was afraid some of the evilness that tainted her soul would make its way through the bond. But if she broke the bond, how could Emmy survive? The hate and evil radiating from the vampyre, in and of itself, would be enough to kill her. Even more disconcerting, it now appeared she would be forced to be the instrument of Emmy's destruction. Angela had no answers. She could not master the darkness that steadily grew inside her.

Even as Angela fought the compulsion, she followed it, gently dressing Emmy in her best clothes and picking her up. "Where do we go, Master."

"That is not your concern," Lukas replied.

The vault was a small stone room located deep under an ornate three-story mansion in the Gypsy Quarter. Against one wall was a fireplace. The heat from the fire made the room uncomfortably warm. Emmy had healed herself of her sickness through her empath abilities, but though conscious, was still very weak and barely able to stand. She looked exhausted and her clothes were drenched with sweat. She had been manacled at the wrists to a wall. Next to her Angela had also been chained. Her skin had taken on an unnatural pallor. She was not sweating, but panting instead.

A vapor appeared through the one door in the room and materialized in front of Angela. Lukas studied her. "Have you changed your mind yet? The hunger will soon be unbearable."

Angela looked defiantly back at the vampyre. Her mind long since cleared of the fog she felt a few short hours ago, "I will see you in hell before I will feed off my daughter!" she shouted.

The vampyre slapped her, "Fool! She is but a herd animal to the likes of us. Just say the word and I will release you so you can eat."

"I am not like you!" Angela screamed.

"If you do not feed, she will die slowly of dehydration. That will take about three days. You will be giving her a last gift. Embrace her! Be what you are now meant to be!"

That stopped Angela. He spoke the truth…Emmy was doomed to a slow death.

Emmy raised her head and looked over at Angela. "No, mommy, don't do it! I do not wish to die…but you will be damned forever!" Emmy went into a brief trance. Suddenly waves of emotion moved between the two through the bond that connected each. The vampyre hissed.

"She uses her empath power!" He screeched.

"No Emmy…you must break the bond," Angela pleaded. "Do not attempt to heal that within me which is broken. The parasite is too powerful for you!"

And indeed Angela was correct. Emmy, though disregarding her mother's words, could not save Angela from the parasite through the bond. She was still too inexperienced, having only just recently come into her power. Emmy, however, refused to break the bond.

Another gaseous cloud appeared and solidified into a female vampyre. Lukas groveled before his matriarch. Bowing low, he said with great deference, "Mistress Polina, Angela resists. How can that be?"

Focusing her attention on Emmy, she moved back. "You're such an idiot! The child is an empath!" she said to the other vampyre. "This can't be! I thought all the empaths had been destroyed!" Turning to Lukas, Polina said, "There is no way her mother can be broken even with the parasite. Her bond with her daughter is too great, her latent empath blood too resistant. Even if the parasite gains control, she will never be truly one of us."

Lukas knew the girl was an empath, but he had purposely neglected to tell Polina. He knew he was treading dangerous waters. "But Mistress, she must feed or she will die! The hunger will break that bond!"

"Perhaps you are correct, but she will always know what she was forced to do and by whom. The mother of an empath can never be trusted," Polina replied as she moved to the fireplace and reached for a half burnt piece of wood. Quickly sharpening one end of the thick stick with a knife, she fashioned a crude stake…the sharpened end of which is still burning.

As she turned and moved back to Angela, she smiled. "According to vampyre lore, a wooden stake through the heart will kill our kind. That is only partially true. A stake through the heart will cause you much pain. I know for it has been done to me. But if the stake is removed before the flesh withers away, the parasite within, over time will reconstitute the damage done to our bodies. The hunger after that, however, becomes primal. You will feed off your daughter. And as you do, you will be aware even though you cannot stop. Then you will be trapped here for all eternity to live with the guilt. Your spirit will be able to caress the bones of your dead child."

Without another word, the vampyre rammed the stake into Angela's body, through the breastbone, piercing the heart. Emmy screamed as Angela convulsed in pain. After a few minutes, Angela quieted, her body becoming limp in pseudo-death.

Turning, Polina said to Lukas, "Go quickly and enlist a brick mason. I want this room bricked up before the light of day. After that work is done, you can do as you see fit with him."

"Yes my mistress." Lukas said as he turned into a vapor and left. His fortune turned quite suddenly. Even so, this mistake would not go easy on him. He judged it was time to remove himself from Polina's presence for a time. Besides, he would still eat this evening.

Removing the stake from Angela's body and tossing it aside, Polina moved to the chained Emmy. "Don't worry child. In a few hours your mother will come alive. The hunger will be so great that she will easily rip the chains from the wall to get at your pretty neck. You will die quickly. Your mother, however, will not be so lucky." Without even another glance, the vampyre followed her disciple and made a misty exit.

Time passed and the fire started to die out. The shadows in the room grew deeper. Emmy - recovered from the initial shock of seeing her mother brutally killed, recovered from the hate filled emotion and evil coming from the vampyre's - started acting upon a plan to try and save her mother. Her empath powers were still too new for her to be able to heal her mother through the bond, but maybe she could through direct contact. She deliberately dislocated her thumb joints. Since the manacles were made for adults, their bigger size made it possible for her to slip her hands through once the thumbs were out of the way. Sobbing because of the pain, Emmy was soon free. She knelt down as the agony enveloped her. After a few moments, however, she quieted and began to concentrate, allowing her empathic power to work its magic. As she did this, she discovered she could disassociate her mind while her thumbs snapped back into place, saving her from even more excruciating pain.

Emmy, thumbs once again uninjured, moved over to her mother and placed her hands over the hole in Angela's chest. After a few seconds, however, she moved her hands away. There was nothing she could do. The parasite could not be vanquished by her power.

Emmy knew nothing about vampyre legend, but she was a very smart little girl and was able to draw some conclusions based upon what Polina had said before she left. Emmy could not save her mother, but maybe she could save her soul. If her mother never fed, thus sealing the pact between her and evil, then her soul could be saved if the vampyre that bit her was destroyed. Who knew when a vampyre hunter or warrior would slay Lukas, freeing her mother? It was her only hope.

As the fire went out, Emmy picked up the discarded stake. Quietly saying, "I love you mommy!" Emmy carefully put the stake back in her mother's chest, ensuring her mother would never awaken. Walking over to a corner of the room and sitting down, crying softly, Emmy broke the bond with her mother which she held so dear. She waited for death to take her, alone in the dark.

Emmy had lost consciousness in the dark vault. A soft blue light suddenly appeared in the middle of the room, taking the shape of a woman dressed in a long silken blue gown. Next to her another light appeared. This one was multi-colored. It formed into the shape of a woman with iridescent wings.

The woman in the blue gown, the deity Althaya, Goddess of Healing, said to her immortal sister Aurora, the 'Angel of the Forest' and Goddess of Rangers, "She is the last of the bloodline."

Aurora winced, for she knew the empath was hunted by some of her own rangers. There was no guilt, for she never condoned the Purge, but she nevertheless felt compelled to join with Althaya to do what she could. Good Althaya. Never did she fear to take a direct part in the affairs of mortals if justice was to be served, though this action was bold, even for Althaya.

"Surely there is still another empath blood in the world."

"At this moment there is not. The bloodline will present itself again, but I do not know when. No, this one must be saved," Althaya answered. Looking down at Emmy, Althaya whispered, "So much responsibility falls upon her shoulders. Yet she is but a child."

Moving over to Emmy, Althaya took off her cloak, knelt down and wrapped Emmy in it, securing it around her neck with an amulet. The cloak magically resized itself to fit the child. Gathering Emmy in her arms, she said, "Sleep, my dear. There is one who will come for you. She will help you save your mother's soul. She will love and care for you as if you were her own. She will be bonded to you and you to her. She will stay by you and protect you until you can stand strong. The world has not seen the last of the empath. On this you have my word!"

With Emmy still in her arms, Althaya silently worked a stasis spell that surrounded the child. It was a spell that, for Emmy, would make time stand still and keep her in a dreamlike state. It would keep Althaya continuously aware of any changes to Emmy's condition. It was a spell that would keep the last empath alive until it is time for the world to once again celebrate the existence of the empath. After gently slipping the sleeping Emmy off her lap, Althaya and Aurora left the vault.

There are mysteries in the universe that even the gods and goddesses fail to comprehend, forces at work they do not control and are often unaware of. Unknown to Althaya and Aurora, fate had already chosen Emmy's protector. As Emmy slept in the stasis field, she dreamed of a strange woman, her skin fair and her intense eyes a golden brown. When those eyes looked back at Emmy, however, they softened with wonderment and love. In her stasis induced sleep, Emmy smiled, deriving solace from this revelation. The woman smiled back and gently placed a kiss on Emmy's forehead as she collected her in a warm embrace. "I will come for you, dear heart."

The woman soon had to take her leave. Emmy did not want her to go, but the depth and warmth of the strange woman's love allowed Emmy to accept her departure. The sudden bond, though very slender, that spontaneously formed between the two came as a great comfort through the long night.

As Emmy slept through the centuries, a name entered her dreams… Kristen.

THE SALVATION OF INNOCENCE

ROBERT E. BALSLEY JR.

CHAPTER 1

On the Mainland

(112 Years Ago)

And the dying man said, 'How did I come to be here?' to which the wind replied, 'You have walked this path to your destiny from the moment you were born.'

— BOOK OF THE UNVEILED

ANNESSA CLEARWATER KUNDENIR was a warrior elf living in the city-state of HeBron. Born to warriors, the warrior life was the only future she was offered. Trained from early childhood, she became a member of one of the mercenary companies that protected the city as well as the interests of its current government. Advancement above this station, however, was impossible as long as she remained in HeBron. Annessa was an elf in all aspects except one, she had sapphire blue eyes. This revealed the taint of human blood, the result of a long forgotten liaison centuries ago. Unfortunately, Annessa's questionable mixed heritage ensured she was labeled as a half-breed and looked down upon by both the elf and human masters she served, good enough for neither.

When Annessa was a young adult, already serving HeBron as a warrior, her mother, Kristen, and her father, Haradion, were both killed in a skirmish between their mercenary company and one from Madeira. Though the two city-states were not officially at war, tensions were always high and little excuse was needed for bloodshed. With her parents dead, the other warriors in her company became her only family. It was not long, however, before Annessa started having doubts about the true intent of HeBron's ruler. As she matured she began to understand that she and her comrades served more for the pleasure of HeBron's ruler than the protection of its people. Consequently, Annessa refused to obey orders that ran contrary to her ethical upbringing. After several such refusals, it became clear to her superiors that she would have to be reprimanded. Her skills with the sword and longbow, however, made her too valuable of an asset to be disciplined as severely as the law required. She was reduced in rank and sent to the borderlands surrounding the city-state. It was during this time that she plotted her desertion.

Life on border patrol was primitive. The barracks that housed the patrol were constructed of logs and dried mud. Toilet facilities consisted of a hole in the ground. The meals, although served in abundance and hot, were tasteless, unappetizing at best, but generally disgusting. The cooks, though very adept at getting the most flavors from moldy grain as possible, failed more often than not. Most of the personnel foraged for nuts and berries to supplement, or replace, their daily rations.

Very few of Annessa's fellow warriors were female, none were elves, and all were there for the same reason, punishment. As a result, she shared her watch with hard men who did not care as much for the fact that she was considered half-breed as much as they appreciated her female qualities. They didn't ask politely before forcing themselves upon her. Fully half a dozen were felled by her blades before the others took her meaning. Each death was ruled self-defense. Each death resulted in furthering her abilities with the sword and made her as hard as the men with whom she patrolled. Each time she took a life, or saw men looking at her, not with the respect she had shown she deserved, but with lust, she became further convinced she would leave. She had an instinctive abhorrence for the type of life she found herself living.

Six months after arriving on the border, Annessa had drawn the midnight patrol which was not uncommon considering her elf abilities to see in the dark as well as a keener sense of hearing. The only friend Annessa had made since coming to the borderlands, a human named Rosilie, was also selected. Rosilie was big for a human female, weighing 160 pounds and standing over six feet. She was very muscular, easily able to pin most of the men she wrestled against. Sadly she was battle-scarred and many turned away from her appearance. Annessa, however, did not care about her outward countenance. Rosilie, even after all the suffering she had endured and all the terrible things she had seen during her tour in the borderlands, was still a good and simple person. Annessa did not know if this was because she was born that way or because she was hit on the head once too often. Regardless, Annessa felt compassion as well as a desire to protect Rosilie, which was reciprocated by Rosilie. The strong Rosilie and the quick Annessa was a perfectly matched pair in battle. The fighting reputation they had earned as a team usually meant that they were the lead scouts when they went on patrol. Their orders were always never engage but report any unusual activity.

This night, unlike most of their night patrols, the two came upon an encampment of elves. Though the elves could see and hear as well as Annessa, she still had the advantage because she knew and understood the terrain, for she had made this patrol dozens of times. Whispering for Rosilie to wait behind while she investigated the camp, Annessa carefully approached. While a large fire was burning, there were several guards positioned so the light of the fire did not interfere with their dark vision. Taking a few moments to study the camp, Annessa returned to where Rosilie waited.

"It's an elven merchant caravan," Annessa whispered. "Although well guarded, our patrol can take it as long as we maintain the element of surprise."

"Why would we? As long as they are peaceful and offer no threat to HeBron, they should be left alone. It is our duty to protect innocents as they cross our lands," Rosilie replied.

"Dear Rosilie! After all this time and everything you've been through, you are still so very naive. A merchant caravan means goods, it means gold. Who's to stop the lieutenant from killing everyone there and taking it all for himself? Oh, he'll reward his men, but it'll be a rich payday for him that's for sure."

Annessa could almost hear Rosilie thinking in the dark. "So you think we should warn them? That's going against our orders," she said.

"If we don't, its murder," Annessa responded. "But by doing this, we can never go back."

"You mean we should desert?"

Annessa nodded her head. "Yes, my friend. It is time. HeBron has lost its way. I no longer wish to be a party to the corruption of its ruler." Pausing, Annessa heard movement not far from their position. Their patrol had arrived sooner than expected. "You must decide. Are you with me?"

"Of course I am, Annessa. You are my only friend!" Rosilie whispered back with conviction.

Reaching over and smoothing Rosilie's ruffled hair, Annessa said, "Thank you. Let's go!"

Running into the camp, Annessa and Rosilie kept their swords sheathed, asking the first guard they met to take them to the caravan leader while identifying themselves as part of a HeBron patrol and saying they had urgent news about an imminent attack. Telling them to wait and instructing the other guards to watch the newcomers, the first guard went to wake up the leader. Annessa did not realize the trap until it was too late. As the first guard was about to enter the largest of three tents, an arrowhead sprang through his back, spewing blood as it appeared between his shoulder blades. Annessa saw immediately that the arrow came from the wrong direction. "Another patrol was out there!" she thought, immediately understanding the tactical disadvantage the camp was in. It was in the middle of a giant pincer. Somehow the borderland guard had intelligence about this caravan and had planned an ambush which she unwittingly was a part of. In the split second it took her to piece together what was happening, two other guards went down, each hit with several arrows.

Dragging Rosilie with her, Annessa dropped down to the ground so she could look around as she gathered her bearings while making as little a target as possible. By now all the caravan guards and travelers were awake and had started to arm themselves. The arrow fire had stopped after the initial volley for fear of hitting the second patrol, her patrol, as it came charging out of the woods and into the camp clearing from the opposite direction. Rosilie shrugged off Annessa's hold on her arm, got up, and charged the patrol. Annessa, calling for Rosilie to stop, a call that went unheeded, took the opportunity Rosilie gave her to go to work with her bow and arrow, giving back a measure of what the caravan guards had been given. But she was only able to get a few volleys off before everything became too convoluted to properly select targets. Tossing aside her bow, Annessa drew her sword and joined Rosilie.

The battle was a blur. As she had done in the past, she used a survival technique taught to her by her father. Her mind moved into a different world, a world of parries, slashes, and thrusts. Her movements were automatic, her entire body performing a dance with the sword which went from killing to providing a barrier of steel against other swords then back to killing again. She did not feel pain as she was cut, she did not feel emotion as she dealt death, she did not feel exhaustion until the last enemy was either lifeless or had fled.

In the end, she was standing with one other whom she vaguely remembered had been fighting at her back, defending it using magical spells which dealt death and destruction as well as her own sword. Turning, Annessa looked to see a male elf, his wise dark brown eyes filled with gratitude and relief. "It is over, my new friend. They have melted back into the forest, richer by far. But they paid a high price for the gold. We too paid a high price, too high in my estimation. If only they had just asked for it."

Annessa nodded, still trying to fathom what had happened. She then looked over to where she last saw Rosilie, spying her still body lying on blood soaked earth. Rosilie had given a good account of herself, but that did not stop her from dying. Walking over to her and kneeling down, Annessa took Rosilie's head and cradled it in her lap, slowly rocking back and forth. Suddenly all the pain and exhaustion caught up with her and caused her to cry out in despair.

The sorcerer knelt down beside Annessa. "I am sorry. Many good people lost their lives today."

"None of them were my friends!" Annessa shouted back. Calming herself, Annessa said, "It was inappropriate of me to say such a thing about the dead. We need to bury them."

"Please, young lady, we must gather supplies and be away from here before they return!" the sorcerer said as he looked around into the night, fearful that someone might come back.

"I must at least put my friend to rest first," Annessa replied through her tears. "She will not be left out here to be wolf meat!"

"We must be away! You need help and there is little else I can do if they should come back. All of my spells have been expended," the sorcerer pleaded.

Annessa shook her head no. "Most of this blood belongs to them, not me. I WILL see to my friend. Help me or not, I don't care."

The sorcerer, who was still looking around for any sign of movement outside the clearing, stopped and focused on Annessa. "Of course I will help." Finding a discarded sword, he started digging furrows in the ground. Annessa got up, moved over to him and placed a hand on his shoulder. "We are in the borderlands. There are plenty of rocks to build a cairn."

Dawn found the two of them safely out of the area controlled by HeBron. They were on foot headed south following the same road the caravan used to travel north. All the horses that pulled the wagons in the caravan were scattered across the countryside, no doubt already claimed by others as their own. The sorcerer did the best he could to bandage Annessa's many wounds, but fortunately all of them were shallow and stopped bleeding before they could become a serious threat. There was little communication between the two during this time, both preferring to concentrate on their escape and still trying to grasp the magnitude of what happened just a few short hours ago.

Finally the sorcerer broke the silence. "I am Rathal Arquen of Havendale which is to the southeast. I was hired to help protect the caravan, its gold, trade goods, and most importantly its smug little self-important owner. It was supposed to be a safe trip, especially once we got past the ruins of Elanesse. We had safe passage arranged with HeBron and felt we were safe once within its borders."

"The borderlands of HeBron to the south are guarded by cut-throats and thieves," Annessa said with little apparent interest in conversation.

"Obviously not all are thus, madam. You and your friend were quite gallant on the battlefield," Rathal replied.

"I led her to her death," Annessa responded sourly.

"Forgive me, but from what I saw as we built the cairn, she had extensive old injuries from past fighting, probably a lifetime of battle in the service of HeBron's ruling elite. She is now free of that control. Possibly you led her to her salvation."

Annessa looked at Rathal. "I would have rather led her to her freedom."

"Many times they are one in the same," Rathal replied. After a few minutes of silence, Annessa said, "I am Annessa. No last name, just Annessa. After this, there is probably going to be a bounty on my head and I'd prefer to leave that part of my life behind."

"It is a pleasure to meet you, Annessa. You will be safe with me, I can assure you," Rathal smiled at having won a small victory by getting her to name herself.

Annessa shook her head. "Like you protected the caravan?"

The suddenly deflated Rathal looked away from Annessa's gaze. "I did not do a very good job of that. You are right and have every reason to be skeptical."

Annessa stopped walking, thinking maybe she was being too hard on the sorcerer. "You had no way of knowing. It was a well-planned trap. The borderland's guard should have been acting as an escort instead of attacking you. I am young, that is true, but my life has taught me that nothing can ever be taken for granted, that no one is ever really safe. Was this your first trip away from Havendale?"

Rathal's face flushed red. "Is it that obvious? I've received years of training in the arcane arts but very little training in the field. This was my first exposure outside the city. If it had not been for you and your friend, it would have been my last. An easy trip, they said. Now I alone survive, but only because of your ability to handle a sword."

Annessa started walking again. "You acquitted yourself well during the battle. Anyone can fall into a trap, but how you handle it is more telling. As for the merchant and the caravan guards, we all die. They knew what they were getting into when they took decided to make the trip. As long as you did your best, there is no guilt."

"Thank you," Rathal whispered. Annessa knew from the tone of his voice that the sorcerer would use this experience to learn from the mistakes he made and from the precautions he did not take. He had unexpectedly become a campaign survivor.

"Rathal, we should find a safe place to stop and rest. We're both tired. Do you have any spells that can ward us while we sleep?" Annessa asked.

"No. I'm sorry," Rathal replied.

"This is the road you traveled going north." Annessa said as a statement of fact.

"Yes. Why?"

Looking around, Annessa asked, "How close are we to the ruins of Elanesse? I've heard rumors it is haunted which probably keeps it deserted. A small building on the outskirts might be a safe place to stop and sleep. I don't think I can stay awake long enough to handle a full watch."

"It's maybe several more hours off the road and to the west. I've never been there of course, but I talked to some of the guards about it. They all seemed to agree that it is not very safe," Rathal replied. "At one time it was a vibrant, magnificent city ruled by the elves, but now it is said to be cursed, that some power controls it and all who enter the city are doomed."

"I think it is a chance we have to take. It's better than staying in the open and it's just for a few hours," Annessa said.

About two hours after leaving the road they found an old farmstead which had several abandoned buildings, all but one reclaimed by the forest. Both spread out bedrolls, ate a quick meal of salvaged trail rations, and settled in for a badly needed rest. It was not long before they were fast asleep.

As the day started to give way to the shadows brought on by the night, Annessa awoke from a nightmare. It was about the slaughter of innocent people, the horror of genocide, and complete isolation. As battle-hardened as Annessa was, her greatest weakness was the fear of loneliness, a loneliness that had been with her since her parents died. Annessa, terrified, sought comfort in the arms of Rathal.

They later continued their journey in silence, both too embarrassed to speak. Though Annessa had had previous liaisons, this felt different, like it had more meaning. By dawn of the next day, Annessa knew she was pregnant, and by the dawn of the following day, all her wounds had mysteriously disappeared.

When they reached Silverstone, they were able to purchase horses for the remaining trip to Havendale. A few miles outside of Havendale the two were met by one of the city's many armed patrols who were scouting the area on horseback and escorted back to the city. Once there, Annessa was given use of a room in a plush inn while Rathal reported to his superiors. Upon his return, Annessa told him that she needed to leave Havendale. She needed to be on her own. Perhaps one day she would return, but she couldn't really say for sure. Rathal didn't try to stop her, sensing she required this to help heal her soul. He made sure that she was given a fresh and sturdy horse, plenty of supplies for her journey, and gold. He deeply hoped she would return to him, but suspected this would be the last he would ever see of her.

Annessa left a week after arriving at Havendale. She did not tell Rathal that she carried his child.

Several weeks later Annessa arrived in the mid-size city of Ascension. She had attached herself to one of the armed merchant caravans heading northwest as a guard. The trip was made without incident and the pay she received added to her already substantial money bag.

As she traveled, she began to feel the presence that shared her body. She didn't know exactly when it happened, but at some point the unborn baby became a person. Annessa started thinking about the day she would finally be able to hold the child and the future the two of them would have together. Buoyed by the child, Annessa's spirit started to recover from the deprivations of her past and continued to do so with each passing day. Her whole heart and soul went into loving the unborn infant living inside of her, intent on being the very best mother she could be. Annessa even made the decision to travel back to Havendale someday so that the child would not be denied knowing his or her father.

As the caravan slowly made its way to Ascension, Annessa thought about HeBron and the mercenary company she betrayed. She was not sure how far their reach would extend or how badly they would want to track her down for desertion. Chances were very good that she would be written out of the company role as a casualty and forgotten, but she could not take that risk now. There was too much at stake. When Annessa reached Ascension, she started to implement certain actions she decided upon during the trip there which would hopefully allow her to find anonymity in the city. She located a modest inn run by a kindly couple and their three daughters. This provided a certain degree of obscurity, it helped to keep expenses down so she could save money, and by building a friendship with the innkeeper and his family, she would have help when it came to the birth of her child, which was something completely foreign to her and which gave her more than one sleepless night of worry.

During this time of peace, Annessa packed away her weapons and started wearing dresses in the fashion recommended by the innkeeper's daughters. Annessa also dropped her last name of Kundenir and started her new life as Annessa Clearwater. Her middle name was known only to her and her deceased parents, so if bounty hunters did come out of the north, they could not locate her by name alone. Finally she needed to find a mundane job which would not only provide a steady source of income but also would not jeopardize the health of her baby. To this end she took employment helping a simple shopkeeper. As her condition became more apparent, this compassionate man would not allow her to do any manual work such as loading and unloading, stocking shelves, or taking inventory. He even started paying her a little extra each week. It was "for the baby's future" he said when Annessa tried to refuse his generosity.

During the middle part of her pregnancy Annessa knew she would have a daughter. She did not know how this was possible, but she was sure of it nevertheless. Towards the end of her pregnancy, almost a year after she left HeBron, Annessa started having flashes of a vision she could not understand. In these momentary flashes, she saw a sleeping child encased in a silvery cocoon. She soon realized, however, that what she was seeing was actually being experienced by her unborn daughter, and that these dreams were somehow being transmitted to her from the womb. Fearful that these visions may cause harm, Annessa made discreet inquiries to determine if there was a wizard or cleric who might be able to answer her questions and to calm her fears. Each time she was told that it was probably her imagination, the result of a long pregnancy and upcoming birth. But something within her knew this was not true, that there was more involved than the simple imaginings of a pregnant female. The dead city of Elanesse was the key to her visions. That much she knew with a certainty. Annessa decided to leave Ascension. She would go to the town of Covington, southwest of the ruins of Elanesse. From there, she would have her child, and perhaps find someone who might understand what drove her to Elanesse...where Annessa had the nightmare that drove her into the arms of Rathal, and the place where her daughter was conceived.

ROBERT E. BALSLEY JR.

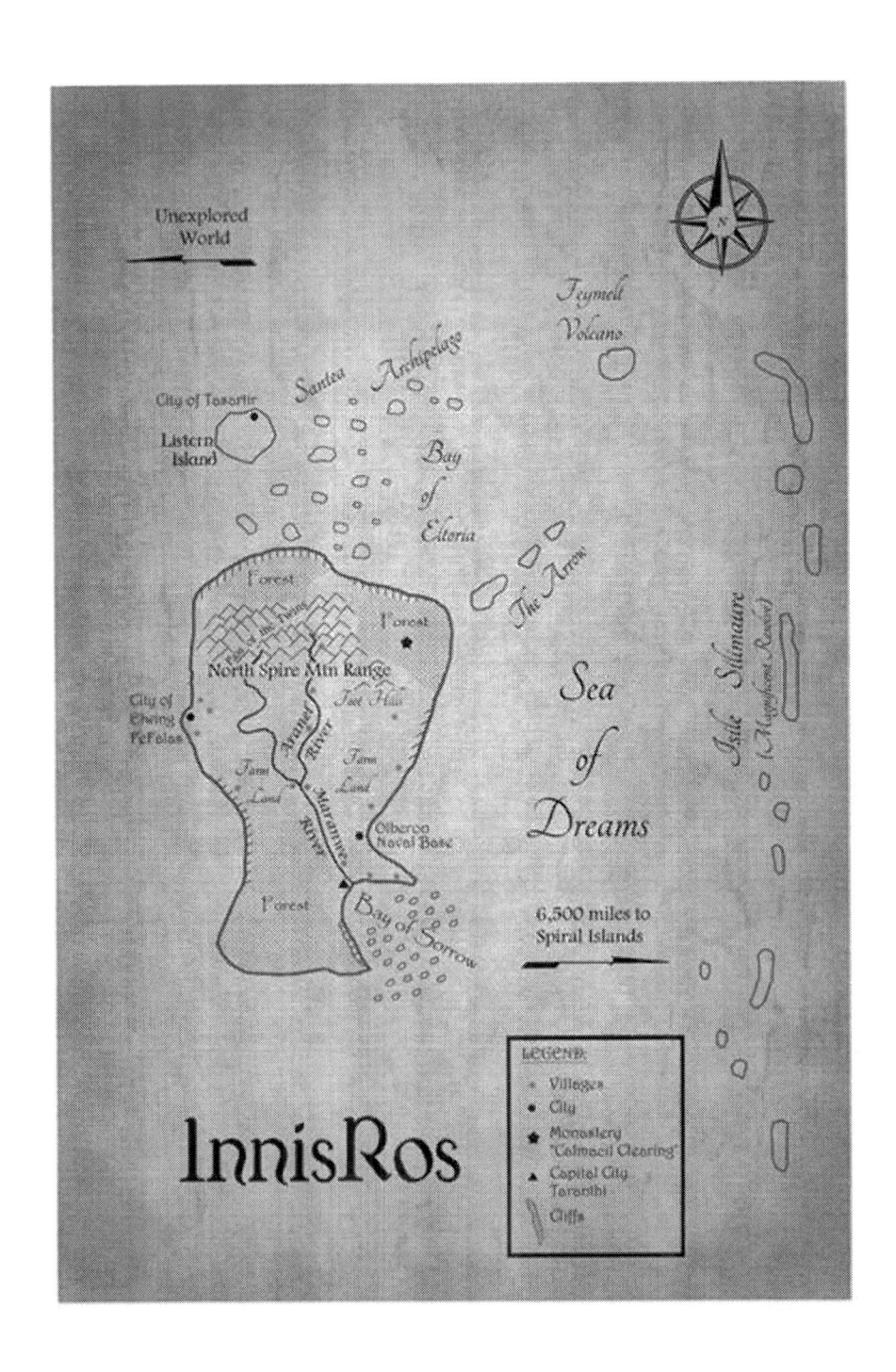

CHAPTER 2

InnisRos

(111 Years Ago)

Given by the poorest of the poor, the King opened the meager offering, and it was the greatest treasure of all.

— BOOK OF THE UNVEILED

INNISROS IS A series of islands west of the largest known continent on the world of Aster. These islands are the primary home of the elves, though there is also a small population of humans who are, for the most part, concentrated in and around the port cities of Olberon and Elwing FeFalas. InnisRos sits in the Sea of Dreams, west of the Isile Silimaure. The Isile Silimaure, or Great Resolve, is a seven-hundred mile long barrier of barren rocks brought forth millennia ago by elven magic used in conjunction with the physical labor of hundreds of elves. Its purpose was to isolate InnisRos from the rest of the world. Though the Isile Silimaure is a great testament to the combined use of both the magical and the mundane, the faulty thinking behind its creation was soon abandoned. Segregation between elves and the rest of the world's races was not possible, though over the generations the isle rulers did everything possible to limit outside influence.

The rumored riches of this island nation are legendary. Over the centuries the navy had become very proficient in stopping invading hordes of pirates...and in some cases other seagoing nations...from establishing a beachhead on InnisRoss' shores. But for all the tenacity displayed by the elves inhabiting the island to stay secluded and therefore outside the sphere of the human influence which was so prevalent on the mainland, smuggling was a reality that could not be stopped. Single boats, if captained well and with stealth, often managed to slide past elven naval pickets and reach the island. Such a thing happened this night. The objective, however, was not to plunder, but to deliver a treasure.

A priest of Althaya, Father Horatio Goram, calmly watched as the embers of his small fire began to go out one by one. Absentmindedly, he waved a hand and pointed a finger. A piece of wood about three feet long lifted from the wood pile Father Goram had made ready, floated over, and gently set down upon the dying embers, causing them to flare up, eager to dance with the wooden newcomer and light the night once again.

Father Goram was an elf of early middle age with long flowing silver hair contrasted by gray at the temples. Clean shaven, he was a pleasant looking fellow, handsome with intelligent silver eyes. They are eyes that can pierce feelings, eyes that can discover reality with but a glance. Elves aged at a very slow pace compared to humans, but wrinkles had begun to appear on his otherwise smooth face, wrinkles that were undoubtedly caused by the worry and responsibility of leadership.

Father Goram came from an aristocratic family, but his station as master of the sprawling monastery at Calmacil Clearing serving the goddess Althaya did far more to earn him his place among kings and queens than his noble birthright ever did. InnisRos was a place of great mysticism, with many temples to various elven gods and goddesses, but his was one of the largest. It was also dedicated to a goddess followed by the humans as well as the elves. Since Althaya's sphere of influence reached past the island shores and over to the mainland, the InnisRos Queen believed she would help protect them from invasion. Consequently, prudence and political expediency dictated Althaya's high priest be given a high place at the Queen's court. In truth, Althaya was a bit put off by elven self-importance, which put Father Goram in an uncomfortable position. In the end, all he ever really hoped to accomplish was mediation between his goddess and his mortal Queen.

At that moment Father Goram was uncharacteristically disconcerted. He stared into the fire, letting the warm flames calm him. "There is a great deal of importance riding on the meeting that is to come," he said to himself. Much had been put in motion since Althaya came to him and told him about the child. For the hundredth time he speculated upon the child and the role Althaya said she was to play when it was time. He was told she would help to serve justice to an injustice done long ago. She would bring back much that had been lost. She would bring back the empath. But about the empath Father Goram only knew what he had read, that they were healers who lived in and around the ruined elven city of Elanesse and were greatly feared and supposedly destroyed several millennia ago.

"Much that can go wrong this evening," he thought. "Fate does not always favor the righteous and can be miserly when meting out justice. And what about the role I am to play? I've never raised a child before, never been a parent. I have so many responsibilities, and now this. But Althaya gave me my orders and I will not disobey her."

Faintly, from a distance, he heard and understood the cry of a dire wolf. A member of a nearby pack that had allied itself with Father Goram's monastery for the mutual benefit of both, the dire wolf was warning him of the approach of strangers. There were three, a human male, a human female, and the little one. His elven hearing allowed him to hear the wolves' message, but even if the humans had heard it, they would not understand it for what it was nor would they be alarmed at a wild animal call from so far away. It was as he planned. Looking out into the darkness of the night, penetrating the even darker shadows, he silently communicated with his dire wolf allies ringing the small campsite. They were ready. They understood what must be done and that the babe must be protected at all costs. Dire wolves, a much larger cousin of normal wolves, understood innocence and the importance of the young to the survival of the pack.

Father Goram heard the careful walking of the two humans stop, and then one continued on. The human male, footsteps heavier than the female, slowly approached until he was just outside the light of the fire. Father Goram could not see him with his elven dark vision, an ability which allowed him to see heat signatures in the dark. The male was undoubtedly using magic to cover his heat source. That came as no surprise, for he was, after all, an assassin. A dreadful fellow to depend upon, but he had certain talents and connections that best guaranteed success. No matter, Father Goram knew exactly where he was.

"Please do me the kindness of showing yourself, Mr. Simon. We have business to discuss," Father Goram said.

A figure stepped out of the shadows and into the firelight. "I suspect it will be an easy transaction. You give me the gold and I give you the brat," Mr. Simon responded.

"Perhaps it shall go as simply as you say. Did you have any problems at the orphanage?" Father Goram asked.

"No, it went very smoothly," the assassin answered. "They won't even know she is missing. There are a lot of children there. I really don't know how they keep track of everyone. Also, per your instructions, no one was hurt - at least not much."

"It is sad but you are right. There are so many children in the world who need a family. Even so, an elf child has no place in the mostly human population of the mainland. She would never have been adopted," Father Goram said while thinking he must send an anonymous donation to the orphanage in Althaya's name as well as recompense to any injured parties.

"It's more than that, priest, and you know it!" Mr. Simon snapped. "She has great importance to you considering the amount of gold you were willing to pay to get her over here."

"You are right," Father Goram replied. "But that is really none of your concern. Now please show her to me."

The assassin studied Father Goram a moment, then called out, "Bring the baby!"

Quickly the human female appeared, standing beside the assassin. She was carefully holding a baby in her arms. "My Lord," she said to Father Goram while gracefully curtsying. "She has fallen asleep. It is strange, for she has been asleep ever since we touched upon this island. It's almost as if she knows she is home."

Father Goram stood. "Indeed she is, my good woman. Indeed she is'" he said. "What is your name?"

THE SALVATION OF INNOCENCE

"I am Mary McKenna. I've taken very good care of her, my Lord. She is quite healthy with lungs like a bass drum and feisty as a wildcat."

"Excellent, Miss McKenna, excellent, though I daresay she sounds like a bit of trouble." Father Goram said.

"Please, my Lord, she wasn't any trouble at all! Not at all! She's a very sweet baby!" Mary McKenna replied.

The assassin sighed, "Oh please, can we just get on with it!" he said testily. "I need to get back to the coast before the tide goes out and I miss my way off this god-forsaken island."

Father Goram looked sharply at the assassin. "On this island we do things my way, Mr. Simon, not yours. You would be well advised to pay attention to that fact." Returning his attention to Mary McKenna, Father Goram said, "Miss McKenna, please show her to me."

Mary McKenna gently uncovered the baby's face and tilted her up in her arms so Father Goram could gaze upon her.

"How did you feed her? I see no milk skin," Father Goram asked.

Mary McKenna glanced down at the baby. "My lord, I just recently lost my own young one to the fever. I am still heavy with milk."

"I am sorry for your loss. It is no doubt why Mr. Simon has involved you in this affair," Father Goram replied, laying a hand on Mary McKenna's shoulder.

"You've seen her," the assassin interrupted. "Now where's my gold?"

Father Goram reached inside his cloak and produced a small bag. "Here's your payment. There's ten thousand gold pieces per our agreement."

The assassin recognized the magical bag and knew its enchantment allowed it to hold much more than it would appear. Grabbing it, he opened it and looked inside. Taking a gold piece out, he bit down on it. Seeing teeth marks left behind, he was satisfied. As for the number, he'd dealt with such large amounts before and judged it to be correct. Besides, he did not have the time to count it all. "If you short changed me, priest," Mr. Simon warned.

"I have not, Mr. Simon. No magic, no sleight of hand, just gold," Father Goram replied.

"Give him the baby and let's be away," the assassin said roughly to Mary McKenna.

As the baby was handed over, Father Goram told the assassin while he cradled the baby in his arms, "I'm afraid I am going to have to amend our agreement, Mr. Simon. Miss McKenna stays with me."

"You can't do that! She's…she's…"

"She's seen your face? That's precisely why she has to stay. If I allow you to take her with you, she will shortly be at the bottom of the ocean," Father Goram interrupted.

"What do you care?" Mr. Simon shouted.

Father Goram's eyes flashed with anger. "What do I care? I AM A PRIEST!" he shouted back. "No innocent shall be murdered for the sake of convenience! Not when I can stop it! You do not want to test me on this!"

Having grabbed Mary McKenna by the arm, the assassin started to pull her away. She struggled but to no avail. "I do as I please, priest!" Mr. Simon said. "While you hold the baby you will do nothing to put her in harm's way. I've dealt with sorcerers before. Without the use of your hands you are powerless!"

"You think because I cannot use my hands I am powerless?" Father Goram responded. "Observe Mr. Simon."

Suddenly five dire wolves trotted into the firelight. Four were massive beasts, five feet high at the shoulders and ten feet long from teeth filled snout to the tip of their tails. Each weighed about five-hundred pounds and they were all snarling at the assassin from four different sides. The fifth, however, was an even more extraordinary specimen, six feet at the shoulders, fifteen feet long and over nine-hundred pounds. The bigger one, the obvious pack leader, ambled up to Father Goram and licked one of his hands holding the baby. Mary McKenna, taking advantage of the assassin's temporary surprise, broke his grip on her and disappeared behind the priest.

Cradling the baby in one arm, Father Goram reached out and scratched behind one ear of the big dire wolf with his other hand. "Mr. Simon, meet Menelaus."

"I have allies to. I was not foolish enough to come alone," the assassin countered nervously.

"It's true, my lord. He has many in league with him," Mary McKenna said from behind Father Goram. "They…they…they all had their way with me!"

"What did you expect? You're nothing but a whore. A prostitute turned out because you were stupid enough to have a child!" the assassin shouted.

Maintaining an outward calm, Father Goram smiled, "Your comrades, at least for the moment, are experiencing the same crisis that so troubles you. It's amazing what a cleric can do without using his hands."

His smile suddenly turned into a very hard expression. Father Goram looked at the assassin and said chillingly, "I suggest you take your gold, Mr. Simon, gather your people, and leave InnisRos before the sun appears on the horizon. Do you understand?"

The assassin, defiant to the end, made a rude hand gesture at Father Goram as he turned and stalked away. From behind Father Goram, Mary McKenna whispered, "That bas…!"

"Now, now, Miss McKenna," Father Goram cautioned with a smile. "Not in front of the baby."

"Yes, my Lord," Mary McKenna replied. "My Lord?" she said after a few seconds.

"Yes?"

"What about the wolves?" Mary McKenna asked.

Father Goram smiled, "Oh! Sorry. Here, reach out your hand and let Menelaus sniff it. It is how a wolf meets people." Mary McKenna complied, and, reassured, stepped out from behind the priest. In the meantime, Menelaus sniffed the baby. Surprising them all, the baby woke up and tugged at Menelaus' ear.

"Oh I think they will be great friends, my Lord!" Mary McKenna shouted with glee.

"Indeed they shall, Miss McKenna," Father Goram said. "Now if you would please take the baby, I wish to have a discussion with Menelaus."

"You can do…yes my Lord."

Father Goram and Menelaus joined with three of the other four a short distance away as the fourth wolf moved to protect Mary McKenna and the baby.

"Mr. Simon is a most disagreeable sort, wouldn't you say, Menelaus?" Father Goram said as he looked deeply into the wolf's eyes. "I truly wish I did not have to use his…special skill set. The fact that I allowed one such as he to walk this sacred ground is unforgivable. With so much at stake, however…but you don't really care about my self-recriminations, do you my four-legged friend? That man and his raping, murderous companions will return, of this I have no doubt. That cannot be allowed to happen."

Taking both hands and scratching behind Menelaus' ears, Father Goram issued instructions he regretted having to give but knew with absolute certainty they were absolutely necessary. "Menelaus, my friend, you must defend your pack. But do not eat my friend. You and your fellow wolves should never get a taste for humankind."

Menelaus, who was staring back into the eyes of Father Goram, did not wish to kill for the sake of killing only, but having been around the elves for such a long time, recognized this distasteful practice was sometimes required. With a howl of understanding, Menelaus turned and ran into the woods, closely followed by the other four.

Satisfied that Mr. Simon would get what he so richly deserved, Father Goram turned and said, "Come, Miss McKenna. Our evening is not done as of yet. We have some traveling to do. How is your young charge?"

"She has fallen back asleep, my lord," Mary McKenna replied.

As the three made their way back to the monastery, Father Goram started to hear the screams.

<hr />

The dawn came fully upon them as Father Goram and Mary McKenna walked through the woods, Mary going first while holding the baby. As they walked, Father Goram studied her. She was about eighteen years old and very attractive. She had long red hair which set off her deep green eyes. There were no signs that she had recently given birth, her form slender and shapely. He watched as she moved lithely through the brush and trees, carefully holding the baby and protecting the child from branches that might get in the way and do harm. This concern for the baby, along with her easy going manner and her ability to function under great stress, as she had already shown and no doubt displayed during the long trip to InnisRos, made her even more beautiful, more worthy. Father Goram suddenly found himself attracted to her.

"Miss McKenna, might I ask you a question?" he said.

"Certainly, my Lord," Mary McKenna answered. "You may ask whatever you wish."

"First we should dispense with all the formality, don't you think? Please call me Horatio."

Mary McKenna shook her head. "Oh I could never do that! I have too much respect for the clergy to ever become so familiar."

"I am not really clergy, you know. I don't have a flock nor do I preach. I am a cleric, a priest of Althaya. I run a simple monastery. We do what we can to help people solve problems, heal them of injury or disease, fight evil where we should find it, and serve Althaya." Father Goram replied.

"If you will excuse me, but I think a monastery that can afford ten thousand gold without so much as a by your leave is not so simple, my Lord...sorry. I mean Father."

"You think I overpaid for the child?"

"Oh no, Father! That is not what I meant at all. I only meant that your resources seem to be more than that of a simple monastery, which means you are much more than a simple backwoods cleric," Mary McKenna replied. "Just your presence demands respect. I can read people, Father. I know who they are by the way they carry themselves, by the way they talk, and by the way they treat a person. In my former line of work it was necessary to develop this skill to survive."

"Mary McKenna, you read true. Forgive me, but I wished to be less formal because I did not want to make you feel uncomfortable, and I want you to understand that you are safe and among friends. We all owe you a great debt for seeing the child safely through to us," Father Goram said as he absently brushed away an errant spider web from his hand. "Will you at least consider it?"

"Perhaps in time, Father," Mary McKenna said.

"I suppose that's all I have a right to expect, Miss McKenna."

After traveling for a few more minutes, Mary McKenna suddenly called out, "Father, there appears to be a path just ahead."

Father Goram nodded. "Yes, Miss McKenna. Please go to your left. That will lead us to the monastery."

The two shortly left the woods and were walking on the path, shoulder to shoulder. The baby was still asleep in Mary McKenna's arms.

"I seem to remember you wanted to ask me a question, Father?" Mary McKenna said, breaking the silence.

"Huh? Oh yes, I rather did, actually. I completely forgot," Father Goram replied. "Now that this ugliness is over, what do you wish to do? Do you want to go back to the mainland? I can see to it that you are safely transported back and given a permanent stipend to live on. I would not see you go back to the life you were living. Or we could set you up here on InnisRos. You would be safe from any of Mr. Simon's friends that might hold a grudge. Just name it, and if it is within my power, I will see to it you have what you want. As I said, we are very grateful."

"Father, I will not take your charity," Mary McKenna responded.

"My dear girl the thought never entered my mind," Father Goram answered. "As I said, we'll do whatever we can to help you move on with your life, but….would you consider staying at the monastery and working for me? The baby seems to like you and I really am afraid we have no practical experience raising such a young person. I daresay I'm probably all thumbs changing diapers. You would be a great help to me. Indeed, to the entire monastery. Will you at least think about it?"

Mary McKenna stopped and looked over at Father Goram. "You will pay an honest wage for honest work?"

"Well of course…"

"No, there is no need for you to answer," Mary McKenna said as she shook her head. "Helping to raise a child, especially one as precious as this, is never work. It is a responsibility and a pleasure. I would be honored to do so even if only for room and board. But listen to me, Father, she must have the best education you can offer... and no disappearing now that you have someone to look after her. She will need a father figure. She will need you as well as the entire monastery to support and care for her as she grows up. I have seen far too many men get a woman with child and never even look upon the child after it is born. That's cowardly desertion."

"Miss McKenna, I would never..."

Mary McKenna interrupted, "Upon your word in the name of your goddess!"

Smiling slightly so Mary McKenna could not see, Father Goram said, "You drive a hard bargain, madam, but I am up for the challenge. Upon my word it is. May Althaya strike me dead if I should ever break this sacred oath! Do we spit in our hands and shake upon it? I have heard that is a human custom."

Mary McKenna rolled her eyes. "That won't be necessary, Father. Actually that's quite disgusting. I trust you. Besides, if you do abandon her, it will not be Althaya you will have to worry about. Oh, with everything going on, I almost forgot. The baby has papers, papers that were also stolen from the orphanage. Mr. Simon told me to hide them. I guess he didn't remember."

Father Goram stopped. "Well, he did have other things on his mind at the time. May I see them Miss McKenna?"

"Of course you can." Mary McKenna said. "I wrapped them up in the baby's blanket. Not so she could feel them, but enough that they were secure. Here, take the baby," Mary McKenna said, handing over the baby to Father Goram, who took her with practiced ease. Mary McKenna raised an eyebrow at Father Goram's apparent expertise. He had been exposed by his effortless handling of the child and, without doubt, had much experience handling children regardless of his claims to be "all thumbs changing a diaper", but Mary McKenna said nothing as she rummaged in the blanket.

"Wait, you put the documents in the baby's blanket?" Father Goram suddenly exclaimed. "I mean, were there not more obvious places to put them? Such as…" But Father Goram didn't finish, his face suddenly reddening.

Mary McKenna paused. "You think perhaps I should have put them in my bodice?"

"I…I…" Father Goram stammered.

Mary McKenna laughed for the first time, a warm rich laugh. "Father Goram, there are three problems with that. One, it is actually the most obvious place for a woman to hide things. Do you think the location on a female body will stop a man from searching there? Father, it's the first place they would look. And the types of people Mr. Simon dealt with were not gentlemen. Also, the reason I was kidnapped in the first place was because I could feed the baby. That meant constantly opening my bodice, not to mention females in my condition have a tendency to….. well, we leak. I haven't worn a dry bodice for six months. The papers would have turned into pulp within a few hours. Finally, if you would quit turning your eyes away, you'd see that there really is not a lot of room to put papers in my bodice anyway."

Completely mortified, Father Goram could only stammer, "Yes ma'am. Please proceed getting the documents out of the blanket."

"OK. Come here and help…loosen that end just so. No not like that. Move a little more to the left."

"Like this?" Father Goram asked.

"Perfect. Here they are." And Mary McKenna handed Father Goram a small packet and then took the baby so Father Goram could break the seal and read the documents.

"Father Goram, she's awake," Mary McKenna said, forcing Father Goram to avert his study of the documents. Looking down, Father Goram saw the baby was indeed awake and staring directly at him with serious golden brown eyes.

"Well good morning, Brighteyes!" Father Goram exclaimed with a laugh.

The baby scrunched up her face then let out a yell that would rival Menelaus. Father Goram cringed, concerned. "I didn't mean anything by it, Miss McKenna, really I didn't. I was only saying good morning! Oh no, I scared the baby!"

"Calm down Father! It's okay. She only needs her diaper changed and then some breakfast."

"You're sure, Miss McKenna?" Father Goram asked.

"Of course I am," Mary McKenna said as she looked around. "I need…perfect! There's a big pile of soft leaves. That will do nicely. Let me take care of her while you read those papers. Maybe she has a name. She dearly needs a name."

"Yes, of course she does," Father Goram said, watching as Mary McKenna changed the baby's diaper. He absentmindedly conjured a protection spell around both to keep them safe while he was distracted. In the back of his mind he wished Menelaus and his pack were here as a further precaution. No matter. This close to the monastery they should be out of harm's way. When Mary McKenna, having changed the baby's diaper, started to undo her bodice to feed the baby, Father Goram politely turned his back.

"Let's see what these papers have to say about our young charge," Father Goram whispered to himself as he opened the papers and began reading.

"Well, what do they say?" Mary McKenna asked. Startled from concentrating on the documents, Father Goram turned to see Mary McKenna standing next him and holding the baby to her breast. She had placed a light rag over her shoulder, covering the feeding baby, to spare Father Goram further embarrassment.

"Miss McKenna! I'm sorry, but you startled me. That's not going to suffocate the poor lass, is it?"

Mary McKenna laughed lightly and smiled. "No, the child is in no danger, at least from the handkerchief. She can breathe through it quite well."

"Well…that's very good, Miss McKenna. From the sounds, it does indeed seem that she was quite hungry."

"Aye, Father. That she was. But I think she's ready for something a bit more substantial. When we get to your monastery, I should need to start mixing and feeding her solids."

"Anything you require, Miss McKenna." Noticing that some of Mary McKenna's long hair has fallen across her face, Father Goram reached over and gently moved it to the side, making eye contact while he did so. Mary McKenna suddenly turned away after a few seconds, looking down at the baby.

"The documents, Father." She reminded him.

"Yes, Yes! Of course! It says that our young lady was found in a forest clearing called Lizardhead Knoll west of Covington. Covington? Why does that name sound so familiar to me? Anyway, a band of adventurers who called Covington home came upon a small skirmish in Lizardhead Knoll. A group of elves were being besieged by small band of the dark elf."

"I have read of the dark elf, Father. A race of elves from another world that come to ours to…..Father, they raid to plunder, kill, and enslave!" Mary McKenna gasped. "This baby has already lived a charmed life!"

Looking at Mary McKenna, Father Goram said, "Yes, she has been most fortunate. I am ashamed to say they are cousins to my own people." Suddenly he paused. "Hold on. You can read? Extraordinary!"

"It's a common misconception about women in my line of work, Father. You should know not to judge people with preconceived notions."

"You are quite correct, Mary McKenna," Father Goram said. "And I'd like to add that you will never again have to be involved in your previous line of work."

"To which I am grateful. About the documents…?"

"Yes…the documents. This is from the hand of the leader of the group that came upon the dark elf attack, a human named Edwin Joseph. This isn't all of it, just the most pertinent part,"

The Salvation of Innocence

'Just before we had reached the end of our patrol area, we heard distant fighting. What we came upon was a dark elf raiding party attacking a much smaller band of travelers. We of course rushed to assist. When the dark elves realized they were outnumbered, outmaneuvered, and could not escape, they started the killing, even those whom they had already captured. There was one female elf that was plainly heavy with child fighting like a banshee. She was the only one still standing. I have never seen such swordplay. But the numbers she fought against were too many, our arrival too late and she was gravely wounded. We dispatched the evil dark elves as quickly as we could, but at the end, we were too late. All were dead save the female, and she would not last much longer. Having no foe left to fight and no further danger to her unborn babe, she sank to the ground. We did not have a cleric with us, a most regrettable circumstance, so all we could really do was bandage her wounds and make her as comfortable as possible. I could see the light fading from her eyes as she started her passage to the afterlife. Taking my hand, she implored me to come closer for she no longer had the strength to speak above a whisper. She told me her name was Annessa. She made me vow to try and save the baby after her death and, if I were successful, to name the child. I, of course, acquiesced. It was a dying declaration and there was no honor in doing otherwise. Upon her demise, I took a knife and opened her belly from which I drew the baby. I have five children of my own, so I knew what had to be done. It was a little girl. Having cleared the child's mouth, I softly rubbed her to stimulate breath. Within a few minutes she was crying loudly. This one was strong, I could sense it. I then held her up in both hands for the world and the gods to see, and I named her as her mother asked, Kristen Rosilie Clearwater.'

"BURP!"

"Indeed, Brighteyes, indeed," Father Goram said as he looked up from the text he was reading. Mary McKenna was holding Kristen over her shoulder and patting her on the back as she stepped closer to read the document over Father Goram's shoulder.

"Well, Miss McKenna, do you want to elaborate upon what it says?" Father Goram asked.

"I'm sorry, Father," Mary McKenna said demurely. "Please go on with your narrative…"

"BURP!"

Mary McKenna smiled. "Good girl! I knew you had another in you. Father, perhaps I'm a little impatient, but I already know she was placed in an orphanage in Ascension. I was with Mr. Simon when he took her so you can skip that part. I'm curious to know why she was sent there in the first place."

"Well, let me see. It appears that her rescuers, after burying her dead mother and all the others, took her to what serves as the council of elders in Covington. They decided to send the child to Ascension. That's odd. Why would a baby be outcast from Covington and taken all the way to Ascension? Surely there were people who would have gladly taken her in. The only clue is a cryptic remark that Covington was close to the ruins of Elanesse. That's where I've heard the name Covington! It's proximity to Elanesse. The papers say that this closeness could be dangerous. I wonder why that is? Why are the ruins of Elanesse a danger to her? We have a mystery, Miss McKenna!"

At about that same time, two elves appeared on the road in the distance. Father Goram placed his hand lightly on the small of Mary McKenna's back. "Come. They are Vayl and Autumn from my monastery. I've been expecting them."

THE SALVATION OF INNOCENCE

The two elves approached Father Goram, Mary McKenna and the baby. One was female and the other male, both with dark long hair and brown eyes. They moved with the customary grace and beauty of the elven people. They carried about them the authority gained through years of study followed by years of experience, confident, capable and completely at ease with their surroundings. Dressed in light armor and covered in splendid blue cloaks to protect against the light morning chill, they each had a mace hanging from their belt and a quarterstaff in their hands. Each had a gleaming holy symbol around their neck which was an identical match to the holy symbol of Althaya worn by Father Goram. They smiled as they drew near the trio. Mary McKenna immediately felt at ease in their presence.

Father Goram shook hands with each. "Well met, my friends. Allow me to introduce my companions. This is Miss Mary McKenna and the baby is Kristen Rosilie Clearwater. Miss McKenna, if you will permit me, this is Vayl Falconclaw and Autumn Vanerious."

Vayl smiled and bowed slightly. "It is my honor to meet you, Miss McKenna."

Autumn, however, immediately rushed over and looked down at Kristen, saying to Mary McKenna, "We are very glad you have been able to keep this little one safe, Miss McKenna, and thankful you are safe as well. Welcome!" Reaching down, Autumn tickled Kristen's belly and made a face, a tradition all adults share with all babies.

Father Goram said to Vayl, "Did one of Menelaus' pack wolves come by?"

"Yes, Horatio," Vayl replied. "The images I got were that all was well with you and the baby. But he was most disconcerted about missing out on a good meal. What was that all about?"

"I'll explain in a bit." Turning his attention to Autumn he said, "Autumn, please escort Miss McKenna and Kristen back to the monastery and show them to the quarters we have reserved. You're going to need to talk to Mister Abraham about moving Miss McKenna in with Kristen, at least until she is old enough to be in a room on her own. And please make sure Miss McKenna gets a good breakfast. And have breakfast ready for me as well. I daresay, we are both famished. At least I am."

"Are you coming, Father?" Mary McKenna asked. Everything had been so unsettled and frightening over the last month and events still continued to happen very fast. Father Goram had quite unexpectedly become Mary McKenna's anchor during this very hectic time.

Laying a hand lightly on Mary McKenna's shoulder, Father Goram said, "I'll be along shortly, Miss McKenna. But there are some things I need to attend with Vayl. Please be at ease. You are going to your new home where you and the baby will be well protected and cared for. You will be one of us."

"I take no charity, remember?"

"Miss McKenna, I have no doubt you will earn your keep doubly so," Father Goram responded.

"Please follow me, Miss McKenna," Autumn said.

"Ma'am, you may call me Mary."

"And you must call me Autumn."

"I should like that," Mary McKenna said, following Autumn back to the monastery.

Father Goram watched the retreating backs of Mary McKenna and Autumn. Vayl touched his sleeve lightly.

"What troubles you, Horatio?"

"You know me well, Vayl," Father Goram said as he continued to watch the two women walk towards the monastery. Autumn was still making faces at Kristen whose laughter could be heard even at the distance separating them. "I did not think this through properly. Because of my stupidity, I caused great harm to come to Miss McKenna."

"You did as you were instructed by Althaya. The baby Kristen is here, safe and well protected. What more is there? Is this not the outcome you desired?"

"The end justifies the means?" Father Goram replied, turning to look at Vayl.

"That is not what I meant, Horatio," Vayl said.

"Did you know that Mary McKenna was raped by Mr. Simon's band of cutthroats and murderers? I'm responsible for that! I hired a known assassin to retrieve Kristen, thinking he had the best chance for success. Did I stop to think how he would keep a baby alive for a month's journey over land and across an ocean? No, I did not, but he did. He kidnapped Miss McKenna, a woman who was even then still grieving over the loss of her own child."

"What else could you do, Horatio?"

"I could have gone myself, Vayl! I didn't because I did not want to leave the confines of our home island! I didn't because I did not want to ever return to the mainland again! How can I be so incredibly selfish?" Father Goram exclaimed.

"You're being too hard on yourself, my dear friend."

Father Goram looked at Vayl with an intensity Vayl was not used to seeing. Finally Father Goram said, "Am I? Self-reprimand is good for the soul, especially if it is so richly deserved as is mine. It is a wonderful thing Miss McKenna is such a strong woman else she would have been broken. But all the protection and care we now offer her does not make up for the depravity she has already endured for the sake of the baby and for the accomplishment of a mission that was given to me. To me, Vayl! The innocent shall never suffer from our carelessness. I have taught this to you, to Autumn, to every acolyte in my monastery, yet I'm the one who broke the very foundation of that imperative."

Vayl looked down at the dirt at his feet. His friend deeply believed in the principles he espoused. As much as it hurt Vayl to see Father Goram in so much self-inflicted pain, nothing he could say would deflect the seriousness of Father Goram's actions and their subsequent consequences.

Looking back up at Father Goram, Vayl said, "And you also teach that mistakes are inevitable since we are mortal. That once a mistake is made, learn from it, try to correct it if possible, and move on with our lives. It's a commonsense principle, but a principle you make sure we never lose sight of. Are you in jeopardy of breaking yet another of your teachings?"

Father Goram smiled in reaction to Vayl's light reproach. "No my friend, I am not. I will correct my error in judgment. In fact, I've already started with help from Menelaus. And, as you have already pointed out, Miss McKenna and Kristen are now safely under our protection and will be for as long as they accept it. I'm very curious, however, as to why Althaya wanted this particular child brought here. Speaking of which, do you have the chapel ready for tonight?"

"All has been prepared. Althaya's instructions?"

"Yes, although I don't know why she wants plants brought in," Father Goram replied.

"Well, whatever the reason, the chapel looks like a clearing in a forest right now. Plants ring the room and spells have been cast to prevent detection and intrusion. Damn odd, that. If our goddess doesn't want an interruption, all she has to do is will it so." Vayl replied.

"Think it through, Vayl. Obviously something very important is going on. Goddess magic has a different scent to it. Sorcerers and clerics scrying at that moment would instantly be drawn to it. They would not be able to eavesdrop, but they would know something is going on and the general location. That could be very dangerous."

Vayl nodded. "While mortal spells would not cause attention because there are so many of those being cast at any given moment. They will be virtually ignored."

"Exactly," Father Goram responded.

Changing the subject, Vayl asked, "Horatio, what happened last night?"

"Vayl, I know evil. Many times I have faced a demon or the undead. To see in a mortal the evil that I saw in Mr. Simon, however, took me completely by surprise. From the moment he came into my presence, I knew he could not live. I knew the band of brigands he led must be exterminated from existence. Althaya preserve me, I wanted to wrap my hands around his throat and strangle the life out of him right then and there. I wanted to watch as the light left his eyes. I wanted him to finally understand that the world held no place for him or others like him. But I was forced to restrain myself because of Miss McKenna and Kristen. I could not put them in jeopardy, indeed, would not, even without Althaya's request that the baby be rescued. As soon as Miss McKenna walked into the clearing with Kristen, I actually felt the importance of the baby. And Miss McKenna, so brave while being so very frightened, willing to give her life for the baby, clutched my heart and captured it. So I took certain measures, Vayl. Menelaus and his pack were happy to comply, though I daresay I used him terribly and owe him an apology."

"You set them on the intruders?"

"I really didn't have a choice, Vayl. I was not going to let them leave the island alive. But I couldn't do it myself. I had to make sure Miss McKenna and Kristen remained safe."

The two begin walking again, neither speaking for several minutes. Father Goram then spoke up and said, "I think I'm going to join Miss McKenna for breakfast, make sure her and Kristen are properly settled in, and then grab a few hours of sleep."

Nodding, Vayl said, "You look like you could use it."

"It's been a hard month," Father Goram responded, every word sounding fatigued.

"Tell me about it, Horatio. You've been like a madman, driving every priest and priestess crazy with all your demands."

"Which has been handled quite admirably by everyone," Father Goram said. "I am quite proud of each person in the monastery."

"We are a product of your teachings." Vayl replied.

"It also speaks of your own character," Father Goram said. "Never sell yourself short. There is still much to do, Vayl."

"We serve at your pleasure, Horatio." Vayl said.

Father Goram raised his eyebrow and smiled. "You're a good second, Vayl. Here's what I want you to arrange. First, I want a sweep of the area. Four squads, each squad with a cleric who is familiar with both healing and animal spells. Send one squad in each direction of the compass. There are going to be members of Menelaus' pack that will need attending to who may not be able to travel on their own. If any of them are dead bring the bodies back for ritual burning. They died on our behest and will get the respect such a death deserves. We must also be prepared to receive injured animals at the monastery. Get the word out that these animals are to be approached very carefully. Everyone should understand how to handle wounded animals, but I want to make sure there are no misunderstandings. I want no more blood on my hands for today."

"I'll see to it, Horatio." Vayl responded.

"Thank you. I promised Menelaus I would do what I could to help any wounded members of his pack."

"By your command, Horatio," Vayl said as he bowed.

Father Goram shook his head in exasperation. "Oh stop that!" He said with a smile. "Next I want you to go with the squad covering the eastern quadrant. That is the direction Mr. Simon was going when last I saw him and the quickest route off the island if he wanted to bypass populated areas. I did not anticipate asking Menelaus and his pack removing the blight of Mr. Simon and his band last night, but now that it has, I'd like to retrieve the gold I gave him for services rendered."

"I should think so, Horatio. That amount put a sizable deficit in monastery coffers."

"Nevertheless, I considered it money well spent for the life of Kristen and, as it turned out, Miss McKenna," Father Goram said. "But perhaps we can get it back. When I sent Menelaus after Mr. Simon, I did not ask him to be careful of the magical bag. I did not want him holding back any attack. Mr. Simon was a very dangerous fellow. Besides, how do you explain to a dire wolf, regardless of how intelligent, the importance we place on shiny metal? But if the bag was not damaged, causing its magic to destroy the contents, perhaps we can reclaim the gold."

"If it is on this island, we will find it." Vayl swore.

"I know you will, Vayl."

Father Goram and Vayl traveled a few more minutes without speaking. They were getting close to the monastery. Breaching the last rise in the road, the monastery of Calmacil Clearing came into view. This sight never failed to bring a sense of well-being and peace to Father Goram. He was coming home.

Nestled in heavily wooded valley, a massive main building sat in the center of a large clearing surrounded by smaller buildings of various sizes. The overall appearance was that of a small city. There were homes, shops, stables, a blacksmith workshop, and many smaller specialty stores. Corrals containing cattle, goats and pigs rimmed the clearing. Large vegetable gardens and fruit groves had been cut into the surrounding forest and both flourished under the hands of expert growers. Running between the smaller structures and the main building was a series of roads and paths, all heavily traveled by clerics, warriors and civilians in all manner of dress. A nearby river irrigated the gardens and groves as well as provided water to all inhabitants.

It was the church in the middle, however, that dominated the city landscape. It gave more the appearance of a fortified castle than a church. It had fifty foot high battlements going around the circumference, reinforced by large one-hundred-foot towers on four sides. The battlements and towers were constantly patrolled by warriors, each of whom carried deadly looking longbows and quivers of arrows. The warriors also had swords encased in decorated scabbards hanging from belts around their waist. As large as the battlements were, they were dwarfed by the main building which they surrounded. Made of granite, this rectangular building stood one-hundred feet from the base of the walls to the roof eaves and was four-hundred feet long and one-hundred feet at its widest point. A tower rose up from the front of the building a full three-hundred feet, from the ground to the top of the symbol of Althaya. Along all sides on the roofs were fantastic carvings of small dragons with eyes shining of silver with a hint of stored vitality, almost as if they would come alive at the slightest provocation. If the city itself were to be attacked, the fortress church was designed to become an impenetrable barrier large enough to accept and protect all from the city that choose to harbor inside.

Rubbing his hands together, Father Goram said with excitement, "I can almost smell the bacon frying from here! By the way, I want you to do one last thing, Vayl, before heading out with the squads. I wish to pen a message to Her Highness the Queen. Somewhere off our coast lies a smuggler ship that needs attention. Please make ready one of our small messenger dragons. It should be one that's flown the route before. I don't want any problems later if that ship gets away because we failed to get the message delivered."

"You're not going to mention you're the reason the ship is here, are you?" Vayl asked.

Father Goram laughed. "No, I think I'll leave that part out."

"Good. You're overly honest and I sometimes worry our Majesty or someone on the council may decide you've crossed the boundary into treason," Vayl said, though he had little actual concern. Father Goram, besides being one of the most powerful priests on the island, was a master politician.

"You know how you beat a treason charge, Vayl? You say its church business. Let them try to prove you wrong."

"I'll be sure to remember that." Vayl replied dryly.

The females and the pups were safe. Menelaus was never overly concerned, they had been well hidden and guarded by several males. But he wanted to make sure. They were the future of his pack, and the men he attacked when the dark was upon the land were dangerous foes. Menelaus normally did not like to concern himself in the affairs of the elves, but the valley elves, especially their pack leader, had been kind to his pack for several generations and trust and loyalty were owed. The battle to kill the strange men from the sea, however, turned out to be deadlier than he had anticipated. Three of his pack was killed and five were wounded, including himself. Fortunately valley elves had come out of their dens and helped his brethren heal. The dead were being taken back to the elf pack leader to be burned, a ritual that showed respect. Menelaus was grateful.

THE SALVATION OF INNOCENCE

Menelaus was pack leader for several reasons. The most obvious was his size and strength. No other male would dare challenge him. A strong pack leader meant full bellies and a safe den. But Menelaus was also extremely intelligent for a dire wolf. He knew the hearts of his pack would be better won if he treated them as family. From that, he found, sprang an intense loyalty to him. He also did not lay claim to all the females. His own mate, Bella, was the only female he desired. She, of course, also claimed him. His son, Romulus, was only a few months old, but he was already the biggest of all the pups, smart, fierce, and dominant. He would someday take Menelaus' place as pack leader. No other male would object. They would welcome him when he was of age.

As Menelaus walked his territory, insuring all was well after such a violent night, he was suddenly accosted by a rich blue light coming down from the sky. Soon, in its place, was a female person, but this female was different from any he had ever seen or met before. Her scent was very subtle, almost to the point of non-existent, yet great power radiated from her. Menelaus understood power and instinctively knew she was his master. For the first time in his life Menelaus was afraid.

Althaya walked over to the wolf who, though leery, did not attempt to scamper away. "You are a big wolf, even by dire standards. What is your name?"

Menelaus was astounded. The blue dressed female was talking in the civilized language of the wolf. "I am Menelaus. Who are you?"

"My name is Althaya. My pack is very large with many elves and humans."

"You are pack leader," Menelaus said, not as a question but as a statement of fact. "Is the elf called Horatio part of your pack?"

"He is, as are all the ones in his pack," Althaya said.

Menelaus considered. "Horatio is a strong pack leader, the strongest of all the people in this valley. He has never talked of his pack leader, however. I did not think one such as he needed one."

"Menelaus, we all need pack leaders to help us. Would you not say this is a wise thing?" Althaya asked.

"I would not have thought so before I met Horatio. People have a different way of…of…smelling things. I am not sure I have spoken that correctly."

Althaya smiled at Menelaus' wolf way of speaking. It was refreshing. "I understand you perfectly, Menelaus. We all must answer to a pack leader, even me. I have a request to make of you, Menelaus. Will you hear me?" she asked.

"Do I have a choice?" Menelaus responded.

"Yes, Menelaus, yes you do. I am not the kind of pack leader that will force my will unless I have no choice, and then only if it is for the greater good," Althaya said.

"So this is not one of those times?" Menelaus asked.

Althaya shook her head. "No. But if you do what I ask, it will bring great honor to your pack."

"Wolves understand honor. What do you require?"

"This will be difficult, but I ask that you give to me your son. The one you call Romulus," Althaya replied.

Menelaus growled. In an instant, all his hopes, dreams, and desires for both Romulus and the pack were being jeopardized. While it was true Bella could still bear litters and sons to be heir, Romulus was a special pup. "This is a hard thing for me to consider, Althaya. He would be pack leader one day."

"There will be other sons, Menelaus. He will still live in this valley, at least during your lifetime, but he will be part of Horatio's pack. I would make him guardian and friend to another person. Her name is Kristen. I will give him long life, for Kristen will live much longer then the dire wolf. He will have many adventures and see many places. He will not only be known as Romulus, but also as the son of Menelaus, pack leader of the Calmacil Clearing valley dire wolves. As I have already told you, he will bring great honor to you and your pack. His destiny will guarantee your pack will never go hungry, even if all the prey in the valley were to leave, for your pack will be brothers to Horatio's pack and they will forever be grateful for this sacrifice. I make this promise to you."

THE SALVATION OF INNOCENCE

Menelaus, carefully considering, decided he could trust this blue person who is Horatio's pack leader, "It will be as you say."

Althaya sighed in relief. She wanted this to happen of the wolf's own free will, for only then could she be sure of the pact now made between them. "Tonight, when the moon is straight up in the sky, you must bring Romulus to the great house where Horatio lives. It will not be goodbye, but after tonight Romulus will be part of Horatio's pack and not yours."

"Will you be there?" Menelaus asked.

"I will but you will not see me. Farewell, Menelaus. Bella will give you many sons and daughters, and you shall grow old in a safe den with a full belly," Althaya said as she slowly faded away.

<hr />

"Horatio, I don't understand," Autumn exclaimed in a voice that was laced through with panic. "I can feel Althaya, she is with me, her power fills my soul, but I cannot heal Vayl. All my attempts end in failure."

"How can that be, Autumn? Healing is your specialty!" Father Goram replied, rushing over to the prone Vayl and kneeling beside Autumn. "There must be something you can do! He is bleeding to death!"

"I have bound him in bandages, but his wounds are too severe! The bandages slow his blood loss but will not prevent it. All I have done is delayed the inevitable," Autumn responded.

"Move over and let me try!" Father Goram said, watching the situation spin out of control. Concentrating, he tried to conjure a heal spell, but, though his call to Althaya was heard, nothing happened. Turning in frustration, he angrily cast a column of fire on an innocent bush, burning it to ashes. "Damn it!" he shouted.

"Horatio, what are we going to do!" Autumn pleaded.

Father Goram took a deep breath in order to calm himself. "Think!" Suddenly understanding flooded his mind, and the implications staggered him. So many lives are going to be lost, starting with Vayl's. Turning to look at Autumn, he said sadly, "We can do nothing, Autumn. No healing or resurrection or magical comfort is possible. The source of healing magic is gone."

"That can't be, Horatio. Althaya would not do that to us, would she?" Autumn, suddenly very fearful, cried out.

"My dear, Althaya had nothing to do with it. We did this to ourselves," Father Goram dejectedly responded.

"No, Horatio, it can't be! Horatio..."

"Father Goram, are you awake?!"

Father Goram was awakened from the dream by a voice and the consistent rapping of a knuckle on his apartment door. "Yes! Yes! I'll be out in a minute," he said, wiping sleep from his eyes. Walking over to a wash basin, he splashed cold water on his face. Looking into a mirror, seeing his reflection staring back, Father Goram thought about the dream he just experienced. No, it was more than a dream, it was a sending. "Maybe I'll get answers tonight," he said to himself. Looking into the mirror, he wondered, "Where in the world did these bags under my eyes came from?"

Twenty minutes later Father Goram walked out of his room. Flagging down one of the many staff personnel going about their daily duties, he asked the girl to draw him a bath. Deciding he had a little time before the bath was ready, he walked down the hallway to the nursery to check on Miss McKenna and Kristen. Remembering that babies sleep at all hours, he gently knocked on the door and whispered, "Miss McKenna?"

Mary McKenna opened the door with a finger to her lips, "Shhhhh. I've just now gotten her asleep."

"Was she being fussy, Miss McKenna?" Father Goram asked.

"No, not at all, but she is so inquisitive! She did not want to close her eyes."

"I see. Have you slept at all?" Father Goram inquired.

"Yes for a few hours. Autumn took Kristen on a tour of the monastery. Autumn is very good with her, Father," Mary McKenna said.

Father Goram nodded. "Healing is her specialty, and the children here get into so much trouble, bumps, bruises, fevers, and all manner of illnesses. She has had a lot of experience. May I see our Brighteyes, Miss McKenna?"

THE SALVATION OF INNOCENCE

Mary McKenna took Father Goram's hand and led him over to the cradle. "Certainly, Father, but please be quiet."

"Miss McKenna, sometimes quiet is my middle name," Father Goram said as he stealthily walked over to the cradle with Mary McKenna to look at the child. Noticing the sound made by his hard-soled boots, he decided he would order the floor covered in soft furs. That would also help to keep away any chill the fireplace missed. Besides, a baby shouldn't be crawling around on stone floors.

Looking down at Kristen, Father Goram's heart immediately melted. Sleeping babies always had that effect on him. He then started thinking about why his little Brighteyes was so important to Althaya. In a burst of inspiration, he recognized that she was not the answer, but the answer to the answer. But what was the question? And since when did Kristen become "his little Brighteyes"?

The moon was straight up in the sky. It was midnight and time for Father Goram's audience with his goddess. He was in good spirits. Vayl found the gold and returned it to the monastery bank, he had for the first time in about a month a full, long sleep, and Mary McKenna seemed to have rekindled romantic feelings that had long been repressed within him. As he stood in the chamber and looked around, again wondering at the importance of the small trees and other miscellaneous bushes, he determined all had been satisfactorily made ready in accordance with Althaya's wishes. A brief rap on the chapel's stout door interrupted his thoughts.

"Yes what is it?" Father Goram answered testily as he opened the door, impatience written plainly on his face. The ranger standing before him gave no ground, however. It was plain that she would not be intimidated. Father Goram quickly calmed himself. The ranger was doing her duty and it was obvious that she would not have been bothered him if it were not important.

"Father, I'm sorry for the interruption, but I think there is something you need to see." The ranger said politely, bowing slightly.

"Safire Renill is it?" Father Goram asked.

"Yes, Father," replied the ranger.

But before Father Goram had an opportunity to apologize for his boorish behavior, her eyes widen and she fell to a knee. Confused by her behavior, he motioned to her with his hand and said, "Please get up, Safire. Surely you know me well enough to know I do not require such formality."

From behind him a familiar voice spoke, "Horatio, I do not believe the obeisance is for you."

Turning, Father Goram saw his goddess, Althaya. Standing beside her was Aurora, the goddess of the rangers. "Now the trees and bushes make sense," Father Goram thought. As Aurora walked over to stand next to Father Goram and Safire, a rainbow of colors flowed from her wings like a multi-colored flag blowing in the wind. "You honor me, Safire, but I do not require adulation. Only that you live an honest ranger life. Please rise."

"Aurora, may I ask you a question? Why do you always appear with wings?" Father Goram queried. "Forgive me, but I've always been curious about that. I mean you're a goddess and don't need them to fly."

"FATHER!" Safire reprimanded.

Althaya chuckled slightly. "Does nothing intimidate you, Horatio?"

"Well, Althaya, I can think of several things, most recent the thought of changing a diaper. Sooner or later I'm going to have to do that. Miss McKenna will no doubt insist upon it. She's a godsend, by the way. I beg forgiveness for inadvertently allowing such harm to come to her, but I'm very glad she is here."

"Why Horatio, you almost sound contrite," Althaya said. "That has been an unexpected yet welcomed development. We shall all strive to make the rest of her life as rich and full as possible in recompense."

Aurora tapped Father Goram on the chest with the tip of one of her wings. "By the way, in answer to your question, I have wings so I can quickly escape irreverent priests. Or perhaps I should fly you up into the sky and let you drop?"

"She is, after all, called the 'Angel of the Forest'. Do not angels have wings?" Althaya asked. "Perhaps you would be best advised to let the whole matter drop."

"Thank you for the timely and accurate observation, Althaya, as well as your excellent advice," Father Goram replied dryly with a raised eyebrow at Aurora and Safire who are nodding in agreement.

Safire smiled, "But say the word, mistress, and I shall smack him with the flat of my scimitars on the back of his hand as one would do to an unruly child."

Both goddesses laughed, but quickly the humor died as Althaya said. "Now, my priest, Safire was going to take you to see something. It is a dire wolf pup, is it not, Safire?"

Safire nodded. "Yes goddess. Menelaus brought him in from the forest and left him at the main doors. It was odd. We're used to Menelaus bringing sick or injured pups or other members of his pack for healing, but this pup is completely healthy. And beautiful! His coat is as black as the night and his eyes are the deepest blue. When we opened the doors to see to him, he bolted inside and went upstairs straight to the nursery. He just sits there in front of the door even as we speak. He lets us examine him, but when we try to move him away from the door, he snaps at us. We thought that peculiar enough to warrant Father Goram's immediate attention."

Althaya said. "Thank you, Safire. Horatio, the pup's name is Romulus and he is the son of Menelaus. Go with Safire, fetch him and bring him back."

"You did hear Safire say the pup snaps when someone tries to move him away from the nursery door, right? Dire wolves, even as puppies, are big, especially if Menelaus is his sire," Father Goram grumbled as he started to head to the nursery. "Don't go anywhere. I'll be right back."

As he followed Safire out of the chamber, Aurora said, "You were right about him," to which Althaya responded "It's why he's one of my favorites. I don't need priests who are afraid to offer me mortal perspectives or afraid to speak their minds. I can live with the occasional backtalk from time to time." Althaya paused. "Aurora, he has never failed me, and what I started with the Empath three-thousand years ago is finally starting to come into fruition. Of all my followers, only he has the fortitude to see this through. That is why I put the child, Kristen, in his care."

When Father Goram and Safire arrived at the end of the long hallway leading to the nursery, three floors above the audience chamber, they found the door open. Looking at each other with concern, they started running. There were several possibilities racing through their minds, none of which ended well. Dire wolves, regardless of this monastery's long association with the particular pack Romulus was a member of, are wild animals, even the pups. They're also big. Even at a young age, a pup, especially one that Menelaus sired, could be as tall as three feet at the shoulders with the strength to rip flesh.

Turning from the hallway and into the room, both priest and ranger were met with a sight that, if not for the seriousness of situation, would have had them doubled over in laughter. Romulus had calmly lain down at the foot of the cradle and was staring up at Mary McKenna who had interposed herself between the pup and the sleeping Kristen. She had a baby rattle raised up over her head, ready to strike if Romulus so much as moved. Romulus, hearing Father Goram and Safire enter the room, looked back at them and yawned. Mary McKenna, eyes never leaving the pup, said, "What took you so long?"

"Why Miss McKenna, it looks like you have this situation well in hand," Father Goram replied with a smile on his face.

"Well...forgive me, Father, but exactly what type of monastery are you running here!" Mary McKenna said indigently. "Wild animals...I mean really?"

"Your point is well taken, Miss McKenna. I shall have the person responsible flogged this very instant." Turning to Safire, Father Goram said, "Safire, please turn yourself in to our master-flogger this very instant. I think twenty lashes should suffice."

"You wouldn't, would you? I mean, really, there's no harm done. Kristen is safe, and it does seem like a rather nice wolf," Mary McKenna responded, suddenly worried for Safire.

"Then allow me to take the wolf from the room before we inadvertently wake up little Brighteyes. We shall forget this ever happened," Father Goram replied.

Breathing a sigh of relief, Mary McKenna said, "Yes, please, Father. Not another word."

Safire whispered, "How are you going to do that? Convince the pup to leave, that is."

"I think I'll just ask him," Father Goram replied.

Kneeling down in front of Romulus, Father Goram presented his hand for Romulus to sniff. He then petted his head and scratched behind both ears. "Romulus, I am Father Goram. Perhaps your pack leader, your sire, has spoken of me. Our packs are friendly to one another. You need to follow me for now, but I am sure Miss McKenna will let you back in once we are done."

"I don't know about that, Father," Mary McKenna said.

"Miss McKenna, a word if you please," Father Goram said as he ushered Mary McKenna away from the cradle to the other side of the room. She went somewhat reluctantly, but Safire took stood next to the cradle to reassure her. Before going with Father Goram, she handed Safire the baby rattle.

Father Goram took Mary McKenna by the shoulders. "Miss McKenna, things are happening that, at least for the moment, go beyond our ability to fully comprehend. I believe I will have some answers shortly, however, and will explain things to you when I can. But for now, I believe Romulus would never hurt Kristen. I believe he is her protector. Perhaps you can think of him as a bodyguard, a bodyguard assigned by the gods."

Mary McKenna did not look so sure. "Assigned by the gods, Father?"

"Yes Miss McKenna, by the gods. Will you be able to handle that?"

"Yes, Father, I think so. I trust you know what is best for Kristen."

"As I trust you do to, Miss McKenna. It is late. Try to get some sleep before little Brighteyes wakes up. I will see you in the morning,"

Father Goram turned and quietly called for Romulus to come. Surprisingly, the dire wolf pup got up and trotted over to the door, ready to follow. Safire, although she knew never to underestimate Father Goram's abilities, was nevertheless astonished. She couldn't wait to tell her friend and brother ranger, Tangus DeRango, about what had just happened. But the telling would probably best be said over a mug of strong ale, for he probably wouldn't believe it otherwise.

Romulus bounded into the audience chamber, leaving Father Goram and Safire striving to catch up without actually sprinting, hoping to maintain their dignity. Father Goram had not dismissed the ranger, sensing she would still be needed.

"Damn puppy exuberance!" Father Goram exclaimed as he walked into the chamber closely followed by Safire.

"The young have such a strong sense of life, don't you think?" Althaya said, not expecting an answer. She was kneeling and scratching Romulus behind the ears, something he seemed to love very much, so much so that he was soon on his back, obviously wanting a good rub on his belly. As Althaya complied, Father Goram saw one of Althaya's hands become insubstantial. Keeping the belly rub going with her other hand, Althaya's ghostly hand reached inside of Romulus to his heart. After a brief instant, a faint glow issued from the wolf, quickly subsiding. Althaya was now using both hands once again to rub the belly of Romulus. "That's a good boy!" she said, laughing.

Safire moved over to where Aurora was standing, watching the scene play out between Althaya and Romulus. Without taking her eyes from the goddess and dire wolf, Aurora said, "A thing to behold, is it not? As goddesses we are always so busy listening to petitions, granting spell use, judging the actions of those who follow us to ensure our dictates have been observed, and playing politics with the other gods and goddesses we never get to simply relax and do something that makes us laugh."

"But, my lady, can't you just...I don't know how to say this...can't you just make it so?" Safire responded, confused.

Aurora sighed. "Dear girl, if it were only that easy. Our long lives seem to be nothing but a constant series of crises. Evil never rests and so we shall not as well."

"Please tell me what I can do to help!"

Aurora looked at Safire. "You are already doing it by being a good ranger. Safire, I am very proud of you. For now, however, take Romulus back to the baby Kristen. Tell Mary McKenna that all is well and that she should never fear the wolf again."

"Father Goram mentioned to Miss McKenna that Romulus is to be one of Kristen's bodyguards," Safire said. "She's important, isn't she?"

"Yes she is, very much so. She is destined to be a priestess to Althaya and those skills are Father Goram's responsibility to instruct. But that is only part of her destiny. Safire, be her friend. Teach her as many other skills as you can, ranger skills, fighting skills, and survival skills. Her future travels will be filled with danger and it is imperative she endure to fulfill that which she is truly meant to accomplish. Lives depend upon it," Aurora said with passion.

Safire nodded her head, knowing she had just been charged with a mission by her goddess. "It will be as you wish, my lady Aurora!"

Aurora placed her hand on Safire's chest, over her heart. "Now attend your duties with my blessing."

Bowing to Aurora, Safire called to Romulus, "Come boy, let's go see Kristen." Romulus' ears perked up, and he quickly followed Safire out of the chamber.

Father Goram watched them go. He then moved to the door and closed it, leaving him and the two goddesses alone. "Althaya, I have done what you have asked. Brighteyes is safely here and under monastery protection, under MY protection. But obviously it does not stop here, does it? You need her for something important."

"Oh? What gave me away, Horatio?" Althaya replied sarcastically.

Father Goram purposely ignored Althaya's sarcasm. "I think it was when you told me to retrieve a specific orphaned baby from the mainland. Something like, and I'm quoting 'Oh, by the way, do whatever is necessary to make this happen'. To which I responded, 'Anything?' and you said, 'Anything!' Does that sound about right?"

"As close as I can recall. And I thank you for this service, Horatio. But as you have already noted, that is not all I require. Please sit with me," Althaya said, walking over and sitting on a nearby bench, patting a spot next to her with her hand.

"Let me guess. You want me to raise her as if she were my own child, teach her to be your priestess, make sure she is trained in the fighting skills, prepare her for the rigors of life, and when the time is right step aside so you can put her in harm's way," Father Goram replied testily as he sat down in the proffered spot.

"Calm down, Horatio, please. She will have Romulus and several other companions to help her see her way," Althaya pleaded.

"Romulus will be long dead before...You did something to him."

Althaya nodded her head in agreement. "I have extended his life line. He will not die prematurely of old age. Horatio, soon you will learn why this is so important. Please trust me!"

Father Goram sighed. "I beg your indulgence, my lady. Of course I trust you. But so much has already happened and, well, if I may speak boldly..."

Althaya smiled, "Of course you may. Since when have I ever tried to muzzle you?"

Father Goram cleared his voice. "Yes, I am a little set in my ways, I admit. It's just that.....Well, this is only the beginning and it disturbs me. I am going to love this little girl, if truth be known I already do, and her future is going to be fraught with great risk else why would she be so important to you. I will not be able to protect her! Can I not go in her stead?"

"You are correct, Horatio. It is only the beginning. What is necessary can only be accomplished by her, however. Yes, it will be hard. It will be hard for both of us and I know I ask a lot from my priest. But recognize that I have come to you with this because it is you I most trust to prepare Kristen for the perils she will face." Althaya laid a hand on Father Goram's arm. "But I will not force you, Horatio. Will you help me?"

"Always!"

Althaya smiled, "I am pleased. What do you know about the empath?"

Father Goram paused, thinking. "Not much really. Only stories probably meant to frighten little children. The stories and histories I have read say they could read minds and control what a person thinks and how a person feels. Supposedly there was a Purge several thousand years ago around old Elanesse on the mainland to destroy all empaths. If they ever did exist, the Purge must have killed them all for there has been no sign or rumor they are here in present time. I have always felt they were myths, but I also know that many myths have factual foundations, though the actual truth is usually lost over time."

Althaya nodded assent. "They are not myths, Horatio. The empath did in fact exist, though perhaps it is inaccurate to call them a race equivalent to elves, humans, or dwarves. They can be human or elves, but mostly human. It is the bloodline that matters and their abilities that make them so distinctive. They do not read minds or control thoughts. They heal people. They protect people through their ability to sense evil. No lie can be told before an empath that will not be furrowed out. The empath is innocence."

"No mortal can be pure innocence. And clerics have the same powers," Father Goram responded. "Where is this leading, Althaya?"

"Horatio…" Althaya started to reply, but suddenly stopped, considering. "I have been hiding something important from you, Horatio - and you as well, Aurora. This is a disservice to you both."

"I'm sure you had your reasons, sister," Aurora calmly responded.

Breathing deeply, Althaya looked at her priest, "Horatio, even the gods must keep secrets. It is how we keep those we love safe. It is how we survive. I am not going to get involved in a discussion about what happens between the gods, suffice to say that the same battles between good and evil occur at our level also. Unfortunately those battles often spill out into the mortal realm and frequently innocents are destroyed as a result. I am not proud of that, none of us are, at least those defending the righteous. Because of this, we are at times forced to be very cautious. Being open and keeping no secrets is a weakness that can lead to our annihilation as well as that of our followers."

"I'm aware of the squabbles the gods have amongst themselves, as well as the suffering it causes in the mortal realm," Father Goram said, his tone serving to scold his mistress. "What is your secret?"

Althaya sighed, but accepted his rebuke. "Horatio, Kristen has Empath blood running through her veins. It is not enough to make her a true empath, but certainly enough to make her very proficient in all healing. It also gives her an extraordinary affinity for all people. But that is only part of her importance. There is one other, a true empath, whom, with the help of Aurora, I have kept safe for over three millennia. She is but a little girl, but even as young as she is, her powers are strong. Her name is Esmeralda Clearwater."

"Clearwater! That's…"

"Yes, Horatio, Kristen and Emmy are bonded by blood. To survive their early years, empaths must be bonded to another. Think of the bond as a hollow tube attaching two objects, or in this case, two people. Through this bond, each can lend strength to the other, each is never alone, each gains the fortitude to keep living through pain and suffering. Usually the bond is with the mother, sometimes the father, but it must always be with an adult that has at least a portion of Empath blood. This bloodline skips generations, however. I have been waiting all this time for it to reappear."

Father Goram looked at Althaya. "And now it has with Brighteyes. That's why she is so important."

Althaya nodded. "That's part of the reason. Kristen does not feel this bond as of yet because she is still too young. However, there will be a time when it establishes itself. Horatio, be warned, when that time comes, Kristen will move heaven and earth to get to Emmy. That is why she needs to be prepared as thoroughly as possible. That is why she will have companions."

"You mean Romulus," Father Goram said.

Althaya nodded. "Yes. But there will be others. She will not be alone. She could not do it alone. There are still many dangers for the empath."

Aurora looked at Father Goram. "She will have one of my rangers to help her."

Father Goram stared at Aurora than shook his head violently. "NO! Now I know the Purge was not a myth. Rangers assassinated the empaths during the Purge! How could you even think of such a thing?"

"Peace, Father. The ranger I have in mind would never hurt Kristen or Emmy. He has never let me down, his heart is true," Aurora responded.

Un-phased by Aurora's assurances, Father Goram rigorously refused to listen. "A ranger is out of the question. Who knows if he will hear the call of the Purge? I know enough about it to understand rangers were given the ability to sense empath blood, which made them the ideal killers they turned out to be. Hell, if it's instinctive, how can even a goddess assure me it won't happen again?"

"Horatio, stop it and listen to me!" Althaya ordered. "The Purge was the result of a terrible spell created by the Council of Priests in Elanesse. We are long past that time and well out of its range. While it may be true there could still be residual energies left in the ruined city of Elanesse, it is most assuredly not strong enough to change a man's heart."

"Tangus DeRango will never betray me, Father Goram," Aurora said, confirming what Althaya just said. "He would die before betraying Kristen, for betraying Kristen would mean betraying me. Free will aside, we still have some precognitive powers concerning actions of mortals. Tangus has walked dangerous roads before and he has never lost his way nor will he. On that you have my word!"

Father Goram, somewhat mollified, nodded assent. He then suddenly understood something that had been bothering him, why Kristen was sent away from Covington instead of being adopted. Since Covington is so close to Elanesse, they would have had direct experience with the

Purge. They must have somehow known about Kristen's empath blood and felt she was in danger from the residual magic of the Purge. Or worse, the Purge might still be fully active!

"There is more, my priest," Althaya said, turning the discussion back to the empath. She was pleased, however, at Father Goram's unyielding defense of Kristen. It was that loyalty to Kristen that would go far to ensure Kristen's success. "The empath bloodline is that of my own."

Aurora, surprised and horrified at the same time, stuttered, "But the Purge…my rangers…I am so sorry, dear Althaya!" She said as she lowered her head in sorrow.

Althaya lifted Aurora's chin with a hand and looked into her eyes. "Please sister, you did everything you could to stop it. I will not have you prostrate yourself so over something that was never your fault. The reason I did not tell you this before was because I wanted to spare your feelings. But I can no longer hold anything back. It is time for action. Unfortunately, however, this is not the only thing I must tell you. Aurora, Horatio, please listen carefully. Horatio, you are correct in that clerics can do most of the things an empath can do with spells and knowledge. The empath, however, is the catalyst, or bridge, for those spells. A cleric prays to a god or goddess for healing spells, but the granted spells will only work as long as at least one empath is alive. That is why I had to save Emmy."

Father Goram suddenly remembered his dream and froze. "You mean…?"

But Aurora finished the thought for him. "She means that without the empath, there can be no healing spells."

Althaya, looked off into empty space and shook her head yes. "That is correct. Without the empath, a cleric will not be able to heal magically. Without the empath, a cleric will not be able to resurrect, restore, or regenerate. Without the empath, tens of thousands of people will die. And even though I am the Goddess of Healing, there will be nothing I will be able to do about it."

CHAPTER 3

InnisRos

(51 Years Ago)

*And so it came to pass that the child became the parent,
the student became the master.*

— Book of the Unveiled

THE FIRST SIX decades of Kristen's life were devoted to her education and the development of the person she was to become as an adult. Father Goram kept his promise to Mary McKenna. To him, Kristen was his daughter, and he was not going to let anything break that relationship. He taught her to be a priestess in devotion to the goddess Althaya. These teachings accentuated all aspects inherent in a holy calling, the duties and responsibilities to the poor, the lame, the weak and all other souls in need of peace, a willingness to tolerate, the ability to heal, and the never-ending dedication to the destruction of evil wherever it may be found. Through Father Goram's instructions, Kristen learned to call upon clerical spells to deal with any given situation at a moment's notice. This response was drilled into Kristen so frequently she was able to instinctively know the exact spell to evoke at the precise moment it was needed. By the end of her sixth decade of life, Kristen was extremely proficient at her craft. But though she spent many hours healing and working with the elves that populated Calmacil Clearing, she had yet to have any practical field experience. Everything she did was with the knowledge that there was always someone more experienced to fall back on should she stumble or fail. Kristen, though eager to prove herself, knew when that time came she alone would be responsible. This was something she greatly feared.

Kristen also received other specialized training. Autumn worked with Kristen to fully develop her extraordinary talent for healing. Kristen had an unusually high affinity for this type of work. This was generally because her empath blood which, as expected, raised her healing aptitude by degrees no other cleric could hope to achieve. But Kristen's healing gift was also reinforced by her ability to understand the nature of the physical body and the many functions within that must work in harmony for life to continue. Even under different circumstances, healing in both the magical and the physical would have been Kristen's calling.

Safire trained Kristen in the art of self-defense and animal handling, although whether or not the latter was required was called in question every time someone saw Kristen and Romulus together. Though forbidden by Althaya from using edged or piercing weapons such as the sword or the bow, Kristen learned the mace, quarterstaff, and morning star. Safire's unique perspective with her weapon of choice, the scimitar, however, ensured Kristen recognized the various forms of slashing attacks and how to parry. Through Safire's guidance, Kristen not only became extremely proficient, but more lethal since she was taught and understood attack and defense against many different weapon types. Though as deadly as a hawk, Kristen's heart was warm. It beat with a balanced sense of right and wrong as well as a desire to ruthlessly seek justice. Kristen's one weakness, a weakness that could be exploited by an opponent, was her willingness to grant mercy. Consequently, Kristen refused to go for the quick kill. Instead she used the knowledge and training Safire provided to develop methods which would allow her to disarm her attacker whenever possible while holding back the killing thrust. Safire hated to think of mercy as a weakness, but in certain situations, no quarter could be given. Safire not only feared for Kristen's physical well-being, but also what it could do to her heart the first time she either had to kill or was betrayed by someone close. Kristen's kindness and compassion was a beam of sunshine in a world that can sometimes be cold and cruel.

THE SALVATION OF INNOCENCE

Kristen's training on the horse was problematic at times, however. Safire, as a ranger, was an expert rider, so the instruction was not the issue, nor was Kristen's desire. Romulus was. As a general rule, dire wolves, especially dire wolves as large as Romulus, and horses did not coexist comfortably. Dire wolves did not normally hunt horses, not due to any lack of veracity on the part of the dire wolf, but because a nervous truce between the two existed since the horse was favored as transportation. This usually resulted in a vigorous defense by their riders, which made it smarter to seek prey elsewhere. Regardless of this truce, however, a horse would never approach a dire wolf except under command of its rider. Though Romulus was a member of the monastery and constant friend and guardian to Kristen as well as all who knew him, he was not allowed in the stables because of the panic that would ensue. When it was time for Kristen to be trained to the horse, however, Romulus' presence became an issue because of the protective instincts he had for her. These instincts would not be denied, so if Kristen were to ride, the horse would have to learn to tolerate Romulus. It was not long before Safire included Romulus in the training of some of the new foals, foals with large, strong and intelligent bloodlines, foals that would be bred to fight in defense of their rider. As a result, the instinctual fear of the horse for dire wolves had in effect been bred out of these particular monastery horses, making selection of the appropriate horse and Kristen's subsequent training possible. Kristen proved to be only a marginal rider at best, however. She preferred to have her feet firmly rooted to the ground.

Vayl prepared Kristen in the art of command. This was perhaps the most difficult lesson Kristen had to learn. Her sympathy for all people interfered with her ability to sacrifice the few, or the one, for the benefit of the group. While Kristen's constant struggle with this frustrated Vayl somewhat, it depressed Kristen greatly. She understood that, as she grew in experience and her powers coalesced fully into a priestess of Althaya, she would be called upon to make decisions of this nature, possibly called upon to decide who might live and who might die in as yet unforeseen circumstances. The other acolytes, however, were given only basic foundational training in these decision making processes, which confused Kristen. Unknown to her, however, Father Goram, Vayl, and Mary McKenna, as much as they wanted to shield Kristen from this soul-wrenching responsibility, all understood the necessity. They knew the road Kristen would someday have to travel. Many a time after a session with Vayl, Kristen emerged from the room they used with tears in her eyes. But she would find no escape. Vayl, Father Goram and even Mary McKenna insisted. "Some lessons in life are hard to learn, child, but they must be learned nevertheless." Mary McKenna would often say as she gathered Kristen in her arms after some of the more difficult sessions. "Pray that you will never have to put these lessons into practice. But do not hesitate if you do. There must be a part of you that is as hard as life itself." As difficult as the training was, Kristen knew there was no hiding from it, that she would never be ready to assume the task of being Althaya's priestess without this fundamental comprehension of her role.

Mary McKenna, though of a different race than Kristen, was in the truest sense her mother during those early years. Mary McKenna loved her as no other. She was by Kristen's side through all; failures, successes, hurts, joy, and every one of the other things that bared the soul of the young for all to see. Mary McKenna was the one true rock in Kristen's life. She was the safe harbor in the middle of the storm; complete love, acceptance, and dedication. Mary McKenna was the one soul Kristen would try to emulate throughout her life. She taught Kristen the value of compassion. More importantly, since Kristen was always gentle of heart, Mary McKenna, because of her human heritage and her own life experiences, ensured Kristen was taught both when, and more significantly, how to be hard, how to defend herself against the realities of life, how to fight for what she believed, and if the circumstances warranted, how to act decisively and with brutal efficiency when protecting the innocent in the face of evil. Mary McKenna was more than a mother. She was a friend, a sister, a confidant, and a mentor. During the first six decades of Kristen's life, she was Kristen's everything. No other had the same degree of effect on the young female elf. Mary McKenna embodied the commitment and sacrifice Kristen herself would one day have to make for another.

THE SALVATION OF INNOCENCE

The natural life-span of an elf, barring disease, accident, murder or war, could be as long as fourteen hundred years, while that of a human was only about seventy to eighty years. It was this disparity between the two races that caused Kristen's first true exposure to deep grief. In Kristen's sixtieth year, Mary McKenna died.

Mary McKenna's death was not unexpected since she was very old by human standards and had been in failing health for many months. There was not a magical remedy for old age. For days Father Goram cloistered himself in the apartment they shared, doing everything in his power to make the woman he loved comfortable. But that was all he could do. Vayl, as Father Goram's selected second, saw to monastery affairs during these times. Father Goram only came out for the most urgent of tasks that required his expertise.

Kristen did not know what to do for either her father or her mother. Though she came and went as she pleased, she still felt she was an outsider looking in. She wanted so much to save her mother and console her father. But she was powerless to do either. Romulus, for the first time in sixty years, stayed with Mary McKenna rather than with Kristen. He had grown to love this human, and fondly remembered their first encounter all those decades ago, how Mary McKenna bravely protected the infant Kristen with a baby rattle raised over her head, ready to strike Romulus should he make any move towards the child. He was, in the way of a dire wolf, now paying homage and saying farewell. When the time came, he would leave the monastery and howl her tribute as he would a favored pack member.

Kristen was in the monastery library studying a history of Elanesse. She did not understand why Vayl was so insistent she read this particular tome that spoke of a long dead city, especially at a time when she felt she should be with her parents. Nevertheless, as she read of the great purge brought down upon the empaths, she became engrossed in the story and all other thoughts were temporarily set aside. She felt she was vaguely familiar with it, though she did not have any suspicion why this would be. With her attention riveted to the story she was reading, she did not notice Autumn, who had taken a seat across from her.

"Kristen," Autumn gently said.

"Huh? Oh, sorry Autumn. I did not see you sit down. I'm doing homework assigned by Vayl," Kristen said as she pointed to the tome. "I'm studying about old Elanesse."

Autumn nodded. "I have read this same tome. It's a history of Elanesse and the story of the purge. It shows the dark side of elf kind, and that for all our haughtiness where humans and the other races are concerned, we suffer from the same prejudices, the same cruelties as they. Your father has made it required reading for all acolytes, usually following that up with lessons in humility."

"How do we know it's true? It happened so long ago, are we sure this history has it right?" Kristen asked.

"It is right, Kristen. We have other corroborating documentation, but the tome you are reading is the most complete history. Also, I have been to Elanesse, sent after you were born to learn what I could. I can attest to the fact that the purge did indeed occur. You can still feel the powerful magic released by Elanesse's clerics even after three millennia." Taking Kristen's hands in hers, Autumn looked deeply into Kristen's eyes, eyes that started to tear up because Kristen knew the real reason for Autumn's visit. "But Elanesse is not my purpose for being here," Autumn said.

"I know," Kristen whispered. "It is time, then?"

Autumn nodded. "Horatio asked me to find you and bid you come. I am sorry Brighteyes. All of us would spare you this pain if we could, but your mother should look upon you once again before she leaves us."

Tears now flowed freely as Kristen asked, "How do I stop this pain? My heart...my heart...breaks."

Autumn squeezed the hands of the weeping Kristen. "We have to accept the pain, Brighteyes. That is the only way we can live with it. It also helps to lean upon those who love us for strength. You are not alone in your grief. Kristen, your father needs you."

THE SALVATION OF INNOCENCE

Sniffling, Kristen took a deep breath and composed herself. "Yes," she said simply.

As the two made their way back to the apartment shared by Father Goram and Mary McKenna, everyone going about their business along the hallways stopped and silently stood aside. Some of the servants more familiar with Kristen gently touched her arm as she passed. The gesture was an attempt to assure her, to tell her they were with her in spirit. Though Kristen was moving automatically, numb, she did have the presence of mind to understand what everyone was trying to do. She took comfort in these simple actions. By the time she reached the room, she had stopped crying and was wiping her eyes dry with the sleeve of her dress.

Stepping in front of the closed door, she paused and looked at Autumn. "My mother told me this time would come." Reaching inside a pocket in her dress, Kristen withdrew a locket on a silver chain shaped in the form of a sailing ship set on a background that represented the island of InnisRos. There were diamonds set at the four locations of the compass. The diamonds represented the purity of the love between Kristen and Mary McKenna. "She had this made for me. It is a remembrance locket. It signifies the new life we found after crossing the ocean. It represents our life on InnisRos together. It…it represents the spirit of her love for me." Taking an end of the chain in each hand Kristen turned her back to Autumn and said, "Would you please lock the clasp? My hands are shaking too much."

With the remembrance locket firmly around her neck, Kristen opened the door to the apartment. Vayl was kneeling in front of the fireplace stoking the fire. A couple of chairs and small table sat facing it. Upon the table was a half-finished glass of wine. There were several rooms in the apartment; the great room, a study, a small kitchen with an adjoining room that served as a green house, and three bedrooms off a long hallway. The door to Father Goram and Mary McKenna's room at the end of the hallway was closed.

Turning at the sound of Kristen and Autumn's entrance, Vayl got up and walked over to greet them, nodding to Autumn and taking Kristen's hands. "How are you?" he asked. He knew she had been crying.

"This is hard, Vayl. How is Papa?" Kristen said as her eyes started to fill again with tears.

Turning his head towards the closed bedroom door, Vayl replied, "He does not show it outwardly, but not well. He loves Mary very much. In all my years with him I have never seen him so despondent."

"I do not know what to do," Kristen said.

Putting an arm around her shoulder to support her, Vayl started walking her down the hallway. "All you have to do is be there for him as he will be there for you." Stopping at the door, Vayl suddenly turned Kristen by the shoulders to face him. "Autumn, I, the whole monastery, and all of Calmacil Clearing will feel this loss. You are not alone." Vayl then kissed Kristen on the forehead before reaching down to turn the door knob to open the door. Inside, Father Goram sat in a chair beside the bed, holding Mary McKenna's hand, while Romulus lay on the floor close by. "Autumn and I will be in the great room," Vayl said as he quietly left.

The next evening, the funeral pyre dedicated to Mary McKenna lit the nighttime sky, bathing it with cleansing light, a radiance that matched the purity of her soul, a brilliance that spoke of her life and the effect it had on every person who'd ever known her. Following elf tradition, the fire burned for three days and three nights during which time Mary McKenna's body was prepared for burial. As the fire burned itself out on the third day, she was laid to her final rest in Father Goram's family mausoleum in a simple yet moving ceremony. On the morning of the fourth day, Kristen, Romulus, and Kristen's favorite warhorse disappeared from the monastery.

※

Tangus DeRango and his daughter Jennifer sat at their favorite table in the Unicorn's End, a quaint tavern on the outskirts of the city of Olberon, approximately eighty miles southeast of Calmacil Clearing. Olberon harbored the main base of the InnisRos navy as well as being the island's second most important port city. Scattered about the table were the remains of a late morning meal. On chairs next to each, within easy reaching distance, were weapons of several sorts; longbows, quivers of arrows, and swords. The two rangers were sitting back in their chairs sipping water while a green and brown-spotted furred elven dog, a cooshee, lay at Tangus' feet. Tangus and Jennifer each wore magical elven chainmail armor and the green and brown cloak which distinguished them as rangers. A silver signet ring shaped in the form of an angel, green emeralds representing the eyes and wings made of small rubies, emeralds, and sapphires representing the colors of the rainbow adorned the right ring finger of both rangers. This identified them as followers of the goddess Aurora.

Tangus was using both his hands and arms to demonstrate the flight of a bird and an arrow. "Jennifer, when sighting a target in flight, you have to lead it properly," he said. "It's not going to be in the same place by the time the arrow gets there if you release on the target. You also need to adjust your lead for target and wind speed, as well as wind direction."

"C'mon dad, that was a crazy impossible shot!" Jennifer exclaimed. "I wouldn't have believed it if I hadn't seen it with my own eyes. That bird must have been one-hundred yards away and going in the opposite direction and at an angle when you fired."

"And yet Jinx had himself a nice breakfast without breaking a sweat," Tangus replied. Jinx, the elven dog, looked up at the sound of his name, wagging his tail just a bit before settling back down into a light doze. "Jennifer, you'll learn to do that instinctively with enough training. No thinking. Just draw and release."

"That's easy for you to say. You're the best ranger on InnisRos," Jennifer responded.

Taking a sip of water, Tangus winked at Jennifer. "You'll learn. Have you heard from your mother recently?"

Munching on an apple, Jennifer nodded. "Yes. She's doing well in Palisade Crest. It also seems that Lionel's paintings are selling much better. The humans seem to be very eager for anything elven."

"I wish he hadn't left. I miss your brother," Tangus responded wistfully.

"Mother could not stay, not with you remaining here on the island. Besides, she always seemed to have the desire to venture to the mainland again. Too many of your tales about your travels while there, I guess. She was intrigued. And Lionel…well, I suspect he didn't want to live in your shadow, especially since he has absolutely no talent as a ranger."

"I never belittled his ability, Jennifer," Tangus said.

Jennifer cut off a piece of the apple she was eating with her knife and gave it to Jinx. "I know that, as did he. It's just that he wanted to make it on his own. I don't think he ever felt comfortable putting the DeRango name on a painting, at least not here on InnisRos. I think he was concerned it would embarrass you."

Tangus sighed. He suspected this, of course. There were plenty of times when he got upset at Lionel for not choosing the life of a ranger. Lionel's mother, though a ranger as well, did not have the same expectations, which is why, when they divorced, it did not surprise Tangus that Lionel decided to stay with her instead of him. "Your mother's probably going to end up back with her family in the small town of Regislar. That's mostly wilderness. I don't think Lionel's going to like that much."

Jennifer shook her head. "Don't worry, dad. He's old enough to make his own decisions and be on his own. He might not be a ranger, but he is a DeRango."

"Point taken," Tangus answered.

Jinx suddenly raised his head and looked at the door. Tangus read no threat in Jinx's actions, so he was not overly concerned. But he did keep his eyes on the door nevertheless. As it opened, Tangus recognized Safire as she walked in, dusting road dirt from her armor, clothes, and cloak.

"Ho, Safire!" Harley, the barkeep and proprietor of Unicorn's End, called out.

"Harley! Good to see you! I'll have a cold mug of ale if you please. Have you seen…..never mind. I see them at their usual table," Safire said as she walked over to Tangus and Jennifer.

Both Tangus and Jennifer got up and clasped hands with Safire. Tangus quickly moved to another table and dragged a chair over. "Safire, what brings you to town?"

"Ale first," Safire said as she sat, grabbed the mug offered by Harley and took a long drink. "Thank you, Harley."

"I'll get you some food. You look like you've been riding hard," Harley replied, briefly clasping Safire on the shoulder. After raising his arm to get the attention of his only waitress, Izzy, he said, "The venison's not quite ready, so how about bread and cheese? I'll look for some leftover bacon, too. It'll just be a few moments."

"That would be great Harley," Safire said.

"It's been a couple of months, Safire. Is everything alright?" Jennifer asked.

"Well, we've been pretty busy at the monastery. But the last couple of weeks have been tough. And now…" But Safire couldn't finish as she was once again overcome with feelings of panic and dread.

"What's going on, Safire?" Tangus inquired, seeing the haggard look on Safire's face and the shadows under her eyes. She had not slept much lately, he decided.

Breathing deeply, Safire regained control over her emotions. "Do you remember me telling you about Kristen?"

"Yes. You're instructing her and the last time we talked you were bragging about her abilities. Let's see, if memory serves, she not much older than Jennifer, very adept in the healing and clerical arts, weapons usage, and extremely intelligent…almost too good to be true," Tangus responded.

"Well, maybe I exaggerated a bit, but not by much. She is going to make an exceptional priestess someday. In fact, she already is, though there are still lessons she must learn. Father Goram has spared nothing in her training," Safire said as she started to pick at the food Izzy had just placed in front of her. After a few mouthfuls, she pushed the plate away. "Maybe I wasn't so hungry after all."

"What has happened, Safire?" Tangus prompted again, knowing something was very wrong.

Safire sighed. "Kristen's foster mother, Mary McKenna, the human female who came over with Kristen from the mainland when she was a babe, has died. It was old age. There was no intrigue involved and from what I have heard she died peacefully with Father Goram and Kristen at her side."

"Sad, Safire, but that is the nature of things," Tangus replied. "We have all had to cope with the loss of a loved one."

"Yes, Tangus, I know, but with some people it's more than that," Safire replied with deep emotion. "They touch your soul. You're never completely prepared for their passing. Mary McKenna was one such person. Her loss has left an emptiness in many people; Father Goram, Vayl, Autumn, me, but most of all in Kristen. True, Mary McKenna was a mother to Kristen. The only mother she ever knew, so we expected this to be hard. But Tangus, I'm telling you there is something different about Kristen. I don't know, I guess it's some special innocence, or vulnerability, or empathy, which has made this so much more excruciating for her, made it even worse than we anticipated." Leaning back in her chair Safire looked at Tangus. "Tangus, Kristen has disappeared. I haven't been able to track her…no one has. She's spelled her tracks well. It's like she has fallen off the face of the world."

"It sounds like she does not want to be found, Safire," Jennifer said.

Tangus agreed. "Jennifer's right. She probably just wants to grieve alone. I'm sure she'll turn up sooner or later. She's got that big dire wolf guardian you were telling me about, right?"

"Romulus," Safire said as she nodded.

"Yes, that's his name. I'm sure he won't let anything happen to her. Just relax, Safire. We'll spend the day fishing and hunting. It'll be good for you. And when you get back, I'll bet she's already returned," Tangus said.

Safire looked at Tangus, her worry for Kristen unabated. "Tangus, what if you're wrong? What if she's managed to get herself hurt and can't get back? You know the dangers in the deep forest for someone not fully prepared or not paying attention. Right now she's acting on impulse and emotion. She's not thinking rationally. She's hurting too much!"

Tangus reached over and put a hand on Safire's arm. "Calm down, Safire. I'm sure it's not nearly as bad as you imagine."

Safire rubbed her eyes. "Sorry. I've had little sleep over the last few days and rode all night."

"You're an experienced campaigner, Safire. That's not it, is it?" Jennifer said pointedly.

Safire looked at Jennifer and smiled warmly. "You're certainly your father's daughter, Jennifer," Safire said as she sighed. "Everything I told you is true...true except for something I'm not sure Father Goram would want you to know."

Tangus gently said, "Safire you can trust us."

"Yes I can. Very well...shortly before Mary McKenna died Kristen tried to heal her. But it was not a normal clerical healing spell, it was something different. Something Father Goram says he's never seen before. He wouldn't be more specific, although I suspect he, as well as Vayl and Autumn, might know what she was trying to do. It all has something to do with when she was a baby. I know Althaya was involved, as well as our goddess, Aurora."

"Aurora! Are you sure?" Tangus questioned.

Nodding, Safire replied, "I spoke to her and she spoke to me. That is not something a ranger forgets or confuses. Anyway, Kristen was not successful in healing her mother and the attempt seemed to sap her soul. She attended the funeral, but I've never seen anyone so despondent! Then, on the morning after the consecration and entombment of Mary McKenna's body, Kristen simply vanished. Tangus, Kristen is special. I mean really, really special. Why else would two goddesses be so involved in the life of one mortal? As deep as her pain has gone, we fear she may try to harm herself. That is why we're all so worried. Father Goram says that she must be found at all costs. You are the best ranger on InnisRos at finding missing persons. We need your help and we will pay double your fee."

Jennifer shook her head, "There will be no fee required. My father will gladly look for your Kristen. You are family!"

Tangus nodded in agreement and got up, as did Safire, Jennifer, and Jinx. "Jennifer, you'll have to handle that affair regarding the livestock poaching," he said as he was grabbing his weapons. "Track the poachers, but leave the arrest to the law keepers. Our standard fee has already been agreed upon. And let them know I'll be out of town for a few days. Make yourself available to them, but nothing dangerous, hear me?"

"Don't worry about it dad. Just find Kristen," Jennifer, nodding, replied as she walked out of Unicorn's End.

"Come, Safire, let's get your horse taken care of. I've got several fresh mustangs you can take your pick of for the ride back to Calmacil Clearing. And don't worry, I'll find her and return her safely home," Tangus said as he started to follow Jennifer out the door.

Safire stopped and clutched Tangus' arm. "Thank you!"

"Dear lady, I would never refuse you. Besides, Jinx could use a good run. He's getting fat and lazy. Harley, payment is on the table. I'll see you in a few days," Tangus called out as the trio left the tavern.

Kristen sat silently on a felled tree in a small clearing near the edge of a bluff overlooking the Sea of Dreams. The sun was settling down for the night, shadows from the trees of the forest were starting to boldly move forward as the sunlight faded. Romulus was lying near a warm, crackling fire which was keeping the chill at bay while Kristen's horse happily munched on what grass he could find. Snuggled in her cloak and drinking tea, Kristen was staring to the east. She could barely see the Isile Silimaure on the horizon. Vayl had told her it meant "Magnificent Resolve" in an ancient dialect, but she felt its name should probably have been "Elven's Folly". The world is not a place that a person, let alone an entire nation, can hide from. Past the Isile Silmaure and across The Ocean of the Heavens was the mainland. Something was there on the mainland, something important. She could not escape this feeling. But what was it? What drove her to make this irrational dash to the coast? Was she hoping to find resolution, some measure of comfort? Or perhaps an answer to the mysterious link that even now she felt coming from the east? So far it only confused her more. It made no sense. Yet the feeling that brought her here could not be denied.

It had come to her as her mother lay dying, the sensation that she could bring forth some power from deep within that could save the woman. It drove away all restraint and reason. She had placed her hands on the side of her mother's face, mentally trying to compel the power that lay hidden within her to come forward. She soon became lost in the effort. She remembered her father grabbing her hands and saying "You are not strong enough!" as he pried them off, robbing her of the opportunity to rescue her mother. As her hands were forcibly moved away, her mother opened her eyes and looked at her. Smiling, she spoke her last words, "Forever my little girl." When Mary McKenna died, a small piece of Kristen had died as well. The attempt to awaken the power, however, opened a link to something or someone that had not gone away. That connection led her to the bluff.

She was brought out of this reverie and back to the present by the distant howl of dire wolves – wolves who were her friends and guardians. Someone was coming. Kristen was not trying to hide from those that would seek her return, although she did take some measures to ensure she would not be found quickly so she could have time to put her feelings in perspective. But she wanted to be forewarned of any approach by either someone she knew or a stranger. The howling amply accomplished this.

Romulus, though still visibly relaxed, pricked his ears up, listening to the message being sent. Looking over at Kristen and seeing her slight nod, he got up and silently disappeared into the forest. He would scout ahead to determine if the one who came was a threat. He was expressly forbidden by his mistress to do physical harm, only to frighten the intruder to a different path unless he determined the intruder was not dangerous. Kristen always trusted Romulus' instincts about such things.

Everything was well in hand when the rider appeared in the clearing, walking his horse that, though being very brave about it, was frightened by the big dire wolf leading the strangers to Kristen's campsite. The elven dog walking at the rider's side, however, gave no indication he was particularly afraid of Romulus. All about there was movement outside the clearing as six dire wolves positioned themselves around the perimeter.

Sensing what was happening and understanding his tactical disadvantage, the rider smiled. "A picket and defensive perimeter established using dire wolves," he said, "most impressive for someone so young!"

Getting up, Kristen looked at the rider and his companions. He was definitely a ranger, completely in control and very self-assured, even given the present circumstances. Though very dangerous looking, there was a kindness in his eyes and his smile handsome and disarming. Kristen knew who he was as soon as she saw the elven dog, for only one ranger on InnisRos had such a travel companion. Tangus DeRango. Safire had talked about him so many times that Kristen almost felt as if she had known him her whole life. For reasons not understood, she felt secure and protected in his presence, as if some aura extended outward with him at the center. Kristen had been able to understand people and read the condition of their soul, both good and bad, since she was a child. Her mother explained that it was a rare and special gift, though sometimes it could be a curse as well. Kristen saw that Tangus' soul was good.

"Part of what I learned from my father," Kristen said in answer to Tangus' remark. "Safire has spoken of you with great admiration, Tangus DeRango."

Tangus smiled. "And you as well, Ms. Clearwater. A very accomplished priestess well trained in many disciplines. I do not think she exaggerates. You hid your passing very well and looking around it would seem you have more than just a fair acquaintance in tactical planning."

"I have taken my training very seriously, Mr. DeRango. Though I have, thus far, lived a sheltered life, I understand that decisions I make have consequences, not only on me, but also on my allies and more importantly my friends," Kristen replied.

Tangus nodded. "Your instructors would be proud." Extending a hand, he said, "It is a pleasure to meet you. Please call me Tangus. May I call you Kristen?"

"Of course you may. Any friend of Safire's is a friend of mine. She's like my sister," Kristen replied as she took Tangus' proffered hand. It enveloped hers. It was big, callused and warm.

"She is to me as well, Kristen. Speaking of consequences, did you consider them when you left the monastery without telling anyone?" Tangus lightly admonished.

Kristen sighed. "Spare me the scolding, Tangus. I'm sure there will be plenty of that in store for me when I get back. For now, however, sit down and relax. From the look of you, you've been traveling hard. Would you like some tea?"

Tangus smiled. "That sounds excellent."

Pointing to a saddle bag lying against a log, Kristen said as she sat back down and poured Tangus a cup of tea, "There's also oats in the saddle bag, as well as some fresh meat for your elven dog. Romulus has had his share. I'm afraid all I can offer you to eat are iron rations."

Tangus went over to his horse, reached inside his own saddle bag and pulled out a couple of sandwiches. "I really hate iron rations! How about some cured venison instead?" he offered before moving to sit across the fire from Kristen. "Jinx and my horse are both well fed, but I thank you."

Kristen took the sandwich and hungrily bit into it. "This is very good! I've had venison before, but this tastes quite different. Is it the spices?"

Tangus, after swallowing a bite, said, "Correct, my own special blend."

Both sandwiches were eaten without further comment. Romulus and Jinx sat down next to their masters, eyeing each other suspiciously. The horses had no such problem, however, and were happily munching on grass. The remaining dire wolves were far enough away to ease the horses natural distrust for wolves, but close enough to defend Kristen if it became necessary.

Tangus poured a second cup of tea for himself and glanced at Kristen, who was looking eastward at the distant horizon across the sea. "Safire thought you might try to kill yourself."

Kristen jerked her attention back to Tangus. "What? That's nonsense! Why would she think such a thing?"

"She said your mother's death hit you very hard, that you became very depressed and withdrawn," Tangus responded. "And to be quite frank, you still have a detached look about you, constantly staring to the east and obviously distracted, lost in your own thoughts."

"She's right about my mother's death. But it is more than that. Something is happening that I do not understand. But be assured I am no threat to myself," Kristen answered. "Tell me, Tangus, have you ever been drawn to something but couldn't explain why? Or felt something inexplicable and unknown resting in your soul? As my mother lay dying, something awoke in me that I can't comprehend. It's…how do I put this in plain words…it's like a little itch that I can't scratch."

"Trauma and pain from loss can often affect people in strange ways," Tangus offered.

"Possibly…" Kristen said as she once again started looking eastward, and then shook her head. "No, that's not right. Whatever it is, Tangus, the answer lies out there."

"Out in the sea?" Tangus asked with a perplexed look on his face.

"No. It's on the mainland. Of this I have no doubt," Kristen exclaimed with absolute conviction. "But I am not yet ready." Redirecting her gaze towards Tangus, she said, "I guess we should probably get back."

"I would prefer not to travel at night, Kristen. Let's rest here and begin our return at dawn," Tangus countered.

Kristen nodded assent. "Maybe that is for the best. Over there, just out of sight, is a freshly killed deer brought down by Romulus. I'll go cut a couple of slabs from the haunch for later. I want to leave the rest for the wolves."

THE SALVATION OF INNOCENCE

Tangus grabbed Kristen's hand as she started to get up. "Kristen, please rest. I'll see to it."

"I'm fine," Kristen replied as she shook off Tangus' grip on her hand and got up. "All I've been doing today is sitting and thinking."

Tangus got up as well and took Kristen by the shoulders, gently forcing her back down. "My dear, you look like you have the weight of the world on you. I want you to relax for just this one night. I'll take care of things, and I'm sure Romulus and his pack…"

"They are his friends, Tangus. I am his pack," Kristen corrected.

Tangus smiled and nodded, "Of course. I'm sure Romulus' friends will offer us ample protection."

Kristen allowed herself to be seated, but then decided to go over to her blanket while Tangus was dressing the meat. Lying down, she was fast asleep before Tangus returned with the venison. Taking his own bedroll, Tangus fashioned a pillow and put it under Kristen's head. As he did so, he started to understand her importance, not only her importance to the monastery but also her importance to something greater. Tangus was a good judge of character himself, nothing innate like Kristen's ability, but rather through a vast amount of experience. He now firmly believed that Kristen was as special as Safire had said. He didn't know yet how or why, but he knew nevertheless her life was paramount. Though emotional decision-making was foreign to him, he made one that instant. Looking over at his elven dog, Jinx, he laid his hand lightly on the slumbering Kristen's shoulder and said, "Jinx, protect!" The utterance of this simple command had the affect of saying to the sleeping Kristen, "Our lives are yours." Romulus, watching this from the other side of Kristen's still form, reached over and, with his snout, shoved Tangus in the shoulder as if to say "In this we are one." Tangus understood the big wolf's meaning and nodded agreement.

Kristen awoke the next morning to the sight of Tangus, hunched over the fire, stirring what she presumed to be breakfast in a pot. Noticing she was awake, Tangus nodded eastward. "You probably picked the one place on all of InnisRos that has the best view of the sunrise. Impressive, isn't it."

Stretching, Kristen looked at the sunrise. "I have been so busy with my own problems I never took the time to stop and notice. You're right, it is beautiful!"

Tangus glanced at Kristen as she stretched. "She's beautiful," he thought. Looking back down at the breakfast he was stirring, Tangus said, "I have found that even when life shows us its worse, there are simple pleasures that make it all tolerable. You just have to pay attention and look for them."

Kristen wrinkled her nose. "What are you preparing? It smells, well, kind of different." Getting up with difficulty, Kristen exclaimed, "By the goddess, my back hurts! I don't think it'll ever be right again!"

"No soft beds in the forest. The trick is to sleep on a good, stiff mattress when you're not on the road. By doing that, your back won't have to make such an adjustment when you find yourself sleeping on the ground," Tangus replied. "Breakfast is about ready."

Looking into the small pot Tangus had warming over the fire, Kristen asked, "Why is it red?"

"That would be the red turnips. As I mentioned last night, I really hate iron rations. But sometimes fresh meat is not always available so I travel with foods that will not spoil quickly, such as cured bacon and venison, bread, nuts, turnips and spices. In the morning it's a breakfast stew. In the evening it's a couple of sandwiches, or cooked meat when I have the time to hunt. Jinx likes turnips almost as much as fresh meat. I'm not sure why that is." Taking a spoon full, he raised it up to Kristen. "Here, take a bite."

"Actually that's pretty good! I'm famished!" she said after sipping the rich tasting liquid on the spoon.

Dishing up a bowl full and handing it to Kristen, Tangus did the same for himself. Both sat next to each other on the tree log, eating and enjoying the sunrise in its full glory. Romulus and Jinx, with a little coaxing from Tangus, made friends during the night and now lay side by side at their master's feet.

Breaking the silence, Tangus asked, "Do you still feel that itch?"

Kristen stopped eating, considering. "Yes. I don't think it will ever go away. But I find I've learned to accept it. Someday, Tangus, I will need to go to the mainland to search for something or someone. However I am not prepared to do so at this time. I still have some growing up to do."

"I don't know, Kristen. We could all use more experience, but you seem pretty grown up to me," Tangus replied.

"It's not just that, Tangus. Where would I even begin to look? And what am I looking for? I think that is still to be revealed. When it does become clear, though, I'm going, of that there can be no doubt," Kristen said.

Glancing over at Kristen and seeing the look of determination on her face, Tangus smiled. Remembering the vow he made with Jinx the previous evening, Tangus decided he would accompany Kristen when that time came. She was going to need him and as many of his allies as he could muster. The mainland could be a very dangerous place.

By the time Kristen and Tangus made their return to the monastery a couple of days later, Tangus knew he had found his soul mate, and Kristen shared that same feeling for Tangus. Within a year the courtship was over and they were married. Wooing Kristen was the easy part for she made no secret of her feelings for Tangus. Father Goram, Vayl and Autumn, however, were not so easily persuaded. They each had to be convinced of Tangus' worthiness, but once that was accomplished, he was accepted as part of their extended family and entrusted with the protection of Kristen's heart and soul, a task Tangus relished.

On the day after they were joined together in marriage, Father Goram asked Tangus into his study and told him that one day Kristen would need to travel to the mainland to seek that which would make her whole. He said this journey would be fraught with grave danger to her and everyone traveling with her, but it was a journey Kristen would insist upon making regardless of the cost. Father Goram also told Tangus that what Kristen must seek was precious beyond imagination. Tangus' enthusiasm for his new life was quelled somewhat upon hearing this, replaced with cold dread for his new wife, and anger that she would placed in jeopardy. The next day Tangus started to take steps that would eventually make him a better ranger, actions which would ultimately equip him to deal with a future that was going to become so very perilous.

Kristen and Tangus established a home in Calmacil Clearing. While Tangus continued to work with the Olberon authorities, Jennifer worked with Safire performing monastery ranger duties. For the next fifty years, Tangus and Kristen built a life together. Tangus trained in secret, honing his ranger skills, turning actions and reactions into instinctive behaviors, learning to read the landscape, and learning to listen to what the world around him was saying. Tangus accepted nothing short of perfection. Kristen also continued to learn, train, and grow as a person. But there was still a part of her that was missing, and that "itch" remained always with her. No one could guess when Kristen would know when it was time to leave, but Kristen, as the years passed, began to feel as if there was a force building inside her. Kristen welcomed the pressure, the feeling that something was about to burst, for it would be at that time when she would realize her destiny.

※

Fifty years after Kristen and Tangus married, Althaya felt the one thing she had dreaded. The stasis magic was starting to fail. Too much time had passed and she had lost control of the magic surrounding the empath. Another conjuring was impossible. Emmy would not survive it. If Kristen did not get to Emmy before the stasis magic failed, Emmy would be lost. Her death would mean all healing magic would be lost as well.

※

THE SALVATION OF INNOCENCE

Fifty years after Kristen and Tangus married, across The Ocean of the Heavens on the mainland, in a cold dark room, a child was dreaming while surrounded by a magical protective stasis spell. Without warning, the soft glimmering of the stasis field was momentarily interrupted. It returned in an instant but was now less radiant. In the brief moment the spell was disrupted, the slumbering child's comforting dreams turned into a nightmare. The terror of the Purge seeped into the girl's dreams, but something even more pervasive and frightening overlapped the darkness of the Purge. For a moment the child felt complete and total hate. She was lost, for she had touched the soul of a vampyre. Before settling back down into a peaceful sleep, after the stasis magic returned, the child broadcast a silent cry for help. It was a plea heard by one person alone, the only person who could save her.

On the island of InnisRos Kristen froze. All the unresolved questions suddenly came into focus, the feelings she could not before identify now clarified, and the link between her and another opened up completely. She heard a terrified little girl call out her name. Her mind, overwhelmed, shut down. Kristen Rosilie DeRango collapsed.

CHAPTER 4

(Present Day)

*How one travels the journey is sometimes as important
as the destination.*

— *Book of the Unveiled*

A MALIGNANT FORCE maintained a vigil deep beneath the ruins of Elanesse. The Purge was constructed by the clerics of Elanesse from magical energies. It was fashioned as a mindless force with no ability to reason, no emotion, and no willingness to bestow mercy. Its creators, long dead, created the Purge to satisfy the mandate to destroy every living empath. In an inescapable irony, the magic created by Elanesse's clerics did the very thing they sought to eliminate - it controlled the thoughts and minds of rangers to use them so that it could realize its compulsion to annihilate the empath. There was also an unintended consequence to the assembly of such strong enchantments, the Purge became sentient.

For over three millennia this force of destruction grew in power, extending its influence up from its underground lair and into the city of Elanesse as well as into the surrounding forest. Its original imperative, however, remained intact. Corrupt and twisted, it saw the empath as an opposing force that threatened its existence, the only force that could destroy it. If the great power of the empath could be absorbed, however, the Purge would be strong enough to move beyond the boundaries of its current limitations. And so it waited for the time when an empath once again walked the earth.

At one point the Purge felt the bloodline of the empath flicker back into existence, but this part of the bloodline was too faint and feeble to be worth consideration. It was not the full power of the empath, so the Purge did not investigate and fell back into dormancy, though a small part of it still maintained its vigil and still sought the empath out. A little over one hundred years later, as time is measured by man and elf, the Purge felt the full presence of the empath appear for the briefest of moments. Shirking off its dormancy, the Purge extended magical tendrils outward, encompassing the entire woods that surrounded the ruins of Elanesse and hunting for receptive minds to invade and dominate. This initial search touched few willing candidates, so the Purge augmented its power, extending the magic, until it judged it had captured the minds of a sufficient number of followers to end the reign of the empath once and forever. The empath was invisible again, but that was unimportant. It would reappear. And when it did, the Purge would drink the empath's essence, leaving behind nothing but a mindless ruin.

It was a quiet night in the borderlands located on the city of HeBron's southwestern flank. The sergeant and his two corporals entered the first of two sleeping barracks of fifty men and women each. It was several hours before dawn. Using swords on shields, the three loudly awoke the warriors from their sleep. This disturbance was met with extreme vocal resistance. To quiet the numerous complaints, the sergeant bellowed for everyone to shut up.

"Alright you scumbags, settle down. We have new orders from the lieutenant. He wants half of the watch to make a new base camp, and I've picked you. So gear up and fall in outside, ready to march in one hour. Don't leave anything behind that you value because I don't think we'll be coming back for a while."

"But sergeant, it's the middle of the night!" one of the warriors protested.

"I got eyes, nitwit! But the lieutenant had some type of revelation and won't wait until morning. The lieutenant says we go now, so we go now. I follow orders, just like each one of you will. Any other questions?"

"Just one. Where are we going?"
"Elanesse."

In another part of the land, leagues away from Elanesse, in a room deep underground, a withered, impossibly old woman, the vampyre Polina, lay on her deathbed. Vampyres are not immortal, even the parasite that inhabits their bodies have a lifespan. After six thousand years, her time had come to meet her eternal damnation. She was afraid. No one ever willingly went to the horror that awaited her, but though she was terrified, she accepted her ultimate fate. It was one she knew she had chosen long ago.

As she lay upon her deathbed, occasionally tortured by the demons waiting to receive her, she unexpectedly felt the presence of innocence. The purity of that faint touch burned into her and caused her to scream out. The empath! As impossible as it seemed, Polina knew this to be true. Revulsion, pure and blinding, filled her whole being, for the empath is the antithesis of the vampyre. The child could not be allowed to remain alive! She must tell Lukas so he could return to Elanesse and obliterate this affront to all vampyre and vampyre-kin. Impatiently she summoned him. He must be told before she died. But he did not answer. Polina continued to call out until she no longer had the strength. She died alone, drowning in hate-filled bile.

Polina did not need to tell Lukas about the empath for he felt her existence the brief moment the stasis magic failed as well. Shortly thereafter he felt the death of Polina. Smiling, he ordered his coven to return from their bloodthirsty lusts. Their hunger could be satiated at another time. He was finally in charge, and the first thing he would do as the alpha vampyre was return to that small room hidden away in Elanesse. With Polina now gone, nothing could stop him from feeding upon the blood of the innocent.

THE SALVATION OF INNOCENCE

It was fall on the island of InnisRos. Although winters on InnisRos were generally mild, the autumn winds blowing in from the north were colder and earlier than usual, indicating that the Island of the Elves was entering a cycle of severe weather. Tangus and Jennifer, along with Bitts, Tangus' elven dog and progeny of Jinx, were in the woods surrounding Calmacil Clearing hunting to refill the monastery larder. Although this was usually the responsibility of monastery rangers, Tangus decided to lend his expertise. Time was quickly running out. Soon the herds of deer and elk would begin their migration south, and the opportunity to hunt, butcher and store meat for the upcoming winter would be lost. It was also a chance to get reacquainted with Jennifer. Both father and daughter had responsibilities which unfortunately keep them apart far too often.

The two rangers were on a hill overlooking a herd of elk grazing in the small valley below. They were biding their time, waiting for Bitts to get around the herd and drive them to within bow range. Below and behind them their mustangs, Smoke and Jewels, watched over several pack horses already loaded with dressed meat from an earlier kill.

"I think maybe a couple more elk will do, father," Jennifer said, breaking the silence.

"You're the boss on this run, Jennifer, but I agree. Besides, the pack horses probably couldn't handle much more anyway." Tangus replied as he kept his eyes on the herd and wondered what was taking Bitts so long to get into position.

"Have you thought any more about Magdalena's offer?" Jennifer asked, looking over at Tangus. "The monastery could always use another ranger. You won't have to spend so much time in Olberon away from Kristen and me. And since this is steady work with a proper salary, you wouldn't have to worry about soliciting clients for work."

"Child, I don't solicit clients, they come to me. My reputation still stands for something," Tangus replied.

"I know that, but still, there are some months when you're not paid because the work simply isn't there. Missing people, poachers, law breakers on the run are not really all that common in Olberon. On many occasions you've had to resort to doing your own hunting to put food on the table. I know, I lived with you, remember? Steady pay from the monastery would resolve all of that," Jennifer countered. "I want what's best for you and Kristen, father, and this job will give both of you stability and security."

"Kristen already has stability, and as her husband, I do as well. Jennifer, everything you say is true, but even so, I have responsibilities in Olberon. Some people there still need me," Tangus said.

"Not paying clients, father. You're talking about people you help even though they can't compensate you." Jennifer sighed. "I'm not asking you to consider stopping the help you provide as charity, only to do it based in Calmacil Clearing. Move your operation here. Take Magdalena's offer."

Tangus, maintaining eye contact with the elk herd during the conversation with his daughter, watched as it suddenly bolted away and out of the valley. "Damn! I wonder what spooked them. And where's Bitts?"

"Over there," Jennifer said as she nudged Tangus and pointed towards the other side of the valley, the side opposite of the one the elk just vacated. Approaching was a rider on a horse. The horse was covering ground at speeds only Tangus' Storm could match. Appearing from deep brush on the other side of the valley Bitts hurried to catch up, growling at the interruption of the hunt. "That's Euranna on Windrunner. Odd, I wonder what she's doing out here?"

"Whatever the reason, she just scattered the herd! She should know better!" Tangus angrily commented as he got up.

Rising to stand beside him, Jennifer said worriedly, "Father, you don't understand. We have no one faster than her and Windrunner. Riding like that could only mean she's carrying an important message."

The rider saw the pair standing on the hill and veered over in their direction. Slowing, she raised her hand in greeting, allowing Windrunner to climb the hill safely. By now, Bitts had overtaken the horse and came up to Tangus, who cupped water in his hands to give his elven dog a drink. Seeing Windrunner was well lathered as he reached the crest of the hill, he looked at the diminutive rider, Euranna. "Perhaps you should see to your horse, young lady."

"Yes sir, but first this is for you," Euranna responded as she reached into a pouch and withdrew a rolled parchment, giving it to Tangus as she dismounted.

Taking the parchment, Tangus broke the seal and unrolled it. It's was written in Father Goram's hand, short and to the point in keeping with his style.

> *"Kristen has fallen ill. She is stable, but unconscious. I fear it is time, and if so, there is not a moment to lose. Please return quickly. HG"*

"You look pale. What is it, father?" Jennifer asked.

Tangus had many different thoughts running through his head, most of which was concern for Kristen. But he knew she probably wasn't in any real danger. He also knew this marked the beginning of something that would draw them to the mainland, the beginning of the quest he had spent the last fifty years preparing for. He started doing mental calculations regarding the logistics of the trip. A ship needed to be hired, supplies readied, his friends on the mainland contacted, obligations satisfied.

Tangus started moving down the hill towards his horse followed by Jennifer, Bitts, and Euranna leading Windrunner. "Jennifer, Kristen has taken sick. Horatio thinks she will be fine, but I need to return as quickly as possible. I want you to stay here with Euranna long enough to rest Windrunner, then return to the monastery with the pack horses. Be on guard. There are still some predators on InnisRos that would love to make a meal of the meat we've taken. I'll leave Bitts to run scout for you on the way back."

Jennifer nodded assent. "Where will you be? In your apartment?" she asked.

"I don't know. Just ask when you get to the monastery." Reaching Storm, Tangus turned and knelt down to Bitts level and rubbed his head and scratched behind his ears. "Bitts protect." Tangus then climbed onto Storm and headed back to the monastery at full gallop without another word.

As both Jennifer and Euranna watch Tangus' ride, Euranna said, "We have a long standing wager in the Messenger Corps on which of us rides faster than Tangus on Storm. I think I know the answer."

"Oh?" Jennifer replied, looking at her smaller companion. "And who would that be?"

Euranna shook her head in awe. "None of us," she whispered in awe.

A soft glowing light encased a sleeping figure, a little human girl. The child was no more than seven years old. Around the slumbering figure was complete darkness. There was no hint of shadows or light from any other source. The child was completely isolated in her magical chamber. Kristen's heart broke with a longing to comfort her, to hold and protect her from all who would do her harm. This fierce need to shield the child seemed like it was a natural, primal desire which sprang up from the depths of her soul. Kristen tentatively touched the surrounding light, desiring to convey through it her presence. Kristen wanted the child to know that she was no longer alone in the world. Kristen wanted the child to know that she was loved. "What have you endured?" she whispered to herself.

"She has endured a lot for such a little girl."

Kristen turned, startled at the voice coming from the darkness. She saw the ghostly figure of a young woman approach. "Who are you?" Kristen asked.

"I was her mother".

"Was?"

Looking with longing upon the child, the figure replied, "Yes. That responsibility now falls upon you, Kristen."

"How do you know my name?"

"I am of your blood. I am a long dead ancestor. My name is...was... Angela Clearwater. We both share the same bond with this little girl. It is that bond that has brought you here."

THE SALVATION OF INNOCENCE

Reaching an ethereal hand out but stopping just short of the stasis magic, Angela said wistfully, "Her birth name is Esmeralda, but she's always been my little Emmy. Now she is yours, at least until she is old enough to be on her own."

Emmy...so familiar, Kristen thought. "I am elf. How can we be of the same blood?" she asked aloud.

Angela shrugged, "How are we to know after so long a time except to say that the blood of the empath courses through both our veins. My mother once told me that the empath was created to serve all races and the bloodline knows no boundaries."

"We also share the same last name," Kristen replied skeptically.

"I do not know how such a thing happened," Angela said. "Perhaps a female elf married a Clearwater male at some time and took his last name. Or maybe the one who named you wanted to establish a link between you and Emmy through some precognitive talent. Did you know your mother?" Angela said.

"I did not know my birthmother. Your conjecture does seem reasonable. Right now however, only Emmy is important. What happened here?" Kristen asked.

"Vampyres, Kristen," Angela replied. "I was taken by one and I could not protect Emmy. I couldn't even control my own actions! The vampyres had me enthralled. But they decided to destroy us instead of forcing me to join their coven. I was killed by a stake driven through my heart and Emmy was left manacled to the wall. Though my mortal body was dead, the vampyre parasite infecting me survived. Somehow my little Emmy escaped and killed the parasite. If not for her, my soul would be forever damned. Kristen, I do not know how it came to be that Emmy has been spared by this strange light that sustains her. I know very little about magic, but I know it is starting to fail. Once gone, Emmy will die in this room, in this darkness, alone. You are now bonded to her, so only you have the ability to save her. But first you must come here. You must find her and you must do it quickly. Kristen, blood of my blood, you must hear my plea! I lost control over what happens long ago. I can only leave it in your hands"

"I feel a strong bond to Emmy. She is what I have been seeking for a very long time and I know she is important, but I don't know why," Kristen responded.

"Kristen, Emmy is a young empath. That is why the vampyres killed us, they loath empaths. They also greatly fear them. You are so important to her survival because you are of the same bloodline which allows you both to bond with each other. The bond will keep her alive, but only if you are with her."

"You need not fear, Angela, I will come for her," Kristen swore, *"and I will love her as you do. In truth, it seems I have loved her all my life."*

Kristen opened her eyes to find Tangus nervously pacing back and forth in the bedroom of their apartment. Her father was seated next to her, calmly reading a tome. Romulus was standing on the other side of the bed she and Tangus shared, looking down at her, his massive snout inches away from her face as he stared intently into her eyes.

"Welcome back, Brighteyes," her father said as he closed the tome.

Tangus stopped in mid-pace, looked over at her, then moved next to Romulus and knelt down, taking a hand. "Move over, Romulus. You're like a mother hen. How are you feeling dear?" Tangus asked.

Sitting up, Kristen said, "Tangus, I dreamed I was in the room with Emmy. I don't know how it happened, but I was there. I met the spirit of her mother. Emmy is the answer I have been searching for all these years. I have finally been able to 'scratch that itch'. But there is not much time. We need to get to the mainland. We need to find Emmy before she is lost!"

Tangus nodded. "Slow down, sweetheart. Your father and I suspected your collapse signaled the time had come for action. Already plans are being made. But who is Emmy?"

Father Goram looked at the two of them. "Emmy is the most important person on this world. Emmy is the last empath."

"So I was informed by her mother while I was with Emmy," Kristen said. "I know about the empath. Vayl had me study their legendary powers and about the purge. But even as an empath, which explains my bond with her, why is she so important to anyone other than those of us who love her?" Kristen asked.

"Shortly after you were born, Althaya came to me and told me to have a baby orphan brought over from the mainland." Father Goram replied. "That baby was you. I did not know of your importance at that

THE SALVATION OF INNOCENCE

time, only that my goddess gave me a task to be performed. I made certain arrangements and within a few months, we had you here safe and sound, although that was mostly because of dear Mary McKenna. I still miss her so."

"So do I, father." Kristen said.

"I know you do, Brighteyes. Anyway, the evening of your arrival I had another visit from Althaya and this time she brought Aurora." Looking at Kristen, Father Goram decided not to mention that Tangus was preordained by Aurora to be Kristen's champion. What good would it do to cause doubt? Besides, the love the two had for each other was genuine. "It was then that I was told about the empath and your relationship with her. The reason you're so important to a goddess is because you're the link to Emmy. You're the link Althaya's been waiting over three millennia for. Without you Emmy cannot survive in the world. Without you, we lose the last empath."

"And if we lose the last empath, father?" Kristen asked.

"Then we lose all of our ability to magically heal," her father answered.

Kristen stared at Father Goram in disbelief that such a thing could be true. "How can that be possible?" she asked in a whisper.

"Althaya told me that the empath serves as a catalyst for the magic. No other full empath lives. She has kept Emmy in a stasis field until one of the bloodline was born to bond with the child," Father Goram answered.

Kristen suddenly remembered her study of the empath. "All young empaths need this bond to survive until they have matured. The bond can only be established with one who also has empath blood."

"That is correct, Brighteyes. And you are that person. We've been waiting for the bond to occur, for the connection between you and Emmy to be fully established. As it turns out, the trauma of your mother's death started the process," Father Goram responded.

"When I collapsed? When I dreamt of Emmy?" Kristen asked.

Father Goram nodded. "I don't think that was a dream, Brighteyes. I think for a moment you were really there, at least your spirit was. What precipitated that is cause for worry and the reason we have to get to the child. The stasis field Althaya put in place to protect Emmy is starting to fail because too much time has elapsed. Emmy will not survive another conjuring. At least that's what Althaya has told me. I know you consider Emmy your little girl, and that is probably as true for you now as it was with her mother when she was alive. But as you can see, there's so much more involved than just a rescue of a child you love."

Kristen looked away. "I know of the stasis field and its weakening. Emmy's mother told me. Her name was Angela. She passed the responsibility for Emmy's protection onto me."

Standing and placing a kiss on Kristen's forehead, Father Goram said, "She knew you were the only one capable of doing it. Now I need to make some arrangements for your trip. Try to get a little rest, Brighteyes. Tangus, I'll see about transportation and funding for supplies. You know better than I what you'll need in the field once on the mainland, however. And since the purge was centered on Elanesse, I suggest you plan on starting your search there." At Tangus' nod, Father Goram started to leave but stopped suddenly and turned around. "Tangus, you're originally from the mainland. If you have any allies over there who will help, it might be a good idea to let them know to expect you."

"How do I do that?" Tangus asked.

"See Rhovalee about using one of his messenger dragons. He's a little overly protective when it comes to them, but he'll get you the best we have. I'll stay in touch. Let me know if you run into any problems." Father Goram turned and left the bedroom.

Tangus and Bitts got up as well. "I guess I need to get going too. I'll go talk to Jennifer and Safire. I know both will insist on coming, so they might as well start getting ready. And I guess I need to see Rhovalee about a dragon."

Kristen mind was racing. "Alright love. I'll see you later," she said.

Tangus paused, seeing his wife frown. He could tell from that sound of her voice and the look on her face that she was clearly distracted. "What's wrong?" he asked.

THE SALVATION OF INNOCENCE

Kristen looked at Tangus and shook her head. "Nothing really... Well, actually it's something Vayl told me a long time ago, but I need to think on it. We'll talk later when father is available."

"As you wish," Tangus said. "Please try to get some rest." Tangus lean over, kissed his wife, and left.

"I don't think I'll be getting much rest, Romulus," Kristen said to the otherwise empty room. Biting her lip, she thought, "The Alfheim...the plane of the Faerie and original home of the elves of light. This whole thing about the last empath and her importance to this world might be a problem if what Vayl told me about the Alfheim is true. There are many elves who would wish to take the empath out of Aster and to the Alfheim so they could control the magic she possesses."

Tangus was staring at the messenger dragon. It had golden scales that gleamed in the candlelight of the dragon stables. It was a great deal smaller than its cousins on the mainland, only about twenty feet from snout to the tip of its tail and weighing approximately two-hundred and fifty pounds. Bred to fly very long distances, the wings of messenger dragons extended thirty feet across and were extremely well developed. The dragon was staring back at Tangus with equal interest, cocking its head to the side and blinking.

Turning to the dragon keeper, Rhovalee, Tangus asked, "So how does this thing work?"

"Please Tangus, he is not a thing. His name is Borum and he's really quite intelligent." Rhovalee then covered his mouth and whispered, "Though not as much as the big ones on the mainland."

"Why are you whispering?"

"I don't want him to hear," Rhovalee replied. "It might hurt his feelings."

Tangus looked at Borum who was still staring at him. "I guess we wouldn't want to do that now, would we."

"No Tangus, not if you want his full cooperation. Sometimes messenger dragons need to be coddled," Rhovalee said as he scratched the skin under Borum's chin.

Tangus looked at Rhovalee dubiously. "They do, do they? How does one go about coddling a dragon?"

"Well…try to speak to it without raising your voice. A messenger dragon can tell a lot by tone inflection. And don't mention the 'you know what' on the mainland. Messenger dragons have an inferiority complex with regard to those," Rhovalee replied.

Tangus looked at Rhovalee, then back at the dragon. The dragon was still staring at him, still cocking his head. "He doesn't really look all that…"

Rhovalee held up his hands. "Please Tangus. Coddling, remember? Euranna with the Messenger Corps will be going. She's had experience with our dragons and will take care of Borum during the voyage, so you won't really have to worry about things until it's time to send him on his mission."

Tangus asked Rhovalee, "What do you think will happen if he ever does see a 'you know what' on the mainland."

"Why I rather think he will fly in the opposite direction as quickly as possible."

"Wonderful," Tangus said with a sigh. "Okay, so how soon can I release him and how do I get the destination locked into that bird…I mean dragon brain of his?"

"As to when to release him, maybe a week from landing, but it depends upon how far inland he has to fly," Rhovalee replied. "Do you have a map?"

Tangus anticipated this might be necessary so he brought his magical map of the mainland he bought all those years ago before he came over to InnisRos. Spreading it out on a nearby table for Rhovalee to look at, Tangus laid the tip of his dagger on Altheros near the Western Coast at the mouth of the Pantera River. "I want to land south. Altheros seems to be the best choice. I want Borum to go up here to Calamity."

THE SALVATION OF INNOCENCE

Studying the map, Rhovalee pointed at Palisade Crest, north of Calamity. "Palisade Crest's a deep water port. Why not just land there and travel south, stopping at Calamity along the way?"

"That will take too much time. No, I want my friends to meet me at Altheros when we make landfall," Tangus replied.

Rhovalee carefully looked at the map and then pointed to three small islands which lie to the southwest of Altheros. "You'll probably travel south of the Spiral Islands and back up. These three islands, the Three Sisters, should be your release point. I don't know if they'll be on your port or starboard side. That depends upon the ship's course into Altheros. But if your scale is correct..."

"It is," Tangus assured Rhovalee.

"Then he should be able to make the trip in about a day," Rhovalee replied.

Tangus nodded. "That should work. Now, how do I go about telling him where he has to go?"

Rhovalee smiled. "That's the easy part. Messenger dragons are very impressionable. All you need is a cleric."

Tangus looked at Rhovalee. "I'm married to one, so that's not a problem."

A look of embarrassment flashed across Rhovalee's face. "So you are. My apologies."

Tangus shook Rhovalee's apology off, "Don't worry about it. Please go on."

"Well, clerics can use spells to communicate with animals, but I guess you already knew that."

"It kind of became obvious living in this monastery. Most of the clerics here talk to animals as if it were their second language. Spells aren't always necessary, however. Kristen communicates with Romulus without magic," Tangus replied. "Rangers do similar things, such as what I do with Bitts. I understand from my wife that Father Goram has developed a spell that makes animal messaging easier. It's a variation of an animal courier spell but created specifically for clerics."

Rhovalee nodded. "That's right. All the cleric has to do is give the animal a mental image of the destination and, since such a far distance is involved, maybe a landmark or two."

Tangus scratched his chin. "That may be a problem. Kristen has never been to Calamity to give the mental image."

"Perhaps you can create a map here, in your head, to relay to Borum through the spell?" Rhovalee said tapping his index finger to the side of his forehead.

"It may come down to that, but a map is hardly a suitable replacement for the memory I have," Tangus said. "Since I know the animal courier spell, perhaps Kristen or Father Goram can teach me the variant. If not I guess the map will have to do, though I hate leaving so much to chance. Is there anything else I should know?"

Rhovalee shook his head no. "That pretty much sums it up. Borum won't let you down."

"Let's hope not." Tangus extended his hand to the dragon keeper. "Thanks for your help. I'll send word to prepare Borum for travel as soon as I know when we are leaving."

As Tangus had thought, both Safire and Jennifer insisted upon going. Tangus made both responsible for securing supplies from monastery stores and preparing all the horses for travel. They also had to get their own personal affairs in order. This was not a problem for Jennifer, Tangus had taught her that rangers must be ready to pick up and move at a moment's notice. The only true home for a ranger was outside in the forest, although having lived with a roof over her head her entire life made it harder. But Jennifer had learned her lessons well and what personal belongings she would need were packed quickly and efficiently. What she had to leave behind she gave to the other young rangers she knew.

It was not quite as easy for Safire. She was as old as Tangus and had lived all her life on InnisRos, working for the monastery since she was very young. Consequently she accumulated much more property and had to make decisions about what she would take and then arrange for the disposition of what she could not. Selling most of the things she would leave behind turned out to be profitable, but many things she dearly loved would be lost forever. In the end, however, she considered it a small sacrifice to help her friends, friends who were her only real family.

Finished with personal preparations and ready to start putting together supplies needed for the trip, the two met in Safire's small apartment to coordinate their efforts. Sitting down with a glass of wine, the two started to make a shopping list.

"Tangus gave me this letter from Father Goram which allows us to purchase whatever we need. The payment will be drawn from monastery coffers," Safire said, unrolling a parchment. "I've never had to anticipate what will be needed while in the field for an extended period of time."

"Father told me most of what we will need for food we can hunt along the way," Jennifer said. "He's been to the mainland and says the game is plentiful, and there are cities and towns to buy anything we might not realize we'll need until we're actually over there. He wants to move fast and doesn't want to be encumbered by a train of packhorses."

"Good. That gives me a much better idea about what we need to take. There will be four of us plus the horses," Safire replied. "You'll be on Jewels, Tangus will be on Smoke and Kristen prefers a heavy war horse. Her favorite is Arbellason. I've seen the two of them together. He might not be able to keep up with Jewels or Smoke in a dead run but he has the stamina to go twice the distance, I'd wager. He's also very protective of Kristen."

"And you, Safire?" Jennifer asked.

Safire shook her head. "I don't really have a preference. I love all horses. I think, though, that I would like one of the mustangs from your father's stable."

Jennifer thought about that for a few seconds before answering. "I think Mercedes will serve you well. She's spirited, fearless, as white as new fallen snow and as swift as the wind."

"That's settled, then. Let's make a list and run it by Tangus to see if we've forgotten anything. That should give us an idea as to how many packhorses we're going to need," Safire replied as she gathered pen, quill and a piece of vellum. "I wonder if we should hold off shopping until we reach Taranthi."

"That's the capital, Safire. How do you know that's where we're going?" Jennifer said quizzically.

"Other than Olberon, it's the largest deep water port on the island. The ship we'll need to get to the mainland is going to be there," Safire replied.

"But everything is more expensive in the capital," Jennifer said.

Safire nodded. "Yes. But it is not our money."

Smiling, Jennifer took the quill and slid the vellum over in front of her. Dipping the quill in ink, she said, "Good point. Item number one..."

By hour's end Safire and Jennifer had put together a comprehensive list of critical supplies. After having reviewed it as the ink dried, cringing at the anticipated cost, the two left Safire's apartment to find Tangus for final approval.

"What do you mean you're not coming back?" Father Goram angrily bellowed at Kristen. It was several hours after she had awakened from her collapse. She, Tangus and her father were sitting around the fire in the great room of her and Tangus' apartment. Father Goram had been issuing orders to just about every person in the monastery, which was now bustling with activity as everyone was working to follow the priest's directions and prepare everything Tangus and Kristen were going to need for the trip to the mainland. He had just come back from sending a message to the docks at the capital city, Taranthi, arranging transport. "I've explained how important she is. You think she'll be safe on the mainland? She needs to be as far away from there as possible!"

"Listen to me, father, please!" Kristen shouted back, trying to talk over her father's outrage. Tangus was looking down at his callused hands, carefully studying his fingernails. Romulus, not really sure what to do, had retreated to a nearby corner and was looking intently at the three. Bitts was sleeping at Tangus' feet, it was a long run back to the monastery earlier in the day. "Our race is disappearing from Aster, some having already chosen the Alfheim! I suspect most of our brethren will make this same choice within the next century. Emmy needs to stay on this world."

"That's ridiculous! The Alfheim…Bah! Do you know how hard it is to transition from one plane to another? The magical spells it requires can only be accomplished by a god-level sorcerer or through the use of a relic. Do you know how rare those are?" Father Goram countered.

"Nevertheless it's happening. You know it to be true, father," Kristen insisted. "Many elves want to leave for the Alfheim. They want to escape the humans and other races deemed inferior. It's another plane of existence, one in which only elves reside, one that has a magic rich environment that's seen as an elven utopia. An empath isn't needed there for healing spells to be effective like she is on this plane. But if I bring Emmy back, chances are very good the Queen, or someone else almost as powerful, will take an active interest in her. You know as well as I how our race values magic, especially magic as powerful as an empath's. The Queen could force Emmy to go with her to the Alfheim she decides to leave this plane. Tell me what I say isn't true!" Kristen demanded.

Father Goram, about to continue the argument, closed his mouth. "In your whole life I have never lied to you, Brighteyes, and I refuse to start now. You are correct. There has been movement to the Alfheim and I do expect it to increase well into our lifetime. Passages are being sold and someone is getting rich off the migration. But staying on the mainland? Live here! You don't have to go to the Alfheim."

Kristen looked at her father. "And if all the elves leave? What happens then? I'll tell you what happens. If all the elves leave, civilization on this island goes with them. No, that's just as risky. Emmy is the last empath and as such she is needed in this reality. As dangerous as the mainland is, that is where she belongs."

Without another word Father Goram got up and left. Kristen called after him, but to no avail. Turning to look at Tangus, she asked, "Am I wrong?"

"Kristen, I'm still trying to mentally absorb the whole idea of the Alfheim. As you explained it just before your father came in was the first I've heard of it. Then again, there is evidence to support what Vayl has told you. There have been missing persons reported lately that I have not been able to locate, whole families. I thought they went to the mainland to avoid something, like maybe debt or prosecution. But now it's starting to make sense. This Alfheim is the one component to the disappearances I wasn't seeing," Tangus answered, shaking his head. "I trust you Kristen. I'm never going to leave your side regardless what you decide. What else did Vayl tell you?"

Kristen was subconsciously gesturing with her hands as she spoke. "You know how stubborn father is. Vayl's very concerned father is not facing reality. Vayl thinks that within a century or two, all elves will have to make the decision to stay or go, that the elven gods will demand it. I follow Althaya and she counts among her followers members of all the civilized races. She will not leave. And Emmy…Tangus, she has to stay! As much as we are committed to each other, so too am I committed to Emmy. She's my responsibility now! But more importantly, I have a responsibility to the healing magic and the people who rely on it in this world and in this plane of existence."

Tangus walked over to Kristen and hugged her close. "You make me proud. Come, we have a lot of things to do with little time to do them. And don't worry about your father, He'll come around. "

Kristen, informed that her father was in the chapel, approached the entranceway doors with apprehension. She's had words with her father before, what child has not, but the look of anger and then fear in his eyes could not be misinterpreted. Still, she knew she must make her peace with him before she left.

Placing a hand on the back of Romulus' for strength, she quietly opened one of the doors and peered inside. He was sitting on a stone bench and reading a tome. Without looking up, he said, "Please, Brighteyes, come sit with me."

As Kristen tentatively approached, he closed the tome and looked up at her. He had quieted considerably since he stormed out of her apartment. "The passages in this tome calm me when I'm worried or angry. The words within remind me to see the bigger picture and stop being selfish. Your mother used to do that as well." Smiling, he motioned for her to sit next to him. As he gave Romulus a good scratch behind his ears, he said, "Brighteyes, you're acting like a child approaching a tiger. We are neither."

Kristen started to speak, "Father…" but Father Goram put a finger to her lips.

Father Goram took Kristen's hand. "As painful as it is for me to accept, I know Emmy should not come back to InnisRos. The empath is powerful magic, perhaps as powerful as any mortal can be, and our race will want her for their own. They will not let her leave once they have their hands on her." Father Goram looked away briefly, not willing to look into Kristen's eyes after this admission. "You are correct about the Alfheim, or maybe I should say Vayl is correct. I see the same pattern he does. Since I serve Althaya, I will not follow my brethren to the Alfheim. Eventually I will have to move the monastery to the mainland unless I can figure out a way to survive here once everyone that's going has left."

Kristen hugged her father closely, allowing tears of relief to flow freely down her cheeks. Father Goram hugged his daughter just as tight. After a few seconds, both pulled back, Father Goram reached over and captured Kristen's tears with his thumbs. "You must leave shortly, my dear. It's several days journey to Taranthi where a ship will be waiting to take you to the mainland. From there weeks on the sea depending on the wind and then even more weeks traveling to get to Elanesse. I have not discussed the overland route with Tangus, but since he's traveled the continent before I'm sure he already has the fastest route mapped."

"Do you think we will be in time, father?" Kristen asked.

Father Goram shook his head. "I don't know. Magic created by the gods is extremely powerful, but it has been over three-thousand years. Even though the spell was created by Althaya, after that long there are just too many unknown variables. It could completely give out within the next hour or last another few decades. I suspect, however, that the spell is more likely to conclude sooner than later. The bond will allow you to…how do I say this…to monitor Emmy's condition. Do you still feel the bond?"

Kristen nodded. "Yes. It's strong. Emmy is safe for now."

Father Goram took both of Kristen's hands in his. "Listen to me, Kristen. It's possible that as the spell gets weaker, Emmy is going to be more and more troubled by those who might wish her harm. Young empaths are extraordinarily sensitive to emotions, particularly ones directed at them. That is going to rebound back at you through the bond. You must be prepared for that."

"I will be. As the hours have passed, I've become more accustomed to handling the bond between Emmy and myself. I'm starting to figure out how to support her, how to comfort her even at this distance. She dreams, you know. When the stasis field collapsed for that brief moment, nightmares invaded those dreams. I think the nightmares came from her experience with the vampyres that killed her mother and tried to kill her. There was also something else, something more insidious and more dangerous," Kristen said.

Father Goram nodded. "That coincides with my belief that the Purge is still very much active and waiting for the stasis spell to end. Considering what we know about the Purge, it will have an unknown number of controlled accomplices in and around Elanesse. No one can be trusted."

"I had pretty much come to the same conclusion, father."

Father Goram smiled. "Good. Now, when the full force of the bond hit you, it caused you to collapse. You can't allow that to happen again."

"I was not expecting it and it took me unaware. I will handle it better the next time," Kristen replied with conviction. "There is something I've been wondering. How do we dispel the stasis field once we get to Emmy?"

"Oh, sorry, that completely slipped my mind." Father Goram said as he released Kristen's hands and started rubbing his eyes. "I completely forgot to mention that. Sorry, so much to do. When you get to Emmy, you only need to touch the field and your bond with her will automatically dispel it since you are of the same bloodline as Althaya. Beyond that, however, is unknown. This type of thing has never happened before."

The two then sat in silence for a few moments enjoying the peace and tranquility of the chapel, listening to the harmony of sounds coming from a small fountain. Father Goram put an arm around Kristen as she laid her head his shoulder. Romulus had fallen asleep at Kristen's feet and was snoring lightly. Both knew this might be that last moments of respite the two would ever share alone together.

Finally Father Goram broke the silence. "We need to get busy, Brighteyes."

"I know, father. But I swear to you that when this is all over, I'm going to have a chapel built just like this one for Tangus, Emmy, and I. It will be our special place. Promise me you will come and see it when it's ready?" Kristen asked.

"I look forward to it. I want you to have something," Father Goram as he took Kristen's hand and placed the tome in it.

"I can't take this father. Mother gave this to you," Kristen said as she started to decline it.

Father Goram put his hands over Kristen's and tightened them on the tome, refusing to take the tome back. "Your mother gave me a lot of things to comfort me in her absence. But this I think should go to you. Besides, there's something I put in the end of it that I think you'll need."

Opening the tome to the end, Kristen saw a spell written out. "This is your Bladebarrier Sanctuary spell."

Nodding, Father Goram said. "I had intended to teach it to you when you were a little more experienced, but time has run out. The spell explanation, its limitations and dangers are all there for you to study. It's crucial you understand the spell before using it. Practice it on the voyage over to the mainland. I think it will probably come in handy at some point. Now let's go find Tangus and see what progress he's made."

The following morning a small group of travelers left Calmacil Clearing heading west. Tangus on Smoke and Kristen on Arbellason led the way, while Jennifer on Jewels and Safire on Mercedes followed a few horse-lengths behind. Trailing the four was Euranna in a cart drawn by two heavy work horses, with Windrunner tied to and trailing behind. In the cart were personal supplies and the replacement weapons Tangus felt necessary as well the crated messenger dragon Borum. Romulus and Bitts were walking alongside Arbellason and Smoke, occasionally running off to scout ahead or to either side, seeking any threat to their masters and the small caravan. Other than the occasional prey animal, however, all real dangers were long ago eliminated by InnisRos rangers and law keepers.

Tangus had decided the quickest route was straight west to the Aranel River. Once they made it to the river, all they had to do was follow it south until they came across one of the many barges for hire that dotted the river's bank. They would travel down the Aranel River to the Maranwe River and, from there, down to Taranthi. This would cut the travel time by half compared to an overland route.

THE SALVATION OF INNOCENCE

As Calmacil Clearing disappeared behind them, Kristen sighed. She was leaving the only home she had ever known for the first time with little hope of ever returning. As important as it was to get to Emmy, her heart hurt from the loss and her eyes began to tear up, though she would not allow herself to cry. Tangus looked over at his wife with concern knowing what she was going through emotionally. Though leaving home was a necessary part of growing up, it still could be traumatic, especially if those left behind are well loved. Tangus knew the sacrifice that all of them, particularly Kristen, were making. He knew how hard and dangerous the road could be. He would spare Kristen, Jennifer, and Safire if he could, but that was just not possible.

"Leaving those we love is never easy, sweetheart. But as the miles widen our separation, we start accepting what has to be and our minds turn to other things. The loved ones we leave behind become a warm spot in our hearts, always there, always helping to light our way."

Kristen sniffed and smiled at her husband. "Thank you. Sorry for being so emotional. I guess I'm acting silly. I should be more grown up."

"Nonsense," Tangus said. "It's completely understandable. When I left home for the first time I cried like a baby. My poor horse...he kept looking back over his shoulder at me. I could see he was wondering what kind of idiot would sob during a perfectly beautiful day for traveling. I didn't even bother to hold the reins. He eventually walked over into a small field and started eating grass."

"C'mon dad, you never cry!" Jennifer called out from behind.

Safire laughed. "That's not entirely true, Jennifer. I've seen him cry once. You remember Jinx? Once we were fishing and Jinx was on a rock batting at a fish with his paw. Suddenly the fish jumped out of the water and scared poor Jinx half to death. He ended up falling in the stream. We had a rather drenched cooshie with dignity problems on our hands. Tangus laughed so hard he was bent over crying, which didn't sit so well with Jinx. I swear Jinx deliberately went over to Tangus and shook all the water off his fur, making Tangus almost as wet as he was, which made Tangus laugh and cry even harder. Old Jinx pouted the rest of the day."

By now all four were laughing. At first Euranna couldn't believe Tangus could be so normal, most rangers on InnisRos looked up to him as the ideal example of what a ranger should be. But within a few minutes, she was laughing as well. After shaking off his amusement, Tangus said to no one in particular, "God, I miss that dog."

By nightfall they had reached the base of the hills which bracketed the Aranel River and decided to stop for the night. Everyone was tired, even Romulus and Bitts, both of whom ended up riding in the back of the cart with Borum the last hour of the day. It was going to be a cold night, so Tangus gathered wood after brushing and feeding the horses and started a fire while Safire, Jennifer and Euranna raided the cart for dry meat and vegetables to make a stew for supper. Kristen, with Romulus following closely behind, walked to the cart to make friends with Borum, something she had neglected because of all the other preparations she had to make before they left. As she was feeding him bits of dried meat, Tangus came up behind her and wrapped his arms around her waist. Kristen leaned back into Tangus' embrace and rested her head upon his shoulder.

"Are you doing okay?" he asked.

Kristen closed her eyes. "It's been a long day and I'm tired, but other than that I'm fine. I can feel the bond with Emmy, and she sleeps peacefully, no nightmares. Tangus I do not know what dangers we will face, but Emmy will not be won easily. Through the bond I have seen Emmy's nightmares. There were vampyres, and something else, something very evil, something very powerful. I'm not only afraid for Emmy but for all of us as well."

"I've been in these types of situations before, Kristen. Life over on the mainland is hard. Remember when I've talked about the Company of the Dagger? None of those stories were exaggerated. During my time with them, we saw a lot of action and we battled many dangerous foes. I know it's been about a hundred years, but some lessons are never forgotten."

"Will they come to help?" Kristen asked.

THE SALVATION OF INNOCENCE

Tangus considered. "When I left the mainland there were only three of us left, Elrond Silverhair, Maximillion Darkshadow and me, so the Company was stretched pretty thin at the time. I've only corresponded with them once since we've been married and they've grown the Company, but they still have obligations to the Duke of Calamity and his sister, Lady Bronwyn. I do not know if they will be in a position to help, but they will if they can."

"If they can't come can we hire other mercenaries?" Kristen asked.

Tangus paused as he considered how to answer. "I don't really want to do that, sweetheart. Hiring someone to fight for money is risky because you never know where their loyalty will lie from one minute to the next. Even worse, without a cause to believe in, they might decide leaving is preferable to dying. Do you want to be in the midst of a fight and see your allies disappear? As a commander it's impossible for me to decide upon the correct tactic if the availability of my force is in question."

Kristen turned to face Tangus. "But you were a mercenary, were you not? You would never run from a fight nor would you do anything other then what was right. You would lay down your life for a good cause. Are not others such as you available?"

"Yes there are. But before I would put the lives of you, Emmy, Jennifer, and Safire in the hands of another person, I would have to know that person's heart. That takes time, Kristen, which is something we simply do not have. I trust Elrond and Max because they are my friends, and by extension I trust anyone they might bring with them. I know their hearts are true, but a stranger? No Kristen. If we have to, we'll go alone. At least then I'll know our limitations and from that I can make appropriate plans."

Kristen put a hand over Tangus' heart. "I know your heart and trust your judgment with my life."

Tangus briefly kissed Kristen and hugged her closely, wondering if he would really be up for the task. If not, he hoped death would come quickly, for he could not live without her. After a few seconds they separated. He took her hand and started to walk back to the fire, but Kristen did not follow, causing him to stop. Tangus turned to Kristen, "What's wrong?"

"Tangus, my love, you must make me a promise."

"From the look on your face I'm not going to like this, am I?" Tangus replied.

Breathing deeply and looking intently into Tangus' eyes, Kristen says, "No you are not. But I need your word on it nevertheless."

"Kristen…"

"I want your word on it, Tangus," Kristen implored. "Please give me your word."

"I can't…"

Kristen put her hands on both sides of Tangus' face. "Tangus, I need your word!"

Locking his eyes on hers, Tangus tried to read what she was going to say in them, but to no avail. Sighing, he nodded his head. "Alright, it is given," he said with resignation.

Kristen breathed a sigh of relief. This was very important to her. "Thank you. If you should ever have to make a choice between Emmy and me, you must choose Emmy. You know how important she is, not just to us but to the whole world. You need to raise her, protect her and guide her."

"Kristen, I cannot bond with her."

"I know that, but if something should ever happen to me, you're all she will have. I need to know you will do that for me." Kristen pleaded.

Tangus leaned back against the cart. "I wish I had a cigar. Nasty things, but they sure do help to calm me." Kristen took both his hands, but before she had a chance to say anything, Safire called out that the stew was ready. Tangus nodded. "It will be as you ask, Kristen. But your death will not come to pass. I will not let harm come to you or Emmy, you have my word on that as well."

Smiling, Kristen led Tangus back to the fire. "I'm counting on it," she said.

THE SALVATION OF INNOCENCE

The next morning they ate a quick breakfast of biscuits and cured venison before continuing their journey. They made their way over the hills and into the valley, reaching the Aranel River by midday. A cold north wind had started blowing not long after they broke camp, and a freezing drizzle was coming down on them by the time they arrived at the banks of the Aranel River. Wet and cold, they turned south. As dusk turned into night, they spied a light in the distance. Within the hour they were comfortably sitting around a fire in large barn, the only protection from the weather that was available to them. The owners, an older couple who operated one of the barges that navigated the Aranel, had provided dry blankets and warm food. Tangus made arrangements to go down river, but the barge owner would only take them to where the Aranel met the Maranwe River. From there they would need to hire another barge to take them into Taranthi.

During the night a heavy snow fell, covering the landscape with a thick white blanket. The winds had calmed, however, giving relief from the bone-chilling temperatures of the day before. After a warm breakfast, again provided by the wife of the barge owner, the horses and cart were loaded onto the barge. The three-man crew set the sails, and the journey down the Aranel River was underway.

Kristen, Jennifer, Safire, and Romulus retreated into a cabin situated towards the rear of the barge just before the tiller, which was being manned by the barge owner, while Euranna covered up Borum's crate with furs so he would remain calm during the journey down river. Tangus, with Bitts at his side, walked to the front of the barge and sat down on a crate. Although they would face many dangers, dangers that would threaten his wife, daughter and friends, Tangus was secretly excited to be on the road again. He missed the traveling he did when younger, all the new things he saw that the world had to offer, and the camaraderie he felt with his friends as they battled the perilous. Tangus, however, also knew this might be his last adventure, and that was not a bad thing. Once Emmy had been rescued and safely borne away from Elanesse, they would have to find a safe place to live, preferably in a nice wooded area. He absolutely refused to believe they would not get through this alive.

Euranna, having finished with Borum, walked to the front of barge towards Tangus, stopping along the way to give each horse an apple she had collected from the barn earlier that morning. Taking a seat on the deck next to Tangus, she wrapped her cloak tightly around her. "I love freshly fallen snow. It makes the ground look so pure, so innocent, like a newborn babe, unspoiled as yet by life" she said.

Tangus turned to look at the youthful ranger. "You have a bit of a poet in you. That's rare for one so young."

"Both my parents were scholars and wanted me to follow in their footsteps, so I was given a scholarly education," Euranna replied. "But I always liked the outdoors. There's a freedom in the forest that can't truly be described, it must be experienced. I never feel so alive than when I'm on a horse running beneath the open sky."

"That was very eloquent," Tangus said. "So what did your parents say when you decided to become a ranger?" he asked.

Euranna looked away. "They were not alive when I chose this life."

"I'm sorry, Euranna. If it's not too personal, may I ask what happened?"

When Euranna turned back to look at Tangus, her face was flushed with embarrassment. "They were executed for murder."

Tangus paused as he considered this revelation. "But there hasn't been...You're Coleen Melundea, the daughter! I always wondered what happened to her...you." Tangus studied the young elf as she was looking down at her feet. "Ahhhhh, now I understand," he said. "I should have known Father Goram would step in."

Euranna nodded, "After the execution, Father Goram took me in, had my named changed to Euranna Kolinda, and placed me with the other rangers at the monastery. All my parents' possessions and holdings were forfeited to the realm. I was penniless and without the means to support myself. I'm not sure what would have happened to me if Father Goram hadn't shown an interest."

"He never told me. I don't think anyone knows," Tangus replied.

Euranna shook her head. "No, but that's by his design. What my parents did, even if unintentional, caused a heinous crime to be committed. They arranged to have certain tomes smuggled in from the mainland, the theft of which resulted in several deaths. But they weren't really bad people, Tangus. They just got too ambitious and made some thoughtless decisions."

"I know the case. They had an opportunity to accept banishment from InnisRos since there was no premeditation. I never understood why they insisted upon a trial knowing what the outcome was going to be?" Tangus said.

"It's my fault, Tangus," Euranna said with great sorrow in her voice. "Banishment to the mainland for capital offenses includes all family members. My parents did not accept that punishment because of me. They knew the eventual outcome as well as anyone, so they made arrangements with Father Goram to take me in after they were executed. Their belief was that it was the only way to keep me safe."

Tangus shook his head. "They did what they thought was best for you, Euranna. You must not blame yourself. It's a shame, though. The mainland is not as primitive as many on InnisRos believe. They probably would have had a great deal of success if they had left."

Euranna nodded. "So Father Goram counseled them, but they refused to believe. Tangus, though my parents paid for their crime, there are still blood-oaths that some feel must be fulfilled."

"Blood-oaths are nothing but an excuse for murder! Where's the honor in that?" Tangus replied heatedly, and then he looked closely at Euranna, suddenly understanding. "You want to go to the mainland with us, don't you?"

Euranna nodded her head. "Father Goram told me to make my case to you and only you. He knows how important this venture is and said you must decide without other influences interfering with your decision.

Kristen's heart is big, but you're more rational and have a better grasp regarding the consequences of someone as inexperienced as me coming along. Please consider carefully. Father Goram says I can never be completely safe on InnisRos."

"Probably a good deal safer than where we're going," Tangus said as he thought about this latest development while Euranna waited patiently. Including Emmy, now there would be five he had to somehow keep safe. But as a ranger she had certain skills he could use. "Very well, you're with us. As the junior member, you better be prepared to take orders. How good are you with that katana?"

"Not as good as I'd like. My strengths are the bow and my ability to ride a horse."

Tangus nodded. "We'll need your bow," he said. "We'll work on your swordplay. I've never actually used a katana before, but it's a good choice. It's light and allows you to make the best use of your speed, as well as it gives you a longer reach than, say, a short sword." Looking out at the landscape going by as the barge moved down the river, he sighed sadly. "Ironic that you're going to the very place your parents died to prevent."

Euranna looked down. Bitts, instinctively understanding her distress, got up and leaned against her, accepting her absent-minded petting of his soft fur, allowing his presence to comfort her. "Yes it is," she whispered.

"Go back to the cabin and warm up," Tangus said to the young ranger. "Tell Kristen and the others that you are coming along and I'll join everyone in a little bit. I want to talk to our host about what to expect when we get to the Maranwe River."

"Yes sir," Euranna said as she turned to do his bidding. "Tangus... thank you!"

"You're welcome, Euranna." As Tangus watched her go back to the cabin he whispered, "But you can really thank me by staying alive."

THE SALVATION OF INNOCENCE

A carriage, windows covered with black paint, was carefully making its way through trees and small bushes. It was late afternoon, but the forest canopy blocked most of the sunlight. The deep shadows, however, were welcomed by those inside. The carriage stopped when the forest opened up to reveal a large, ruined city that was only partially reclaimed by woodlands. Here and there smoke rose from fires, each revealing the location of treasure hunters searching for the riches or relics believed to have been left behind when the city was abandoned. Men were frequent visitors, for their quest for fortune and fame was never-ending. They did not concern themselves with the underlying malevolence that prevailed within the city and the surrounding forest. Sometimes that lack of fear for the unseen evil in Elanesse lead to death.

The carriage driver called out, "We are here master, but the night has not yet returned!"

"Wait and let us know when it is fully dark!" A deep rich baritone voice from within the carriage replied.

"Very well, Lord Lukas," the carriage driver said.

CHAPTER 5

The proud mountain stood mighty and tall, a majestic lord over all the land. The raindrop caused little concern. Over time, however, the raindrop and its brethren became an ocean, swallowing and sending the mountain to its doom.

— BOOK OF THE UNVEILED

NIGHT HAD FALLEN by the time the barge reached the point where the Aranel River flowed into the Maranwe River. The shores at this intersection point were dotted with several small inns, each of which had docks and barges available for hire. Finding a barge to complete the river journey into the capital city of Taranthi could be accomplished without much difficulty, however, none of the barge owners would make the trip in darkness. Having no other acceptable options, Tangus, Kristen, and the others decided upon a comfortable looking inn in which to spend the night.

After having made arrangements with the innkeeper, Tangus gave Jennifer and Safire leave to go inside and get warm while he led Kristen, Euranna, the horses, and the cart into the stable built into the side of the building. Telling the young stable boy they did not need help, Tangus started to get the horses ready for the night. The stable boy bowed his head in quick assent, never taking his eyes off Romulus, before quickly disappearing into the darkness.

After untying Windrunner from the cart and backing it into a stall, Euranna unhitched the two horses. She then opened the cage and placed a cover over Borum's head. "This will stop him from trying to fly away. Normally he can be trusted, but, in a strange place, if he were to get startled who knows what might happen. I have to open up his cage to feed and water him, and from the smell, he could use a good rinse," she said as she went to get a bucket of water from the inn's nearby well.

"Won't he get cold in this weather if you get him wet?" Kristen asked after Euranna had returned.

Euranna shook her head. "No, the cold does not bother these dragons. They are equipped to handle it. They have to be, considering the height they fly when delivering messages. I'm told it gets colder the farther up you go."

Tangus, as he was brushing a horse, nodded. "You have that right, Euranna. Kristen, the mountains on InnisRos aren't nearly as high as some of the ones on the mainland. I can't tell you the number of times I've seen snowcapped mountains in the middle of summer over there." Changing the subject, Tangus turned to Euranna. "Euranna, when you're done getting Borum and Windrunner bedded down for the night, go inside, warm up, get something to eat, and catch a few hours of sleep. We can't risk losing any of the horses or Borum, so I want to post a guard. I'll take first watch with Bitts. I want you, Jennifer, and Safire to take the second. I think two four-hour shifts will be sufficient. Under no circumstances do I want any of you to be alone. I'm not expecting trouble, but these are troubling times. Besides, I want everyone to start getting a feel for standing watch throughout the night. It's tough to stay awake after an exhausting day of traveling. It's a lesson that needs to be well-learned. Lives may soon depend on it."

"Yes Tangus," Euranna replied.

After Euranna left, Kristen asked, "Do you really think there's any danger of having the horses or Borum stolen?"

Tangus shook his head. "Not really, but I don't want to take any chances."

"I'll take first watch with you," Kristen said.

"No, Kristen, I want you to sleep through the night. I've been around sorcerers and clerics long enough to understand that they need plenty of sleep to be able to work their spells," Tangus replied. "Trust me when I tell you that using magic will fatigue you much quicker than using a sword ever could. But you can come over here and give me a hand with the horses before turning in for the night."

Kristen was happy to comply. She loved horses and learned to care for them when she was very young. Oftentimes she found comfort in brushing brambles out of their manes and tail. It allowed her mind to focus elsewhere, to address problems and seek resolutions. After thoroughly brushing Arbellason's mane and coat, she lifted each leg to look at his hooves, making sure the horse hadn't picked up a rock that might cause it to come up lame. After she was done with her Arbellason, she moved to one of the heavy work horses while Tangus silently worked Jennifer's Jewels. When all the horses had been brushed and their hooves checked for stones, Tangus and Kristen fed and watered them.

"Where did Romulus and…never mind," Kristen said as the cooshie and dire wolf came running around the corner of the stable. Tangus' elven dog Bitts was in the lead and was being chased by Romulus. The two had developed a strong bond of friendship and spent a good deal of their spare time chasing each other if they weren't wrestling. Bitts, as the fastest and quickest, normally won the chase, but when it came to wrestling, Romulus, with his size, easily pinned Bitts, though he never was able to hold on for long. Though the two had never been forced to fight together in defense of their masters, they were going to make life extremely difficult for Tangus' and Kristen's enemies when that time did come. In a flash they both disappeared around the opposite end of the stable.

"That's a lot of stored up energy!" Tangus laughed. "I guess it comes from riding on a barge all day."

Smiling, Kristen said, "What are they going to do after a few weeks on the ship?"

"Terrorize the crew!" Tangus said as he sat down on a bench and leaned against a post. "How are you holding up?"

Kristen sat down beside him, tucked her arm underneath his while grasping his hand and laid her head on his shoulders. "I'm okay. I just worry that we will not get there in time. Already two days traveling and we still haven't reached Taranthi. How long will it take to cross over to the mainland?"

THE SALVATION OF INNOCENCE

"Three to four weeks depending upon the prevailing winds. The trip can be made faster, but we won't be taking a speedier cutter since we'll have horses with us."

Kristen closed her eyes. "I wouldn't want to do this without Arbellason. He's steady, dependable and knows how to fight."

"I feel the same about Smoke. Besides, our horses are used to Romulus being around. I imagine from a horse's point of view he's the bogeyman," Tangus responded. "It would be difficult to get another horse to accept him without taking time to train the fear instinct out of it."

Kristen did not reply. Looking over at her, Tangus saw that she had fallen asleep. About that time Bitts and Romulus came barreling around the stable corner again. Tangus raised his finger to his lips, "Shhhh!" Both stopped and went over to sit down next to their masters, breathing heavily with tongues lolling out of their mouths. For the next few minutes Tangus sat quietly looking up at the stars. It was a clear and cold night, but it was also a time of peace and solitude. Though he knew he should awaken Kristen and ask her to go inside, he loved the feel of her against him and thought, "Just a few more minutes."

Suddenly Kristen awoke with a sharp intake of breath. "What is it, sweetheart?" Tangus asked.

"I just shared a dream with Emmy, a nightmare, actually. Somehow, through her dreams, she can sense danger, and that danger is close by her," Kristen replied.

"Is the stasis magic getting weaker?"

Kristen shook her head. "No. It hasn't lost any more of its power to protect her. But something's reached Elanesse that, before now, was just a terrifying memory. Angela told me about the vampyres. They're coming for Emmy!"

"As long as the stasis magic is functional she cannot be harmed. That much we know. Can you somehow keep her from having nightmares through the bond?" Tangus asked.

"The bond with Emmy is still too new to me," Kristen said. "I'm not sure yet what can or cannot be done. Tangus, I'm pretty much playing this by instinct. But in answer to your question, no, I don't think I want to do that. I can minimize her distress and support her through the bond, but I wouldn't want to take the nightmares away, even if I knew how. They act as a warning. I think it will help us in the long run, and I think Emmy is strong enough not to be traumatized by them. We won't be going into Elanesse unaware and perhaps it will allow me to locate just where in Elanesse she lies."

"That sounds reasonable. Try to relax. Go inside and get some sleep. I'll be in after my watch," Tangus said.

Kristen yawned. "You're right. I am sleepy," she said.

Tangus and Kristen got up and exchanged a kiss and a brief hug before parting. Romulus closely trailed Kristen as she went into the inn. "Well old friend, I guess we wait," Tangus said to Bitts, sitting back down on the bench and scratching the dog behind the ears. "I never get tired of looking into the night at the stars. I have a confession, Bitts. I've missed my life on the mainland. Your grandfather, Jinx, and I had plenty of adventure over there. It was dangerous, true, but it was exciting. And through it all it was more than just being a mercenary hunting for treasure. We were actually accomplishing good. We saved a lot of lives, Bitts, and in our own way actually made the world a better place to live. God, I loved it! And to this day I have never figured out just why I left and came to InnisRos. But if I had not, I would never have settled down long enough to have had a daughter and son. I would never have met Kristen. Funny how life sometimes knows what's better for you than you do yourself. I wonder why that is? Kristen probably has some idea. She's a pretty deep thinker, Bitts, even as young as she is. Me, I'm just a ranger. I see the world differently and I don't try to reason out why things happen. Philosophy! I never really got the hang of it. But I think if I ever did discover the answer, it would probably drive me insane."

Bitts patiently sat and listened to his master's soliloquy. When Tangus fell silent, still looking up at the stars, Bitts laid his head on Tangus' knee and stared up at him. Looking down, Tangus petted Bitts on the head and smiled. "I think it's time to make our rounds, boy." Getting up, Tangus and Bitts roamed the inn and stable perimeter.

THE SALVATION OF INNOCENCE

The rest of the night passed without incident, though Jennifer, Euranna and even Safire had a hard time staying awake. At dawn, Tangus came out of the inn with hot breakfast sandwiches for each. "A gift from our hosts," he said without further comment as he started eating.

"Where's Kristen?" Safire asked.

Swallowing a bite of a breakfast sandwich, Tangus muttered, "She's still sleeping. I've talked to the innkeeper who also owns the barge. I'm going down to the docks to inspect it and arrange a price. It'll actually be his son, Samuel, who will be behind the tiller. We didn't meet him last night, but he's down there right now along with the rest of his crew. While I'm gone feed and prepare the horses and Borum for travel." Licking his fingers, Tangus started towards the dock. "C'mon boy!" he said over his shoulder to Bitts.

"Well ladies," Safire said, "time to get this show back on the road. Euranna, are you going to need any help?"

"A little with the two work-horses would be much appreciated," Euranna replied.

Nodding, Safire said, "Jennifer, help Euranna after you've taken care of Jewels. And I guess you better see to Smoke as well. I'll get Arbellason ready when I'm done with Mercedes."

Kristen and Romulus appeared from the inn. Kristen was eating a breakfast sandwich in one hand and carrying her pack in another. Romulus was smacking his lips. He had won favor with the innkeeper's wife and had been given a handsome piece of meat which was promptly consumed. By this time the horses had been fed and were ready for travel. Safire, Jennifer, and Euranna were sitting on the same bench Tangus and Kristen had sat on the previous night.

"Where's Tangus?" Kristen inquired.

"Down by the...wait, here he comes," Jennifer answered looking in the direction of the river.

Tangus and Bitts made their way to where the rest waited and Tangus gave Kristen a kiss. "Morning, sweetie," he said.

"Gee dad, you never kiss me anymore," Jennifer said playfully.

Safire shook her head. "Parental abuse!" she said, "so very sad. Does he even tuck you into bed at night?"

"No, he doesn't do that either. I swear Smoke and Bitts get more attention than I do," Jennifer replied.

"Alright, alright," Tangus said holding up his hands. Walking over to Jennifer, he gave her a kiss on the forehead. "Satisfied?"

"And will you tuck me into bed tonight?" Jennifer asked.

"No, but Bitts will, won't you boy," Tangus laughed.

"Woof!"

Tangus ruffled the fur on Bitts head. "There you go Jennifer, Bitts will be happy to do it. Now, are we ready to travel?"

Safire nodded, "We're ready to go."

"Kristen?" Tangus asked.

"I left my gear in our room, Tangus. I'll be right back," Kristen said as she rushed back to the inn carrying a glass vial in her hand. Romulus was following close behind.

Tangus looked at Kristen's pack lying on the ground and turned to his three fellow rangers. "That's funny, all her gear is right here. Get the cart and all the horses down the hill and loaded into the barge. Kristen and I will be down in a few minutes." He then followed Kristen into the inn, but when he got to their room, she was not there. "Kristen, where are you?" he called out.

"I'm in here, Tangus," he heard her call.

Following the direction of her voice, he entered a small bedroom to find his wife kneeling beside a bed. Sitting in a chair next to the bed was the innkeeper's wife, Bonnie. In the bed was an old female elf, frail and sickly. Tangus had never seen someone looking this ancient. Turning to look at Tangus, Kristen said, "This is Glassada, Bonnie's mother. She is dying. I'm trying to make her comfortable." Redirecting her attention to Bonnie, Kristen said, "I've done all I can with magic. When the spell wears off, give her a sip of the healing potion I gave you. There should be enough to last a week or so."

Bonnie looked down at her sleeping mother. "I don't think she'll live even that long, but thank you, Kristen!"

Getting up, Kristen went to Bonnie and took both her hands. "I wish I could do more. It's just your mother's time. Celebrate her long life." Turning to Tangus she said, "I'm ready to go now. Farewell Bonnie."

"Farewell, Kristen."

The two left the inn and walked down the hill to the dock, holding hands, but not speaking. Shortly thereafter the barge was heading down river.

The Maranwe River ran much faster to the coast then did the Aranel. Knowing time was of the essence, Samuel had his crew set the main and secondary sails to capture as much wind as possible. He expected to reach Taranthi by the early afternoon.

Although still quite cold, the sun shone brightly. Its light transformed the snow, turning the ground and trees into a bright, sparkling wonderland. Everyone preferred to remain outside, doing their best to stay out of the way of the barge crew while still enjoying the brilliant scenery as it sped past. As they were traveling downriver, a question gnawed at Tangus. With Kristen at his side, he went to the stern of the barge to have a conversation with its captain.

Acknowledging Tangus and Kristen's approach with a nod and a smile, Samuel said, "Good morning Mistress Kristen. Master Tangus. Is there a problem?"

"Not at all, Samuel," Kristen said. "Please, call me Kristen. My husband and I don't really stand on formality."

"As you wish, Kristen," Samuel replied. "It is a beautiful day, is it not? The river runs fast and we have a little wind at our backs. A perfect day for traveling, though I think if it gets much colder we may have a little ice on the river."

"Is that generally a problem?" Tangus asked.

"You mean the ice?" Samuel asked. Tangus nodded. "No," Samuel said. "The river runs too swiftly for it to ever ice over completely, but some patches can develop closer to the shore. A sloppy barge captain can find himself grounded on ice quickly enough."

"Samuel, I know you're busy, but I'm puzzled by something," Tangus said. "It's just a thought that has been nagging me ever since we started out this morning. How do you get this barge back upriver?"

Samuel laughed with delight. "I have been on the river for most of my adult life and I have never been asked that question before."

"My husband is a very inquisitive fellow, Samuel," Kristen responded with a smile.

"Please call me Sammy, madam. I value passengers taking an interest in how we do things. Most just pay me to get down river as quickly as possible and then they disappear into the cabin, not coming out until we've reached the end. Some go as far as treating my crew as simple servants, never once trying to understand or appreciate all we do to make their trip as quick and comfortable as possible. I hate arrogance, but I can't turn away a fare if I want to stay in business. I generally over charge those people, however. Forgive me. I know it's not ethical, but they can afford it and it gives me a certain amount of comfort knowing I made them pay for their boorish behavior."

Tangus nodded and replied heatedly. "There's nothing I like more than kicking an arrogant bas…"

Kristen grabbed Tangus' arm and hand. "What my husband is trying to say is don't let people like that force you to become jaded. Weren't you, honey?"

"Well…yes, I guess I was, sweetheart," Tangus replied a bit sheepishly.

Kristen continued, smiling pleasantly at Sammy. "He was also trying to say that there are a lot of good people in this world, people who are always trying to do the right thing by other people. Isn't that right, dear?"

Tangus glanced at Kristen who was now looking at him pleadingly, squeezing his hand to emphasize her point. "Yes, sweetheart, that's exactly what I was saying," he finally said, while inwardly smiling. She was his moral compass and she apparently knew it.

THE SALVATION OF INNOCENCE

Kristen grinned as did Sammy. He was married too and understood the meaning of what often silently passed between husband and wife. "Okay...so, getting a barge up river...come over here, Tangus," Sammy said. As Tangus approached, Sammy raised the tiller completely out of the water. The tiller was approximately twenty-five feet long, the last fifteen of which had a massive rudder attached. Made of sturdy oak, it looked as if it weighed several hundred pounds. "Take the tiller," Sammy instructed Tangus.

Tangus hesitated.

"It's okay, Tangus, the barge isn't going to run amok. Go ahead, take the tiller," Sammy repeated.

Tangus did so, ready to support its weight. But to his astonishment, it was as light as a feather. "It feels like balsa wood!" he exclaimed.

"But as strong as steel," Sammy said as he took the tiller back out of a very surprised Tangus' hands. "Magic and damn fine engineering is the key, Tangus. Pardon my language, Kristen. Our barges are engineered from sturdy oak. Fins, like a fish, are built along the bottom, and horizontal planes run along the hull, below the waterline, to provide stability. Then the sorcerers take over. They spell the barge to harden the wood while at the same time making it very light. I don't understand everything they do, but it's been working for centuries. Going downriver all we really have to do is steer it as the current takes over. We use sails when the wind is right for extra speed. Going upriver, again we use sails, but we can also power it by moving the rudder back and forth. It's like a giant oar. Mount a couple more of these oars in those two brackets on both sides of the main rudder and we can get this thing moving upriver at a decent speed."

"That's amazing!" Tangus muttered.

"I don't know if it's amazing," Sammy replied. "It's like most everything else, I imagine. Figure out what you want to do and then figure out how to do it using the tools or magic available to you. If we didn't have magic, then we would have figured out something different. Either way, we'd do what we needed to do to get the job done. I guess that's pretty much how everything works."

"I never really thought about it in that way," Tangus said.

"That's because on the river you're a user, not a maker. You just want to get down the river. You're a ranger, right? And you, Kristen, a priestess?"

Both Tangus and Kristen nodded.

"Tangus, I bet if you're in the woods and had a problem, you'd know how to figure it out using your knowledge as well as the tools at your disposal. In the woods you'd be a maker. I'm sure the same is also true for you, Kristen, when it comes to people's soul or healing needs."

"That's very perceptive, Sammy," Kristen said.

Sammy shrugged. "Standing behind a tiller all day gives one plenty of time to think."

For the rest of the trip Tangus and Kristen stayed with Sammy and engaged in light conversation. True to his word, the barge reached the capital Taranthi in early afternoon. Tangus gave Sammy additional gold to reward him for getting them to Taranthi as quickly as he did. Sammy refused at first, but Kristen insisted, and he did not care to argue with a priestess who was also a wife. Sammy intended to contemplate that combination as he went back upriver.

As Tangus, Kristen and the others made their way off the barge, they all knew they were leaving behind a new friend.

Taranthi was located where the Maranwe River runs into a deep water bay, the Bay of Sorrow, called that because of the inordinate number of ships that, during bad weather, smash against the rocks that lay on either side of the bay. The docks of Taranthi are extensive. As with any island nation, InnisRos depended upon commerce to meet some of its needs, mostly indulgences that couldn't otherwise be found on the island. InnisRos also exported items, most of which were elven-made luxury items such as tapestries, carved wood art, wine, and musical instruments which were prized and considered the best on all of Aster.

THE SALVATION OF INNOCENCE

The business of export and import with InnisRos had become profitable for many merchants and therefore was an around the clock operation. All the barges that came down the Maranwe River were docked at the river's mouth. The large merchant vessels coming from the mainland, however, were docked south of the city.

"Everybody listen up!" Tangus shouted. They had just disembarked from the barge and had gathered together next to a stack of crates on the dock. Each was holding the reins of their horses. "Safire, Jennifer, you have the list of supplies we're going to need?"

"I have it safely tucked away along with Father Goram's letter of payment guarantee," Safire replied.

"I want the two of you to rent a cart and buy all the supplies on the list…"

Before Tangus could finish his instructions, Euranna interrupted. "Excuse me, Tangus, but we already have a cart. Why don't we get Borum and our supplies loaded onto the ship, after which Safire and Jennifer can use our own cart? No real point renting something we already have."

Tangus paused and then sighed. "Of course you're right, Euranna."

Kristen put her hand on Tangus' arm. "It's okay, dear. You can't be expected to think of everything."

"Yeah, dad, it's kind of why we're along. You know?" Jennifer quipped.

"Shush, Jennifer. You don't want to hurt Tangus' pride, do you? Only Kristen is allowed to do that," Safire said with a smile.

Kristen laughed. "You are kind of outnumbered, my love. But don't worry. We female folk will take care of you."

Tangus looked at each of them. Even shy little Euranna was smiling. Sighing again, he held up his hands. "I, of course, surrender. Shall we go find the ship then? It'll be one of the bigger ones at anchor in the southern part of the city. It's called the *Freedom Wind*."

Tangus hesitated as everyone else left and bent down to Bitts eye level. "You understand me boy, right?"

"Woof!" Bitts replied.

Tangus stared at the cooshie. "Well that sounded rather dubious."

"C'mon, Dad, you're falling behind!" Jennifer yelled.

The *Freedom Wind* was one of several deep water vessels currently in port. She had four masts, including the bowsprit, and three decks plus the quarter-deck. The waterline to the top of the main mast measured two hundred feet. At two hundred and fifty feet long by fifty feet wide and displacing three thousand tons fully loaded, she was the largest of the deep water merchant vessels in port. She was also the most heavily armed with seventeen ballistae on each side as well as two each on the bow and stern. Three heavy catapults were set on metal plates at equal intervals along the main deck. The plates rotated, which allowed the catapults to be fired in any direction. Large cranes on the dock were loading various sized crates into the *Freedom Wind's* several holds. A large gangplank ran up from the dock to the top deck of the ship.

Everyone was standing on the dock, feeling a little intimidated by the sheer size of the *Freedom Wind*. Everyone, that is, except Tangus. He had sailed on a ship this size before when he came over from the mainland.

"The crew is human!" Euranna suddenly exclaimed.

"That's not untypical, Euranna," Tangus replied. "Elves are fine serving aboard ships in coastal waters as our navy does. However, our kind has problems spending weeks upon weeks out in the ocean with no land in sight. No doubt there are exceptions, but we are mostly too enamored with our forests, rivers, and lakes to be willing to make a career of being away from them for long periods of time. Humans, however, take to the high seas very well. Their shipwrights are the best in the world. If I'm going to take a long ocean trip, I want the ship to be crewed by humans."

Tangus stepped forward, cupped his mouth, and yelled, "Ahoy the ship!"

A lone figure leaned over an elaborate banister from the quarter-deck and looked down. Tangus was surprised to see a female elf. She was wearing a cream-colored shirt with long wide sleeves ending in a buttoned cuff. Coming out of the top of the shirt was a wide lace scarf. Her pants were tight-fitting with gold strips going down each pant leg, ending in calf-high boots. Her long blonde hair was tied back, but strands escaped the ribbon and blew freely in the wind.

She looked at Tangus and then everyone else before straightening back up and disappearing. "Belay that last order. Mr. Krist, please prepare to receive our passengers," she bellowed. As she looked back down, she was putting on a deep blue jacket with gold buttons and gold epaulets on each shoulder. "Tangus DeRango?" she shouted.

"Yes, madam. You're the captain?" Tangus asked.

"That is correct, sir. Jasmine Dubois, Captain of the *Freedom Wind* at your service. I'll send down some of my crew to help with the horses and the cart. My First Officer, Mr. Krist, will accompany them. He'll also arrange anything else you might require. When you are situated, please come to my cabin for a meet and greet." Turning her head to look over her left shoulder, she said, "Mr. Krist, if you will."

"As you wish, Captain," Mr. Krist was heard saying, though no one on the wharf could see him.

Within a few short minutes Mr. Krist led a group of men down the gangplank. He too was an elf. Mr. Krist and his men stopped, however, when they saw Romulus, who had stepped in front of Kristen and started to growl. Taking a deep breath, Mr. Krist stepped forward.

"Madam, we were informed there would be a dire wolf accompanying your party, but nothing was said about the size. Will you be able to control that beast whilst on board?" he asked.

Kristen moved up to stand beside Romulus and put a hand lightly on his back to quiet him. "Mr. Krist, his name is Romulus!" she said heatedly. "I do not wish to cause trouble for your captain, you or the crew of this ship, but I WILL NOT suffer my friend being referred to as a BEAST! Can we be clear on that?"

There was complete silence as both groups stared at each other. Tangus knew from experience that there was nothing in Mr. Krist's posture that indicated any threat to Kristen. He also was a bit surprised at his wife's stern defense of Romulus. Usually she would just politely set the record straight regarding her wolf. Tangus now worried the strain of the bond might be having a greater effect on her than she was showing.

Mr. Krist broke the silence. "Certainly, madam, you have my most humble apologies. If you would permit me?" he said, gesturing at Romulus.

Kristen hesitated, but then nodded. Mr. Krist walked over to stand in front of Romulus and extended his hand for Romulus to sniff. Romulus, for his part, relaxed and sniffed the proffered hand. Mr. Krist then took both hands and scratched Romulus behind the ears. "I've never seen a wolf as big as you, Romulus. It is indeed a pleasure to make your acquaintance." Turning, Mr. Krist ordered his men to start helping with horses and supplies in the cart.

"Mr. Krist, I apologize for my rude behavior. Your reaction to Romulus is quite typical. I normally handle my response more, shall we say, diplomatically," Kristen said.

Mr. Krist turned to Kristen and bowed. "No apologies are necessary, madam. Perhaps if I show you to your cabin so you can freshen up? I am sure the captain will understand the delay."

Kristen wiped her brow with her hand. "You have my gratitude, Mr. Krist. I would like that very much."

"Very well, madam, whenever you are ready."

Tangus turned to Safire, Jennifer and Euranna. "Please help these gentlemen get the horses and Borum onboard, all except the cart and the two work horses. When that's done, Safire, I want you and Jennifer to take the cart and buy the supplies on the list. When you get back, I'm sure some of the crew will help with their loading and securing. Is that fine with you, Mr. Krist?"

"Certainly, sir," Mr. Krist replied. "If I may, I'll have one of our junior officer's go along. We've been to this port-of-call on numerous occasions and know where the best places are to buy supplies. Most of the shops in the area are run by good, honest folk, but there are some charlatans as well." At Tangus' nod, he called out to one of his men. "Ensign Carlowe, please be so good as to accompany these ladies. I think probably you should start with Pelior's Merchandise and Supply."

THE SALVATION OF INNOCENCE

"Aye aye, sir," a young man called out as he walked over to the cart.

Turning to Tangus, Mr. Krist said, "Ms. Pelior is a very honest trader. Her items are high quality and she charges a fair price."

"Thank you, Mr. Krist," Tangus said. He then looked at Euranna. "I want you to oversee the loading of Borum onto the ship. Please stay with him for the time being. I'll come down into the hold after we get situated to see how he's doing. I hope he does not require someone to be there constantly."

Euranna nodded. "Yes sir. I think he will be fine once he gets settled in. Messenger dragons mostly sleep anyway."

"Excellent. Anybody have any questions?" Tangus asked. Everyone shook their head. "Mr. Krist, we're ready."

"Very good sir, if you will follow me."

As Tangus, Kristen, Bitts, and Romulus went up the gangplank, everyone else got busy with the loading of the horses and supplies. Euranna put the cover over Borum's head and then wrapped the entire crate in furs to keep the dragon as calm as possible. Within the hour the horses and supplies had been efficiently loaded and secured in the middle hold. Of *Freedom Wind's* five holds, this was the only one that had a ramp which made it easily accessible to the horses and other animals. Safire and Jennifer, with Ensign Carlowe in tow, had left with the cart to buy supplies. Euranna was tending Borum. He had survived the loading none the worse for wear and was happily eating some dried fish.

Meanwhile, Mr. Krist led Tangus and Kristen on board the *Freedom Wind* and to a lavish stateroom one deck below. There was considerable worry that Romulus would have problems negotiating the ladder, but he did fine, though several of the steps cracked under his weight. Mr. Krist ordered a nearby member of the crew to fetch the ship's carpenter, "I want these steps fixed and strengthened without delay," he told the crewman. Once they were in the room and Mr. Krist was sure they did not require anything else, he said, "By your leave, I will inform the captain that the lady requires a spot of time to freshen up before your meeting."

Kristen smiled. "Thank you, Mr. Krist. You are too kind."

Bowing, Mr. Krist said, "Not at all, my lady." Turning to Tangus, he gave him a quick salute. "Sir," he said as he left the room and closed the door.

Kristen sat down on the large bed. Tangus went over and sat down beside her, putting an arm around her shoulders. "What's wrong?" he asked.

"Nothing really," Kristen said. "The bond is solid, Emmy hasn't had any more nightmares, and the stasis field is holding steady. I'm not sure why I snapped at Mr. Krist."

Tangus hugged Kristen tight. "You're just tired. This is your first real trip on the road. It wears on a person."

"That's probably it," Kristen replied.

Tangus kissed Kristen on the forehead. "Of course it is. Eventually you'll get used to it. Why don't you lie down and rest a few minutes before we go meet the captain."

A slight trace of energy resonated above. A rope of magic, very faint, traveled the Ether and was striking the dead city of Elanesse, leaving behind an echo. Like a spider web, the vibration caused by the magic alerted the Purge to its existence. It recognized the enchantment of the bond. Although the nearest end-point was invisible, the Purge was able to follow the magic to its other end and found it connected to a mortal, the one who was bonded to the empath. Backing away, the Purge waited, keeping an imperceptible hold on the connection between the two. It knew the bonded mortal would come for the empath. Then it would achieve that for which it was created.

THE SALVATION OF INNOCENCE

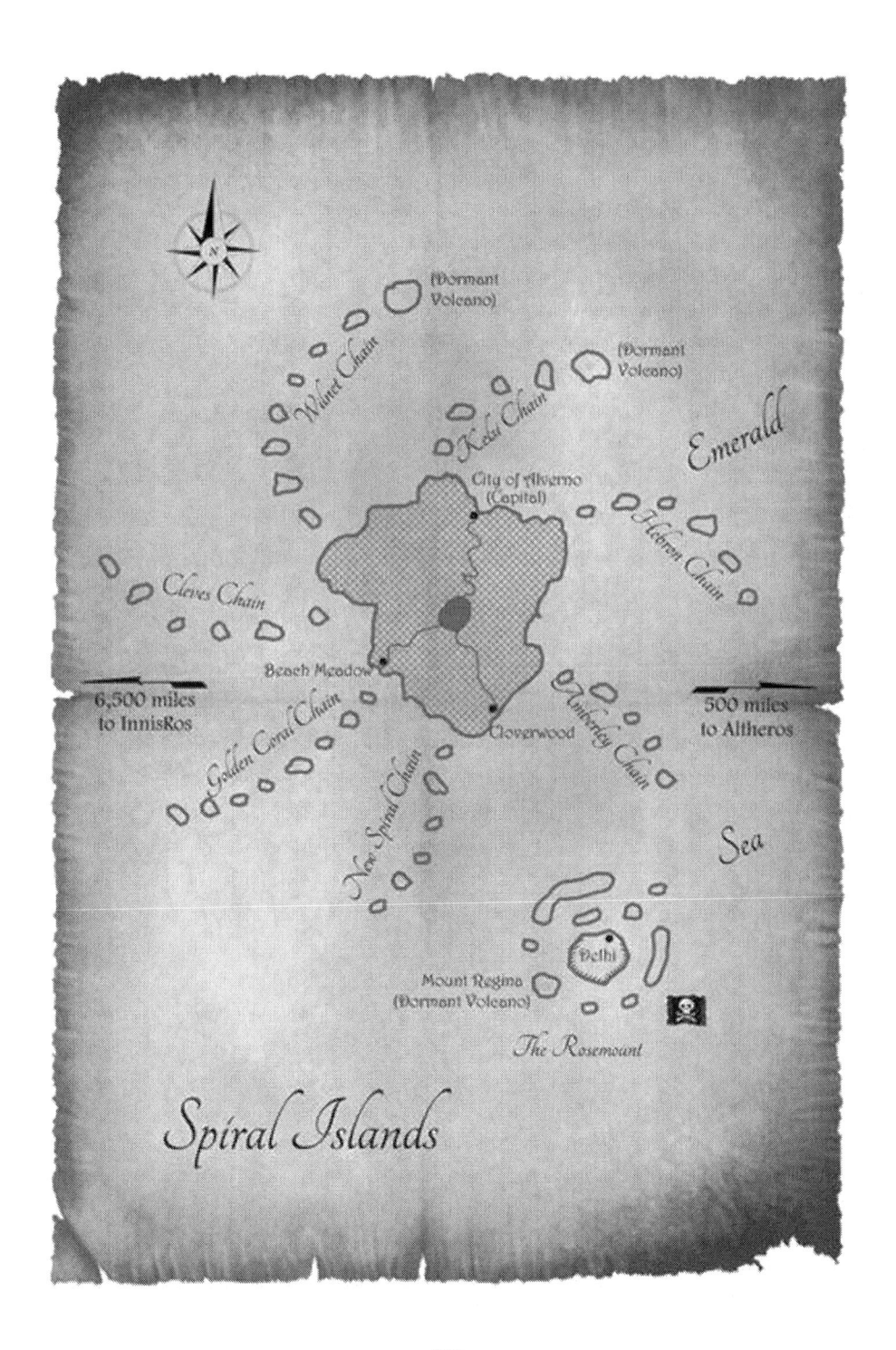

CHAPTER 6

Be always cautious of the sky when travelling far. Its vastness hides many dangers. Even on a clear day the unwary can be blinded to its hazards.

— *Book of the Unveiled*

Kristen fell into a deep sleep. Tangus, as he stared at her, continued to worry. The last few days were not physically challenging, but Tangus knew there was much going on within Kristen that she would not talk about, at least not yet. The pain of leaving her loved ones, Father Goram, Vayl, Autumn, and all the others at Calmacil Clearing, the bond between Kristen and Emmy, the responsibility placed upon her by Althaya, and the fear she most certainly felt for the world, should she fail, all had to be weighing very heavily on her. Tangus covered Kristen with a soft fur, then, with Bitts and Romulus lying by the door, settled into a chair to watch over her. The captain would have to wait.

Looking around the comfortable stateroom, Tangus spied a book on a table on the other side of the bed. Quietly getting up, he went over and looked at the title, *"A History of the Freedom Wind."* "This might be interesting," Tangus thought to himself. Over the course of the next hour Tangus learned that the *Freedom Wind* was the flagship of one of the largest and wealthiest merchant families in Palisade Crest, the Dular family. She was the largest of her class of cargo ships and the gem of the small fleet belonging to the family. Built five years ago, Captain Dubois was her first captain, a position she still held. Prior to this command, Captain Dubois had led a squadron of fast cutters that patrolled the Emerald Sea on the western coast of the mainland, and engaged piracy wherever she found it. The *Freedom Wind* was crewed by approximately six hundred officers and sailors as well as one hundred marines from Palisade Crest's City Watch. Since commerce was so important to the metropolis, members of the Watch were frequently used on privately owned ships unless a merchant preferred to use one of the several mercenary companies who based their operations in or around the city. Besides the captain, officers and crew, the ship's complement also contained two experienced and powerful sorcerers as well as three clerics. Looking at the section of the book that described the ship's armament, Tangus whistled softly. "This ship could probably beat off a whole flotilla of pirate ships," he thought. "That is if she didn't just outrun them instead. Damn she's fast! Twelve knots at full wind and canvas! But not surprising since that was the whole reason she was designed this way. Transporting and protecting valuable cargo was the entire reason for her existence. Father Goram certainly spared no expense getting us to the mainland!"

Tangus was so engrossed in the book he did not hear the first knock on the stateroom door. Kristen, just wakening, was stretching. "How long did I sleep?" she asked.

Tangus looked out the porthole, gauging the shadows of the sun. "Not long sweetheart, maybe a little over an hour. How do you feel?"

"Better I think," Kristen replied. "But now we're late for…"

There was another knock on the door, this one a bit more insistent. "Madam, sir, is everything alright?" Mr. Krist called from the other side. "I do apologize for the interruption, but the captain is making inquiries."

Tangus got up, went to the door, and opened it. "Please extend our apologies to the captain, Mr. Krist. We completely lost track of time. Kristen will be out in a few minutes, but I need to go up now to see how things are going with our supplies and check on the rest of our party."

"Very good, sir," Mr. Krist said, bringing his hand up to his cap in a brief salute.

Tangus looked over his shoulder at Kristen. "See you in a few minutes?"

"Yes, love, I'll be up shortly," she replied.

Closing the door behind him and Bitts, who had followed, Tangus turned to face Mr. Krist. "Lead the way," he said.

"Begging your pardon, sir, but will the madam require assistance finding her way topside?" Mr. Krist asked.

Tangus shook his head, "No Mr. Krist, she'll be fine. She has Romulus who could sniff his way out of a maze. Besides, the door out is just down the hallway, around a turn and up some stairs."

Mr. Krist shook his head. "That would be a ladder, sir."

Tangus started down the hallway. "Of course it is. I don't suppose we can stop all the 'sirs' and madams', can we?"

"No sir, we really can't. Passengers are just as important to us as cargo. It would be most improper to take them for granted, or to be so familiar. And quite frankly, most of the passengers we ferry are either noblemen or those with more than a modest amount of wealth. So they demand it. Believe me it is quite beyond my ability to do otherwise…sir," Mr. Krist replied.

Tangus sighed, "As you wish Mr. Krist."

When Tangus stepped on the deck, he saw Safire supervising the loading of the supplies that she and Jennifer had purchased. Judging from the size of the pallet, he judged they would probably need a couple of pack horses for the trip to Elanesse. Noticing Tangus watching, Safire walked over to him. "Don't know why I'm overseeing this, the crew is remarkably efficient." Pointing at the pallet, "That's everything on the list."

"Jennifer?" Tangus asked.

"As we were shopping, Bernie - that is Ensign Carlowe - told us about a place that would give us a good price for the cart and work horses. He was right. She's there right now arranging the sale. She'll be back in a bit, certainly in time for supper."

"Which is?" Tangus asked.

"In navy parlance, four bells during the first dog watch," Safire replied.

"Huh?"

Safire smiled. "Six o'clock. Trust me. Bernie told us all about telling time on a ship. It's quite fascinating."

Tangus decided not to inquire further about ship time. "Have you checked on Euranna?"

"I was going to do that after I was done here," Safire responded.

"Don't worry about it, I'll go down. Kristen should be up shortly, so that's where I'll be if she asks," Tangus said. "By the way, what 'bell' is it right now?"

Safire laughed as did several crewmen who were working nearby. "What 'bell' is it? That's cute, Tangus. It's currently eight bells on the afternoon watch. That's four o'clock as we know it."

Tangus sighed, shook his head, and then went to find a crewman to direct him to the hold Euranna and Borum were in.

Kristen and Romulus made their way topside a few minutes after Tangus went below to check on Euranna. Kristen did not see Tangus anywhere on the top deck, but did see Safire talking to some of the ship's crewmen. Safire glanced her way during the discussion and waved, but did not disengage. Kristen waved back and then looked around. Everywhere the crew was working to prepare the ship for sea, or so she presumed. Not wishing to be in the way, she moved over to the side of the ship that overlooked the bay. Romulus followed close behind. The view was spectacular! Not quite as striking as the view from the cliff where she had first met Tangus, but enough to warrant admiration.

Kristen heard someone approach and stop beside her. Looking over, she immediately recognized the captain. The two silently stared outward for a few minutes. Finally the captain broke the silence.

"Mr. Krist tells me that you were not feeling well earlier. I hope all is well with you now," Captain Dubois said.

"Yes, Captain Dubois. I was only a little tired. A short nap was all I needed. I apologize for missing our meeting," Kristen replied.

"Please, do not concern yourself. There's plenty of time for talk. You, your husband, and the rest of your party are invited to dine at the Captain's Table with my officers this evening. That also includes your wolf and your husband's cooshie. I have to admit, I've never seen a cooshie before, or a wolf the size of yours." Turning to look at Romulus who was sitting on the other side of Kristen, Captain Dubois said, "May I?"

"Of course, captain. His name is Romulus. There is nothing you or your crew has to fear from him, except maybe when he starts chasing Bitts. Then heaven help anything that gets in their way!" Kristen replied, smiling.

"And Bitts would be the name of your husband's cooshie?" the captain asked, smiling back.

"Oh! Sorry. Yes, that's correct. Those two have formed a surprisingly strong bond, like brothers."

Captain Dubois let Romulus sniff her hand and then petted the fur on his back. "He's got a thick coat."

"It's his winter fur. When the spring comes he sheds like you wouldn't believe," Kristen said as she too started to pet Romulus.

Giving a last scratch to the top of Romulus' head, the captain returned to her place on the other side of Kristen. "The *Wind* is close to being completely loaded and ready for sea. We'll set sail on the morning tide. How are your accommodations?"

"They're really very luxurious. I would never have guessed a ship could be so comfortable," Kristen replied. "Actually, everything I've seen so far speaks of wealth, yet looking around I see that your ship is extremely well armed, as much a fighting vessel as a cargo ship."

"She is both. The owners are very wealthy and quite concerned our cargoes get to their destinations safely, particularly the lords and ladies who pay a small fortune to book passage," Captain Dubois replied. "Have you ever traveled the sea before?" she asked.

"No. Of all of us, I think only Tangus has. He's originally from the mainland," Kristen responded. "His daughter, Jennifer, was born on InnisRos. I can't really say for sure about Safire, but I don't think so. Why?"

THE SALVATION OF INNOCENCE

"Some people are born to ride the waves, but most have to, as we sailors say, get their 'sea legs'. Until they do, they can be quite sick. Clerical spells can provide temporary relief from the nausea, but are limited in that their effect doesn't last all that long, at least when you stop to consider we'll be at sea for three to four weeks. We do have medicinal remedies that will help, however. I'll have Mr. Bowen, our master cleric, give you the medicine tonight. You can then treat your husband and friends as needed. It even works on animals, though horses, dogs, and, I presume, wolves seem to be somewhat immune," the captain replied.

"That would be appreciated, Captain," Kristen said. "What time do you want us for dinner?"

"Four bells. Right, Captain?" Tangus said as he approached the two with Bitts at his side.

Turning, Captain Dubois smiled. "That's correct, Mr. DeRango! How did you know?"

"Safire educated me after having been first educated by your Mr. Carlowe." Giving Kristen a quick peck on the check, he said, "That's in about an hour and a half, sweetheart." Turning to the captain, he continued, "In 'landlubber' parlance, Captain."

Captain Dubois laughed. "Of course," she said. "Well, I have a lot of work to do, so I'll take my leave. We'll talk at dinner. Afterwards we'll have an after dinner drink in my parlor. I want to have a discussion with both of you and your friends. It will be a kind of 'do and don't do' briefing. Oh, and you can bring Romulus and Bitts along."

After the captain left, Tangus looked out over the bay with Kristen and said, "She's got a parlor? Unbelievable! Maybe we should buy a ship like this and sail to ports unknown. We could certainly live in style."

Kristen chuckled. "Captain Tangus! You would make such a handsome swashbuckler!"

"The world is filled with possibilities. Once we have Emmy safe and sound, we could go and do what we want," Tangus exclaimed lightheartedly.

Kristen became serious, "I wish, dear. But it's never that easy."

Tangus put his hand over Kristen's. "I know. What's troubling you, Kristen?"

Kristen turned to look at her husband. "I'm not sure. We've both been so concerned for Emmy, and I'm learning to deal with the bond and how to protect her through it. When we got to the docks, however, something changed. Somehow the bond was suddenly...tainted. Not much, just very lightly. It's really hard to explain to someone who has never felt the bond before. I fear what this portents for Emmy. What happens if I can no longer reach her, or if the bond is broken? What happens if the bond actually starts to hurt her?"

Tangus sighed. He wasn't going to try to pretend everything would be okay to placate Kristen, she understood the situation as well as he did, perhaps more. "I don't know, Kristen. Sweetheart, we're doing all we can."

"I know," Kristen said. "But what if it's not enough?"

Dinner in the captain's cabin turned out to be a formal affair. Tangus, Safire, Jennifer, and Euranna all wore their best clothes, green tunics, black pants tucked into knee-high brown boots and ceremonial hooded cloaks secured by an angel brooch made of platinum, emeralds, sapphires, and rubies. There was no mistaking each for the rangers they were. Kristen looked stunning in a midnight blue floor-length dress. The only adornment on the dress was a beautiful round blue amulet, set in gold, pinned to her left shoulder, closest to her heart, a gift from her goddess Althaya. The locket, given to her by her mother all those years ago, hung around her neck and rested on her chest. Kristen's long, straight auburn hair hung down to her waist, loosely tied by a blue ribbon. A sharp intake of breath escaped from more than one of the men surrounding the table when she entered. The captain and her officers all wore their dress uniforms. The meal itself was fit for a king.

The dinner conversation was limited to small talk. Tangus could tell the captain and the ship's officers often entertained high-ranking officials, as Mr. Krist had earlier mentioned, and were quite comfortable in that kind of setting. Though Tangus, Kristen and the others knew they were not royalty - though Kristen certainly looked as beautiful as any queen - they were made to feel that way. By the time they had finished dinner, the captain and her officers had skillfully drawn their guests into conversations while at the same time being very unobtrusive. Tangus marveled at how adeptly they were questioned.

After concluding the meal with an after-dinner coffee, Captain Dubois dismissed her officers with the exception of Mr. Krist. As each officer left, they paused, bowed, and kissed the back of Kristen, Safire, Jennifer, and Euranna's hands, causing each to cringe with embarrassment.

Captain Dubois smiled and said, "They were quite taken with all of you. If you will pardon me, there's a bit of a mystic about elven females where human males are concerned. At least that's what I've come to believe. If not for the discipline I demand on this ship they would probably have been falling all over themselves when you ladies walked into the room, especially you, Kristen. Blue suits you very well."

"Thank you, captain," Kristen replied demurely, embarrassed by the compliment.

"Get used to it, dear," Tangus laughed. Turning to Safire, Jennifer and Euranna, "You three as well. The captain's correct. Elven females seem to hold some sort of spell over human males."

"What would you do to them, Captain?" Jennifer asked seriously. "That is, if they fell all over themselves when we entered."

"Why I'd keelhaul them of course. Shall we adjourn to the parlor?" the captain suggested as she rose from her chair at the head of the table, winking at Tangus.

"Please, right this way," Mr. Krist said, using a hand to direct them to one of the doors off the side of the cabin.

As they were going into the parlor, Jennifer whispered to her father, "What is 'keelhauling'?"

"I'll explain later. Just don't get on the captain's bad side," Tangus whispered back.

"Don't worry about that!" Jennifer said looking worried. Tangus smiled as she went into the parlor ahead of him. Kristen, walking next to Tangus and holding his hand, asked, "What was that all about?"

"I'm just playing along with the captain's joke. Actual keelhauling is a punishment that's lost its appeal, at least with civilized captains," Tangus replied.

The parlor, though richly furnished, was not as large as the captain's mess. It had a sturdy table at its center which was surrounded by comfortable chairs, all of which could be firmly secured to the deck when the occasion necessitated it. The table contained a couple of crystal decanters filled with wine. Matching glasses ringed the decanter. Mr. Krist seated Safire, Jennifer, and Euranna while Tangus seated Kristen. The captain and Mr. Krist took their chairs after their guests were comfortable. One of the stewards who served dinner came in and poured each a glass of wine.

"Will there be anything else, Captain?" he asked afterwards.

"No Mr. Jenkins. You are dismissed for the time being with my thanks. Mr. Krist will tell you when you are needed again. And please pass on my compliments to the ship's cooks." Captain Dubois said as she nodded her head acknowledging his salute.

"Very well madam," Mr. Jenkins said as he bowed to the rest of those in the room.

"This ship astonishes me, captain. This is my first time at sea, but never in my wildest imagination would I have believed what I'm seeing," Safire said.

Captain Dubois nodded. "Her owners are very rich, Ms. Renill."

"Please call me Safire."

"And call me Jennifer," Jennifer suddenly blurted out. Everyone turned to look at her as she suddenly covered her mouth with a hand, her eyes widening in surprise.

"She is fearless, is she not, Tangus?" Captain Dubois asked with humor-filled eyes.

"Painfully so, Captain," Tangus replied with a smile.

"Very well, Jennifer. And may I call you Euranna?" The captain said, re-directing her attention to the diminutive ranger.

Euranna, who had been trying to avoid attention, nodded, "Yes, Captain. Of course you can."

Tangus, desiring to draw Euranna out of her shyness a little more, remarked, "Euranna is one of the best I've ever seen on a horse, Captain. She seems to have a natural talent for it."

"Really?" the captain said, directing her gaze back at Euranna.

Euranna dropped her head and stared at the deck. Kristen, who was sitting next to her, took Euranna's hand and said softly, "We're all your friends here, dear."

Euranna looked up demurely, "Yes ma'am."

Still holding Euranna's hand, Kristen looked at the captain. "I've never had a meal like that. If this is how we're going to eat, I suspect our bellies will be so bloated by the time we cross we won't be able to even get on our horses."

"Don't worry about that. The first meal we serve is always a bit pretentious. Afterwards, however, it's hardtack and jerky," the captain replied.

Euranna finally broke into a smile. "Good for you, Euranna!" the captain said. "It's comforting to know someone appreciates my sense of humor!"

"So that was a joke?" Jennifer asked, causing everyone in the room to laugh.

"It's time to talk a bit about our upcoming voyage. Mr. Krist?" Captain Dubois said.

Mr. Krist went over to a wall cabinet and pulled out several small books, handing one to every person in the room, excluding the captain. "These are yours to keep. As you look through them, please keep in mind that they were written for dignitaries, lords and wealthy passengers. Most of the rules and regulations are common sense, something you already have as fighting men and women, so please try not to be insulted. Nevertheless, we must maintain certain tenets whilst at sea."

"We understand completely, Mr. Krist. We have no problem with that," Kristen said.

"Very good, madam. Please read over them tonight so we have no misunderstandings once underway. I will, of course, be available to answer any questions you may have. Now if you will allow me, I'd like to direct your attention to pages nine and ten. As you can see, it is a landscape drawing of the *Freedom Wind*. As you can also see, it has been redacted somewhat. These are places on the ship that are restricted. We have marines stationed at each entry point to remind anyone who might stray. I would also be remiss if I did not point out that there is to be no interference with the crew going about their duties while at sea. Finally, on this ship, Captain Dubois has complete authority. I know, this is all so tiresome and dreadful, and I would never insinuate any of you would disregard the rules of the sea, but we of course must always strive for clarity. Have I covered everything, Captain?"

"Yes, Mr. Krist, you have, as always, given us a wonderful briefing. I do have a few comments to make, however." Captain Dubois replied. "First, I want to express my agreement with Mr. Krist in that these policies are not intended in any way to be an affront to your intelligence, experience, or instincts. For the most part, our passengers are mostly spoiled little twits lacking any semblance of what the rest of us call brains. I guess that happens when everything you ever needed has been simply handed to you." Pausing, the captain briefly glanced at each person in the room. "There are dangers inherent with all crossings. You noted our defenses as you boarded? All essential, I assure you."

"Sea monsters, Captain?" Safire asked.

"Perhaps, well, I wouldn't actually call them sea monsters. There are some large creatures in the world's oceans and seas. But our route is heavily traveled and most of the bigger underwater predators have long since vacated the area or have learned that taking a sailing ship is no easy task. I'm really talking about pirates, bad weather and dangers from the skies. This brings me to my real purpose for this conversation. All of you are warriors. How experienced I cannot say, but I suspect you know how to use the swords and bows you brought aboard."

Tangus nodded. "I'm the only one with any real combat experience, but we all know how to use our weapons, including my wife, who, if pressed, will make an extremely dangerous adversary. Although I would have to say that she is best suited for healing the wounded."

"Tangus, Captain, you're both starting to scare me. I've only been thinking about the dangers we will face on the other side. I never felt we would be in harm's way during the crossing," Kristen said.

"There are always perils, my love." Looking at Safire, Jennifer and Euranna, Tangus went on. "We all need to understand that, but that's not to say it's going to happen."

"Precisely, Tangus," Captain Dubois replied. "But if we do run into trouble, say from pirates, I'll take any help I can get."

"Who would attack this ship?" Jennifer asked.

The captain shook her head. "No one in their right mind unless they had a very strong force. Dogs can take down an elephant if there are enough of them."

"If it comes to that, we would of course be happy to help," Tangus said. "But Captain Dubois, these people are under my command, not yours. Our mission has to take priority. I understand that we depend on you getting us over to the mainland, but it would be to no avail if we could not carry through once there. Is that going to be acceptable?" Tangus asked.

Mr. Krist shook his head. "Master Tangus, on this ship the captain has complete control. She won't…"

"Mr. Krist, if you please," Captain Dubose interrupted. "When it comes to leading and fighting his people, Tangus would know better than either of us how it should be done. I'm sure in all other things regarding this ship Tangus will defer to me. Is that correct, Tangus?"

"Of course, Captain," Tangus said.

The captain looked at Mr. Krist. "As you wish, Captain," he said.

"Then your terms are perfectly acceptable, Tangus," Captain Dubois agreed.

Tangus nodded. "Kristen, you will stay below and help with the wounded. Safire, I know this will be disagreeable, but you will stay below as well. After me, you're best suited to get Kristen to Emmy."

"Tangus!" both Kristen and Safire barked.

"I'm sorry. That's the way it has to be. There are certain realities we all need to face. What to do if something should happen to me is one of them," Tangus said. The tone in his voice told them all he would brook no argument.

Captain Dubois raised an eyebrow. "It's true, ladies. That's why I have Mr. Krist."

From above, the ship's bell rang twice. Safire smiled, "Nine o'clock, Tangus."

Tangus sighed. The captain got up from her chair. "It's getting late and I still have many things to do before I can turn in, so I think we should adjourn for the evening. Do you require escort back to your staterooms?"

"We'll be fine, Captain." Kristen replied.

"Excellent. Then I will see you out. Mr. Krist, please have Mr. Jenkins come in and clean up."

Mr. Krist saluted. "Very good, Captain."

The next few days were a time that Kristen, Safire, and Jennifer would rather forget. Seasickness struck all three within a day after setting sail. Tangus won his sea legs many years ago, and Euranna, strangely, was not affected. For two days, Tangus and Euranna were extremely busy taking care of their stricken comrades, as well as all the horses and a ravenous messenger dragon. The medicine given to them by the ship's master cleric, Mr. Bowen, relieved the three from the vomiting, but did nothing to help them regain their strength. They would need solid food for that, and none of them would even entertain the idea of food in their current condition. Each subsisted on warm broth for several days.

Captain Dubois ran a very tight ship, and although her crew was well trained in all aspects of sailing, she continually held drills to "keep the edge on" as she described it. After Kristen, Safire and Jennifer's seasickness had subsided and they regained their strength, they, along with Tangus and Euranna, took orientation instructing them on the subject of ship terminology. This was critical if they were going to be involved in the defense of the vessel. It was not long thereafter that they were all participating in the captain's call to general quarters with the rest of the crew. Kristen and Safire reported below to the ship's sick bay, while Tangus, Jennifer and Euranna were stationed on the quarterdeck with bow ready, scabbard swords for close-in combat hanging at their sides. The call to general quarters occurred at all hours, so there were several nights when warm beds had to be vacated as everyone rushed to their duty station. Kristen, hair mussed, realized she did not like to go out in public without putting on her "dignified priestess" look, but she quickly learned to accept it. Everyone else looked just as mussed in the middle of the night as she did. Everyone, that is, except the captain. She always painted a perfect picture, standing on the quarterdeck, holding court and judging whether or not the crew posted themselves in an acceptable time. Even Tangus was not immune to her displeasure during these drills.

After receiving permission from Tangus, the captain asked Euranna if she would be willing to take a few night watches. Lithe, sure-footed, and equipped with dark vision, an ability common to all elves, the captain reasoned she would make an excellent lookout. Tangus and Kristen both felt this might help her gain confidence outside her expertise with horses. Tangus suspected from Kristen's concern for Euranna's well-being that the girl had been informally adopted by his wife, whether Euranna realized it or not. Though this was not at all surprising considering Kristen's kindhearted makeup and Euranna's past, Tangus would have preferred keeping away from a strong emotional attachment with her. If something were to happen, it would tear Kristen apart. But Tangus also knew that these types of bonds were unavoidable. He had unexpectedly also developed strong protective feelings for Euranna. Tangus discovered, over the years spent with Kristen, his heart had gone through a readjustment. His gruff, untrusting exterior gradually gave way to the ability to examine what was in a person's heart before judging a person's actions. Sometimes, life forces people to do things to survive that go against their innermost character. There are times when one must look past circumstances before judging actions. Tangus found that, because of Kristen, he was just as incapable of resisting caring about others as she was, though he still resisted repeated outward displays except toward Kristen or Jennifer.

Two weeks into the voyage, Tangus, Kristen and the others were well integrated with the ship's crew. They had become more than just passengers. Tangus especially enjoyed occasionally spending time below deck with crewmen and playing games of chance. Euranna, as hoped, had started coming out of her shell and began tearing down the walls she had been building for herself ever since her parents were executed. She admitted to both Tangus and Kristen that she loved being in the crow's nest on star-filled evenings, the freedom and beauty of the night were intoxicating. She was also starting to use the katana with a greater level of expertise. Tangus was unrelenting in his training. It would keep her alive. Jennifer and Safire also participated in the instruction, sometimes pitting themselves against Tangus and Euranna with wooden training swords. After a week, Euranna was no longer a liability to Tangus. After the second week, Euranna and Tangus won as many bouts as they lost.

The fourteenth day of travel was much like all the others. The seas were a little rough because of a stiff wind, but this allowed the *Freedom Wind* to speed through the white-capped waves close to her maximum velocity of twelve knots. The sky was generally clear with a few billowy clouds moving swiftly on air currents, and the sun was halfway through its descent into the western sky.

THE SALVATION OF INNOCENCE

Captain Dubois and Mr. Krist were on the quarterdeck taking navigational measurements to ensure there had been no deviation to their course. Lt. Farnsworth was officer of the deck and stood on the railed edge of the quarterdeck, hands clasped behind his back, watching forward as the crew went about the business of sailing the ship. Set underneath the quarterdeck and directly below the spot where Lt. Farnsworth was standing was the ship's wheelhouse, the wheel manned by four helmsmen and Ensign Carlowe. The calm of normal ship operations was broken by a shout from the main mast lookout.

"Dragon dead astern!" the man shouted.

Captain Dubois looked to the west and into the sun. "Mr. Krist, man the telescope if you please. Lt. Farnsworth, ring to general quarters." Quickly moving to the edge of the quarterdeck and leaning over, she shouted, "Ensign Carlowe, make your course north by northeast."

"Aye, Captain. Making my course north by northeast."

"I've got it spotted, Captain." Mr. Krist said. "It's coming out of the sun."

"Range, Mr. Krist?"

"About one mile, Captain," Mr. Krist replied.

"Belay that order, Ensign Carlowe. Hold your course steady."

"Aye, Captain, holding my course steady."

"Lt. Farnsworth, time before the stern ballistae arrows are changed out?"

"A couple of minutes at most, Captain. And then another to set elevation."

"Range one half mile, Captain," Mr. Krist said. "We don't have time to get a shot off."

"Thank you, Mr. Krist, I'm aware. The color if you please."

"I'm trying, Captain."

Ten valuable seconds passed. "Color, Mr. Krist," the captain asked again.

"It's…red dragon, Captain, red dragon!"

About that time the crew had responded to general quarters and taken their battle stations. Captain Dubois allowed herself a second to smile her satisfaction. Tangus, Jennifer, Euranna, the two sorcerers, and several young boys who were runners came bounding up the ladder to the quarterdeck, their assigned positions. Looking at the dragon, which by now could be clearly seen, the captain said to the wizards, "Well?"

"Not enough time to do anything other than magic missiles, Captain."

"See to it as soon as it is in range. Tangus do you and your folks have any kind of magic arrows?" she asked.

All three were already notching arrows with slightly glowing tips. "Yes Captain, we do," Tangus replied.

"You have command of your people, Tangus," the captain said. "You may fire when the range is appropriate. Lt. Farnsworth, I want all archers to fire at that beast as soon as it's in range. It doesn't matter if they have magic arrows or not, anything that might distract it."

"Aye, Captain!"

"We're not going to be able to stop it from making a pass on us, Captain," Mr. Krist said.

About that time several magic missiles hit the dragon while several others veered away at the last minute to fall in the ocean. The dragon didn't even flinch at the pain caused by the explosions of magic that came with each successful hit. "Some magic resistance, Captain," one of the wizards said. Both wizards then started incantations for another spell.

Mr. Krist turned to one of the runners and said, "I want fire damage control standing by." Looking at another runner, he said, "Get a cleric up here."

The dragon was closing the ship quickly. As Tangus was watching the dragon's approach, he judged it to be about middle age from its size. The body was about one hundred feet matched by an equally long tail. The wingspan of the brute had to be at least one hundred fifty feet. Bitts started growling as the dragon neared. Suddenly realizing Safire,

THE SALVATION OF INNOCENCE

Jennifer and Euranna had never seen a creature of this magnitude, Tangus calmly said, "Hold steady."

The captain shouted, "Ensign Carlowe, make you course north by northeast on my mark."

"Aye, Captain. Will make my course north by northeast upon your order."

When the dragon flew within range of his longbow, Tangus shouted, "SHOOT!" Along with Tangus, Jennifer, and Euranna, all the archers of the *Freedom Wind* released their arrows. A flock of about fifty arrows ascended to meet the beast. Most had no effect, but several did, though they did not slow the dragon's approach. Before another volley could fly, the dragon used its terrible breath weapon.

In an instant, one half the length of the mizzenmast had been completely disintegrated along with all the men working the sails and the archers posted to fire arrows. The remaining half was burning, flaming pieces of sail falling upon the deck. Screaming men, set afire but unlucky enough not to have been instantly killed, dropped into the sea or onto the deck. Though the flames eating each man were quickly smothered, it was too late to save them. Their cries of agony and fear died as they did. As the dragon passed over, leaving destruction in its wake, another volley of arrows followed it.

"Hit it on the left side after it clears the ship," the captain said to the wizards. "Ensign Carlowe," she shouted, "set your course!"

"Aye, Captain! Making my course north by northeast!" Ensign Carlowe shouted over the shrieks of the dying men.

"Mr. Krist, I'm going down to the ballistae. You have the command."

"Aye, Captain!" Mr. Krist walked up to Lt. Farnsworth. "You are relieved, sir. Please lead the fire damage control party."

"Aye, Mr. Krist! You have the deck." Lt. Farnsworth replied, saluting smartly. He rushed down the ladder from the quarterdeck to take over the fire control damage party.

Mr. Krist, after returning Lt. Farnsworth's salute, shouted. "Helm, is your course north by northeast?"

"Negative, sir," Ensign Carlowe called out. "She's handling sluggishly, another minute."

"Very good, Ensign, please spare no effort." Turning to Tangus, Mr. Krist said, "I expect you'll be getting another shot off before long. Unfortunately, a good number of our archers were on the mizzenmast."

Tangus nodded as he watched the dragon that, by this time, was about one hundred feet off the bow, but the mainmast prevented him from taking another shot. As the ship slowly turned, the dragon came into clear view once again. Three arrows streaked outward, along with two blue bolts of lightning from the wizards' hands. Both bolts hit the dragon on its left side, shortly followed by the three arrows. The impact of the lightning bolts turned the dragon to the left. It roared in pain. Hovering for a few seconds while searching the ship, its eyes alighted on the two wizards. Again roaring, this time in anger, the dragon flew directly toward them.

By this time, the ship had made its north by northeast course, allowing her to bring all of its starboard side ballistae to bear on the dragon. Captain Dubois had cleverly manipulated the dragon into attacking the ship from the side. With the captain on the main deck directing fire, seventeen magic-tipped large arrows fired on the dragon as it once again closed the ship, most of which hit. The dragon staggered, but roared again and picked up speed, heading directly for the quarterdeck. With the ballistae being re-loaded, only three arrows streaked out in defense of the ship.

The quarterdeck exploded when the dragon hit it. Large splinters of wood flew outward in all directions. Everyone on the quarterdeck was violently thrown off their feet, which was the only thing that saved them from the hail of splinters. Tangus, as he got up shaking his head to clear it, had a hard time seeing through the smoke brought on by the still burning mizzenmast. Looking around, he saw Jennifer starting to get up as well. Bitts went to Euranna and started licking her face. Mr. Krist was helping a couple of the runners back to their feet while at the same time yelling for damage control. Of the wizards there was no sign.

THE SALVATION OF INNOCENCE

Tangus then heard the dragon roar, but it was not close. Looking westward toward the source, he saw the dragon retreating, three limp bodies hanging from its two massive claws. Within seconds the dragon was out of sight. As quickly as it had begun, the battle was over.

Captain Dubois arrived on the quarterdeck and appraised the scene. "Mr. Krist, report!"

"The dragon carried away both our wizards, as well as one of our clerics who happened to arrive just as the dragon hit us. Everyone else on the quarterdeck at the time of the attack is accounted for captain."

Looking at the wreckage on the quarterdeck as well as the crew's efforts to finish putting out several small fires on the main deck, the captain nodded. "Very good, Mr. Krist," she said sadly. "Get the ship's master carpenter up here and begin repairs immediately. Raze what's left of the mizzenmast and get a new one in its place as soon as possible. Bring me a status report within the hour. I'll be in my cabin."

"Aye, Captain," Mr. Krist said.

The captain then went over to Tangus. "Thank you for your help. I'm…"

"Father," Jennifer shouted urgently. "Euranna."

Tangus, looking over, saw Jennifer kneeling next to Euranna. Bitts looked up at him with sadness in his eyes. Both Tangus and the captain rushed over to the three. Euranna had a large wooden splinter sticking out of her side. There was also a deep gash along the side of her head. She was unresponsive but still breathing, though shallowly. She looked very pale. Tangus, kneeling down beside her, knew that she had gone into shock because of the amount of blood she had lost.

"Don't touch the splinter!" The captain warned as she went over to a small box fixed to a railing. From it, she took out a length of white linen and knelt down next to Tangus. "Taking the splinter out will cause the wound to bleed even more," she said as she gently wrapped the linen around Euranna and immobilized the splinter so it would not move. Using her teeth to split one of the ends, she tied a specialized knot around the splinter to further secure it.

"Thank you, Captain," Tangus said. He was well adept at dressing field wounds but had no experience with an injury such as this.

"Has you wife ever had to perform surgery on someone?" the captain asked.

Tangus shook his head. "I don't understand."

"Withdrawing the splinter is going to leave behind smaller pieces of wood in the wound. Wood can fester and cause the wound to become infected. It should be removed surgically so it doesn't break off during extraction and also so the wound can be inspected for other contaminates. A cleric can heal infections with spells, but as long as wood remains, the infection will keep coming back."

"That makes sense. I don't know if Kristen has ever done that sort of thing. She's never mentioned it to me, but I know she does much more to heal people than just casting healing spells," Tangus said as he carefully cradled Euranna in his arms and got up.

"Take her below to sickbay. My clerics perform surgery regularly if your wife cannot."

Tangus nodded and went to the ladder going down from the quarterdeck, closely followed by Jennifer and Bitts.

"Mr. Krist."

"Yes, Captain?"

"Set our course back to our original heading. Also, let's make it two hours in my cabin instead of one. I want damage control assessment and status. I also want a casualty list. Have all the department heads present except for those otherwise occupied."

"Aye, Captain," Mr. Krist replied.

As Captain Dubois walked past Mr. Krist to exit the quarterdeck, she paused and laid a hand on his arm. "I'm very glad you survived, Thomas."

"Too many didn't, Jasmine," He responded looking into her eyes.

She nodded and left.

THE SALVATION OF INNOCENCE

In far away Elanesse, Emmy was still safely enveloped in the magical stasis field. Though she dreamed, she was also vaguely aware of Kristen's distant presence. Through the bond she felt Kristen's pain, her fear, and her insecurities. Emmy, though slumbering, felt intense distress coming from Kristen. Through the bond Emmy sent a sense of herself to calm Kristen, to give her strength. Through the bond, Emmy returned the warmth and love that she had so often received from Kristen. In her dreamlike state, Emmy was perplexed. She had never been able to do that before.

Outside the chamber where Emmy slept, three figures stood and watched while a fourth used a sledgehammer to smash stone and mortar. Before the night was through, they would be through the wall and into the room.

The Purge, maintaining a conduit between itself and the empath bond, felt power emanating through the bond back to the distant bonded partner. The empath, though still invisible to it, was already strong, and her strength was growing. The Purge had never known of such a thing ever happening.

When Kristen saw Tangus carrying Euranna into the sickbay, she thought she was going to faint. The thought of that dear girl dying brought tears to her eyes. All she could think was "No! No! No!" as she rushed over to intercept Tangus. Without warning, a feeling of great calm came over her. The warmth and love that washed her soul took away all of her anxiety and allowed the professional healer in her to take charge. As Kristen worked to save Euranna's life, she marveled at what Emmy was able to do.

CHAPTER 7

The never ending struggle of good versus evil brings with it a long list of past and future casualties. All will eventually perish for the outcome will never be decided. Giving the highest measure of devotion to the cause, however, earns an honored place in the hearts of those whose turn to sacrifice has yet to come.

— BOOK OF THE UNVEILED

WHEN TANGUS ARRIVED at the ship's sick bay, he found it in a state of organized confusion. There were about a dozen crewmen, most with burns but some with other injuries as well, receiving treatment. Several other less injured crewmen were patiently waiting their turn. Kristen and Mr. Bowen, the ship's master cleric, were caring for the most serious, while the lone remaining cleric was working with those whose injuries were not as extensive. Crewmen orderlies were at the healer's beck-and-call. With so many people in sick bay, Romulus, his massive size too much for the crowded area, had laid down outside in the hallway. Safire had assumed her position as Kristen's body guard alongside him. When she saw Tangus carrying Euranna coming down the hallway, she rushed to meet them and escort them into sickbay.

As soon as Kristen saw Tangus, Jennifer, and Safire come in with Tangus carrying Euranna, her heart skipped a beat. The crewman she was healing needed some more work, but he was stabilized and not in pain. As Kristen rushed over to Tangus, she felt a calming reassurance coming through her bond with Emmy. Though puzzled by this new development, she did not take time to consider its implications.

"Put her over here, love," she said as she went to an empty bed. "Jennifer, Safire…I'm sorry but it's too crowded in here for you. Please wait outside."

THE SALVATION OF INNOCENCE

First looking at the wooden splinter extruding from Euranna's side, she saw that the bleeding had abated, although she knew from the coloring of Euranna's skin that she had already lost a lot of blood. Turning her attention to the head wound, she said, "This is pretty bad also. It looks like she may be concussed." Feeling Euranna's pulse while listening to her heart, then placing her hand on Euranna's chest to measure breaths, Kristen shook her head, "Weak pulse and shallow breaths. She's in shock. Tangus, we're close to losing her."

"The captain said she needs surgery," Tangus said.

"Yes, I agree. I'll consult with Michael...Mr. Bowen. Let me stabilize her," Kristen responded. She closed her eyes and said a prayer to Althaya, asking her goddess to grant healing spells. Blue light appeared where Kristen touched Euranna. The young elf immediately started breathing easier. Kristen then repeated the same process with the head wound, closing it and removing any trace of injury. "She still has brain issues that need deeper healing, but I want to get Mr. Bowen over here to see about removing that splinter first. My stamina is quickly failing, so we may not be able to completely heal her today."

"Is there anything I can do?" Tangus asked.

"We have plenty of help in here, love. Why don't you go wait outside with Jennifer and Safire?"

Tangus started to move away. "Okay, I'll..."

Kristen turned to Tangus, "No wait!" she said. "The other cleric, Mr. Huarte I believe, went top-side. You could go and find him and ask him to come back down if he's available. We could use another healer in here."

Tangus shook his head. Kristen asked, "What's wrong?"

"I'm afraid Mr. Huarte did not make it. We lost both of the sorcerers as well."

Kristen paused, "It's pretty bad, isn't it?"

Tangus nodded. "Yes. We could have lost the ship. As soon as we realized it was a red dragon, we knew we were in deep trouble. The captain fought the *Freedom Wind* well and that not only saved the ship but minimized causalities. Even still, we were hit pretty hard."

Kristen sighed and then re-directed her attention back to Euranna. "I will pray for their souls later," she said.

Tangus turned and was walking towards the door leading out of sickbay when Kristen softly called his name. She had come up behind him and put her arms around his neck after he turned to face her. He pulled her in close. They stood for a few seconds before parting. Kristen dried tears with the back of her hand as she went back to work on Euranna.

"I'm going top-side to help with the damage. Don't try to do too much. There's always tomorrow," Tangus said.

"Maybe not for everyone...love you," Kristen replied, already absorbed in the work she was doing to try and save Euranna's life.

"Love you too, sweetheart."

***

Tangus, Jennifer, Safire, and Bitts came on deck to witness a beehive of activity. Safire was briefly taken aback by the extensive damage to the quarterdeck. The blackened unsalvageable parts of the mizzenmast had already been removed and thrown overboard. New lengths of thick-columned wood had been brought topside and were lying next to the mizzenmast base, carpenters prepping them for installation. Looking into the open wheelhouse directly below the quarterdeck, Tangus recognized Ensign Carlowe who was studying the ship's compass while four sailors manned the wheel.

Directly above, Lt. Farnsworth stood at the edge of the quarterdeck, hands behind his back, overseeing the work and other ship operations. From his position, Tangus didn't see as much as he heard the efforts to repair the damaged and broken quarterdeck. Lt. Farnsworth looked down and saluted Tangus. "Sir," he said.

"Lt. Farnsworth," Tangus answered as he returned Lt. Farnsworth salute with a nod. "We've come to offer any assistance."

"Thank you, sir, but that's unnecessary. We have everything under control. Besides, we'll be losing light soon, not much more can be done today topside."

THE SALVATION OF INNOCENCE

"Very well, lieutenant. Can we remain topside for now if we promise to stay out of the way?" Tangus asked.

"Of course you can, sir. Oh and sir, on behalf of the crew and myself, thank you for your rigorous defense of the ship. We...honor your efforts, particularly those of your wife. I'm told she's helping to save many lives," Lt. Farnsworth said.

It was Jennifer who spoke. "Kristen is remarkable and deserving of your thanks, I'll certainly grant you that. All we did, however, was fire off a few arrows."

Lt. Farnsworth shook his head. "It's much more than that, madam. We've been in tight spots before, but guests rarely help. And it cost one of your own grievous injuries. How does the Lady Euranna fare, by the way?"

"My wife thinks she will mend, but they have to perform surgery to remove the splinter. That's going to be risky, and she also has a severe head wound. We are all still very concerned," Tangus answered.

"I'm sure she will be fine, sir. If you would be so kind, please try to keep me posted on her condition? Sometimes my duties keep me out of touch," Lt. Farnsworth replied.

Safire nodded agreement. "We will," she said.

"Thank you, madam. Now if you will excuse me." Lt. Farnsworth disappeared from view and could be heard having a discussion with a carpenter about the priority of a railing over decking. "Well, Mr. Smythe, you can't logically have a proper railing without a deck to put it on." Tangus, Jennifer, and Safire turned their attention elsewhere.

Ensign Carlowe waved and walked over to them. As he passed the sailors manning the ship's wheel, he said, "Maintain your present course." "Aye sir!" one of the sailors responded.

"Good evening, Mr. DeRango, Miss Safire..." he said as he saluted Tangus and Safire. Taking Jennifer's hand, he bent over and kissed it. "...and to you, Miss Jennifer." Jennifer flushed. "I do beg your pardon, but I overheard your conversation with Mr. Farnsworth. It is my most fervent hope Miss Euranna recovers from all her wounds."

"Thank you," Tangus said. "We are all optimistic."

"Sir, may I ask you a question?" Ensign Carlowe said. Tangus nodded. "Have you ever fought a dragon before?"

"Yes, but it was many years ago," Tangus replied.

"I've seen them from a distance but this was the first time the ship has ever been attacked by one, at least since I've been aboard. I wonder what made this time different from all the others. And where did it come from? It attacked from out of the sun, how did it know to do that?" Ensign Carlowe asked.

Even though it was many years ago, Tangus was well versed in the habits of and dangers posed by a red dragon. He had hoped he would never see one again. "Red dragon's are particularly aggressive and no doubt saw us as a target of opportunity. I think this was nothing more than a random encounter. They are very intelligent and can fly high and for very long distances. It knew we would be most vulnerable if we had little time to respond to its first attack, so it came at us from out of the sun. Had it not been for the captain and the wizards, we probably would not have survived. It's fortunate we were able to disappoint it."

"Do you think it will come back?" This came from Safire.

"No, I don't," Tangus answered. "We proved to be more difficult prey then it expected. But red dragons are easily enraged. The wizards hurt it and the only way we were going to keep it off them was to kill it. I'm sorry we did not get that done. Once it had them - had what it no doubt saw as its revenge - it wasn't going to stay around and risk further harm or worse. As I mentioned, they are very intelligent."

"Ensign Carlowe, return to your station if you please," Lt. Farnsworth said from above.

Looking up at the lieutenant, Ensign Carlowe saluted. "Yes sir!" Turning to Tangus, Jennifer, and Safire, he said, "By you leave," before going back to his place in the wheelhouse.

Tangus looked around the deck and spied an out-of-the-way place that would give them a good view of the setting sun. "Over there," he pointed. As the sun was just starting to touch the horizon, a team of cooks came on deck with sandwiches, fruit, and hot coffee for everyone working to repair or sail the ship. As the sun slipped below the horizon, all three had plenty to eat and plenty of coffee to drink. The cooks even remembered to bring Bitts some raw meat and a bowl of fresh water.

Tangus turned to Jennifer and Safire. "I'm going to check on Kristen and Euranna. Why don't you two go below and make sure Borum's doing okay. He probably needs to eat."

Safire nodded. "Euranna showed us everything that needs to be done. We'll take care of him, Tangus, until Euranna is back on her feet."

"Mr. DeRango!" an all too familiar voice called.

"Yes, Mr. Krist?" Tangus answered.

"Sir, your presence is required in the captain's cabin."

Tangus looked at Jennifer and Safire. "I guess there's a change of plans...see to Borum. I'll get down to sickbay as soon as I can." Directing his attention back to Mr. Krist, he said, "Lead the way, Mr. Krist."

Mr. Bowen had a small room adjoining sickbay that he used for surgeries. Euranna had been carefully moved into the room by orderlies. Although she was still unconscious from her head wound, Mr. Bowen gave her a general anesthesia to insure she would not awaken during the surgery.

"Kristen, have you ever performed surgery?" Mr. Bowen asked.

"Yes, but only on very minor and superficial wounds, Michael. My father was a very accomplished healer and insisted I gain a working knowledge of it. There's so much more to healing than, as he would put it, 'waving a magic wand'. He taught me that proper healing is the combination of both magical and physical treatment. That sometimes magic is either not required or not available, and it is my responsibility as a healer to know the distinction and act accordingly to save a patient's life. Performing surgery is part of the physical treatment. Besides, we don't really have a choice. I have long ago expended all my healing spells."

"As have I, Kristen," Michael said. "But, as you say, there is still much to do. We can't just stop to rest so our spells come back. People are going to die. When you healed Euranna's scalp wound, did you get a sense of the seriousness of the damage to her brain?"

Kristen nodded. "It's severe and probably what's keeping her unconscious, although blood loss could also be the cause. I don't think it's as critical as the splinter, however. The longer that thing stays in her, the better her chances of developing an infection. Without immediate treatment she will probably die before night's end."

"I agree with your assessment. I have medicine we can use for infection. Let's remove the splinter, clean out the wound, and get her stabilized. Then I want you to take a nap so you can magically heal her head wound. Normally I'd just give you a magical scroll for that, but head injuries are so complicated. You really need to do it with your own magic," Michael replied.

"Agreed," Kristen said. "We'll do the surgery and then perhaps get a few of hours sleep before I try to heal Euranna's brain, though I hate leaving that brain injury unattended even for a couple of hours."

"Don't worry. Someone will keep a close watch over Euranna while you sleep. I think after we've removed the splinter she'll be stable enough so we can afford the couple of hours it will take you to rest up," Michael responded. "Now, are you ready to help with this surgery?"

Kristen nodded.

Turning to an orderly, Michael said, "Surgical tray if you please, Mr. Sanderson."

For the next hour Kristen and Michael worked to remove the splinter, inspected the wound and surrounding tissue, and cleaned it of pieces of wood and other particulates such as cloth from Euranna's clothing that were carried in by the splinter. Kristen mostly watched and took mental notes, learning how to tie off bleeding blood vessels, how to make precise incisions, and how to remove bits of foreign matter. She decided to ask Michael if he had a spare surgical toolset, and if not, where she could get one once they docked at Altheros. Something like that would be very useful in the field and should be part of every cleric's healing kit.

The surgery was going well when all of a sudden a spray of blood flew out of the wound. "Damn! Where did that come from?" Michael said. "I thought I had everything tied off."

"Mr. Bowen, her heart rate is getting slower," Mr. Sanderson, who was monitoring Euranna's vital life signs, said.

"She's already lost too much blood. She can't afford to lose any more. Damn it! My field of vision is gone with blood filling the wound. Kristen, can you see anything?"

"I can't see anything either, Michael," Kristen replied worriedly. "Both Michael and I are dead tired" Kristen said to herself. "How are we going to save Euranna when we can barely stand on our own feet?"

Mr. Sanderson called out, "We're losing her, Mr. Bowen. Her heart rate is very weak and starting to skip beats."

"Thank you, Mr. Sanderson," Michael said as he inserted his fingers into the wound to try and find the bleeding artery. "Come on, show yourself!"

"Mr. Bowen, she'll be gone in a few seconds. I can barely pick up any heartbeat at all."

"Kristen," Michael said, shaking his head and removing his hand from the bleeding wound. "I'm out of options. I can't find the bleeder."

Kristen stroked Euranna's forehead, brushing aside an errant strand of hair. "Michael, do you have a healing scroll or magical ointment?"

Michael shook his head. "They've already been used up. Kristen, I'm sorry."

"Please, Euranna, no." Kristen whispered.

The captain, sipping on a mug of coffee and nibbling on a sandwich, was sitting at the head of the same large table used for her formal dinners. Several vellum sheets were stacked on the table in front of her. A large tray sat in the middle of the table with several coffee pots, mugs, and stacks of sandwiches. The steward, Mr. Jenkins, was standing off to the side and back against a wall, ready to do the captain's bidding. There were many empty chairs, however. Including the captain, Mr. Krist, and Tangus, only two other officers were seated, both of whom Tangus recognized.

Captain Dubois and the other two men rose when Tangus and Mr. Krist walked into the room. "Thank you for coming, Mr. DeRango. Please allow me to reacquaint you with Mr. Gilbert, my ship's chief carpenter, and Major Etherton, commander of my marines," she said. "Mr. Bowen, our master cleric, is otherwise detained, and of course, sadly, you know what happened to Mr. Randel and Mr. Townes, our two ship's wizards."

Tangus shook hands with each man. "Mr. Randel and Mr. Townes fought very bravely," he said as he took his seat.

The captain, taking her seat as well, nodded. "Indeed they did." Pointing at the tray of coffee and sandwiches, the captain said, "Please help yourself, gentlemen. Before we begin, Mr. DeRango, I'd like to thank you again for all the help you, your wife, and your associates gave us during the battle with the dragon and are in fact still giving us. How is Miss Euranna by the way?"

"When last I spoke to my wife it was still too early to know for sure, but she thought Euranna was going to make a full recovery," Tangus replied.

"Excellent! Please let me know if there is anything you or your wife need."

"I will. Thank you, Captain."

The captain took a sip of coffee before speaking. "The reason I've asked you to attend, Mr. DeRango, is because part of what we are going to discuss will have a direct impact on your arrival time at Altheros. I know how important that is to you." The captain paused and looked around the table. "Gentlemen, we've suffered a disastrous attack. The mizzenmast was virtually destroyed and the quarterdeck heavily damaged. But most painful are the men we've lost. Going to sea means living with all its inherent dangers. We all accept this. And even though we as officers do everything in our power to ensure the safety of our crew, death is not uncommon despite our best efforts. Though not easy for any of us, we've been through this before. I require each of you to act accordingly. We now need to think about the living and how to best get this ship to Palisade Crest safely while at the same time fulfilling our obligation to Mr. DeRango and his people. We cannot afford time to mourn while we tend our most pressing duties. That time will come later. That also goes for each crewman in your departments. Pass this along to your officers. For now, we go about our business. Does everyone understand?" the captain asked.

A chorus of "Aye, Captain!" rang throughout the room.

"Very good, gentlemen," the captain said as she turned to Mr. Krist. "Mr. Krist, report."

"Captain, before you is the causality report. Seventeen crewmen not counting marines are confirmed dead and another thirteen are unaccounted for, presumed to be dead as well. We have five in sickbay who, if they survive the night will probably live, although each has severe burns and will need continued care once we make landfall. Twelve were treated and returned to full duty."

"Thank you, Mr. Krist. Major?"

"Captain, all the archers I had posted to the mizzenmast were on the top half. None of them survived. Ten killed, madam," Major Etherton replied.

"Thank you, Mr. Etherton. Mr. Krist, please carry on."

Nodding, Mr. Krist continued, "With the loss of the mizzenmast, our maximum speed has been reduced to eight knots. Our maneuverability is also affected, the ship responds sluggishly to the helm. We now ride the waves with, how should I put this, with less grace then before. Though replacing the mizzenmast and jury-rigging sails won't increase our speed by more than one or two knots, it will stabilize us, especially through rough waters. The loss of speed also means one other thing, captain. We need to change to a more northerly course. We need to sail north of the Spiral Islands instead of south."

Tangus looked at Mr. Krist. "That's going to take us way off course, Mr. Krist. We'll lose at least three or four days on that heading."

Caption Dubois responded for Mr. Krist. "You're correct, Mr. DeRango, but the southerly course takes us too close to The Rosemount and the pirates that sortie from there. Without a fully functional mizzenmast, we can't outrun them or outmaneuver them. If enough of them try to stop us, we probably can't fight all of them off with our armament. Pirate ships have also been known to carry wizards, and with the loss of Messrs. Randel and Townes, we have no magical defense. We are a valuable prize, not just for the cargo we carry, but also the ship itself. No, Mr. DeRango, I can't take that chance."

"Why…because of your employers, Captain?" Tangus replied heatedly. He did not want any delays. The stasis field protecting Emmy could collapse at any moment. Bitts ears perked up in reaction to the anger in Tangus voice.

"Because of my crew, Mr. DeRango," the captain calmly responded. "Pirates do not treat captured sailors very well. Usually it's torture for information followed by beheading or hanging. It would be worse for your wife, Safire, Jennifer, and Euranna. Wouldn't you prefer to not take such a risk and get there safely, albeit late, than to risk not getting there at all? I am the captain of this vessel and the crew, passengers, and cargo will always be my primary concern. We go north. Mr. Krist, please have the course set accordingly after this meeting."

"Aye, Captain." Mr. Krist replied.

"Thank you. Do you have any other comment about this matter, Mr. DeRango?" the captain asked, turning her attention back to Tangus.

Tangus shook his head. "No. I'm sorry, Captain. I know you're doing your job, and you do it very well. It's the dragon I should be upset with, not you or any man on this ship."

"There are no apologies necessary, Mr. DeRango. I share your frustration." The captain re-directed her attention back to Mr. Krist and nodded her head. "Please go on."

"Thank you, Captain. We're in the process of gathering all the belongings of the dead crewmen. We'll conduct the auction after the memorial services. When can I say the services will be performed?" Mr. Krist asked.

"I think tomorrow on the afternoon watch, shall we say six bells? Mr. DeRango, that's three o'clock if you, your wife, or any of your companions would like to attend."

Tangus nodded, "Certainly, Captain. May I ask a question?"

"By all means," the captain responded.

"Isn't auctioning off items belonging to the dead a bit callous?" Tangus asked. "Shouldn't they be returned to the families?"

"Tradition, Mr. DeRango. Certainly all personal effects such as diaries and lockets are returned to the families. But each crewman has other items that revolve around the performance of their duties, items that the families would not want or need, but items members of the crew could use, such as shoes or clothing. Some crew just wants remembrance tokens of their friends who have died. All proceeds of the auction are gathered up and evenly distributed to the families. It's just a little extra besides the death benefits paid by the Dular family," Captain Dubois said.

"Thank you, Captain," Tangus said a bit sheepishly, thinking he should have known there was a logical explanation. The captain and her entire crew have thus far been consummate professionals.

"How's crew morale, Mr. Krist?" the captain asked.

"A bit shaky at first, but during the battle everyone performed as they were trained. You know as well as I that after the battle, when men have a chance to think about what just transpired, the real problems begin. Many of our men have never seen an actual dragon before, and the ship was set to fire, every sailor's nightmare. That plus the realization some of their friends didn't make it…" Mr. Krist shrugged his shoulders. "But with the work to repair the ship, however, things are starting to get back to normal. Morale-wise, the ship is back to running tightly, ma'am."

"Thank you, Mr. Krist. Anything else?" the captain asked.

"No, Captain."

"Major Etherton? Do you have anything to add?"

"Nothing really, Captain. You're already aware of the losses we sustained. But we're still very much capable and willing to defend the ship to the death," the major replied.

Mr. Gilbert leaned over and whispered into Tangus' ear, *"He's a bit of an ass, but absolutely capable. And he would go through Hell itself if the Captain were to ask."*

"We're also all quite capable of hearing, Mr. Gilbert," the captain said sternly.

Mr. Gilbert looked like a child caught with a hand in the honey jar. "Yes, well, so sorry Major," he said as he looked down and studied the calluses on his hands.

"Please do not concern yourself, Mr. Gilbert. You're right. I am an ass, an ass with a very sharp sword," the major answered with a grin.

The captain sighed, "Enough, gentlemen. Mr. Gilbert, please give me an update concerning the repair of my mizzenmast and quarterdeck."

"Yes, Captain. We'll finish raising the temporary mizzenmast tomorrow sometime in the early afternoon. I estimate having the sail jury-rigged the following day. You should have your stability back then. As for the quarterdeck, those repairs should be completed late tomorrow, sooner if I rig some lighting and work through the night."

"No, Mr. Gilbert, there will be no work after dark. Have your men stand down within the hour. It's too dark to work on the mizzenmast and I won't have your men hammering the quarterdeck when most of the crew is trying to get some sleep. It's been a long day."

"Aye, Captain."

"Anything else, Mr. Gilbert?" the captain asked.

"We also have fire damage on the main deck that concerns me. I'll do a more thorough inspection when it gets light. Other than that, there's nothing else," Mr. Gilbert replied.

"Very well," the captain said. She then looked around the table, making eye contact with each person sitting there. "Gentlemen, we fought well today. I'm proud of each of you as well as each man in the crew. Please pass that on. For now, I need to get down to sickbay and look in on our injured men. You may carry on with your duties. Mr. Jenkins, please straighten up in here. Mr. DeRango, I suspect you'll want to come along to sickbay as well."

Jennifer and Safire threw chunks of raw meat, thoughtfully provided by one of the ship's cooks, to Borum. The small dragon happily chomped away as if nothing had happened. He needed his crate cleaned, so the two rangers were waiting until Borum had finished eating. Dragons usually became lethargic and liked to take a nap when they had a full belly. Cleaning a dragon's crate is far easier when the dragon is either cooperating or in enough of a stupor they didn't really care. Safire looked over at Jennifer. "You've been awfully quiet. Care to talk about it?"

Jennifer stared off into nothing before replying. "That was a huge dragon, Safire! And Dad acted like it was no big deal!"

"He's seen them before, Jennifer."

"We could have died! If it had not been for those sorcerers making it so angry, we probably would have!" Jennifer said.

Safire laid a hand on Jennifer's shoulder. "But we didn't, did we," she said.

"What about the next time," Jennifer said quietly.

"We're not on InnisRos any more, child. We're in a race to save a little girl from dangers only the gods could know. It is not going to be a nice quiet walk in the woods," Safire gently admonished. "This was your baptism under fire, and you reacted very well. But there is much more to come."

"My father tried to prepare me for this, but he always tempered that by saying no amount of training can truly portray what the battlefield holds, that there is no sight as terrifying as that of seeing your first dead body…especially if it is someone you know." Jennifer picked up a bucket of water and opened the crate of the sleeping Borum. "He's right. He's right about so many things."

Safire nodded, "Yes, he usually is. Here, give me a brush." As she started to scrub the parts of the crate Borum was not lying on, she said, "You'll be fine, Jennifer."

※

Kristen stood looking down and watching Euranna die. Euranna was so young, but one thing Kristen learned from a very early age was that there is no answer to the riddle of life. When Michael said there was nothing more he could do as Euranna's heartbeat slowed to become barely imperceptible, Kristen started saying a prayer to Althaya. If Euranna's death was to be, then perhaps her soul could find peace with the Goddess of Healing.

Kristen took several deep breaths and closed her eyes to begin the ritual prayers. When she opened them, however, she did not see Euranna lying on a bed bleeding to death. Instead she saw the wound made by the splinter. She saw it in a clarity that she would never have thought possible. The wound was still drowning in a pool of blood, but that did not interfere with Kristen's vision whatsoever. She could see with precision the location of the bleeding blood vessel. She saw through the blood, past the skin, muscle, and other blood vessels. Reaching forward with her finger, she touched the vessel. A purple glow appeared on the spot of the touch and the offending laceration in the vessel closed. The glow then raced up the vessel to the heart. Kirsten clearly saw the path it took and watched as the heart, surrounded by a purple aura, gained strength and slowly started to beat regularly. As Euranna's heart beat ever stronger, her breathing stabilized and her complexion turned from pale to a more healthy pink.

Kristen then felt the pain in her own body as a blood vessel opened up and she began to bleed internally. She felt herself go down to her knees, sweat breaking out on her forehead. Then slowly she started to feel better. The broken blood vessel in her body sealed itself of its own accord. The lost blood reabsorbed into her body. Kristen now understood that Emmy had somehow saved Euranna. For the first time in over three millennia, the world had felt the healing touch of the empath.

※

Emmy felt Kristen's distress through the bond. Though she still slept, her instincts for healing reached out. The knowledge and power so often used by the empath traveled the leagues separating the two, finding Kristen and mingling with the faint trace of empath blood that coursed through Kristen's own veins, revealing, if only temporarily, the full empathic power. As Euranna was healed, the universe sang out, endorsing the return of the empath. Emmy blissfully slept on, but a smile appeared on her slumbering face.

※

Lukas and his coven of two female vampyres and a human male slave stood over a recumbent child surrounded by a shimmering field of magic. Lukas looked down and studied the magic, but he could get no "feel" for its strength, except that it must be very powerful to have lasted this long. When last he saw the little girl, she was manacled to the wall next to her mother, whom he had bitten. Of the mother, only bones remained. That one was long dead, even the parasite he had introduced into her had not survived.

"Gyorgy, touch the girl," Lukas commanded his human slave.

"Yes, my Lord," and without hesitation Gyorgy tried to touch Emmy. The stasis field flared white and Gyorgy was flung across the room by the power of the spell and hit the opposite wall. Stunned, Gyorgy was otherwise unhurt as he got up and walked over to stand next to his master, waiting further commands.

"Luminista, touch the girl," Lukas said to one of the two female vampyres.

"I don't want to do that, Lukas. I do not want to cross whoever built this spell!" Luminista protested.

"Oh please! You're nothing but a coward!" the other female vampyre, Drina, said as she reached down to touch the girl. When her hand made contact, the magic flared once again, but this time it was black. Drina screamed. Starting with the offending hand, her body began to disintegrate, moving up her arm. Within a few seconds Drina's screams were echoing off the walls of the small room. Of Drina, there was nothing.

Both Lukas and Luminista stared. Unnoticed in a dark corner, the ghost of Angela Clearwater, Emmy's mother, smiled.

The Purge felt the empath power travel the Ether through the bond. It felt the magnitude of its strength. The last empath was the most powerful of them all. All must be made in preparation for its arrival.

The fifty mercenaries from the HeBron guard who had traveled into Elanesse had made a temporary bivouac in the approximate center of the dead city. As is customary, guards were posted around the perimeter of the camp. In a tent at the camp's center, the commanding officer, Lieutenant Arnish, and his second-in-command, Sergeant Warfel, were going over the results of the day's search of the city ruins and discussing strategy for the next day. Sergeant Warfel was not sure what they were looking for, just that they would know it when they found it. Hearing commotion outside the tent, both looked up.

"Warfel, see what's going on," the lieutenant ordered.

Going outside Sergeant Warfel saw groups of men coming into the camp. He knew these men were prospectors, all hoping to strike it rich by finding a legendary treasure said to be hidden in Elanesse. Walking over to the nearest man who was kneeling down next to one of the camp fires and warming his hands, he asked, "Why are you here?"

The man looked up at Sergeant Warfel with a puzzled look on his face. "I'm not really sure. I just have this feeling I should be here, helping you do whatever it is your doing. I've talked to some of the other men as I was coming here and they all said the same thing."

CHAPTER 8

The man looked down upon his comrade whose head he held in his lap. Upon the face of the other man was pain, but also acceptance of the severity of his wound. He was dying. 'I am sorry, my friend. I cannot save you.' the kneeling man said, to which the mortally wounded man replied, 'There is no need for sadness, brother, for I shall soon find peace.'

— *Book of the Unveiled*

"*Kristen! Kristen! Kristen!*" Kristen heard Michael's voice, but it seemed to be coming from very far away. At first it was barely perceptible, but gradually it became louder and more persistent. After what seemed like an eternity, Kristen's senses started to become more and more focused. Her vision moved from the micro-world of blood vessels, muscle tissue, and bone in Euranna's body to the macro-world of beds, patients, and medicine in the *Freedom Wind's* sickbay. Romulus was licking Kristen's face, but she didn't respond. She was thinking of the penalty empaths must suffer each time they heal another person and the incredible devotion to life they must have in order to endure such pain over and over again.

"Kristen! Are you with us?" Michael said.

Kristen grabbed Romulus by the ears and moved his head away from her face so she could look at Euranna. Mr. Sanderson was bending over Euranna, checking her breathing and heart rate. Michael, who had knelt down next to Romulus said, "I don't know how you did it, but you managed to stop the bleeding. Her breathing and heart function appear to be close to normal, and the incision I made to remove the splinter has been completely healed without a scar. She even regained consciousness

THE SALVATION OF INNOCENCE

for a moment. Other than having a headache, she was not feeling any pain, just a deep general weakness. Kristen, what did you do?"

Kristen grabbed Romulus around the neck, closed her eyes and laid her head on his shoulder. "It's a long story," she said. After a few brief seconds, she got up using Romulus for support. As she looked down at Euranna to check the girl for herself, a great weariness came over her, forcing her to sit down on the edge of the bed.

"Are you okay, Kristen?" Michael asked.

"Yes, just a little dizzy. I think I may need to lie down. I'm so tired," Kristen replied. "Would you please send someone to get my husband? I need to go to our stateroom."

Michael nodded, "Mr. Sanderson, please see to it." Michael then turned to Kristen and said, "Tomorrow, after you've slept, you have to tell me how you healed Euranna. I've never seen anything like it."

"Mr. Bowen..." Mr. Sanderson said, but before he could finish Tangus came into the room, followed by Captain Dubois and Bitts.

"Kristen! Are you alright?" Tangus asked with deep concern as soon as he saw Kristen. He pushed Romulus to the side and knelt down next to the bed beside Kristen and the recumbent Euranna. "You look like death has claimed you."

"I'll be fine, love. But I need sleep more than anything right now," Kristen replied as she closed her eyes and started to nod off.

Captain Dubois laid a hand on Tangus' shoulder. "Take her to your stateroom and the two of you get a good night's sleep. You've both earned it."

Tangus nodded and got off his knee, helping Kristen up. "How's Euranna?"

"She's going to be fine," Kristen said wearily. "We'll need to see if she needs more healing for her head wound tomorrow, but my guess is probably not."

Hearing the fatigue in Kristen's voice, Tangus picked her up and cradled her in his arms. "Tangus no, I can walk," Kristen insisted.

"Hush sweetheart. Bitts, Romulus, let's go." With Bitts and Romulus leading the way, Tangus carried Kristen from the sickbay. Kristen was already deep asleep when they met Jennifer and Safire on the way to their stateroom. Tangus assured them that both Kristen and Euranna were going to be okay and suggested that they retire for the night.

After Tangus had left the sickbay with Kristen, Captain Dubois said to the cleric, "Mr. Bowen, please give me a report…including what just happened here with Mistress DeRango. I also wish to visit with the injured."

"Certainly, Captain, right this way. You're never going to believe what I just saw," Mr. Bowen said.

"I'm sure you'll tell me all about it," the captain replied.

Kristen and Tangus awoke the next day to the sound of hammers, saws, and Mr. Gilbert screaming orders to the men working them. Mr. Gilbert, though jovial-seeming in appearance and personality, was very serious regarding carpentry and how the finished product should look. If the work did not suit the regal nature of the *Freedom Wind*, it was redone. Captain Dubois, knowing the nature of her ship's carpenter, always carried extra lumber to make up for those pieces thrown overboard because they were not up to Mr. Gilbert's expectations.

Tangus looked over, yawning, to see Kristen up on one elbow studying him. "How are you feeling?" he asked.

"I feel…amazingly refreshed. It's like I've slept for days, although I'm not sure I have any dignity left after being carried to bed like a little child," Kristen replied with a smile.

Tangus laughed. "You remember that? I would say the problem you have with your dignity was not being carried to your bed but rather your loud snoring."

"Ha! Ha! I'm hungry and I really need to wash up and change clothes. I can't believe you let me sleep in these."

"Yes you do…and so do I." Tangus reached over and kissed Kristen on the forehead. "Relax for a bit. Let me clean my teeth, shave, and change clothes and I'll go make arrangements for breakfast and a bath. Together?"

"Breakfast," Kristen asked with a puzzled look on her face.

"Bath," Tangus said with a smile.

"You're naughty!"

The day was overcast. The occasional sunray broke through the clouds and streaked downward to the waiting waters below. A blustery breeze came out of the north. To catch wind, Mr. Krist had the ship set on a zigzagging course. Concerned that this was reducing the ship's already slowed speed, Tangus voiced his concern. Mr. Krist, in answer to Tangus' query, explained that tacking, or angling the sails to forty-five degrees when no direct bearing was possible due to wind direction, was how they were able to make headway. Somewhere in the explanation Mr. Krist mentioned the rudder, off-wind, the keel using water resistance, and other things a ship can do to sail against the wind. It was too nautical for Tangus, who stopped Mr. Krist after a couple of minutes and thanked him for his time. Tangus politely retreated before Mr. Krist noticed his eyes glazing over.

Part of Tangus' everyday routine involved going down into the hold with Bitts and brushing down the horses. Though the captain assigned crewmen to do this, Tangus felt more at ease doing the work himself. He always carried with him a bag of either apples or carrots to give each horse as a treat before combing their coats. He cherished the time he spent grooming these noble steeds. Other than Kristen, horses made the best listeners, and Tangus had a lot of apprehension about the dangers everyone faced on the road to rescuing Emmy. What happens afterwards? Since they were not returning to InnisRos, they would have to settle down on the mainland. They would have to build a new life. Doing this was not always easy when the only support system you had was yourself and your small band of family and friends. Then there was the importance of Emmy and her ties to Althaya. Could she ever be safe? This was a question Tangus had been pondering ever since he learned of Emmy's existence, the bond between his wife and her, and their relationship to Althaya. The gods and goddesses made enemies, enemies who were other gods and goddesses. How can a mortal protect those he loves against that? As always, Tangus could find no answers. Smoke looked at him with big brown eyes, nudging Tangus on the shoulder, reminding him that his mane was not quite up to standard. "To a horse, everything is so simple," Tangus thought.

Kristen with Romulus trailing behind made her way to sickbay to check on Euranna and see how Mr. Bowen was doing with his patients. Along the way she passed several crewmen who, without exception, made way for her with respectful bows. Each and every one of them understood the impact she had the day earlier helping to heal the injured. One, however, did not move aside as she walked down the corridor. He was an imposing man, dressed in the uniform of the ship's marines. He wore the epaulets of a captain on his broad shoulders. Upon closer inspection she saw that he was not human, but half-elf. He looked at her as she neared with intelligent and kindly eyes. Ordinarily Kristen would have found such a combination unusual in a man trained to kill, but that was before she had met Tangus.

"Sir…" Kristen started to say.

"Please madam. May I have a word?" the half-elf said, gently interrupting. After Kristen nodded, he introduced himself. "My name is Christian Baltzli. You probably do not remember me, but you healed me yesterday after the attack."

"I'm sorry, I'm trying to place your face, but there were so many people in sickbay at the time," Kristen answered apologetically.

"You had no need to look upon my face," Christian said as he raised his hands up to show Kristen. The palms of both had terrible burn scars on them. "I lifted a burning piece of the mizzenmast off one of the crew. He did not survive."

"I'm so sorry your sacrifice was in vain," Kristen said sadly.

"It was not in vain, madam. One must never give up regardless the cost. Though in terrible pain, he was no longer burning, and he did not die alone. It was a price I would pay again if so necessary."

"That's very gallant, Mr. Baltzli. I'm not sure I know what to say," Kristen said as she took his hands in hers to more closely inspect them.

"Pardon me, madam, I was not trying to gain favor. What I did, the sacrifice I made, was no more noteworthy than what many others did and sacrificed yesterday. I still have my life. But I would ask you a question, if I may," Christian said.

Kristen let go of his hands and looked up at his face. "Of course you can, sir," Kristen replied.

Christian nodded. "Thank you. I've heard some of the scuttlebutt – rumors - surrounding you, your husband, and your companions. It's said that you have very important business on the mainland…very dangerous business."

Kristen's eyes narrowed. "Tangus warned me about ship 'scuttlebutt' as you put it. But in this case it is correct, although I will not divulge the nature of our need to get to the mainland."

"I would not ask such a thing." Christian said as he shook his head. "As a military officer, I understand how the 'need to know' works. What I ask is that I be allowed to help you in your quest. My enlistment ends after this voyage and I have no family to speak of. I think it's time for me to do other things. I've been watching how you, your husband, and your friends Jennifer, Safire and Euranna interact. I…well, as only one of two marine officers onboard the *Freedom Wind*, I don't have that kind of camaraderie. I do not say I am deserving of your friendship, you hardly know me. But I would like the chance. I want to do right in this world. This ship does not really give me that opportunity. In my heart I know there is great good in the quest you and your husband have undertaken. If you are going into harm's way, you could use a person with my abilities."

Kristen, using her clerical senses, searched the man's face looking for any trace of duplicity. She could find none. He was being truthful, and he was also right. They could use another sword arm to help rescue Emmy. "Thank you, Mr. Baltzli. You make very valid points, but my husband makes these types of decisions. I will speak to him. I'm sure he will seek you out soon to discuss it. In the meantime, let's go to sickbay. I'd like to rid you of those scars."

"Please call me Christian, madam. And thank you for offering to talk to your husband about my request. I will not let either of you down if you should consent to let me accompany you. As for my hands, they cause no pain and you healed them so that they are fully functional. For now, I think, I should like to keep the scars as a reminder of the lives lost yesterday."

Kristen nodded. "I understand, Christian. We all carry scars from yesterday."

Christian bowed slightly and stepped to the side of the corridor. "I should not keep you away from sickbay any longer, madam."

"We'll be talking soon, Christian," Kristen said as she smiled and walked past him. Suddenly stopping and turning around, she asked, "When would your duties allow for that?"

Christian paused, considering. "Probably sometime after the memorial services would be best."

Kristen nodded, "Very well. Be careful today, Christian."

"And you as well, madam."

As Kristen made her way into sickbay, her thoughts turned from Christian to Euranna. Before going through the door, she told Romulus to wait outside with an admonishment. "And don't growl at anybody. The poor crew is scared to death of you." Kristen could swear that Romulus was smiling when she went into sickbay.

"Kristen!" Michael called.

"Good morning, Michael," Kristen said as she studied him. "Did you get any sleep at all last night?"

"Enough. We lost one of the more severely burned. I really thought he was going to pull through."

THE SALVATION OF INNOCENCE

"What happened?" Kristen asked.

"Circumstance," Michael said with a shrug of his shoulders. "We had so many injuries as you well know. I've been using spells non-stop until I had no more to use, even after a nap. He developed an infection. It was just too massive, even the medicine would not work, though I didn't use all of it. We've still got a week of sailing before we drop you off, then another week up the coast to Palisade Crest. I couldn't use the remainder on one man when I have the entire crew to consider. Without it I couldn't save him. I'm not sure I could have even if I had."

"I'm sorry, Michael. I'm surprised you didn't have more medicine available to use after all your spells were exercised," Kristen said.

Michael shook his head. "This attack was unprecedented, Kristen. I've never before heard of a dragon attacking a ship this size. We were simply not prepared for casualties of this magnitude." Michael paused for a moment. "We will be the next time, however. I've spent part of the night drawing up a protocol for a ship's healing requirements based upon ship size and the number of crew, additional medicine, clerics, healers, even an onboard apothecary with all the plants necessary to make new batches of medicine. I'd appreciate it if you took a look at it and let me know what you think…when you have a chance, of course."

"Certainly, Michael, I'll take a look at it after I check in on Euranna, unless you need my help with the more critically injured?"

"Thank you, Kristen, but the remaining badly burned are stabilized and in no pain. What they are going to need now is therapy which will have to wait until we dock at Palisade Crest. Now go see Euranna. I think you'll be happy with her progress. Come see me when you're ready and we'll go over my protocol," Michael said.

Kristen nodded. "I'll see you in a few minutes."

Euranna had been moved from the room where her surgery was performed to a corner area of sickbay. She was propped up on several pillows and studying a copy of the ship's manual. Looking up as Kristen approached, she closed the manual. "I asked for something to read and this was all they had. I never knew how complicated sailing a ship was! During the battle the captain was shouting order after order. Now I have a notion what some of those orders were meant to accomplish."

Kristen took the manual and put it down on a table next to Euranna's bed. She leaned down and held open Euranna's eyelids as she studied the pupil, first the left and then the right. Satisfied, Kristen placed her hands on Euranna's chest over her heart. Euranna started to say something but Kristen shushed her. Kristen then exposed the side where the splinter had entered. Nodding, Kristen covered Euranna's side back up. Finally Kristen placed both her hands on the side of Euranna's face, closed her eyes, and concentrated, using her clerical healing ability to gauge the damage deep inside Euranna's head. "Excellent," Kristen said to no one in particular.

"You know Mr. Bowen did all these same things just a little while ago. He too was happy. He said I didn't need my brain healed after all," Euranna said. "I guess I'm going to live."

Kristen smiled. "Yes, child, I guess you are. How do you feel?"

"Fine. The headache is gone and I feel no other pain. But I still feel weak."

"That's normal," Kristen said as she gave the manual back to Euranna, then, with the back of her hand, felt her forehead checking for fever. Sitting down in a chair next to the bed, Kristen made herself comfortable and looked at Euranna. "I think bed rest for today. Tonight we'll help you to the stateroom you share with Jennifer and Safire. Tomorrow you should be able to come up on deck. Have you had breakfast?"

"Yes ma'am. They brought me eggs, bacon, turnips, and coffee," Euranna replied.

"Good. You need to eat to regain your strength. You're body went through a lot yesterday. We almost lost you."

"That's what Mr. Bowen said. When the dragon attacked the sorcerers, I felt a sharp pain in my side and remember thinking as I was falling that I'm going to hit the railing with my head. That's the last thing I remember until this morning," Euranna said.

THE SALVATION OF INNOCENCE

Kristen looked at Euranna. "Do you have any other memories from yesterday?"

Euranna started to shake her head no, but paused. "Wait...not a memory, but I did have a dream, well not really a dream as much as a feeling of warmth, you know, the kind of warmth you feel on a cold morning lying in a warm bed with your head under the covers, safe and secure. Why? Is it important?"

Kristen smiled. "I don't know, dear."

About that time Jennifer and Safire entered sickbay and walked over to them. Safire asked, "How are you, Euranna?"

"Kristen and Mr. Bowen said I'm going to live, but I have to stay in bed until tomorrow," Euranna replied with a grin.

"Well I have just the thing!" Jennifer said holding up a small bag. "Chocolate! Mr. Carlowe gave me these with his compliments. He said, 'I do so hope the Lady Euranna has recovered. Please pass along my regards.' There's enough for all of us."

For the next few moments everyone gathered in Euranna's corner of the sickbay enjoyed the rare treat. "I think this would go good with cherries," Safire commented.

"Or peanuts," Jennifer said as she was licking her fingers.

※

The ship's bell rang six times. It was time for the memorial services. Several hundred crewmen who were not on watch had gathered on the main deck and were looking up at the quarterdeck. The sails of the temporary mizzenmast had been struck...so many more were in the sail rigging of the mainmast. Along the port side of the ship's railing ten flat boards had been erected on brackets so they could be tilted. Lined on the deck next to the railing where forty-four bodies wrapped in sail canvas, one for each man lost. Ballast rocks were put at the feet of each wrapped body. For the bodies of those who had died in the water and not recovered, or those disintegrated by dragon breath, straw and rocks filled the canvas bags.

Tangus, Kristen, Jennifer, and Safire, along with Romulus and Bitts, were also on the main deck, just below the quarterdeck in front of the wheelhouse. When the captain came on deck, officers yelled for "call to quarters" as the ship's bell rang five times. All crewmen in attendance came to attention. The captain crossed the quarterdeck to the center, faced the assembled crew, and also came to attention. Standing next to her was the ship's First Officer, Thomas Krist. "Mr. Krist!" the captain said, turning to face Mr. Krist. "Please call the roll!"

"Aye, Captain!" As Mr. Krist read the names of those who had died, the ship's bell rang once for each. When he was done, he turned to the captain, said "All present and counted!" handed the roster to the captain, and saluted as she accepted it. Unrolling the long vellum roster, the captain deliberately reviewed each name. Rerolling it, she handed the roster back to Mr. Kist. "The roster is correct. Mr. Krist, please post the roster to the ship's log." Mr. Krist took the roster and saluted. "Aye, Captain." The captain then turned to face the crew once again, as did Mr. Krist, both remained at attention. From behind them a drum started a slow roll. The captain, Mr. Krist, and all officers present for the ceremony saluted and held the salute as the bodies were put on the boards. As one, all ten boards were tilted. This was repeated five times. As each body slipped into the sea, it sank out of sight. A moment after the last body disappeared from view, Mr. Krist shouted "At ease!"

The captain waited for her crew to settle themselves. The captain presented herself with dignity, grace, and power. The distinctive gold of the buttons and epaulets contrasted the deep blue of her dress uniform. Her knee high boots were shined to perfection. Her captain's cloak rippled slightly in the wind. The clasp that secured it around her shoulders gleamed slightly of magic. Though her appearance alone would breed confidence, her bearing and conduct during and after the battle with the dragon demanded it. As she stood on the quarterdeck surveying her crew, it appeared as if she were making eye contact with each one of the men. As one, every person on the deck and hanging from the riggings became silent, giving the captain their upmost attention.

THE SALVATION OF INNOCENCE

"My father was a very wise man, a philosopher, a teacher, an orator. When I was a young girl, we would often talk about things that could only be conjectured upon, things that had no answer such as magic and why it is, or the meaning of life, or why the innocent are so cruelly savaged in far too many parts of the world. These, of course, are the types of conversations all children have with their parents as they grow and try to understand the world around them. And I must admit, like most children and even most adults, I never really made much sense of some of the things I saw or heard. Not until one day…a day when my father made a simple statement. Everything suddenly became very clear to me."

"He made the analogy that life was only a temporary bridge spanning between the beginning and the end. For all of us, how we cross that 'bridge of life' as he called it, ultimately determined the eternity we earn for ourselves, for the final disposition of our souls, the essence of who we are, depends upon the choices we make during our time spent on the 'bridge'. It does not matter whether we are peasant, high-born, or somewhere in between. It does not matter if our lives are short or long. What truly matters is the journey we made, how we crossed the 'bridge' when the other side comes into sight."

"These men choose to sacrifice their lives so others may live. It is a choice we all would have made, a choice we all still may have to make sometime in the future. What more can be said about the way these men lived their lives, the way they crossed their 'bridge', and the way they died except to say that we, as witnesses, can be assured eternity will look kindly upon them."

"These forty-four men now resting on the bottom of the ocean have found peace. Their passage is complete. But each of you is still crossing the 'bridge', still living your lives. Each of you must still carry on. Do so as your conscience dictates so that when you reach the end of your 'bridge', eternity will look as kindly upon your journey as it no doubt looks upon the journey of our fallen shipmates."

At this point the captain paused and once again looked out upon her crew. "I am your captain, but I have no sovereignty over your fate.

There are never guarantees as to when we will reach the end. But rest assured, as long as you are on my ship, you will never be alone. God's speed to each of you," Captain Dubois said as she turned to Mr. Krist. "Mr. Krist, you may dismiss the men."

"Aye, Captain. Crew! Attention!" Mr. Krist bellowed.

As one the entire compliment on deck came to attention and remained so until the captain disappeared into her cabin through a door behind the wheelhouse. "Crew dismissed!" Mr. Krist shouted.

※

The next few days passed without incident, the ship's officers and crew going about their duties professionally and efficiently. But a somber mood had settled in. The laughter, joking, and light-hearted banter normally associated with men working together was absent. Crewmen smiled and tipped a finger to their head as a salute whenever they passed one of the ship's passengers, but Tangus noticed a reserve that was not there prior to the attack. Even the captain and officers were solemn.

These men, particularly the officers, were of good character. Tangus considered them friends, the type of comradeship that is forged in battle. Both Tangus and Kristen were concerned the loss of so many men had affected everyone very deeply and they needed emotional healing. "Tangus, all of the men who died were considered brothers. The captain probably thought of them as sons. They are hurting," Kristen said. "Maybe I can help in some way. I know how I felt when I lost my mother, so I can relate to them. But I don't know if I'd be allowed. Even Michael has been closed-lipped. These are proud men."

"Sweetheart, people deal with loss in different ways. I've lost many friends over the years. There's a mourning process that we have to go through. As you mentioned, you know because you went through it with your mother," Tangus said.

"I know, Tangus. But it still breaks my heart," Kristen replied.

Tangus took Kristen's hands in his. "That's one of the things I love about you. But if you took the pain away, you would be doing them a disservice. We all must learn to cope with death."

"I guess it's the cleric in me," Kristen said as she shook her head in acknowledgment.

Tangus smiled and put his hand over her heart. "No…it's the compassionate spirit within you."

Euranna made a complete recovery and was taking care of Borum the second day after the attack. Tangus continued with her sword training after he was assured by Kristen that Euranna was completely healed. Her progress with the katana was outstanding. She more than made up what she lacked in brute strength with her litheness and speed. The katana, light and made for cutting, was the perfect hand-to-hand combat weapon for her. She learned to dance around Tangus, slashing whenever she found a break in his defense, never going for a killing blow but instead scoring hit after hit that, if real weapons were being used, would leave him cut in many places, slowly losing stamina as he bled. Whenever Tangus started to feel Euranna was getting cocky, though, he quickly disarmed her and put his wooden blade to her throat. Her speed was no match for his experience, and a good dose of humility would serve her well. Tangus prayed she'd be ready when she faced a truly talented and knowledgeable foe.

Tangus, as promised by his wife, sought out Christian Baltzli. Sitting down with him in the officer's mess and drinking a mug of grog, Tangus and Christian talked for the better part of an hour. Like Kristen, Tangus decided that he liked the big half-elf and gladly accepted him. Though certain aspects of Emmy's importance and her relationship to Kristen were not discussed, Tangus gave Christian a very thorough briefing regarding the overall nature of the mission and its inherent dangers. Tangus also made sure Christian understood who was in command and that the safety of Kristen and Emmy were paramount. Nothing Tangus said dissuaded the marine, he was ready to go. Tangus was inwardly happy to have another person with leadership experience along. Whenever his duty permitted, Christian spent much of his free time with Jennifer, Safire, and Euranna in particular. As an experienced marine, Tangus felt he could take over her sword training. Within a few days he had successfully melded into Tangus and Kristen's small group.

The *Freedom Wind* continued to sail north, west of the Spiral Islands. Tacking against the wind slowed her speed down to six knots. After a couple of days, however, she turned east, putting the islands on her starboard side. After sailing past the Wilnet Chain, the northern-most spiral chain of the islands, the *Freedom Wind's* took a southeasterly course and her speed picked up to eight knots.

When the ship made her southerly turn, the mainland came into sight on the horizon. Tangus, studying his map, decided it was time to release Borum. He had written the message to his brothers of the Company of the Dagger days before. He knew they would help if they could. His only concern was that the messenger dragon would fail or be otherwise distracted. After discussing the situation with Kristen, they decided they would wait one day in Altheros before starting their trek east to Elanesse. If his friends did not arrive by then, they could not afford to delay longer.

With the help of some of the crew, Mr. Krist, Christian, and Euranna, the crate with Borum inside, his eyes covered, was brought up on deck. "How does this thing work?" Mr. Krist asked curiously.

Tangus laughed. "That was my question as well. A messenger dragon is very easily impressed. We use spells to plant an image in his brain. Even the image of a well drawn map will work. It's as easy as that, as long as you can use the magic required."

"I assume you can, Tangus?" Mr. Krist replied.

"Well, usually it takes a cleric," Tangus replied. "But in this case, Kristen has never been to the mainland, so we think, considering the gravity of the situation, it be best that I impress Borum. Rangers have some limited spell ability and Kristen's father taught me the spell. Let's see if I've learned my lesson well."

Tangus slowly removed the eye cover from Borum. The small dragon cocked his head and blinked. "SCREECH!" it shrieked.

Tangus cleared his mind and concentrated on the spell Father Goram had taught him. When he knew Aurora had granted his request, he reached out and touched Borum. Upon contact, he envisioned in his mind the location of the Company of the Dagger's small keep, local landmarks, and its relationship to the ship on her current heading. Through the power of the magic, Tangus knew that his mental vision had impressed itself on the dragon. Borum looked at Tangus and blinked. Turning to Kristen and extending his hand, he said, "Message, dear." Kristen took a rolled piece of vellum and gave it to Tangus, who secured it in a pouch hanging on a harness put on Borum for this purpose.

"Okay, buddy, do your thing." Tangus said as he stepped out of the way of the open crate. In a flash Borum was in the sky. He circled the ship one time before heading east. Kristen whispered, "Be safe Borum."

Maximillion Darkshadow and Lester Trueblade represented exactly one half of the Company of the Dagger. It was early evening. Having gorged themselves upon a dinner of beef stew, bread, and sweet cakes for desert, the two were up on the battlements of the small fortified keep they called home to enjoy an after dinner cigar, a vice they would partook only occasionally.

"Looks like a storm coming in from the north," Lester said.

Maximillion nodded his head after blowing out smoke rings from his cigar. "Probably right," he said. "I can already feel the chill in the air. I hope it doesn't snow. I hate snow. Did I ever tell you about the time Elrond, Tangus and I were up north on the other side of the Dragon Teeth Mountains?"

Lester sighed. "Yes, Max, several times in fact."

"Huh? Can't remember, but if you say so. The Light at the Top of the World looked like we could reach out and touch it. By the gods that's a big mountain. And the cold! I didn't think I'd ever thaw out. Been allergic to cold weather ever since." Looking at Lester, Maximillion asked, "When was the last time we were out in the field? Sitting around the keep day in and day out is wearing on my nerves."

"And your mind," Lester said quietly to himself.

"What was that?"

"Nothing, Max. I was just thinking out loud. We nearly died the last time we went on a mission for the Duke, remember? He told us to take the rest of the year off and recover. We're lucky. If it was me, I'd have fired us," Lester replied.

Maximillion grunted. "He'll calm down, he always does. He needs us. Besides, it wasn't like we deliberately let that shipment of gold be stolen."

Lester shook his head. "We kind of did, actually."

"The odds were against us. No amount of gold is worth my life or the life of my friends," Maximillion said as he waved his cigar. "But perhaps he's right. Maybe we're slipping just a bit. It seems we get little practice anymore."

Looking at his own cigar, Lester replied, "When I joined the Dagger, our name was known from Palisade Crest all the way down south to Altheros. Now we're just another small mercenary company. If it wasn't for the Duke's patronage, I'm not sure we'd still have a job."

"The whole damn world's gone civilized on us, Lester. But just wait. Somewhere out there adventure waits. It always has. Then we'll get our chance again," Maximillion said. But as he finished talking, something in the sky caught his attention. "What the hell is that?" he said as he pointed west.

Lester looked in the direction Maximillion was pointing and saw something flying toward them, but couldn't quite make it out through the light of the setting sun. Both elves put their hands over their eyes and squinted, hoping to see enough to identify whatever it was that flew their way.

Maximillion suddenly called out, "Dragon!" and dropped to the stone floor of the battlement. "Lester, get out of sight before it sees you!"

"Looks awfully small to be a dra...", but before Lester could finish his thought, Maximillion had grabbed the end of his cloak and pulled. Lester sighed and dropped down beside his friend.

"Shhhhh. Dragons have very keen hearing AND eyesight. We need to stay out of sight and hope it passes us by." Lowering his voice to a whisper, Maximillion said, "Did I ever tell you about the time a dracolich dropped boulders on the main house?"

Lester rolled his eyes. Maximillion was a very good friend, but if he had to keep hearing the same old stories over and over again, Lester decided he'd let the next ogre they came across bash him with a club to end his misery.

Maximillion, not really paying attention to Lester's displeasure, launched into the dracolich story. "The thing was bombarding the main house with boulders. You know about dracolich's, right? Vicious undead dragons! Wasn't any way we were going to come out, well at least not until it became apparent the roof of the main house was starting to crumble. Boy-oh-boy did that take a lot of gold pieces to fix! I thought Elrond was going to go into convulsions! You know how he is with his gold. Anyway..."

"Max, I've heard this story before, as well as its embellishments. I..."

There was suddenly a thump and a "SCREECH!" on the battlement ledge directly above them. Maximillion calmly said, "Oh crap!" as he drew his sword. "Nice knowing you, Lester."

Both Maximillion and Lester looked up to see a small dragon sitting on the ledge, looking down at them and blinking its eyes, "SCREECH!"

Getting up, Maximillion said, "That's not a dragon!"

"SCREECH!" the dragon screamed as it tucked its head under a wing.

"I think you hurt its feelings," Lester said.

"I mean it's a dragon, but a smaller messenger dragon. I've seen these things being used by some of the highborn in Palisade Crest. It must have wondered off course," Maximillion replied.

Lester pointed to the pouch attached to a harness. "Since this is a messenger dragon, maybe you should read the message and find out."

"Good idea. Think it'll bite?"

"There's only one way to know for sure." Lester reached over and unclasped the pouch. The messenger dragon bravely looked at him, "SCREECH!"

"Here you go," Lester said as he handed the pouch over to Maximillion.

Maximillion quickly opened the pouch and scanned the parchment. "I'll be damned! It's from Tangus! I need to get this down to Elrond." Pointing at the messenger dragon, he said, "Take care of him, will you? He might come in handy later."

As Maximillion hustled down the stairs to the inner courtyard, Lester sighed. He suddenly realized he's been doing that a lot lately. "But it belongs to someone else!" Lester shouted to Maximillion's retreating back.

"Not anymore! Finders keepers…first law of the mercenary."

Lester shook his head. "More like first law of Elrond and Maximillion," he thought as he turned his attention back to the small dragon. The messenger dragon was looking at him, head cocked. "How do I take care of you?" Lester asked.

"SCREECH!"

Lester sighed. "Screech indeed!"

The mortally wounded red dragon was flying low over the water heading northwest. She had long ago dropped the three dead humans into the sea, her rage toward the two wizards gone as she now fought for her own survival. Ahead of her the island of InnisRos appeared. On the very northern tip of the main island was a clearing in an uninhabited part of the forest. There she would meet the wizard Mordecai Lannian. As she circled the clearing, she saw two elves awaiting her arrival, the wizard and Amberley Siloratan, Mordecai's assistant and lover.

Landing clumsily, the dragon staggered over to the pair. "I have done what you have asked. The ship has been destroyed."

"Is it now, Tirith?" Mordecai said. "I wonder."

"Yes. Now release my babies and heal me!"

"My spies inside the monastery report nothing out of the usual. Do you think Father Goram would not know if the ship went to the bottom of the sea as you say? It did, after all, have his precious daughter aboard," Mordecai replied. "But no matter, my allies will verify it soon enough."

"Please Mordecai, heal me and release my babies." Tirith pleaded.

Mordecai smiled as he shook his head. "Tsk. Tsk. Begging does not become you, Tirith. Those ballistae bolts appear to be dreadfully painful. And it looks like you've lost a lot of blood. Oh look! I recognize the fletching of this arrow. Tangus DeRango had a hand in this." Grasping the shaft of the arrow, Mordecai shoved it into the body of the dragon even further. Tirith, too weak from blood loss, could only roar in pain.

Drawing his brightly gleaming sword, Mordecai raised it to strike. "You can go to be with your little monsters now!" he said as he brought the magical blade down and severed Tirith's head. Wiping the blade on a cloth handed to him by Amberley, Mordecai, as he absentmindedly kicked Tirith's head, laughed. "We need to get back to the council before the queen misses us, my love," he said as he turn and walked away.

Lukas and Luminista looked at the sleeping Emmy inside the stasis field. "What do we do now, Lukas?" Luminista asked.

Lukas, however, wasn't really listening. He was studying the magic warding the child. It did not kill Gyorgy, but it did seem to lessen slightly in brightness. When Drina touched it, the obvious drain was even more significant. Lukas did not know how long the stasis magic would continue to last, but he did know how to deplete its power.

"Listen to me, Luminista. There are plenty of men in Elanesse. I want you to bite one and infect him. Then lead him back down here. Gyorgy, go help her."

"Yes, master," the thrall said.

"But Lukas…"

Lukas held up his hand to silence Luminista. "For once stop arguing and just do what I say!"

Luminista knew when Lukas would be pushed no further. She left the room, Gyorgy following close behind.

Lukas smiled. "I shall have you soon, my little innocent."

CHAPTER 9

Friendships newly made are often as endearing and everlasting as friendships that have stood the test of time.

— *Book of the Unveiled*

Tangus, Kristen, Jennifer, Safire, Euranna, and Christian were leaning against the quarterdeck railing looking out at the coastline. Romulus and Bitts were lying down taking a nap. Unbeknownst to anyone except some of the crew, the wolf and elven dog had just come up on deck after a good chase around one of the holds. "Ladies, I give you the mainland," Tangus said.

The ship had come to a stop about three-hundred yards from the shore and dropped anchor. It was the nearest a ship as massive as the *Freedom Wind* could safely get to the shore without the risk of running aground. Large barge-like boats were being hoisted over the side.

"Why can't we dock at Altheros, Dad?" Jennifer asked.

Tangus, as he maintained his gaze upon the vast expanse of the mainland, said, "Would you like to answer that question, Christian? You're probably more qualified."

"Certainly, sir," Christian replied. "It's really pretty simple, Miss Jennifer, Altheros lies on the Pantera River miles inland. The *Freedom Wind* is too large a vessel to navigate such shallow waters. It would also be very difficult to turn the ship around once on the river. This really is as far as we can safely go."

"That all makes sense, Christian. But how are we going to get the horses unloaded?" Jennifer replied.

"With great difficulty, Miss Jennifer, but we have done it before. Try not to worry. This crew is very adept. Your horses will be safe," Christian said.

Kristen turned and smiled. "OUR horses, Christian," she said.

Euranna hit Christian in the arm. "Yeah, marine, you're one of us now. And quit being so formal." The two had been spending a lot of time together lately.

Kristen shivered. "It's cold." The sky was clear, but winter was starting to settle in. Even this far south the days were still chilly, the nights even more so.

"I'm sorry everyone. But the cold is going to be a fact of life as we travel overland. We'll be able to spend most nights in an inn or some farmer's barn, but expect to sleep under the stars also. We can't afford the time it would take to pitch tents and take them down. We take only what a couple of pack horses will carry. Once we're on shore, we control how fast and under what conditions we travel. Considering everything that's at stake, I'll be pushing hard," Tangus said. "Christian, still want to come along?"

"Of course I do!" Christian replied enthusiastically. "Ship duty has only come recently for me. For most of my career, I've been what we like to call a 'grunt' or 'boots on the ground'. I've experienced campaigns much colder when I was in Palisade Crest's militia. Major Etherton has already accepted my resignation and I'm all squared away."

"Squared away?" Safire asked.

"Ready to go, madam," Christian replied.

Euranna punched Christian in the arm again. "What did I say about formality?"

Christian smiled.

Kristen nudged Tangus and whispered, "She does that to get his attention. I think they're sweet on each other."

"Great. I've been worrying about Jennifer and Ensign Carlowe, but that's going to end today. Now these two," Tangus whispered back.

"It's natural, my dear. Let it happen."

As they watched, ship balustrades were removed and a large gangplank with sturdy rope hand railings had been lowered from the main deck onto one of the two barges that had been lowered into the water.

THE SALVATION OF INNOCENCE

A crewman came up the ladder and saluted Lt. Farnsworth, the Officer of the Deck, and reported. Returning the salute, Lt. Farnsworth said "Very good. Thank you." As the seaman went back down the ladder, Lt. Farnsworth looked over. "Mr. DeRango, if you please. They will soon be ready to have your horses brought on deck. We are more than capable of carrying this out, but I assume you would want to at least oversee it."

"Thank you, Lt. Farnsworth. Yes we do." Turning to his wife and the rest of his companions he said, "Let's get to work."

After a couple of hours of work, all the horses had been brought up on deck, transferred to a barge and taken ashore. Several of the crew along with Christian stayed on shore to watch over the horses while Tangus, Kristen, and the others went back onboard to say their farewells. Mr. Krist met them as they walked up the gang-plank. "The captain would like the pleasure of your company in her cabin for a going away drink."

"We would be honored," Kristen said. "Can Romulus and Bitts come along?"

"I'm sure the captain would have it no other way," Mr. Krist said, smiling. "More than one sailor is going to miss their chases below deck."

Following Mr. Krist, they made their way through the wheelhouse, into the captain's ready-room and through a door to the dining room. Captain Dubois was sitting at the far end of the table. To her left was another gentleman wearing the epaulets of a lieutenant on his shoulders. There was a stack of papers sitting in front of him. In the middle of the table was a decanter of wine with crystal glasses. Next to that was a bag which appeared to be filled with coins. As they entered, both the captain and the lieutenant rose. "Please, have a seat," the captain said as she gestured to the chairs surrounding the long table. Mr. Krist came over and sat next to the captain on her right.

"Please allow me to introduce Mr. Berry, my ship's purser. I have decided, because of all the assistance every one of you rendered during this voyage, that your payment should be returned. I made this decision independent of my employers, the Dular family. I have discretion in matters such as this," Captain Dubois said with a smile as she glanced at Mr.

Berry, who had a slight frown on his face. "They may own the ship, but I am its captain."

"Here! Here!" Mr. Krist suddenly blurted out, totally out of character. "Sorry, Captain."

"See! I have Mr. Krist's full support," the captain said with a grin. "To refund your passage fee, however, there are certain formalities Mr. Berry insists upon. I turn the floor over to you, Mr. Berry."

"Aye, Captain. This top document says the captain hired Tangus and Kristen as consultants and that you agreed upon the price of two-thousand gold pieces. I need your signatures, or mark, here, here, and here," Lt. Berry said indicating the places that needed to be signed by Tangus and Kristen, "in triplicate. Everyone else, for the purpose of this transaction, is considered sub-contractors working for you. As such, they are paid from your resources and not the ship's."

"Captain, returning our payment isn't really necessary," Kristen protested.

"Thank you, dear girl. But from my perspective, as well as that of my crew, it is. I'm sure, however, that after your done signing all the paperwork, you're going to feel like you did in fact earn it."

"Captain, may I continue?" Lt. Berry asked a little impatiently.

"Of course, Mr. Berry," the captain replied. "Please carry on."

Placing the paper in front of Tangus, Lt. Berry handed Tangus a quill and slid over a small jar of ink, saying "Everything is in order, Mr. DeRango."

Tangus took the proffered quill, dipped it into the ink and started signing his name. Kristen did the same. Once done, Lt. Berry produced another document.

"This one says that the consulting work you both have performed was accomplished as per the agreement between the captain and yourselves and that neither party takes grievance with the other. Again, please sign here, here, and here."

As Tangus and Kristen were signing the second document, Mr. Berry produced a third. "This is the final document. This one is a receipt for the gold. I only need one signature each right here," Lt. Berry said pointing to at the bottom of the page.

THE SALVATION OF INNOCENCE

After Tangus and Kristen had signed all the documents, Lt. Berry studied each one to make sure there were no discrepancies. He then initialed the bottom right corner of each sheet, blowing on the ink to dry it. Satisfied, he gathered and tapped the stacked documents against the top of the table to straighten them out, pulled out a leather satchel from underneath the table and placed them inside. "Captain, with your permission I'd like to place these in the ship's vault. I'll file them with the magistrate when we get to Palisade Crest."

"Very good, Mr. Berry," the captain said. "If that is all, you are dismissed,"

"Thank you, ma'am," Lt. Berry said as he left the captain's dining room.

"What a strange man," Safire said as the door to the room was closed.

The captain laughed. "He's the ship's accountant. Actually, he has more contact with our employers than I, and is probably more important to them. He's the one who keeps track of cargo, which as you know is the life blood of the Dular family business and the reason this ship sails. He's very good at it, probably worth his weight in gold to the family. By the way, he completely approves of refunding the transit fee to you. He keeps to his ledgers, but he also keeps track of what happens on this ship and who did what. He was very impressed by your help when the dragon attacked, particularly you, Kristen. He figures the number of crew you helped to heal saved the Dular family much more in death benefits than what's in that bag. It's about the bottom line, my friends. He would call it 'profit margin'."

Rising, the captain leaned over and grabbed the decanter of wine. "Please, let me pour each of you a glass." After doing so, she raised her own glass up and out. "I want to make a toast!" Everyone around the table stood and held their glasses out.

"May your days be calm, your nights be peaceful."
"May your road be smooth, your trails unmolested."
"May you find the answers you seek."
"May you find everlasting tranquility."

"May the wind be forever at your backs."
"To good friends! To steady comrades!"

"Salute!" Mr. Krist shouted. "Salute!" everyone else shouted as seven glasses were tapped together. Sitting, the fine red wine was sipped and enjoyed as was the quiet conversation of friends, but eventually they all knew it was time to leave. Tangus rose and offered his hand first to Captain Dubois and then Mr. Krist. Kristen, Jennifer, Safire, and Euranna preferred hugs.

As the captain walked to the door of the dining room, she paused and turned to look at each one before opening the door. "It has been a pleasure to have you aboard my ship. Every one of you has earned my trust, my gratitude, and my friendship. As you know, our home port is Palisade Crest. If you are ever up that way and should require assistance of any kind, please know that you can always call upon either Mr. Krist or me. If we are available, we shall endeavor to help you however we can."

Kristen walked up to the captain and hugged her again. "Thank you, Jasmine. We shall remember. And although we are nothing but 'land lubbers', as so many of your crew call us, we offer the same invitation." Taking a small gem out of a pouch on her belt, Kristen looked over at Tangus who nodded. "Take this. It is a small communication crystal my father gave me. I have its opposite. If you should ever need to contact us, just say the word "cummunicare" and we'll be able to talk briefly."

Captain Dubois accepted the crystal and nodded. "Maybe, once you've completed your task and are safe, you could let me know?"

"We will," Kristen replied.

"Kristen, we have to go," Tangus said as he took Kristen's arm to lead her out of the room behind the captain and Mr. Krist with Jennifer, Safire, and Euranna following closely behind.

Kristen whispered, "I'm going to miss those two as well as this ship."

"As are we all, sweetheart," Tangus whispered back.

As they came out of the captain's cabin, they looked upon a virtual sea of men. As one, all the men parted to present an aisle from the wheelhouse to the gangplank. Lt. Farnsworth, above on the quarterdeck, shouted, "Boatswain! Pipe if you please!" Immediately a shrill whistle called out and the crew stood at attention. The captain smiled and said, "You've earned this." As the party started to the waiting gangplank, the crew presented arms. After boarding the waiting boat to be rowed ashore, Lt. Farnsworth shouted, "Man the rails!" then "Hip! Hip! Hooray!" to which the crew lining the side of the ship responded three times.

On shore everyone checked their horses and then saddled them. Christian would ride on Windrunner behind Euranna until they reached Altheros where they would buy him a horse, saddle, bridle, and blanket of his own. Before riding off the beach, they each turned their horses around to look at the *Freedom Wind*. The captain was standing on the quarterdeck with Mr. Krist and Lt. Farnsworth at her side. She glanced over at them and saluted before returning her attention to the running of her ship. Turning their horses to begin an easy gallop to Altheros, they could clearly hear the captain as she shouted orders. "Recover the boats, Mr. Farnsworth." "Hoist the gangplank!" "All hands, prepare to make sail!" "Mr. Krist, weigh anchor if you please." She and Mr. Krist could still be heard issuing orders as Tangus, Kristen and the others breeched a small hill and rode down the other side.

In a space deep within the *Freedom Wind*, a space few crew bothered to go, a man sat hunched over a small communication crystal lying in the palm of his hand. Whispering the word "sermo", he waited for a response. The crystal brightened and a voice said *"Report!"*

"Mordecai, they have left the ship," The man said. "The nearest city is Altheros, so I believe that is where they are going."

"Still the five of them?" Mordecai asked.

"No, wizard," the man said. "One of the ship's marines has joined them. He has a very formidable presence."

"*Very well, your services are no longer required. Make sure you immediately throw the crystal into the sea. Your payment waits in Palisade Crest.*" The crystal then went dormant.

The man looked at the crystal. He would throw it into the sea as instructed. It was incriminating evidence that would get him arrested and tossed into the brig. He then decided he didn't want to be on the ship when it docked at Palisade Crest because he suspected payment was probably going to be the end of an assassin's blade.

In InnisRos, Mordecai leaned back in his padded chair and took a sip of wine. Amberley was still sleeping in his bed. As he admired the curves of her body underneath the bedding, he began to rethink his approach to capturing the empath. "Maybe I've been going about this all wrong. Elanesse is a very large city, and the bond between the empath and that priestess Kristen is strong. No, I shouldn't be trying to kill the priestess and those she travels with, but instead have them followed. They'll lead me right to the child."

Mordecai reached into his robe and withdrew another crystal. Laying it on the table next to him, he cleared his mind and then commanded the magic within. "Nightshade," he said.

"*Yes.*"

"Where are you?" Mordecai asked.

"*Where do you wish me to be?*"

Mordecai sighed. This demon assassin he had called up from the abyss was the very best, but communication with the killer was never easy. "There has been a change in plans. I no longer wish you to kill the targets, at least not until after they have led you to the empath. Go to Elanesse and wait. When the empath has been released from the protection of the stasis magic, take it. You may kill the others at your own discretion, but safely acquire the child and bring her to me. Do you understand?"

THE SALVATION OF INNOCENCE

"We have an agreement so it shall be as you say. I will contact you when I have the empath," the voice replied through the crystal.

Mordecai broke contact. "I need a backup plan," he said to himself.

Tangus estimated it was approximately fifty miles from the sea shore to Altheros. He thought if they pushed the horses they should be able cover the distance and arrive by midnight, but only if they rode straight through without stopping for any length of time. Since they would be traveling inland along the shore of the Pantera River, the terrain shouldn't be too much of a problem for the horses even at the pace Tangus was going to demand. As for Romulus and Bitts, it will be a hard run, but nothing they haven't done before.

Reigning in Smoke, Tangus waited while everyone gathered around. It was cold, the exhaled breaths of the horses could be seen as they snorted, pawing the ground. Each, after having been restrained on the ship for so long, was eager to run, especially Tangus, Jennifer, and Safire's mustangs. Looking at Windrunner, Tangus saw an immediate problem. Windrunner was built for speed, and his rider, Euranna, was very petite. Could Windrunner maintain the speed Tangus was going to set with Christian also on his back?

"Altheros is about fifty miles east up the Pantera River," Tangus said. "I want to try and get there by midnight, which shouldn't be a problem for the horses. However, I think we need to make one adjustment. Kristen, do you think Arbellason will carry Christian? You can ride with me on Smoke."

Kristen smiled and patted Arbellason on the neck. "He'll do anything for me, won't you boy. Husband, I have him eating out of the palm of my hand."

Safire chuckled, "Kristen, you would have most males eating out of the palm of your hand if you so desired." She then looked pointedly at Tangus.

"I'm married to her, what would you have me do?" Tangus replied in his defense, then just sat on Smoke, hands gripping the saddle horn as he waited for everyone one to quiet down. Sometimes mirth was overrated, especially at his expense.

"Christian, when was the last time you rode a horse for any period of time?" Tangus asked.

"Probably about five years. That's how long I called the *Freedom Wind* home. But I've ridden whenever I was on leave or she was in port. Prior to that I spent time campaigning on horseback. I know what you're thinking, and you're right. I'm going to have a sore backside come the morning," Christian replied.

"I know what that feels like, Christian. I have a cure for it," Kristen said.

"Thank you, madam."

Tangus nodded. "Tomorrow we'll resupply and buy you a horse."

Christian patted his moneybag as he dismounted from behind Euranna. "Thanks for the offer, Tangus, but I had a lot of back pay coming to me. I thought Mr. Berry was going to have a fit as he was counting it out."

Kristen demeanor suddenly changed as she was helped up onto Smoke by Tangus. "We can't afford to stay long. When we were on the ship, we had no control over how quickly we traveled, but now we do. Tangus, we need to get to Elanesse as soon as we can."

"I know sweetheart. We all know," Tangus said, holding her close in front of him as he grabbed the reins. "But I want to give my friends at least one day to meet with us. It's a long trip from Calamity to Altheros. Believe me, when we're engaged in the battle for Emmy, we're going to be thankful we waited for them."

After Christian had settled on the back of Arbellason, Tangus nodded. "Let's ride!"

The trip to Altheros was uneventful and proceeded as Tangus had hoped. It was an hour before midnight when they stopped on the outskirts of the city at a tavern with rooms for rent above it. Tangus dismounted with the others after first helping Kristen down. As expected, Christian got off Arbellason stiffly, rubbing his backside with one hand as he led the big warhorse into a nearby stable.

Tangus, petting Smoke's forehead, said, "Everybody listen up. I know I don't have to tell you this, Christian, but everyone else, this isn't InnisRos. We certainly have our share of pickpockets, cutthroats, and thieves over there, but not even close to the extent we'll find here on the mainland. The cities are particularly dangerous if you're caught in the wrong part of town. Until you've had a chance to adjust your thinking, and subsequent view of your surroundings, I don't want anyone out alone. We won't be leaving until morning after next, so I'd prefer you not wander into the city proper. We've got a long road ahead so rest up. This might be the real last chance we get. Christian, you're more familiar with the mainland, does that about sum it up?"

Christian agreed, "Certainly, sir! You very accurately stated the potential risks. For the uninitiated, caution is the best course of action."

"Understand Jennifer and Safire?" Tangus asked.

"What about Euranna?" Safire queried.

"Yeah, Dad, why single Safire and me out? We like the bad kids or something?" Jennifer chimed in.

"Speak for yourself, Jennifer. I'm at least as old as Tangus," Safire countered.

Tangus sighed. "I brought this on myself. Why do I keep doing that?" he thought to himself. Out loud, "Do you understand, Euranna?"

"No way am I going into the city by myself, Tangus." Euranna replied shaking her head.

Tangus nodded, hoping that was the end of Jennifer and Safire's quipping. "Very good," he said. "All of you please rub the horses down and see to it they get hay, and feed if you can find any. I'll settle with the tavern owner. Kristen, let's go in and arrange for food and a warm place to sleep for everybody. Christian, let's talk a little later." Romulus and Bitts lead the way as Tangus and Kristen walked hand in hand into the tavern. A few moments later several drunken patrons stumbled out mumbling something about a "damn big wolf".

Inside Tangus and Kristen were apologizing profusely to the tavern owner for running out all of the paying customers. They had gotten so used to the big wolf and elven dog being around they sometimes forgot the impact the two made on the unwary.

"That's all right, sir. I was about to run them out and back to their families anyway," the tavern owner remarked.

"You're sure?" Tangus asked.

Nodding to once again assure Tangus, the tavern owner said, "Because of the lateness of the hour, I assume you'll require a room to rent. How else may I help you?"

"Actually we'll need food enough for six as well as our two companions lying down over there by the fireplace. We also need an equal number of warm beds if they are to be had. And we're stabling five horses outside," Tangus said.

"Let me get the wife going on some stew and fresh baked bread. I have raw meat for your four-legged friends. There's plenty of hay in the stable and I'll bring out some feed. If you and the missus would have a table, I'll start seeing to everything."

"That's very kind of you," Kristen said. "Can I help your wife with anything? It's late and I'm afraid we might be overwhelming your family."

The tavern owner shook his head. "No ma'am. You're guests in my establishment. Sit down and enjoy the fire. Oh and sir, you might want to move a couple of tables together for your friends. My name's Jackson, by the way. My wife will be serving you. Her name is Matilda."

"It's a pleasure to meet you Jackson. I'm Kristen and this is my husband Tangus. We'll make introductions with the others when they are done bedding down the horses for the night. How much do we owe you?"

"We'll settle up before you leave. Offhand I think probably five gold pieces per night total which includes food and water. Stronger drinks will be an additional charge," Jackson replied.

"That will be fine, Jackson," Tangus said.

"Then if you'll excuse me."

A couple of hours later everyone but Tangus and Christian had retired to their rooms for the night. Bitts was snoring under the table. Tangus, after clearing away dishes and mugs, reached down and brought up his backpack. Reaching inside he brought out a small rolled tapestry. It gleamed with powerful magic. Spreading it out revealed a map of the entire mainland in astonishing detail.

"Tangus," Christian said as his breath caught, "that's beautiful! I've seen nice maps, both land and nautical, but none as incredible as this."

"It better be! It cost me a small fortune…more than everything else I own combined. My days as a mercenary were at times extremely profitable which made it possible for me to purchase it. This map is solid gold to a ranger. The magic not only keeps it pristine, but also reflects the mainland in real time. Everything that happens to change the landscape is also documented on this map. If a volcano were to erupt destroying a mountain, this would show it as it happens. I've seen a small town drop into a crevice caused by an earthquake. This map no longer shows that town. And watch this." Tangus took out a small wand and laid the tip of it on Altheros. Instantly the whole city grew until it was the size of the entire map showing buildings, streets, the harbor, even parks and cemeteries.

"Extraordinary!" Christian gasped.

"I believe it's the only one of its kind. I didn't have much use for it on InnisRos. Obviously things have changed. Have you ever been to Altheros?" Tangus asked.

Christian shook his head. "I wish I could say I have. But this isn't a deep water port as you know, so I never had occasion to visit while assigned to the *Freedom Wind*. The rest of my soldiering days were spent farther north."

"Neither have I." Tangus said. "I've been this far south but more inland. As you know I'm expecting some friends to meet us here, at least I hope they show. Being unfamiliar with Altheros, however, I wasn't sure where to tell them to meet us. Poor planning, I know. So now I need to figure out the most likely place to meet them. Looking at the city, do you have an opinion?"

Christian turned his attention to the map and shook his head. "I still can't believe this map!" he said. "Let's see...I think our best bet would be to circle around and intersect the north road going into the city. If they have not already arrived, this is the road they have to come south on. If they are here, my bet is they will be in the northern part of the city. Either way I think that's our best chance."

Tangus studied the map. "Agreed," he said. "Rather obvious, I suppose. Now the trip...we need to go from here," Tangus said as he pointed to Altheros on the map, "to here." pointing to Elanesse. "It looks like we should take the Pantera River to Ordenskyr and then pick up the Alpine going north. We turn east and go through this pass, Knights Lament, in the Olympus Mountains and then over to Ascension. The only problem I have is that I've gone up the Pantera aboard a barge before. It takes a long time pulling those things up-river. It's not like they handle barges on InnisRos."

"Oh? How do they handle barges on InnisRos?" Christian asked.

"You wouldn't believe it. They use magic to...never mind. The point being it would probably take less time if we travel across land," Tangus replied. "We'll follow the river all the way to Ordenskyr."

Christian studied the map. "I don't see anything wrong with your route. Once we get to Ordenskyr the rest of the trip will be on established trade roads which are generally safer, better maintained, and will have places to stop and rest so we can get in out of the cold, particularly in the mountains. Yes, I think that will work."

Tangus, still studying the course he just proposed to Christian on his map, said, "My friends, if they come, are more attuned to this landscape, so I'll go over this with them and see what they think, but it looks to be the best approach. I've spent a lot of time studying this on the way over from InnisRos, but wanted to get the opinion of a seasoned campaigner. Thanks." Tangus yawned. "Let's go upstairs and get a few hours of rest. You and I are getting up early to buy supplies and you a horse. I want to be on the northern side of the city by mid-morning."

The next morning the four ladies, with Romulus trailing behind, came down the stairs from their rooms to the main tavern area. There were no customers, nor did they find Tangus or Christian. Jackson was standing behind the bar inventorying his bottles of alcohol. "Good morning!" he called to them pleasantly.

"Good morning, Jackson," Kristen responded. "Have you seen Tangus or Christian?"

"They were up and gone early, probably about three hours ago," Jackson answered. "Tangus didn't want you awakened and he told me to make sure you and your friends had a hearty breakfast. You know your husband is a good man, gave me twenty gold pieces for a five gold piece bill. He also told me to close the tavern and take Matilda somewhere nice today. Yes madam, a good man. Please, be seated. We'll have your breakfast out in a little bit."

Kristen smiled, "Yes he is. Thank you, Jackson." Turning to Jennifer, Safire, and Euranna, "Well ladies, it would appear we're on our own for the moment. Shall we?" she said pointing to a waiting table.

Tangus, Christian, and Bitts walked into the tavern not long after breakfast had been served.

"I can't believe you didn't buy that stallion, Christian," Tangus was saying, "a beautiful horse! Powerful...he looked like he could travel all day without breaking a sweat! But instead you bought a mare. I still don't understand."

"She's a Shire, one of the finest breeds of horse one could find anywhere, in my humble opinion. They have wonderful discipline, speed, stamina, and the smell of blood or the sight of monsters will not spook them. And at eighteen hands, she's bigger than most,' Christian replied. "Besides, the stallion you liked so much was a bit too jumpy for my taste."

"I'm not arguing with your reasoning, but I'm a pretty good evaluator of horses myself. The stallion would have been great, especially considering he would have cost about one half of what you paid for Penny," Tangus argued.

"You're probably right, Tangus, but I wanted to go with a proven commodity. All the horses I've had during campaigns were Shires. Penny was the only one in the stable. She's worth twice what I paid for her," Christian countered.

"So you bought a horse," Euranna said as the two came over and sat down on offered chairs. Tangus kissed Kristen while Christian grabbed Euranna's hand under the table.

Tangus nodded. "Yes, as well as more supplies and a couple of packhorses. They'll slow us down a little but we need them. As I was out with Christian I felt a hint of snow in the air. We need to leave as soon as possible. I don't want to get caught out in the open in a snowstorm."

"What about your friends?" Kristen asked.

"As soon as you're done with your breakfast we're going to go and wait for them at the northern edge of the city. If they have not arrived by dawn tomorrow, we're leaving. I'll not delay any longer than that," Tangus said.

Kristen pushed her plate away. "I'm ready to go now," she said. "We've already waited too long as far as I'm concerned. Every minute puts Emmy in that much more danger."

Jennifer, Safire, and Euranna also had their fill of food and stopped eating as well. Christian, however, finished up what Euranna had left behind. Taking a mouthful, he suddenly noticed that all talking had ceased and everyone was staring at him. "Oh! I am so sorry! I don't know what came over me! Old habits, I guess. Marines on campaign eat as much as they can when they can because they never know when they'll have a chance to eat again."

Euranna punched Christian in the arm. "You're just like Romulus and Bitts!"

Christian was still blushing as everyone got up from the table, smiling at his discomfort. Jackson and Matilda came over with a large sack. "I've made some food for you to take on the road. Just heat it up over a fire," Matilda said.

Tangus shook hands with Jackson. "Remember, someplace nice."

"I know just the place," Jackson replied grinning.

By noon they were on the northern side of Altheros. Tangus, Jennifer, and Bitts stayed in a small copse of trees directly beside the main road going into the city, while the rest decided to wait in the relative comfort of a warm inn just on the outskirts.

It was late afternoon when Tangus spied a couple of familiar figures on horseback coming down the road. With them were two others, one an elf, though large in stature, and the other a dwarf. Following the dwarf was a scraggly looking dog, barking at the dwarf's heels while the dwarf was desperately trying to kick it. Fortunately for the dog, the dwarf's leg was too short to reach it from the back of the horse he was riding. The dwarf could be heard yelling, "Get away you mangy, dim-witted excuse for a dog before I come down there and put you in my supper pot!"

"Dad, please tell me those aren't your friends," Jennifer said.

"Girl, I wish I could."

In Elanesse, Sergeant Warfel stuck his head into Lieutenant Arnish's tent. The lieutenant was eating breakfast. "What is it, Warfel?" he asked.

"Sir, I just completed morning roll. Another man is missing," Sergeant Warfel replied.

"So? These prospectors can all leave as far as I'm concerned," Lieutenant Arnish said without looking up from his breakfast.

"But Lieutenant, this time it's one of our own men."

Lieutenant Arnish stopped eating and glanced at his second-in-command. "Come in sergeant. I think it's time to try and figure out what's happening."

As Sergeant Warfel took a seat and started to stare at the food on the table, the lieutenant waved his hand over his breakfast. "Eat what you want, Warfel," he said with resignation.

In a small underground room in Elanesse, four figures stood in front of the stasis field containing Emmy. Luminista pointed to a man dressed in a ragtag uniform that had seen better days. "Touch the light!" she commanded. "Yes mistress," he replied woodenly.

As expected, there was a terrible pain-filled scream as the man disintegrated. The light emanating from the stasis field dimmed. "Yes! This is working quite nicely," Lukas said.

CHAPTER 10

*The greatest transgression is treason against friend or country.
The price a traitor pays is the loss of all identity.*

— BOOK OF THE UNVEILED

ON INNISROS FATHER Goram was paging through a script of ancient writings that astonishingly had passages about the empath. This particular manuscript had just been brought to Father Goram's attention by Autumn, who found it in a long abandoned wing of the monastery. Titled '*Magical Properties and Its Effects on the Planes*', it was placed there by one of his predecessors, mixed in with other manuscripts that were either nonsensical or non-relevant, such as outlandish prophecy's of long dead clerics and autobiographies of those same long dead clerics. But this manuscript, written over two-thousand years ago, made several references to the empath and the Svartalfheim, the plane of the dark elves.

If what was written could be taken as fact, and Father Goram was very skeptical on this point, when the empath's pure white magic is mixed with the strong dark magic of the Svartalfheim, there would be a momentary outburst of pure magical energy. It would be magic with no contaminates and no limits. Anyone able to control that brief explosion of magic would have instant access to unlimited power which would magnify astronomically any spell cast. There may only be time to wield the magic once, but with careful planning a wizard could conceivably make himself ruler over all the Svartalfheim. With control of the dark elf armies, Aster would certainly be threatened. With the combined armies of both the Svartalfheim and Aster, the Alfheim itself could become a target.

As he continued to read the manuscript, Father Goram came upon a passage that made his blood turn cold. *'The release of empath power in the Svartalfheim will most certainly be fatal to the empath as well as all in the bloodline.'*

The manuscript slipped from his hands. "By the gods!" he thought. "If this is true, then not only would Emmy be destroyed, but also Kristen…and Althaya. They are of the same blood. There's even more at stake than we could possibly have imagined!"

Picking up the manuscript, Father Goram wondered if anyone else had access to this information. There was probably at least one copy, almost certainly the original, in the Royal Library. As he left the deserted wing, Father Goram decided to travel to Taranthi and visit the Royal Library to find out. As valuable as these works are, they must all be destroyed to prevent that which was described within its pages from falling into the wrong hands.

When Father Goram walked into his apartment, a servant was straightening up. Father Goram didn't particularly care about the condition of his living quarters, especially after the death of his wife, Mary McKenna, all those years ago. Vayl had made arrangements to have someone clean up after Father Goram once a week. As it turned out, this didn't amount to much work since Father Goram very rarely stayed in his apartment except to sleep on the sofa in the main room. He had not slept in his bed since his wife died in it.

"Good afternoon, how are you today?" Father Goram asked.

The young female elf was doing light dusting and had been taken by surprise. She hardly ever had any interaction with the priest and was unsure as to the proper respect that should be shown. Vayl never really said anything about it. Straightening, she turned towards Father Goram and bowed slightly. "My Lord," she said.

"Please Miss…I'm sorry, what is your name?"

"Sandis, my Lord."

Father Goram shook his head, mentally lambasting himself. He'd seen her before and he should have remembered her name. "As I was beginning to say, please don't do that. None of my priests, me included, require such formality. If you're at the Queen's court I would recommend it, but not here. I don't need your services anymore today. Go out and have some fun."

"As you wish, Father," Sandis replied. As she turned to leave, Father Goram stopped her and gave her several gold pieces. "A little encouragement," he said.

Sandis smiled. "Yes, I think a little shopping is called for! Thank you, Father!" Before she knew what she was doing, she ran up and kissed him on the cheek.

Blushing, Father Goram smiled. "Yes, well, off with you now," he said.

As the youngster was closing the apartment door behind her, Father Goram paused, momentarily thinking about all the times Mary McKenna gave him a quick peck on the cheek. He thought that, as much as he loved her even still, he must move on. He was tired of living alone. Sighing wistfully, he walked over to the fireplace and stoked it to take the chill off. Sitting in a chair, Father Goram poured himself a glass of wine from the decanter on the table next to him. Taking a sip, he waited for the flames to fully establish themselves. When they did he took the manuscript and threw it in the fire.

Father Goram was awakened by an insistent knock on his apartment door. He had fallen asleep in the chair. The fire still had some burning embers left, so Father Goram estimated he had been asleep about three hours. Looking over at the bottle of wine, he saw that about half of it was gone. "Be right there!" he called out. Before going to see who was at the door he put a couple of logs into the fireplace.

On the other side of the door was Vayl. Standing beside him was Rhovalee, the monastery's messenger dragon keeper. Both were looking very worried.

"Please come in gentlemen," Father Goram said. "Would you like a glass of wine? Or perhaps you would prefer something stronger."

Both men just stared. Father Goram nodded, "Something stronger it is, then. Have a seat while I get you two a glass of whiskey." Both settled in the two chairs facing the fireplace. Rhovalee was nervously bouncing a knee while Vayl was tapping the table with his fingers. Handing them their glasses, Father Goram decided against the sofa and grabbed a chair from the formal dining room and put it beside them. Sitting down, he asked, "What's going on?"

Each man drained their glasses. Rhovalee and Vayl looked at each other and then Vayl looked at Father Goram. "We have a problem, Horatio."

"I can see that from the look on your face, Vayl. And since you dragged our dragon-keeper along, who looks absolutely horrified, I can only deduce it involves dragons. The floor's yours."

"Early this morning we discovered that one of our messenger dragons had gone missing," Vayl said. "Rhovalee here keeps close tabs on all our dragons. He knows at all times which dragons have gone where. Since yesterday's head count, one disappeared. And before you ask, there's no chance it was somehow overlooked."

"Is that true, Rhovalee?" Father Goram asked.

"Oh yes, Father!" Rhovalee exclaimed. "As Master Vayl said, there's not a dragon in our stables I don't know the whereabouts of at all times. Every dragon taking flight and every message sent goes through me. Frances, that's the name of the missing dragon, vanished and I have no explanation."

"You've talked to your assistants?" Father Goram asked.

"All have been interviewed, Horatio. I truth-checked each man myself," Vayl said.

Father Goram shook his head. "That can be countered if you know the right spell."

"I know, Horatio. I don't think any of Rhovalee's assistants are powerful sorcerer's incognito, though. Anyway, we'd just begun our investigation when Francis turned up about an hour ago."

"So he's not missing after all."

"He's dead, Horatio, his body found by poachers. It was only by luck that our own rangers caught them before they had a chance to dismember the corpse and put the parts on the black market. From where Francis was, we think he was heading back from the capital. We believe he was sent with a message early this morning. Though we don't have that message, we do have the reply." Vayl handed over a message scroll to Father Goram.

> *"I have booked passage on the Sea Wyvern to the mainland. The ship is leaving three days hence. Be on it. The captain has your payment of 5,000 gold. Hire however many men you need and locate the empath on the mainland. I will give you further instructions at that time."*

Father Goram's paused, thinking, "This is very troubling in light of what I just learned. Someone on InnisRos, someone powerful and wealthy, wants the empath. If they've read the same passages from another manuscript, they'll want to take Emmy to the Svartalfheim."

"Horatio, are you still with us?" Vayl asked, bringing Father Goram back into the conversation.

"Yes, yes, my boy. Please go on."

Vayl nodded. "More bad news, I'm afraid. Autumn is missing. I knew she would want to be in this discussion so I tried to locate her, but she's nowhere to be found. I checked her quarters and some of her clothes are missing, like she packed in a hurry. She hasn't been seen since early this morning."

Father Goram looked at Vayl. "You think Autumn is a traitor? Impossible! I've known her since she was a child. She's like a daughter to me, Vayl. You know that. And she loves Kristen like a little sister. No, she would never do this. No. Not her," Father Goram said as he shook his head.

"I don't know what else to say, Horatio. I can't explain her packing up and suddenly leaving. She has too many duties here to just disappear without so much as a 'by your leave'," Vayl replied. "I don't want to believe it either, but what other explanation is there? It just seems like too much of a coincidence."

As Vayl continued talking Father Goram wondered. "There has to be something else going on that I'm not seeing. Autumn was the one who brought the manuscript to my attention. Why would she do that if she was working for someone who wanted the empath, especially knowing as do I the consequences if the empath is taken across to the Svartalfheim?"

"...but all the evidence seems to be pointing at her," Vayl finished.

Returning his attention to Vayl, Father Goram said, "But if she got the message, Vayl, why would she leave it behind. It's rather damning evidence don't you think? It makes no sense, none at all. I want to question the poachers."

Vayl suddenly looked uncomfortable. Shaking his head he said, "I'm afraid they all resisted. They're dead."

"Then take me to their bodies so I can dead speak them," Father Goram demanded.

"I've already done that, Horatio," Vayl responded apprehensively. "They didn't know anything except they saw an opportunity to butcher a messenger dragon and did so. There was no hint that someone else was with them, though one did think he saw someone in the brush as they were cutting the dragon up. It was about then our rangers appeared." Vayl paused to take a breath before continuing. "It looks like Autumn lay in wait knowing the dragon's probable return flight path and killed it herself. After all, she wouldn't want the dragon to show up back at the monastery, particularly after it went missing. No doubt it would be easier to just pretend ignorance at its disappearance, who would suspect her? The poachers probably saw the dragon go down, saw an opportunity, surprised her, and caused her to run, leaving the message behind. That chance meeting with the poachers ruined her plans. People make mistakes. Many times that's how they are caught."

Father Goram considered. "Very well, Vayl, we'll figure it out later. I assume you have already initiated a monastery-wide search for Autumn?"

"Yes Horatio. That's underway even as we speak. I also have rangers tracking south to see if they can pick up her trail to Taranthi," Vayl replied.

"I do not want her harmed, understand! I want to know why she did what she did and who was paying her," Father Goram said.

Vayl sighed. "I want those same answers."

"Thank you, Vayl. Find her for me."

Vayl nodded. "Don't worry, Horatio. We will. But if Autumn does escape us and gets to Kristen, there's no way Kristen will know Autumn's a traitor. With Kristen's complete trust, she'll have Emmy spirited away before Kristen or Tangus would even know what happened. We need to somehow get a warning to Kristen and Tangus."

"I'll take care of it, Vayl. You do what you have to do. I want a progress report in three hours," Father Goram ordered.

"As you wish, Horatio," Vayl answered as got up and left the apartment with Rhovalee trailing behind. Father Goram followed and closed the door behind them. Walking over to the chairs in front of the fireplace, he sat down and poured himself another glass of wine, lost in the dance of the fireplace flames while he thought about everything Vayl had said. He finally came to the conclusion that Autumn was innocent, silently exclaiming to the listening fire, "Autumn did not do this. She's being framed, but by who? When I find out I'm going to shred them into little pieces and let Ajax and his wolves have what's left. And if she's been hurt or killed, I'll do even worse."

Father Goram then frowned. "I need to somehow find her," he thought. "Then I need to find out who the real perpetrator is and warn Kristen."

The answer to locating Autumn suddenly came to him. "The locket Autumn's mother gave me!" Father Goram suddenly said out loud. Getting out of his chair, Father Goram rushed into his bedroom and over to a painting of Mary and Kristen hanging on the wall. Whispering a spell command word, "Ianua patescit" the picture moved out from the wall on hidden hinges. Behind the picture small double doors opened to reveal darkness. Removing a small magical ruby laden dagger from a sheath attached to his belt, he cut the palm of his hand. When his hand broke the plane of the darkness, a compartment revealed itself. Inside were Father Goram's most prized possessions, including a small glowing locket shaped like a tree with leaves at the base of the trunk, a common representation of the autumn season. Withdrawing the locket, Father Goram rubbed a finger across it. It was warm. Autumn was still alive. He commanded his secret compartment to close and went into the main sitting area. Sitting down, Father Goram said out loud, "Let's see where you are, my dear."

※

Autumn awoke in pain. She was tied to a post, naked, in a small rock and log hovel. Her clothes, now barely recognizable tatters, had been stripped from her body and were lying in a far corner. Her head throbbed from the beating she had taken. Each breath was agony, ribs had been broken. A small pool of blood was spreading at her feet as several knife wounds bled. Slowly her memories started to come back to her.

The day had started early as she led five rangers on horseback into the surrounding forest to scout for what Vayl told her were missing children. He said her presence was necessary in case the healing spells of a priestess were required. Several miles out of Calmacil Clearing, she felt the sting of an arrow as it grazed her thigh. Looking back at the rangers, they had all stopped and were smiling. When she tried to ask them what had happened, the words would not come out. The last thing she remembered was her vision graying and the ground rushing up to meet her as she fell from her horse. When she awoke, the rangers were brutalizing her, using their fists and knives to savage her body. She had already been stripped of all her clothes and belongings, including several magical items that would have allowed her to fight back. She was powerless. After what seemed like an eternity, the beating and cutting was soon replaced by something even more sinister. The ropes holding her against the post were removed and she was roughly thrown to the ground. Her head slammed into the hard-packed soil which hammered her into merciful oblivion.

As she thought about what had happened to her, she began to pray to Althaya for death. She did not want to live with the humiliation. As she once again began to drift into unconsciousness, she hoped her supplication to Althaya would be answered.

Autumn was jerked awake by a bucket of freezing water thrown on her. She had been retied to the post. Shivering uncontrollably, she looked up to see two dirty human rogues grinning as they studied her naked body. These were not the rangers who had drugged, beaten, and raped her earlier this morning.

"What have we got here? Oh missy, we're going to have so much fun. Now my friend here says we should kill you first, but I'm a bit more discerning then he. I guess it doesn't really matter though, does it, at least not for you."

The rogue approached. His breath stank and he had terrible body order. He only had a few teeth left and those were black and rotting. His tongue was sticking out as he licked his lips. The thought of either man's mouth on any part of her body disgusted her. So much so that she wished that they would indeed kill her first as the second man had suggested.

"SUCCENDENT IN INFERNUM!"

The rogue nearest Autumn was suddenly standing in the middle of a column of ghostly searing fire. She knew the spell well, *Spiritstrike*. She also recognized the voice commanding it, Father Goram. She watched as the second man was attacked and quickly dismembered by a huge dire wolf. Ajax! Four big yet smaller dire wolves ran to create an impenetrable wall of snarling fur around Autumn. The second man was killed quickly by Ajax. The first, however, was still alive after the *Spiritstrike* spell ended, though he was screaming in terrible agony.

"SUCCENDENT IN INFERNUM!"

It was another *Spiritstrike*. Autumn heard the anger in Father Goram's voice. The only mercy being offered by the priest was death. After a few seconds the screaming rogue quieted as he finally succumbed to the fire. Walking quickly to Autumn, Father Goram used a knife to cut her bonds. As she fell, he grabbed her and gently laid her down on the ground. Using clerical spells, he healed Autumn's physical wounds. Autumn felt the pain slip away, but she was still freezing from the cold. Father Goram then took his cloak and wrapped her in it. Whispering another spell, the area around both warmed up. Lifting Autumn, Father Goram carried her over to the burned man and shoved him with his boot. Turning to Ajax, he said sharply, "You know what to do." Ajax looked over his shoulder and barked a couple of times. The other wolves barked once in acknowledgement and dragged the two corpses out and away from the shack. Ajax then looked up at Father Goram who nodded. The three walked out into the late afternoon sunlight, heading for Ajax's den. Autumn, in Father Goram's strong arms, lost consciousness again.

Vayl, with four of the five rangers who assaulted Autumn earlier in the morning, and two clerics, dismounted his horse in front of the small shack. The ranger left behind as a guard was slumped against the wall, his throat cut so deep it nearly decapitated him. Stepping inside, he saw plenty of blood on the walls near the door as well as burn marks in the hard soil that served as the floor. The ropes that were holding Autumn were cut and lying at the base of a post. There was a lot of blood there as well. Wondering what happen, Vayl bent down and ran his hand over the burned soil. He knew immediately a *Spiritstrike* had been cast. "Damn!" he shouted. "Horatio found her!" Getting up, he walked out of the shack. "Track the priest! I want to know where he took the girl!" As the rangers turned to do his bidding, he called out, "Wait!"

and reluctantly said, "I want them both killed when you find them." As one his rangers saluted and disappeared into the woods. The clerics remained behind. "ALL OF YOU!" Vayl screamed. The two snorted in contempt, but turned their horses and followed the rangers. Vayl knew Goram had the help of Ajax's pack from the blood splatter inside the shack. There was no doubt the two were safely away and he had just sent everyone on a fool's errand, but he needed time to be alone.

Walking back into the shack, he pulled a communication crystal from out of a belt-pouch. "omilia" he said. The crystal emitted a soft glow. After a few seconds, a voice spoke through it.

"What is it, Vayl?"

"Mordecai, Goram didn't buy the cover story. He has Autumn and he'll know she was framed. He's too smart to not make the connection between me and her kidnapping. And if he knows, you can bet Kristen will soon know as well. I can't infiltrate as we planned. Tangus would probably kill me on the spot if I go over there to join them now."

"How many have you recruited?"

"I have four rangers and a couple of ambitious priests whom I don't trust. We all follow elven gods so there's no problem with Althaya or Aurora."

"Good. I've given you plenty of gold. Book passage to the mainland as soon as possible and recruit men over there. Be my army and take the empath by force."

"I do not want to kill Kristen. She's a good soul. I've known her for so long," Vayl said. "I trained her and was one of her mentors."

"Vayl, her soul may be good, but yours is not. You want the monastery? You must do this."

"Yes, I still want the monastery and will do what is necessary to attain it. But I want to change our agreement. I want you, not me, to kill Father Goram and Autumn. They cannot be allowed to remain alive, but now that they know I'm the traitor, I won't be able to get close. He's too strong for me. Neither knows about you, however," Vayl replied.

There was a pause until finally Vayl heard *"Agreed."* Contact was broken from the other side.

Father Goram, carrying the unconscious Autumn, entered Ajax's den, a spacious cavern with fresh spring water and a natural break against the wind at the entrance. Small rocks spelled with light dotted the walls, a long ago gift from Father Goram. Ajax's mate, Cassandra rushed up to Ajax and rubbed noses, then over to Father Goram. Finding a bed of straw, the priest lay Autumn down and inspected her for any wounds he did not have time to heal earlier. Several pups came up to the two and sniffed curiously. Father Goram absent-mindedly petted a few heads as he continued his examination of Autumn. Satisfied that she had no surface wounds, he gathered his will to heal her head wound. Within a few moments, she opened her eyes.

"How do you feel?" Farther Goram asked.

"Okay all things considered. Where are we?" Autumn replied.

"I've taken you to Ajax's den. There's a secret tunnel from here to my study we can use to get back." Father Goram searched Autumn's eyes. "Dear, we need to talk about what happened. Do you think you're up to it?"

Autumn gave Father Goram her arm. "Help me sit up, Horatio." With Father Goram's help, Autumn leaned her back against a wall. She closed her eyes, but when they came back open, they reflected steely determination. "I'm very tired, but I want to talk about it."

Father Goram nodded and sat down besides her, allowing her to rest her head on his shoulder. "Autumn, you were betrayed by Vayl," he said. "I know that's painful to hear, but it's the truth nevertheless."

Autumn whispered, "I know." She was sad, but not surprised.

"What happened this morning?" Father Goram asked.

"Vayl came to me and said some children were missing in the forest and he was sending a squad of rangers to search. He asked me to go along in case harm had befallen the children and they needed clerical healing. Of course I immediately agreed. When I met with the rangers, however, I didn't recognize any of them. I inquired and they told me

Vayl had recently hired them. Thinking about the children and having no reason to question Vayl's judgment in such matters, I didn't give it a second thought."

"I thought all new rangers were hired by Magdalena?" Father Goram asked.

"That's correct, Horatio. Perhaps I should have known something was up then. Now that you mention it, though, I haven't seen Magdalena for several days. She has Tangus' complete trust so I know she wouldn't just disappear. He's such a good judge of character," Autumn said.

"There are just too damn many things going on that I know nothing about! When did I lose control?" Father Goram said more to himself then Autumn.

"Horatio, when a traitor is second in command that happens. Don't be so hard on yourself over it," Autumn replied.

Father Goram nodded. "We have to find Magdalena if she's still alive. What happened next?"

Autumn looked down. "I allowed myself to get ahead of them. Pretty stupid, huh? I was looking for signs and didn't even notice they had fallen behind until I felt a sting on my left leg. An arrow had been shot at me, Horatio, a poisoned arrow. They didn't intend to kill me, at least not then. I remember losing consciousness and waking up tied to a post in the shack from which you rescued me. The two you killed, I believe, just happened to be there by circumstance and were not associated with Vayl's treachery."

"I believe that also. The ranger left as guard was dead, no doubt killed by those two rogues," Father Goram replied.

"What I don't understand, Horatio, is why the rangers didn't just kill me," Autumn said. "Why was I still living for the rogues to find?"

Father Goram thought for a moment. "At the time you may still have had value to Vayl alive, maybe a bargaining chip. There's not much I wouldn't do to get you back and he knows it."

Autumn thought about it for a moment. "A bargaining chip for what, Horatio?" she asked.

"That much I think is pretty clear. He wants the monastery. To get that, I have to be eliminated, but he's not powerful enough to do it himself, so he was going to use my feelings for you to force me into a trap. Vayl's probably working for someone powerful enough to have me removed and the monastery is his reward. My guess would be Vayl's mission is to capture Emmy for whoever has bought his loyalty. With you and me out of the way, he has a direct line to Kristen. She trusts him with her life. And she would trust him with Emmy's as well." Looking at Autumn, Father Goram said, "You recall that obscure manuscript you found yesterday with passages about the empath?"

"Yes. I didn't read much of it, but from what little I did see, I had a feeling you would want to," Autumn replied.

"Your instincts were correct," Father Goram acknowledged. "The manuscript had passages about the empath. According to the manuscript, taking an empath to the plane of the Svartalfheim will release unimaginable power that can be briefly harnessed by a sorcerer. Also within its pages are incantations that would allow a sorcerer to capture that magic. I do not know if there are more copies of the manuscript, but I'm starting to get the feeling that there are and at least one has been found and interpreted. What we are possibly seeing is a power play for the Svartalfheim. If that should be successful, not only would the empath be destroyed, but also all of the empath bloodline, at least according to the manuscript."

Father Goram could see the connections being made in Autumn's mind, and he saw her eyes widen as soon as she understood the implications. "Vayl has told someone of Emmy, someone powerful, probably a wizard. Also...by the goddess, Kristen and Althaya would be destroyed!" she whispered.

Father Goram nodded. "We can't afford to disregard the manuscript as hearsay or prophecy. We must assume it speaks to what will happen. All of a sudden Kristen getting Emmy away from whatever evil she faces on the mainland is only part of the equation. We must do our part over here to ensure Emmy is never taken to the Svartalfheim. That starts with finding out who has seen the manuscript," Father Goram said.

"And the one I gave you?" Autumn asked.

"I burned it. It had nothing else to offer about the empath. It was dangerous and would continue to be so until destroyed."

Autumn yawned as she nodded. "I need to sleep, Horatio."

Father Goram agreed. "We have a few hours. I'll wake you when it's time to go. You can sleep all day tomorrow in my apartment."

"Find Magdalena…" Autumn whispered as she fell into an exhausted sleep. Father Goram straightened her hair with his hand. "Don't worry. I will. And then I will have my vengeance," he said quietly.

※

After midnight they began the long trek back to the monastery through a series of underground tunnels. Father Goram, as he did with the wolves' den, had placed light-spelled stones in the walls at intervals to give light as well as to ensure the correct path was never lost. Items spelled with light magic would never diminish unless so wished by the spell caster, so there was no chance they would lose illumination or their way through the tunnels. The myriad of passageways between Ajax's den and Father Goram's apartment was extensive, even an experienced underground traveler, with the possible exception of a dwarf, could get lost.

Autumn, still deeply exhausted, leaned heavily on Father Goram as they moved through the tunnel system. Ajax was in the lead and two of his four wolf "honor guard" followed behind. About two hours later Autumn was sleeping in Father Goram's bed. He had covered her with a blanket and started a slow burning fire in the long unused master bedroom fireplace. Magically placing a ward around her, he slipped out and went into the main room, which had been taken over by three large dire wolves. Father Goram got them some water and fresh meat he kept for such occasions. It was not unusual for him to have wolf "guests", so he was always prepared.

After stoking the main room fireplace, he poured himself a glass of wine. By now the three wolves were lying down. There was only room for Ajax to rest in front of the warm fireplace, but the other two made themselves comfortable on thick hides scattered about the floor around the room. Father Goram pulled out a communication crystal from one of his pockets. This one was attuned to a crystal Kristen was carrying. After taking a sip of wine, he said "loguor locutis", commanding the magic of the crystal.

After a few moments, Kristen spoke through the crystal. *"Father?"*

"How are you, sweetheart?" Father Goram asked.

"We've had a few difficulties. I know the crystal drains quickly so I won't go into detail. We're at Altheros waiting for Tangus friends to get here, if they're coming that is. We leave for Elanesse tomorrow morning."

"I'm afraid I have bad news. Vayl tried to kill Autumn," Father Goram said, blunt and to the point. "It's part of a much larger game going on over here. There appears to be a movement to capture Emmy. Someone with very high connections, someone very powerful, is behind it. I do not know who as of yet. Your fears about the Alfheim, though probably correct, are not the reason someone wants Emmy, however, but rather the Svartalfheim. Kristen, there is some evidence that if they get Emmy to the Svartalfheim she will be destroyed in a powerful burst of magic. As a consequence, the Svartalfheim could come under the control of the person wielding that magic. That same evidence indicates her bloodline will be destroyed as well. That means you and Althaya."

"Father, how could Vayl…this is a lot to digest. Is Autumn alright?"

"She will be, but you would not believe what was done to her. She's going to need a long time to recover emotionally." The anger was starting to be heard in his voice, so Father Goram paused while he regained control over his emotions before continuing. "The crystal is draining quickly. Heed my words, beloved daughter. If Vayl should ever show up, he will be there to take Emmy. Have no mercy. He must be killed. I will try to see who's behind this here in InnisRos and try to stop it at its source. But you must be extra cautious. Rescue Emmy and go someplace safe, someplace where you will not be found. Trust no one. If anything should ever change, I will let you know."

"Yes father. I love you. And give Autumn my love," Kristen replied.

"Be safe, dear one," Father Goram said as he broke contact. Putting down his drained wine glass, he got up and went to his bar and poured himself a small glass of whiskey. Draining it in one gulp, he grabbed his cloak which he discarded on the couch and put it on. Ajax took that as his cue to get up from his spot by the warm fireplace. Yawning, he walked over to Father Goram. Father Goram scratched behind his ears. "Let's go find Magdalena big boy." Pointing at the other two, he said, "You two stay and guard." Ajax put emphasis on Father Goram's request with a bark of command.

With Ajax in the lead, Father Goram went into the hallway outside his apartment, quietly closing the door behind him and locking it. Looking at Ajax he said, "I guess we need to start by going to Magdalena's quarters so you can get her scent."

CHAPTER 11

The road of life is oftentimes filled with obstacles which must either be maneuvered around or avoided altogether. The secret to succeeding against these challenges is to never let them lead you to the road's end.

— BOOK OF THE UNVEILED

ELROND, MAX, AND the other two in their party suddenly stopped on the road about one-hundred yards north of where Tangus and Jennifer waited. The dwarf had finally convinced the wayward dog to abandon the chase and annoy someone else. "Well there goes my supper!" the dwarf shouted.

Wondering why his friends had stopped, Tangus and Jennifer moved out of the copse of trees and started to walk towards them. As they were walking down the road, Elrond suddenly pointed behind them and shouted, "Behind you!" At about the same time Tangus heard the sound of several horses approaching from behind. Turning, he saw a mounted patrol of the city's guard moving up the road to intersect Elrond and Max. "Please excuse us good sir and madam. City business," the leader said as the column rode past.

Tangus and Jennifer stepped aside to allow the horsemen to pass and watched as the column rode up to his friends and stopped in front of them. Looking over at Jennifer, Tangus shrugged his shoulders. "There were always certain…uhhhh…shall we say allowances one must make in order to work with them. And it looks like nothing much has changed."

Jennifer kept her attention directed at the meeting occurring ahead of them. "You mean your friends are rogues," she said.

"I wouldn't exactly call them...well yes, I guess you could say they're rogues, at least Elrond and Max are. I don't know about the other two. But honey, they're good rogues. I mean they don't rape, pillage, or steal...well, they don't rape. At least I don't think so."

"I wonder how Kristen is going to take this," Jennifer retorted. "She sets a pretty high moral standard you know."

Tangus looked over at his daughter. "And I'm morally challenged? Jennifer, I'm married to her! Of course I know!" Tangus looked back at his friends and shook his head. "She's going to kill me, isn't she?"

"Don't worry dad. I'll put in a good word for you," Jennifer said with mock encouragement.

"Gee thanks," Tangus replied grimacing. "Shall we go see what's going on?"

"Indeed we should!" Jennifer said hiding a smile.

Cautiously walking forward, Tangus and Jennifer could hear the leader of the guard patrol talking. "If it were up to me, Elrond, I'd let you in the city. But it's not up to me. Duke de Silva said you and your companions are to be arrested. Duke Redle is simply enforcing Duke de Silva's decree. You do remember Duke Redle's my boss, right?"

"C'mon, Peter, they'll never know. We've ridden a long way and could use some rest and a little drink. That's my friend there behind you," Elrond said as he pointed at Tangus and Jennifer. "You'll vouch for us, won't you, Tangus!" Elrond called.

The leader identified as Peter shouted from over his shoulder. "Please do not interfere, sir. This is Purple Cloak business."

Jennifer asked, "Who's the Purple Cloak?"

All conversation stopped and everyone looked at Tangus and Jennifer. Peter turned his horse around and went over to the pair. "Not from around here, are you," Peter said as he looked down at Jennifer from his perch on top of his large warhorse. "Madam, the Purple Cloak Mercenary Company is one of the largest mercenary companies in the realm. We keep Altheros safe for travelers such as you, as well as guard the trade routes for miles around. Duke Redle is our leader. Every man in the Company would die for him. When the Duke gives an order, it is followed. If you are friends with these miscreants, we will have our eyes on you as well."

"Hey wait a minute, Peter!" Max called. "Miscreant is a bit harsh, don't you think?"

Turning his horse back around, Peter pulled out a document and held it up for all to see. "You're probably right. But it says so right here on the arrest warrant." Unrolling the warrant, Peter studied it for a few seconds, his lips moving as he read, "Ah yes, here it is…miscreant." As Peter re-rolled the document, he looked at Elrond and Max and said, "Please don't go into the city or I will be forced to serve it."

"All we want is a drink," the dwarf said, "a glass of your finest red. Elrond's willing to pay handsomely."

Peter sighed. "I don't recognize you, good dwarf," he said, "but it was drink that got your friends banished in the first place." Redirecting his attention back to Elrond, Peter continued, "Elrond, you don't bed the high priest's daughter in a drunken stupor and expect there not to be consequences. If you go past the wall and into the city I will be forced to arrest you. You will then be escorted to the temple house where you will be held until all preparations for a wedding have been made. Then you will be forced to marry that young woman who, as I understand it, is still pining away for you. Sure as hell can't understand it, but she is."

Elrond held up his hands. "That's a sentence I don't really want to serve. We'll respect the warrant, Peter."

"Thank you." Turning his horse, Peter and his men rode back into the city.

"I just don't understand," Max said shaking his head.

Elrond looked over. "What?"

"Why women find you so attractive and don't even bat an eye at me," Max replied.

Jennifer looked at her father and sadly shook her head. Tangus wouldn't meet his daughter's gaze.

THE SALVATION OF INNOCENCE

As Tangus renewed old friendships, and began new ones, Jennifer studied the four strangers. The one called Elrond was a big half-elf. He was ruggedly handsome and carried himself with confidence as well as a bit of self-importance. Dressed in gleaming chain mail, tunic, pants, and knee high boots, he had multiple weapons dispersed on his belt and a harness draped around him. The sword at his side hung in an ornate sheath. Both the sheath and sword radiated strong magic. His cloak was hooded and heavy. A staff and several wands hung from the saddle his horse, a big warhorse only a little smaller than Arbellason.

Next to Elrond was Max, a full elf on a light warhorse. Like all of his kind, he was lithe and rather small. He moved with a grace that was most uncommon, even for an elf. He was outfitted much like Elrond, except his weapons of choice were lighter to take advantage of his natural quickness and dexterity. He too had a sword that radiated strong magic.

The two behind Elrond and Max were an oddly matched pair. One, like Elrond, was also a half-elf, but bigger and huskier. Outfitted in field plate armor with a huge two-handed sword strapped behind his back, the hilt of which jutted up and over his head, and a heavy white cloak, instead of black worn by the other three, he calmly sat on his horse as Tangus, Elrond, and Max were becoming reacquainted. His horse was the largest warhorse Jennifer had ever seen, maybe nineteen hands high at the shoulder. He looked kind, but at the same time he looked very dangerous. Her father had spoken often about paladins, or knights of the realm. She wondered if he was one such, and if so, why would he align himself with Elrond and Max, two rather dubious characters?

The last of the four Jennifer scrutinized was the dwarf. She had never seen one of dwarven race before, but her father described them quite well, and she had also learned about them in her studies. Known as natural miners, their haven is below ground much as the elf's is the forest. Riding a horse that looked like a pony compared to the horse the knight was riding, he was impeccably dressed. His chain mail armor, tunic, pants, and cloak were pristine, his black beard neatly trimmed, and his long hair tied with a black ribbon behind his back. From what her father had described as well as what she had read, he was everything a dwarf was not supposed to be, at least in appearance. The huge battle axe strapped to his back and the large mace hanging from his horse's saddle bespoke of great power and strength. Jennifer wasn't even sure if she could lift the axe, let alone swing it in battle. Noticing Jennifer studying him, the dwarf smiled and tipped his head to her. Jennifer couldn't help but to shyly smile back and wave. For reasons she did not understand, if she had an uncle, she would want this dwarf to be it.

Jennifer's attention was brought back to Elrond as he said something to the knight and the dwarf. Both dismounted and shook hands with Tangus. Tangus turned and said, "Jennifer, come up here. I want you to meet my old friends."

Putting an arm around Jennifer's shoulder, Tangus said, "Jennifer, this is Elrond Silverhair and Maximillion Darkshadow." Both came up to Jennifer and shook her hand. "Are you as good with a bow as your father?" Elrond asked.

"No one is as good with the bow as my father. But I keep trying," Jennifer replied.

"Don't let her kid you, Elrond. She's awfully good," Tangus said. "She hit a dragon in flight on the way over here from InnisRos."

"That's a story I want to hear," Max said. "You look like your mother." Turning to Tangus, "How is Winnie, by the way?"

"I think she's in Palisade Crest, but I'm not really sure. We parted ways a long time ago. Neither of us was really ready for marriage at the time. The marriage gave me Jennifer and my son Lionel, but that's about all," Tangus responded. "Kristen is my soul mate. You'll meet her soon." Addressing the other two who had been politely standing in the background, Tangus said to Jennifer, "This is Lester Trueblade."

The tall half-elf bowed deeply to Jennifer. "It is a pleasure to meet you, my lady." Jennifer nodded, "For me as well, Sir Knight."

"And this is Azriel Demonspawn," Tangus went on. Azriel took a hand of Jennifer's in one of his own large callused hands and kissed the back of it. "I am grateful to make your acquaintance, young lady."

Jennifer couldn't help herself. "What kind of name is Demonspawn?" she asked.

"I made it up. It scares the peasants. BOO!" Azriel replied with a smile.

Tangus laughed. "I think we've just been called peasants, dear. The famed dwarven sense of humor I had thought I left behind. Go back and get Kristen and the others. Tell them we're going to spend the night outside the city since Elrond isn't allowed in on pain of matrimony."

"Of course father," Jennifer said as she turned to do her father's bidding.

"Looks to be a chip off the old block," Elrond said after Jennifer had moved out of hearing distance.

Tangus nodded. "She's much more than that." Tangus looked up into the sky. "The weather's not too bad yet. We need to find an inn outside the city before dark so we can rest up. I also want to talk to you about the route we're going to take to Elanesse. Your banning from the city complicates things a little."

"I know the perfect place to stay the night," Elrond offered. "It's an inn just east of the city, only about a mile away. It's called the Amare Casa Inn. Very secluded, the staff minds their own business, and the rooms are comfortable and warm. A little pricey, however, and the maitre d' expects a generous donation…"

"Amare Casa…Amare Casa…that means Love Cottage! Wait a minute!" Max shouted. "You're talking about the place you took that priest's daughter, aren't you?"

"Well…"

Max didn't give Elrond a chance to finish. "And the donation to the maitre d' is a bribe, isn't it? That didn't work too well, now did it?"

"Alright Max, now simmer down. You're scaring the natives," Elrond said.

Max scoffed. "Tangus knows all about you! As for Lester and Azriel… well I suppose they need to figure things out for themselves anyway. I can't believe you would recommend…"

Tangus interrupted. "It's better than a night out in the cold. I don't want to move my wife, daughter, and friends out of the city just so we can suffer with you if there wasn't any other choice. If this place will have us, I say let's go."

"Oh, they'll have us, Tangus. They speak the universal language," Elrond said.

"What language is that?" Lester asked.

Azriel laughed. "Why it's the language of gold, my dear boy."

Several hours later the sun was beginning to set. An entire wing of The Amare Casa Inn had been rented out compliments of Elrond. Tangus decided to provide the donation to the maitre d' since the man had grave concerns about Bitts and Romulus, which required a substantial nonrefundable down payment against the possible damage that might be caused by the two. After everyone brushed, watered, and fed their horses, taking advantage of the inn's well stocked stable, they all made their way indoors to the main dining room.

Tangus had introduced Kristen and the others to Elrond, Max, Lester, and Azriel. Christian and Lester immediately became friends and, joined by Safire and Euranna, took their own table. Jennifer sat next to the dwarf, Azriel, listening to him as he regaled her with story after story. Kristen, also at ease with the dwarf, joined Jennifer and Azriel while Tangus renewed his friendship with Elrond and Max. Bitts had lain at Tangus' feet and fell asleep. Romulus was not as calm, however. He was unsure about the newcomers, particularly the dwarf who sat next to his mistress. The huge dire wolf growled a warning when Azriel attempted to scratch him behind the ears. He finally accepted the scratch after Kristen assured him Azriel meant no harm or ill will towards her or any of her friends. As he allowed Azriel to scratch him, he extended his senses to check for himself. The dwarf did not seem to harbor any evil intent to those Romulus loved. Satisfied that Kristen was safe, Romulus shrugged off Azriel's scratching and lay down at Kristen's feet, still alert to danger.

"Alright Tangus, we're all here, so what's the story?" Max asked.

Tangus sighed. "Where do I start?"

"The short version is fine, my friend. You can fill in any gaps later," Elrond replied.

Tangus gratefully smiled and nodded. "Have you ever heard of empaths and the purge which resulted in their genocide?"

"Ancient history," Elrond said. "Supposedly it happened in Elanesse, but the stories I've come across about them and their demise were more fantasy than proven truth."

"They are not fantasies, Elrond," Tangus said. "The empath did in fact exist and the purge was real. It took place about three millennia ago during Elanesse's golden age. At the time the popular belief was that the empath had the ability to control the minds and thoughts of a person. Though the basis for the purge, it was, of course, ridiculous. It's possible this fabrication was fostered for political expediency, to either eliminate a perceived threat, or divert people's minds from real issues such as poverty and racial inequality. The clerics and priests of Elanesse came together and created a magical force which, through the enchantment, was imparted into Elanesse's rangers, giving them the ability to sense and track the empath. As you know, most, though not all, rangers follow the goddess Aurora. All rangers who either did not follow, or who had denied the teachings of Aurora, made the destruction of the empath their primary mission. All empaths were eventually killed with the exception of one. Even though all the empaths except this one were destroyed, the bloodline did not die completely."

"Because of the one that survived," Max said.

"It's a bit more complicated than that, Max. Apparently the empath bloodline can skip generations." Pausing, Tangus took a drink of wine.

"The last remaining true empath, a child, is now resting in a stasis field that was spelled around her by Althaya, awaiting the time in which another with the blood, regardless of how diluted, was born. That person is Kristen."

"And this is critical because?" Max said.

"A young empath is very much impacted by emotion. A young empath needs to be bonded to an adult with empath blood to help protect and shield the child from emotions of hate. Young empath's are completely unequipped to handle strong emotions. If they are not bonded to another, their hearts can actually be stopped by such raw passion. Kristen has bonded with this last empath, essentially taking the place of the empath's mother. Her name is Emmy and she's about seven years old. Both Kristen and I consider her our daughter, which gives you some idea how important she is to the both of us." Tangus looked at his friends. "The stasis field now protecting her in Elanesse is starting to fail. We know this through Kristen's bond with Emmy. We also know there are forces gathering in Elanesse who want to either kill or capture Emmy. That's why it's so important we get to her as soon as possible."

Max whistled. "Is that it?"

Tangus shook his head. "No. I haven't told you the most important part. The empath, and my wife to a lesser extent, have the same blood flowing through her as does Althaya."

This time it was Elrond's turn to whistle. "You mean Kristen and Emmy are goddesses?"

"No.....not at all. They're as mortal as you and I, though the empath's ability to heal is like no other. What makes the empath so important is that, if she is destroyed or removed from this world, the ability of clerics to heal magically is forever lost. The empath serves as the bridge between all healing power and its ability to interact within this world."

Elrond and Max stared at Tangus. Both knew the impact this would have if what Tangus had just told them were true. Both had experienced the warmth and relief that came with magical healing. Both knew that they would have long been dead if not for the succor provided by this all-important magic. It's imperative considering their line of work as mercenaries and treasure hunters.

"Is there any chance you are mistaken?" Elrond asked.

"No chance whatsoever. Kristen is an orphan, born by a mother unknown and put into an orphanage in Ascension when she was only a babe. Althaya ordered a priest on InnisRos, Father Goram, who is now her foster father and my father-in-law, to arrange she be brought to InnisRos. Why? Because Kristen is the first to have empath blood flowing through her veins born in over three thousand years. Kristen is the only person now alive who can bond with Emmy. What I just explained about healing magic and the empath's impact on it, as well as her relationship with Althaya and my wife, came from Althaya herself."

"I would think Althaya would have every one of her clergy and all her followers drop everything and help since this is so important," Max said.

"Yes, except for one thing. Althaya doesn't know who to depend upon," Tangus replied. "The goddess I follow, Aurora, was betrayed by many of her rangers during the purge, a lesson she will never forget. Aurora is closely aligned with Althaya. I'm sure what happened during the purge gave both goddesses reason to pause, as well as it gave them some severe trust issues. We all see them as immortal and very powerful, but one thing that not too many people understand is there are limits to even what they can do. They are not omnipotent, and nothing trumps a mortal's free will."

Laughter suddenly came from the table shared by Kristen, Jennifer, and Azriel. Tangus smiled. "It's good to hear Kristen laugh. The bond between her and Emmy is very strong and it wears on her. She getting better at bearing the responsibility, but I still worry."

Max laid a hand on Tangus' arm. "Rest easy, my friend. We've been through bad situations before and we've always managed to beat the odds. We will do so again."

Tangus nodded. "Thank you, Max."

"Yes, well, let's see what you have planned," Elrond said as he cleared away a place on the table.

Tangus, anticipating this, had unpacked his magical map of the mainland and had it with him. He laid it out on the table. There was a point of light at the spot on the map indicating the location of the Amare Casa Inn.

"I really should have bought that map from you before you left," Elrond said.

Tangus smiled. "You don't have enough gold to buy this map my friend."

"That's why I should have stolen it!" Max countered.

Tangus ignored Max's quip and pointed to Altheros, using his finger to follow the route as he explained. "We'll travel east along the Pantera River to Starr, at which point we cross the river to the south side for the trip into Ordenskyr. From there we go north through the Olympus Mountain foothills then turn east and go through Knight's Lament pass and over to Ascension. We'll have to go through The Hammer before we clear the pass heading for Ascension. Continuing east, we turn northeast at Silterstone for the last leg of our trip to Elanesse."

Elrond studied the map. "Max and I have been through Knight's Lament pass before. The Hammer shouldn't be a problem. It is indeed a formidable fortress, but its purpose is to protect the lands beyond from invasion. I don't think they'll consider us an invading army. But Tangus, why not just take a barge up the river to Ordenskyr instead of riding along the river?"

Tangus shook his head. "That will take too much time. You know how slow those barges are." Tangus looked at his friends. "Gentlemen, we do not know when the stasis field is going to fail. Every second we take to find Emmy could be crucial."

"What do you think we'll find in Elanesse?" Max asked.

Tangus looked at Elanesse on the map. "I'm not positive, vampyres for sure, and probably remnants of the magic created to bring the purge into existence. I'm not sure, however, how the Purge will show itself, though I think it's a possibility it could use mind control similar to what it used with the rangers to destroy the empath. Whatever we face will definitely require sacrifice. But this is probably the most important thing any one of has ever done or ever will. Emmy must be saved at all costs, and Kristen kept from harm. Those are my two primary concerns. Everything else is secondary to me, including our lives. Is that going to be a problem for either of you? If it is, you don't have to come along. I'd understand completely."

Elrond and Max looked at each other. "You're a Dagger Company brother. We'll stand with you," Max said.

"Hell, we've faced worse odds before," Elrond laughed.

Tangus didn't smile at Elrond's levity. "Somehow I don't think any of us really have," he said.

Later that night Tangus, Kristen, Jennifer, Safire, Euranna, and Christian met in Tangus and Kristen's second-story room. The room was very spacious with several chests, a couple of desks, a large fireplace, and a huge round bed. The walls were pink with a pattern of red roses. Before the fireplace was a small sofa. On tables that bracketed each side of the sofa were a dozen red roses in ornate vases. A small table in front of the fireplace contained a bottle of white wine with two stemmed crystal glasses. A vellum brochure lay on the table next to the bottle of wine.

The Rose Room
For the discerning couple.
Make your stay with us memorable
and filled with much laughter and love.
And remember, Amare! Amare! Amare!
Please enjoy this bottle of wine compliments of the owner
and staff of The Amare Casa Inn.
Long life!

As the group filed into the room, Safire whistled. "Elrond didn't spare any expense for you two, did he?"

Tangus smiled. "It's called the 'Honeymoon Suite'. Apparently Elrond has used this room before. Please find a chair." After everyone had seated themselves, Tangus asked, "So, impressions?"

"Before you start, husband, I've received some very disturbing news from my father. I didn't want to mention it earlier but it really can't wait any longer," Kristen said.

"Father Goram contacted you? How was he able to do that?" Jennifer asked.

"A communication crystal," Tangus said without taking his eyes off Kristen, immediately concerned about what Kristen was going to say next.

Kristen nodded and said without preamble, "Vayl is a traitor. He tried to kill Autumn."

"Is she okay?" Several voices asked at the same time.

"My father thinks she will be fine. He told me he believes Vayl is coming over here to take Emmy. Tangus, he said if Vayl should ever show up, kill him immediately. No mercy."

"No one threatens my family, I don't care who it is," Tangus said. His voice was hard. "As Horatio's second, Vayl knows a good deal about you and Emmy which makes him extremely dangerous. He will receive no mercy from me. Did your father say anything about his motive?"

"My father believes it is part of a larger conspiracy by persons, as yet unknown, to capture Emmy. He's going to investigate to see who might be behind it and why," Kristen replied.

Tangus thought about that for a few moments. "Good. Horatio has substantial resources at his disposal with which to work. As surprising and disturbing as the news about Vayl's attack on Autumn is, it's even more disconcerting to know there are others we know nothing about actively trying to harm Emmy. Will he keep you appraised, Kristen?"

"Yes, he said he will," Kristen replied.

"Good. How are you holding up?" Tangus asked.

"I've known Vayl all my life. It's so hard to believe and it saddens me. He was such a good person until…"

"Until he wasn't," Tangus said matter-of-factly. "To turn on those who loved him makes him a traitor doubly so. Let's table this conversation for now and continue our discussions about your impressions of our new allies. We can evaluate the repercussions of Vayl's treachery later. Right now I don't think there's any immediate danger, especially since we've been warned. So, who wants to begin?" Tangus responded.

Everyone who knew Vayl, particularly Safire, was too stunned to even begin to consider the implications. They all remained silent and in a state of shock.

"May I?" Christian asked. At Tangus' nod, Christian continued, "Lester is a former knight from Astoria, a small monastery in the Mahtan Mountains. He's quiet, humble, and polite, all the things you would expect of a knight. I did not inquire as to why he is now a member of a mercenary company, which does seem to run counter to what a knight would normally be doing. I didn't want to be rude. But I caught no hint of duplicity, only sadness, and a willingness to atone for something in his past. I like him, but I fear he may be eager to sacrifice himself. I've seen men like that before…ferocious in battle but always dying before their time."

"I don't want any martyrs in the group. Christian…"

"Tangus, I'll watch him," Safire said before Tangus could finish his thought. "He's a good man who only needs to be shown that the best way to make amends is to keep fighting for what he believes. Death serves no purpose."

Tangus nodded. "Euranna, do you agree with Safire and Christian's assessment?"

"Yes, Tangus, I do. I don't know if he's searching for a cause to die like Christian says, but I do like him."

Tangus got up and grabbed the wine, opened it, and poured himself a glass. "Sweetheart?" he asked Kristen.

"Please," she said.

Tangus poured a glass for Kristen. "Anybody else want some wine? I think we have more glasses here somewhere."

As everyone agreed that a glass of wine would serve them well as a nightcap, Tangus searched for more glasses but eventually gave up. "I guess I was wrong. Here, pass the bottle around," he said as he handed the bottle to his daughter, Jennifer. "Alright, what are your impressions of Azriel?"

Kristen smiled for the first time since coming into the room. "What a delightful little man! He's courteous to the extreme and funny, though a bit bawdy."

"I liked him from the moment I met him, Dad," Jennifer said.

"Okay, that works for me," Tangus replied.

"What about Elrond and Max, Tangus?" Safire asked.

Tangus shook his head. "Not much has changed with those two. Elrond apparently continues to chase females who, to my amazement, are attracted to him. Max, as usual, pretty much stays in Elrond's shadow, which isn't very surprising since he's one of the better thieves in the land…..at least to hear him tell it. I think he's close to being right, though. I've seen what he can do. Elrond is a fighter and a sorcerer, though, at least when I was part of the Dagger Company, he relied more on his magical items than his skills as a spell caster. I think that's probably for the best, however. Using spells takes time, and time is something we don't usually have in battle. His skill with his weapons is pretty good, but I always felt they would be much better if he devoted more time to practicing. Maybe that's changed, but I don't really think so." And with that Tangus finished the last of his wine. "All in all they have weaknesses as do each of us, but as a group we cover each other's individual flaws well."

"Tangus, I get the feeling Elrond is used to being in charge," Christian said.

Tangus laughed. "That's an understatement, and also a very acute observation, Christian."

Christian nodded. "Thank you. I read people pretty well. How is he going to respond to your leadership, do you think?"

Tangus smiled. "I haven't told him yet. Does anyone have anything more to add?" Tangus asked. Everyone shook their head. "Good. Tomorrow is going to be a long day in the saddle, as are the next few days. Go and get a good night's sleep, all of you. We rise at dawn."

After everyone had left, Kristen went to the bed and sat on the edge. Tangus kissed her and grabbed his cloak. "Where are you going?" Kristen asked.

"Just down to check the horses, sweetheart," Tangus replied. "Want to come?"

Kristen paused, thinking. Tears began to run down her cheeks as she said brokenly. "Not tonight. I want a bath and then I want to go to bed and sleep. I'm tired and I want to forget about Vayl for a while."

Tangus sat down next to her and held her while she cried. Finally she said, "Go. I'll be alright, love."

Tangus kissed her again on the forehead and got up. "I won't be long. Let's go Bitts." As he closed the door behind him Romulus walked over and laid his massive head in Kristen's lap. She hugged him tight around the neck for a few minutes before going to the bath tub and magically heating the water already in it.

Tangus found Azriel outside sitting on a bench smoking a pipe. "May I join you?" he asked.

Looking up, the dwarf smiled. "But of course, my good man. What brings you out in the cold of the night?"

"I just wanted to do a quick check on the horses. And you?" Tangus replied.

"You needn't bother with the horses, I've already done so and they're fine," Azriel said. "In answer to your question, whenever possible I like to end each day smoking my pipe and being alone with my thoughts."

Tangus started to get up, "I'm sorry to have intruded."

Azriel grabbed Tangus' arm. "Nonsense," he said. "Sit with me a while. New found friends are always welcome. Besides, sometimes I have thoughts I really don't want to think about. This is one of those times."

Settling down on the bench, Tangus looked up at the sky. "Snow's coming soon. If not tonight, then tomorrow," he said.

Azriel shook his head. "I wouldn't know about that, but there does seem to be a cold chill in the air. I've always wondered how elves could tell such things. I guess dwarves spend too much time underground to develop those instincts." After a silent moment Azriel said, "Your wife and daughter are both very charming ladies, though your wife seemed sad for some reason."

"She received some bad news earlier," Tangus said. "We're all still trying to process it. However, I must say they both seem rather taken with you as well. I can read people, but my wife can feel them. In many respects she's the best judge of character I know. She seems to have an innate sense about their nature." Tangus shrugged. "Whatever it is, I trust her."

"Perhaps it is her connection with the empath," Azriel replied.

That stopped Tangus briefly before he replied. "From what I have learned regarding the empath, her name is Emmy by the way, they have the ability to judge people by the state of their soul," Tangus said, hiding the surprise in his voice. "In some respect that talent has probably been passed onto Kristen through the bond."

Turning to face Azriel, Tangus studied him for a moment and then had a realization. "You know more about Emmy and empaths than what I've told Elrond and Max, don't you?"

Azriel nodded. "I didn't know about the bloodline relationship between Emmy, Kristen, and Althaya until tonight, nor did I know the effect the loss of the empath would have on healing magic. But I know about the rest. I know about the purge and the consequences to young Emmy if she is not rescued and joined with your wife."

"How do you know this?" Tangus asked.

"My people have a small mining operation under Mount Repose northeast of here. As the purge was unfolding in Elanesse some three thousand years ago, an empath mother and her daughter accidently found a tunnel entrance at the base of the mountain in which to hide from the rangers seeking them out. They were barely alive when we found them, suffering from exposure and arrow wounds. Unfortunately we could not save them, but before they died the mother, knowing she was not long for this world, gave my people a diary she had been keeping. Not only did the diary talk about her struggles, thoughts, and fears, but also about the nature of the empath. My people still have that diary. I have read it myself."

"You mean to tell me you knew about us through some sort of prophecy?" Tangus queried suspiciously.

"No, no, dear sir. I'm here quite by accident. Actually, I thought the diary was the ramblings of a woman out of her mind and near death. I never thought there was any substance to it until today. I was wrong, although considering the consequences if we do not successfully win Emmy away, I wish I wasn't." Azriel then tapped his pipe, clearing out the smoked tobacco from the bowl. "Think I'll go to bed now. And you?"

"Yes, I think I will as well," Tangus replied.

Azriel put a hand on Tangus' shoulder. "Don't worry, we'll get Emmy," he assured Tangus before he left.

Tangus, now alone with his own contemplations, stared into the cloudy sky for a few more minutes. Snow was starting to fall. "I hope your right," he said to himself as he got up and followed Azriel inside.

In Elanesse Lukas was waiting for Luminista and Gyorgy to get back from their nightly kidnapping foray. Lukas was very pleased with their success thus far. By sacrificing infected men to the stasis spell, he was successfully draining away its power. Lukas estimated he had reduced the magic to about half-strength. When Luminista and Gyorgy returned, however, they were alone.

"Where is the thrall?" Lukas asked.

Luminista looked worriedly at Gyorgy. "Lukas, they've changed tactics."

"How, Luminista?" Lukas asked. "And please keep in mind your life depends upon the answer."

"They no longer patrol alone. They now travel in groups of five or six. Gyorgy and I can't handle that many at once," Luminista replied.

Lukas slapped her. "I DON'T CARE HOW YOU DO IT!" he screamed. Calming, "Go back out and get me a thrall. Sooner or later you will find one off alone. We're close to having the empath. I WILL NOT let anything stop me! DO YOU HEAR?!"

Cringing, Luminista looked down. "Yes Lukas." She then silently left the room. Lukas looked at Gyorgy and nodded. Gyorgy turned and followed Luminista.

Looking through the stasis field, Lukas stared at the little girl inside. "You are safe for now, empath. But not for much longer."

CHAPTER 12

The good man will gladly sacrifice himself while the evil man will sacrifice everyone but himself.

— BOOK OF THE UNVEILED

AUTUMN CAME OUT of a deep, healing slumber. She was in a lavish bedroom, but the reddish light coming from the fireplace didn't reveal much more. Snuggled under the covers, Autumn felt safe and didn't want to come out. Then the memories flooded her, memories of betrayal, torture, rape, and rescue from death by Father Goram. She suddenly realized she was now in his bedroom. Getting up, she put on a plush robe that was lying on a footstool at the end of the bed. Moving over to the fireplace, she added a couple of logs, then went to a closed door. Opening it, she looked down a hallway. It was dark except for a reddish glow coming from the other end. All was quiet except for the occasional snap and crackle of burning wood coming from the main room fireplace. Moving down the hallway, her bare feet walking on thick rugs, she looked into the main room to see Father Goram sleeping on the sofa in front of the fireplace. Ajax was lying on the floor nearby. Ajax looked up at Autumn, then rose to greet her. Petting his soft fur, she sat down in a chair and watched the priest sleep.

Father Goram suddenly opened his eyes and saw Autumn staring at him. Sitting up while yawning, he said, "How are you feeling, Autumn?"

"Alive thanks to you, Horatio. How long has it been?"

"Three days. You went through a lot and needed some time to recover," Father Goram replied as he got up. "I'll make us some coffee. I've completely lost track of time sitting here and buried in my own thoughts. What time is it?"

Autumn got up and looked out a window into the night sky. "From the positions of the stars I'd say it looks to be about three in the morning."

"Not too early for breakfast then. How about some fried eggs and venison sausage?"

Autumn suddenly realized she was famished. "That would be great! What have I been eating for the last three days?" she inquired.

"Warm soup," Father Goram said from the kitchen as he was bringing the small fireplace up to a suitable heat for cooking. "I'd wake you up to eat, but almost as soon as you were done you went back to sleep. Come here, Ajax!" he called to the big dire wolf as he slapped a slab of fresh meat down in a large metal dish.

"It feels like I haven't eaten a thing." Autumn said as she sat down at the dining room table and watched Father Goram cook some eggs. "It snowed during the night Horatio. It's so beautiful outside. I..." But Autumn couldn't finish as she started to cry silently.

Father Goram, looking over Autumn, took the eggs off the flame and sat down next to her, taking her hands in his. "You are alive, dear girl. As long as you are, there is hope. We'll work through what happened together. Trust me. Also trust me when I say I will never let it happen again." He then embraced her as she began to sob uncontrollably.

After a few minutes she quieted. Ajax, deeply concerned, had placed his paw on Father Goram's knee and whined slightly. Autumn laughed between sniffles. "Sorry, Horatio."

Father Goram shook his head. "No need for that, not between us, Autumn. Still want these eggs and sausage?"

Smiling, Autumn said, "More than ever!"

Father Goram returned to preparing breakfast. Autumn suddenly had a thought, "How's Magdalena?"

"Safe," Father Goram said as he turned to face her, the sausages, sizzling in the steel frying pan over the fire, still needed another minute or so to be fully cooked. "Vayl found a labyrinth beneath the monastery. It probably dates back some three to four-thousand years. This wasn't always a monastery. People were tortured and died down there. We've also found a treasure-trove of old manuscripts and magical tomes as well as an armory full of mostly rusted weapons, but some were magical. I can't even begin to understand why someone would leave all that, or even more puzzling, why would Vayl? It looks like he didn't even explore the other rooms. I suppose that's what happens when one gets tunnel vision. He was probably so wrapped up in his deceit that he didn't pay attention to anything else." Father Goram put the sausages on two plates and cracked a couple of eggs. "Anyway," he continued as he cooked the eggs, "Magdalena had been drugged but not harmed otherwise. They either just hadn't gotten around to it or intended to let her die down there. She's already back on duty and determined to see if Vayl has any more rangers on his payroll. Autumn, she is very angry."

"I know how she feels," Autumn replied.

Father Goram set a cup of coffee in front of Autumn and one at his place next to her. "Breakfast coming up," he said as he went back to the fireplace and finished filling their two plates with food.

Autumn dug into her food as soon as the plate hit the table. For a few moments Father Goram just watched, smiling. An appetite was a good sign that she was healing. In between mouthfuls, Autumn said, "What about Vayl." The last word was spoken with several small bits of food flying out. Autumn swallowed her mouthful and looked contritely at Father Goram. "I guess I got a bit carried away," she said as she wiped away the bits of food that hadn't landed on her plate.

Father Goram took his napkin and wiped away a bit of egg on her chin. "Not too surprisingly Vayl has disappeared. My contacts at Taranthi spotted him and several others boarding a deep water ship. I'm sure he's heading for the mainland. Kristen's already been warned about him."

"You used a communication crystal?" Autumn asked. Father Goram nodded. "How's she taking it, could you tell?"

Father Goram sighed. "No not really, but he's been a big part of our lives for a long time. I'm sure she's extremely sad. What scares me is that Kristen, if she and Vayl ever do meet, may try to salvage him. You know how big her heart is. She'll only want to see what the person was, not what he has become."

"Tangus is with her, Horatio," Autumn replied. "I've grown to know him well over the years. I sense in him an unwavering desire to do whatever is necessary to protect those he loves. He'll kill Vayl, of that I have no doubt. He may feel bad about it, but nothing will stay his hand if Kristen, Jennifer, Emmy, or any of his friends are in jeopardy. And I think he'll sleep just fine at night with a clear conscious afterwards." Autumn paused. "How do you feel about it?" she asked.

Father Goram looked deep into Autumn's dark brown eyes. Autumn could see the anger building in his eyes. "How could I have so misjudged his soul?" Father Goram asked. "I don't understand how someone can be your colleague, your friend for all those years and turn on you like he has done. He did unspeakable things to you and now he threatens Kristen and Emmy. I'm sorry Autumn, and Althaya forgive me, but I wish I could be the one to kill him. I want to send his soul to the blackest reaches of Hades. I want to look him in the eyes so he sees how much I hate him!"

Autumn took Father Goram's hand in hers. "There should be no room for hate in your heart, Horatio. You are a priest. Perhaps we shall help each other to heal."

"That doesn't make me immune to feelings, Autumn! Nor does being a priest stop the rage I feel towards Vayl for his treachery, and, more importantly, the harm he caused you!" Father Goram exclaimed emotionally. "My dear, I need no healing. I need justice! I need vengeance!" Taking a deep breath to retake control of his emotions, he said, "Finish your breakfast. Later this morning I want you to see Cameron."

Autumn shook her head. "I'm not crazy, Horatio."

Father Goram touched the side of Autumn's face with his hand. "Child…"

"I'm not a child, Horatio," Autumn said. "I'm all grown up, a very accomplished priestess and an adult."

Father Goram drew back a little. "I realize that, Autumn, which is why I'm making you my second."

"Horatio, I don't want to be your second. Give that to Cordelia. She's more than capable."

"I'm confused. Do you want to leave?" Father Goram asked.

Autumn sighed in exasperation. "Of course I don't want to leave. That's not what I'm saying at all." Autumn bit her lip, not really sure how she should proceed. So much had happened and she wasn't sure how best to approach it, or even if it was the right time to express her feelings for Father Goram. But, after her vicious beating and near death, the only thing keeping her from a complete collapse was the love she had for Father Goram and the calm in the storm he offered.

"Autumn, what is it?" Father Goram asked.

"Horatio let me explain it this way. Mary McKenna holds a place here," Autumn said as she laid her hand over Father Goram's heart. "I too want to be held here. But not just as a colleague or friend."

Father Goram stared at Autumn, he could not deny his feelings for her. He did not want to say goodbye to his beloved Mary, but he also was very tired of the emptiness he felt. Mary had taught him the value of love and the sharing of one's life with another. Perhaps it was time to put those lessons to use.

Autumn sensed Father Goram's hesitancy. "Horatio, I'm not asking you to forget about Mary," she said. "I loved her like a sister and will always remember her. But there is room in a person's heart for more than one occupant. I'm broken now, that is true, but I've loved you for some time. More than ever I need to be open with you, more than ever I need to admit the truth held within my heart."

Father Goram smiled and nodded. "I think Mary would approve of you. And I know Kristen would." Father Goram looked off into the space of his mind for a few moments before returning his attention back to Autumn, who was waiting patiently. "I've been hiding behind my duties far too long," he said. "But I really couldn't commit to another person until I knew within my own heart that my commitment would be absolute. You're very special to me, and when I knew you were in danger I was terrified…and livid someone would wish to harm you. Is that love?"

"That is a question you must answer for yourself, Horatio. My feelings for you will not change and I'm willing to wait as long as you need," Autumn replied.

Father Goram embraced Autumn. They sat in silence for a few minutes, enjoying the miracle of companionship. "I still want you to talk with Cameron," Father Goram said, breaking the quiet. "We can do it together if you prefer, but I think you should do it alone. What happened to you should to be addressed and talked through so it does not permanently damage your spirit. You may not see them now, but the emotional wounds are there and will continue to bleed if not properly mended."

Burying her head into Father Goram's shoulder, Autumn said, "I know you're right. I have nightmares, Horatio."

"As do I," Father Goram said as he held on to Autumn tightly.

Mordecai Lannian and Amberley Siloratan walked out of the Queen's council chamber and down a deserted hallway toward the building exit. As First Councilor to the Queen, Mordecai was required to be at all meetings and briefings that affected the realm, but Mordecai had very little real interest in the daily operations of the island of InnisRos. Removing his councilor's robe and handing it to Amberley, he put his outside cloak on and said, "I hate these meetings. Very little ever gets accomplished. And why should I care about the quibbling of two land owners over who has a right to water their pigs at a waterhole. By the gods, it all makes me sick. I mean, Amberley, that's why we have administrators!"

"You'll live, lover. It's not like we have a choice. The Queen commands it. Besides, every once in a while a small kernel of information comes out that can be of use against our adversaries," Amberley replied.

Mordecai laughed, "Those imbeciles on the Council, idiots every one of them, except maybe for Erin Mirie. She's cunning and has the Queen's ear, and she's in opposition to me on everything I try to do. It's bad enough I have the constantly plead with the Queen to get my agenda pushed through, but I also have to counter every argument Mirie makes against my proposals. I think she disagrees with me out of spite. She will be Nightshade's next assignment after I've been brought the empath."

THE SALVATION OF INNOCENCE

"Have you mentioned the manuscript we found to anyone?" Amberley asked.

Mordecai shook his head. "No, that's our secret. The Liberian who found it and brought it to my attention has met with an unfortunate accident and all traces of the tome have been removed. No one knows it ever existed in the Queen's Library." Arriving at the front door of his family mansion, which was across the street from the council building, he unlocked the door and went into his spacious and luxurious home. "Go and pour us a glass of wine," Mordecai told Amberley as he hung up their cloaks and his councilor's robe. He then threw logs onto the waning fire in the great room fireplace. After stoking the fire into life, he lifted a rug off the floor and whispered the spell command word "aperire". A part of the stone floor disappeared, revealing a large book, *'Magical Properties and Its Effects on the Planes'*. After Mordecai removed the book, the stone floor once again became solid.

Setting the book on a table, Mordecai opened it to the bookmarked page where it spoke of the empath. Amberley brought over two glasses of wine and sat down next to him. Taking a sip, Mordecai pointed to writings on the page outside the margin. "See these? The book is filled with additions in freehand, like the author or authors came across additional information and updated it over the years. This is not in the same language the tome was originally written and consequently, as I have mentioned, I've been having a hard time translating this passage."

"We've discerned it's probably an ancient elven script, probably Quendian," Amberley said.

"Yes, Amberley, that's correct. But this is a specific dialect I've never seen before. But I believe I've finally worked it out last night," Mordecai said. Getting up, Mordecai went over to a bookcase and removed two books. "This one is my personal copy of *'Disguising the Magic's of Death'*. It's written in Quendian. But I also found the identical book in the Queen's library, completely by chance, that's exactly the same as mine except it's written in the same dialect of Quendian that's written on the pages of the tome." Opening both books, Mordecai pointed to different words. "Look. Some of the words are the same in both books but in different dialects of Quendian. These books are my translation keys."

"So you've worked out the conversion, Mordecai?" Amberley asked.

Mordecai nodded as he pulled out a folded piece of vellum from a pocket in his tunic. Written on the vellum in Mordecai's handwriting was *"The secret to releasing the power of the empath in the Svartalfheim is to break the bond between the empath and its protector. But this can only be done once both the empath and the protector are in the Svartalfheim. If the bond is broken elsewhere, the magic will not come."*

Mordecai smiled. "You see, Amberley, it's not enough to just take the empath to the Svartalfheim. That by itself will not release the power. The bond must be broken in the Svartalfheim, which means we need both the empath and the priestess. The tome even tells me the spells and incantations required to capture the magic released when that bond is broken. I've already contacted Nightshade to change her mission. She understands she must bring the priestess to me as well as the empath."

"How do we break the bond, Mordecai?" Amberley asked.

"That part is pretty straightforward. We must kill the priestess after we've crossed over into the Svartalfheim," he replied.

After breakfast Father Goram and Autumn sat on the sofa in a comfortable silence, enjoying the fire crackling in the fireplace as well as each other's presence. Ajax was lying on his back, mesmerized by the flames. His body length easily covered the entire width of the fireplace, allowing him to take full advantage of the heat. Autumn suddenly felt exhausted. She didn't want to go back to bed but, as she sat nestled against Father Goram, her eyes grew heavier and heavier. At one point she found herself nodding off only to jerk awake and see Father Goram looking down at her. "You need to go back to bed, my dear," he said.

"I don't want to, but you're right. Even with magical healing, bed rest is frequently necessary. That's usually what I prescribe to my patients at the hospital," Autumn replied.

"Then perhaps you should follow your own counsel. I'm going to need you strong for the days ahead," Father Goram said.

"Can I stay one more day?" Autumn asked.

"You can stay as long as you need, dear girl," Father Goram replied. "My home is your home. When you wake up, don't be surprised to see some of Ajax's pack lying about. I have things to do today but I want you well protected. Two or three dire wolves will be ample, I think. I will talk to Cameron and see if he can talk with you tomorrow."

Autumn sighed. "It will be hard talking about it, both the betrayal by a beloved friend and…and the other thing. But I know I need to do it."

"Good. The realization you need help is the first step to healing. Now let's get you back to bed," Father Goram said as he got up and helped Autumn. Ajax reluctantly turned over, but didn't get up. In Father Goram's master bedroom, Autumn climbed under the covers of the big bed and was asleep almost immediately. Father Goram re-stoked the fireplace and quietly left, leaving the door partially ajar.

Walking back into the main room, Father Goram looked at Ajax. "You're starting to get just a little too comfortable in front of my fireplace, my big friend." The dire wolf stared back at him somewhat defiantly. Father Goram smiled and went over to him, bent over and scratched him behind both ears. Soon the wolf had flopped back over on his back as Father Goram gave him a good belly rub. Ajax, as did his father and father before him all the way back to Menelaus, enjoyed nothing more than good belly rubs. "Okay, enough now," Father Goram said as he collected his will. Releasing the magic he needed to further communicate with Ajax, Father Goram instructed the wolf to return to his pack. "Cassandra's probably a bit worried and maybe a little angry that you haven't been around to keep your pups in line. Hey! I just realized…you sly wolf! That's why you've spent so much time here! Your mate's going to be mad at me for keeping you away." Ajax looked at Father Goram and grinned. Father Goram laughed, saying, "Give me Razor and Finley to guard Autumn." Ajax licked Father Goram's hand in acknowledgement. Keeping his hand on Ajax's back, the two walked over to the wall perpendicular to the fireplace. "*Solvo!*" he said. A portion of the wall moved out, revealing the underground passageway back to Ajax's den. Father Goram said to the wolf, "Be off with you now." Watching the dire wolf scamper around a turn in the tunnel and out of sight, Father Goram, leaving the secret door opened for the returning wolves, went to the kitchen and started to clean up.

Rhovalee was in his office. His assistants were going about the daily routine of cleaning up after the monastery messenger dragons while he was trying to do routine paperwork, but his mind kept drifting back to what had happened a few days before with Vayl and the death of Francis. Vayl actually had him believing Autumn was a traitor and instead it turned out Vayl was the one who betrayed Father Goram and the monastery…as well as having Francis killed and almost killing poor Autumn. Rhovalee was deeply troubled by the inadvertent role he had played in the whole affair. Outside he heard a sudden commotion. Stepping from behind his desk and opening the door, he saw Father Goram walking straight towards him. Rhovalee's assistants had all stopped what they were doing and stood aside. There was something in Father Goram's gait that told Rhovalee that this was not necessarily going to be a pleasant chat. In Father Goram's hand was a thin book.

Letting the priest into his office, Rhovalee said, "Please, Father, have a seat."

Father Goram nodded and seated himself saying "Thank you. Close the door." Father Goram's response was a bit too brusque for Rhovalee's comfort. After closing the door, Rhovalee started to go around his desk to sit down. Father Goram motioned "no" and pointed to the other chair opposite the one he was sitting. "That chair and desk are reserved for the keeper of my dragons. I'm here to determine if you're going to still be that person," Father Goram said.

Rhovalee swallowed hard. "Yes, Father," he said taking the indicated chair.

"Magdalena gave me her report," Father Goram said.

"She was quite thorough, father. And angry…"

"Of course she was angry!" Father Goram snapped. "She was kidnapped by Vayl as well. If it had not been for Ajax, she probably would have died in that underground maze." Father Goram stopped and threw the book he was holding onto the desk. "In her report she clears you of any duplicity. That's your copy. It makes for good reading. There are recommendations within that you might want to think about putting into practice. That is if you're still here when I'm done with you." Father Goram paused for effect before continuing. "As a ranger, Magdalena has to rely on her investigative skills as well as her 'gut feelings' to arrive at conclusions. I'm not saying that she's wrong. She's good enough to have been offered a law-keeper position in Taranthi. But I have certain skills that are not available to her. I will not allow my people to be jeopardized ever again, so I have decided to take certain steps."

"Certain steps, Father?" Rhovalee asked apprehensively. "How could things get any worse?" he thought to himself.

"Don't worry, Rhovalee. You have nothing to worry about if you've been completely forthcoming. If not, well…" Father Goram shrugged his shoulders. "I want to cast a spell that will allow me to determine if you are truthfully answering all my questions. Are you willing to cooperate?"

"Of course, Father. I have nothing to hide. Is it going to hurt?" Rhovalee cautiously replied.

Father Goram smiled for the first time since entering the aviary. "No. You'll feel a slight tingle, that's all. Are you ready?"

Rhovalee nodded as Father Goram grabbed his arm. A slight tingling sensation radiated along the length of his arm and eventually involved his entire body just as Father Goram said, "Feel the magic, Rhovalee? It knows you now. You can speak whatever falsehoods you want, it will not prevent that. But it does tell me. Each time you lie I will know it. And after each lie, I will ask the same question again and you will be compelled to answer truthfully. I'm not concerned about any secrets you are keeping that do not involve the kidnapping of Autumn and Magdalena, so rest assured on that score. Any questions before we proceed?"

"No, Father."

"Tell me what happened the day Francis was killed and Autumn was attacked," Father Goram said.

Rhovalee cleared his throat. "Well, I was late coming in that morning. You see, I had to see a healer about a particularly nasty bout of hemorrhoids…"

Father Goram interrupted. "That's in the report, along with a truthfully sworn statement from the healer who saw you. What about after the visit?"

"Well, as soon as I was finished, I headed straight over here. I arrived to find all my assistants running amok, talking about Francis being either stolen or sent on a mission without consent," Rhovalee replied.

"How did you know he might have been sent on an unscheduled messenger mission instead of just 'flying the coop' as it were?" Father Goram asked.

"Because his harness was missing, Father," Rhovalee replied. "You see, harnesses are used to allow the dragon to carry the message pouch attached. Sometimes messenger dragons are easily distracted. We wouldn't want to rely on them holding the message pouch in their claws. They're very dependable getting from one place to another, but they might divert from their course if they see prey. They're meat eaters after all and use their talons to attack." Rhovalee saw Father Goram staring at him and decided he needed to get back on point. "Anyway, each dragon is carefully measured for their harness so that it doesn't chafe them when they fly."

Father Goram nodded. "How could someone other than yourself, or one of your assistants, know which harness to put on Francis?"

"All the harnesses have the name of the dragon on it. That's so no mistakes are made because each harness is tailor made for the dragon. You have to understand, Father, all my assistants are really just young boys and girls, forced into this work by parents who want them to gain experience and character shoveling crap…I mean dragon droppings. The responsibilities are much more than that, however, but unfortunately the job has a bit of an image problem. The life of a dragon keeper is not something to which most people aspire," Rhovalee said.

"And Francis," Father Goram asked. "How did he get spirited away?"

"As I told Magdalena, one of the night assistants fell asleep."

"That's in the report," Father Goram said. "I assume you did your own investigation?"

Rhovalee nodded and said, "Yes I did, Father. It was Jasper. I've had this problem with him before."

"So why didn't you punish him at the time?" Father Goram asked.

Rhovalee shrugged. "Two reasons. His parents are both rather influential."

"Not more so than me," Father Goram said harshly.

Rhovalee swallowed again. "Understood, Father," he said.

"And the other reason," Father Goram prompted.

"Who wants to steal a messenger dragon, Father? Everything we do here is so mundane. Why discipline Jasper when no real harm was done? After that first time, I talked with him and he assured me it wouldn't happen again. I didn't push the issue because he's rather sensitive and I didn't want to hurt his feelings. I'm sorry, Father, but I allowed myself to become complacent and lowered my guard. Jasper's not really to blame here, I am." Rhovalee looked down at the floor. He didn't want to meet his superior's gaze.

"Go on, Rhovalee," Father Goram said after a few moments.

Rhovalee took a deep breath before speaking. "Technically I report to Vayl, so I went to him with the problem as soon as I discovered Francis was missing. He told me not to worry, he said he would send rangers out to search and get whatever information they could. He also said that he could use a spell that would allow him to determine Francis' destination and whether or not he was just sent on a mission or actually stolen. He told me to go about my business and not say anything to anyone because he didn't want any unnecessary attention. When we spoke next he told me basically what he told you. We stopped by Autumn's apartment on our way to brief you so she would know what happened, but she was gone, and it looked like a lot of her belongings were missing as well. I allowed myself to be deceived by Vayl and for that I'm sorry, Father."

Father Goram released Rhovalee's arm and sat back in the chair, thinking. "I want a tighter control on your operations, Rhovalee. Understand?" Father Goram asked and waited for Rhovalee to nod. "I don't blame you for this nor do I blame young Jasper. He may have fallen asleep, but I'm quite sure he was kept sleeping by magic. Actually, falling asleep probably saved his life. Magdalena recommended we place an experienced ranger discretely on guard duty each night. I concurred. We've actually already started that as of a couple nights ago. It is something we are going to do permanently."

Father Goram studied Rhovalee. "Cordelia is my new second, so you will report to her from now on. But you have access to me as well. I want that understood."

"I understand, Father," Rhovalee replied.

Getting up, Father Goram shook hands with Rhovalee who had also stood. "Perhaps we both got a bit complacent with the dragons. Read over the report and implement each of Magdalena's recommendations. If any of the parents of your assistants give you any trouble, please refer them to either Cordelia or me. In the short term you may end up having to replace some of your assistants, but I'm sure you'll keep the situation stabilized. Do you have any questions?"

"No, Father," Rhovalee said with a good bit of relief.

"Very good…you may return to your duties," Father Goram said as he turned and left the room. He never really thought Rhovalee had anything to do with Vayl's plan, but Rhovalee, as well as everyone in the monastery, needed a swift kick in the rear to remind them of the importance of their duties.

Amberley got out of Mordecai's bed and wrapped a thick robe around her. Moving into the main room, she found Mordecai sitting on the floor in front of the fireplace, once again studying *'Magical Properties and Its Effects on the Planes'*. Coming up behind him she knelt and wrapped her arms around Mordecai's neck. "Have you found anything else of use?" she asked.

Mordecai shook his head. "No, nothing more," he said. "And I believe we may have a bigger problem now. With Vayl gone, I'm left with only one asset with eyes and ears on Goram, and she's limited in what she can tell me about his movements. He's probably the smartest person I know, and he's definitely going to be a problem."

"But you told Vayl you were going to kill him. Problem solved, right?"

"I don't really care what I told Vayl," Mordecai replied. "You think once I have the empath and the priestess that I will still care about him? If he betrayed someone he's known and been friends with most of his adult life, he'll betray me as well if the price is right. He's probably going to get himself killed on the mainland anyway, but if not, Nightshade's going to have that one when I no longer require his services. Killing Goram, on the other hand, presents another problem altogether. I'm not sure even Nightshade can handle him," Mordecai said.

Amberley seductively kissed Mordecai's neck while purring, "Why don't we discuss that later?"

Mordecai smiled, turned, and forced Amberley into his lap. "Yes. Why don't we?" he said, thinking that the distraction was just what he needed.

Father Goram returned to his apartment after spending a busy day talking to monastery personnel and discussing plans to increase vigilance with his council of leaders - Cordelia, his new second, Magdalena, his top ranger, Cameron, his master healer, and Landross, a paladin of Althaya and chief of security. Autumn was now awake and sitting on the sofa, legs curled beneath her, reading Father Goram's original copy of Magdalena's incident report. In one hand she had a glass of wine. Razor and Finley were doing what most of Ajax's pack liked doing most when in Father Goram's apartment, lying stretched out before the fireplace.

"How are you feeling, my dear?" Father Goram asked as he walked over to the sofa, sitting down next to Autumn.

After setting her glass on the end table, Autumn interlocked her arm with Father Goram's. "Well rested, Horatio. Magdalena's report makes for fascinating reading. Poor Rhovalee! You weren't too rough on him, were you?"

"Only enough to force him to take his job a bit more seriously. Actually, no one has been spared today. You could say I've been on a bit of a rampage," Father Goram replied.

Putting the report down, Autumn laid her head on Father Goram's shoulder. Father Goram put his arm around her. "You probably shouldn't have read that just yet."

"It's fine, Horatio. I know I have to deal with everything sooner or later if I'm ever to become fully functional again. Tomorrow I'll go see Cameron. I hope he can help me," Autumn responded.

"I talked to him at great length today and I think he will. He's expecting you tomorrow around noon," Father Goram said. "I'll go with you, but he said he wanted to talk to you alone."

The two sat in silence for several minutes until Father Goram said, "Well, I better get these two lazy bums back to Ajax before he shows up wondering why they're still here." Both wolves looked up.

After persuading the two wolves to leave via the tunnel back to Ajax's' den using slabs of meat as a bribe, Father Goram sat back down next to Autumn saying. "I want you to consider moving your things here."

Autumn looked up at Father Goram. "Horatio, are you sure?"

"Very much so, if you feel you're up to it. I can be a lot to handle sometimes, so be warned," he replied.

Autumn smiled and nodded. "I would like that very much! And I believe I'm up to the challenge."

"Then it's settled. We'll take care of that first thing in the morning," Father Goram said.

After a few minutes of comfortable silence, Autumn asked, "Horatio, what do you have planned next?"

Father Goram thought about that question for a few moments. "I think I'm going to take a trip to Taranthi and have a look in the Royal Library. I need to see if it has *'Magical Properties and Its Effects on the Planes'*, and if not, find out if it ever did."

"I'm going with you," Autumn said.

"Autumn, it could be dangerous," Father Goram replied as he shook his head.

"No argument, Horatio. I'm either going with you or I'll follow you. This is not up for discussion," Autumn said as she sat up and met Father Goram's gaze.

Father Goram studied the very determined Autumn. "You still work for me, you know," he said. But Autumn kept staring, not giving in. Father Goram finally capitulated. "Oh, very well then...but only if Cameron says you're ready to travel. Agreed?"

Autumn studied Father Goram. "You'll make no prior arrangements with Cameron to hold me back?"

Father Goram shook his head. "No, my dear, I will not speak nor have I spoken to Cameron about this" he replied.

Autumn smiled. "Then we have an agreement," she said as she thought about the conversation SHE was going to have with Cameron.

CHAPTER 13

The misty covered landscape revealed little to the traveler. Its blacks and grays drifted without purpose, its existence undetermined. Engulfed, the traveler soon lost his way. The mist does not return that which it has claimed.

— *Book of the Unveiled*

THEY HAD BEEN traveling for five days. Snow had fallen the night before they left Altheros, and the land was covered in pure white - beautiful, serene, and innocent. Following a well established gravel road along the Pantera River, the group had made good time the first three days of the expected five day journey to reach Esterling. Since river barges often stopped at night rather than risk running up and down the river in the dark, there were plenty of inns available along the way to spend the nights indoors and protected from the cold. On the morning of the fourth day they awoke to freezing rain, which had fallen for a good portion of the night and was still pouring down when they set out after a hot breakfast. The travelers were determined not let the weather conditions slow them down.

The first half of the day they made little headway. The road had become so iced over and slick they were forced to ride their horses off the road and on the more uneven ground that flanked each side. This was the only way their horses could find true purchase. Slowly the journey continued. As the day progressed, long shards of ice grew down from the branches of the trees, the long grass forced over, every bit of exposed flesh on the travelers turned to red, every beard doubled in length, every voice silenced to the point that the labored breaths of the horses and their riders were the only sounds heard above the constant pattering of the freezing rain.

THE SALVATION OF INNOCENCE

"Damn it!" Elrond bellowed in frustration, "I'm ready to call down a ball of fire upon myself just for some heat."

"You'd just make yourself wet by melting all the ice on you," Tangus replied. "And then you would re-freeze. Don't you have a magical cloak for warmth?" Tangus asked.

Elrond snorted. "I'm using it!"

"Maybe we should consider stopping until this blows over," Max said.

"I think this is going to keep up for at least another couple of days. We can't afford to stop that long. Besides, we're making some progress, and that's better than sitting on our backsides in front of a warm fire," Tangus replied.

Christian agreed. "Tangus is correct, gentlemen. This weather system is going to last at least that long. I've had experience in conditions like this, both on the sea and on the land. Sometimes you just can't let it dictate your response. You work with it, if possible you use it to your advantage, and you press forward."

"Look…it's Christian right?" Elrond asked.

"Yes," Christian replied.

"Well Christian, I don't mean to sound disrespectful or anything, but I barely know you and I'm sure as hell not going to take directions from you until such time as I do," Elrond said.

Christian started to respond. "I understand, sir, but…"

"Elrond, did you not see his hands?" Azriel asked, joining the conversation. "They're burned terribly. Look at his cloak, standard marine issue. Look at the way he carries himself and rides a horse. My guess is he's more than earned his way," Azriel said pointedly.

Kristen stopped her horse and turned to face Elrond. "Indeed he has, Mr. Silverhair."

"Madam, please," Christian pleaded.

"No Christian, do not ask me to stop. You've earned every bit of the respect I give you. Rest assured Mr. Silverhair, Christian Baltzli is a fine and courageous fellow. He received the injuries to his hands by lifting a piece of burning wood off a crewmate on the ship as we crossed from InnisRos. I would trust him with my life!" Kristen said heatedly.

"Kristen, I'm sorry. I didn't mean anything personal, certainly no disrespect. However, in my line of work, trust must be earned lest it kill you. Tangus, can you help me here?" Elrond asked beseechingly. Azriel was trying to hold back a snicker.

"Sweetheart, Elrond's correct," Tangus remarked. "You've had no experience with the way things are here on the mainland. Trust is something that, by necessity, must be given grudgingly. But Elrond, you can trust every one of my friends as I have trusted yours. Christian was a captain serving in Palisade Crest's marine contingent. For the last five years he served onboard a sailing ship, and before that extensive campaigning here on the mainland. Don't worry. I've vetted him very closely with his superiors. Kristen's also provided input. We've talked about how well she reads people. She can also use clerical magic which allows nothing to be hidden. He can most definitely be trusted. On that score you have my word."

Elrond nodded and brought his horse up to Christian and offered his hand. "Had a taste of that clerical magic myself, so I know what it's like…I don't like my secrets exposed. I offer my apologies, Christian."

Christian smiled. "No apologies are necessary, sir."

"Good, now let's move on," Tangus shouted as he turned his horse and started forward again, Kristen at his side.

"Thanks for having my back," Elrond said to Max who was riding beside him towards the end of the small column.

Max looked at Elrond incredulously. "Have your back!? Elrond, when you start down one of those tangents, I want to be as far away as possible."

Elrond looked at his friend. "Those 'tangents', as you call them, have saved our lives more than once, my friend."

"True," Max reluctantly agreed.

By the time the travelers reached Esterling they were a day and a half behind schedule. Tired and cold, they spent the night in Esterling before continuing on to Starr, their next destination. The following morning the ice storm had given way to a clear and sunny sky, though the temperature remained cold. The icy landscape, glimmering in the bright sunlight, painted a surreal picture of trees, grasses, and bushes, all wearing an invisible skin.

As the sunlight melted the ice, the ground on both sides of the road became water soaked and muddy. Fortunately the graveled road saved them from becoming bogged down and enabled them to move at a fast yet easy pace. During this time, everyone took advantage of the opportunity to learn more about each other. Euranna, each night, continued her training using the katana. Lester, however, was now the one providing instruction while Christian and Safire always watched and offered input. Lester's weapon of expertise was a massive two-handed sword. Properly fought, the katana, though much lighter and smaller, also required two hands…a form of fighting style neither Christian nor Safire specialized in. Euranna was quickly becoming as good with the katana as she was with her bow.

Kristen and Jennifer spent a lot of time with Azriel, who regaled them with tales of long-ago heroics, the never-ending battle between good and evil, and dwarves' principle role in each, though both knew Azriel tended to exaggerate about the dwarf involvement. Kristen and Jennifer often found themselves laughing as Azriel spun his stories. Soon they were comfortable enough that all three started to discuss details about their own lives. Azriel, with his previous knowledge of the empath and the disaster that befell them, could sympathize with Kristen and her fears for Emmy. Kristen told him of the bond with Emmy, how she could feel Emmy's presence as she knew Emmy could feel hers, and how that comforted each. Kristen told Azriel how Emmy healed Euranna through her, of the incredible sacrifice an empath must make to heal, and the satisfaction that the healing process brought.

Azriel never went to bed without spending time smoking his pipe and thinking of each day's events. He realized over the last few days he had come to the remarkable conclusion that his new mission in life was to be Emmy's special protector once the child was set free of the stasis field. Like she had done with every other person rushing to save her,

Emmy had managed to give purpose to his life. Each morning Azriel sharpened his huge two-handed battleaxe to a razor's edge in anticipation of her defense.

It was not long before Tangus, Elrond, and Max meshed into the same patterns of the past. They spent most of their free time, along with Christian, hunched over Tangus' map, anticipating and planning for obstacles offered by the road, as well as discussing battle tactics. They knew with a certainty that one or possibly more vampyres were involved. Kristen, through her bond with Emmy, had also told Tangus of something else, something potentially even more dangerous than the vampyres that awaited them in Elanesse.

Elrond refrained from insisting things be done his way during the planning sessions, instead usually relenting to Tangus' point of view. Elrond and Max both noticed a distinct change in their friend. Having a daughter involved, as well as his marriage to Kristen, was certainly affecting Tangus' decision making process, but by no means was it the complete story. Tangus had become a better ranger. His assessments and subsequent choices were inspiring. Even Christian, an experienced battlefield commander, mostly deferred to Tangus, seeing the logic, or as Christian liked to call it the 'beauty', in Tangus' conclusions and tactics.

They arrived at Starr late on the third day after leaving Esterling.

Starr was a large, vibrant city resting at the junction of the Pantera and Southern Way rivers. Even at their late hour of arrival, the city was bustling with activity. Built around merchant trade and the profitability the industry brought with it, the availability of services within was endless. Finding a barge to make the river crossing, however, would have to wait until daylight. All agreed the few hours this would allow them to rest were welcomed. Locating a comfortable, yet reasonably priced, inn took little time and soon most of the travelers were asleep. Even

THE SALVATION OF INNOCENCE

Azriel decided to forego his pipe for one night, preferring the feel of a warm bed after a long, tiring day. As usual, Tangus, Elrond, Max, and Christian stayed up afterward to study Tangus' map before retiring. The map, with its magical enhancement, captured and revealed any recent changes to the landscape. Tangus started to depend more and more on this invaluable asset, even though, as Elrond cautioned, it could be magically sabotaged. Tangus felt the chance of that happening was slight. He believed he had unknowingly obtained a relic all those years ago and that it would take almost god-level magic to affect it. But he considered the possibility nevertheless and always worked that prospect into his decision making.

Their next destination, Ordensyr, was on the south side of the Pantera River. Deciding it would be best to cross the river now instead of later, the following morning everyone rose early and ate a substantial breakfast before saddling their horses for the ride down to the dock area of Starr. Lining the docks were warehouses, shops, taverns, and inns of various sizes, from the very basic to establishments that catered to the extremely wealthy. Every attempt was made to accommodate each income level of potential clientele. Tangus took Kristen, along with Bitts and Romulus, to negotiate a barge for the river crossing. Azriel followed at a discrete distance, ready for any sign of trouble. Jennifer, Safire, and Lester took the packhorses and bought replacement supplies for those that had been expended. Elrond and Max used this time to become better acquainted with Christian and Euranna. Through their late night planning sessions with Christian, they had come to develop respect for the big marine. He had a solid tactical mind and his handling of his sword was impressive. The diminutive Euranna answered their questions politely, but it was clear to both that Christian was her main point of focus.

Within a couple of hours Tangus and Kristen had procured a barge large enough to take everyone across in one trip. Both large pack horses were fully loaded with supplies. As the party stood holding the reins of their horses, waiting for the commissioned barge to be prepared for the river crossing, Tangus turned to Kristen. "How is your bond with Emmy holding up," he asked.

Kristen, standing beside her husband, shook her head. "Things are not so good. My bond with Emmy remains strong, but there has been a slight corruption to it over the last few weeks, as if something foreign is infiltrating it. Don't ask me how because I don't understand it fully, but both Emmy and I feel the presence and we both have been trying to remove it. Nothing seems to be working. It's just too subtle…kind of like trying to grab a greased hog. I believe whatever is causing this corruption is somehow aware of our progress. As for the stasis magic, it is somehow being drained."

Tangus grabbed Kristen's hand. Turning his attention to everyone else, Tangus saw that they were all looking at him. "Through the bond Kristen feels the stasis magic protecting Emmy being drained," he repeated for the benefit of those not hearing his conversation with his wife. "Time has become even more critical, and I will be pushing very hard. But traveling isn't all we'll be doing the rest of our time on the road to Elanesse." Redirecting his attention to Elrond, Tangus said, "Elrond, you have the floor."

Elrond nodded. "During the next few days we are going to have, for want of a better word, war games. Some of us are new to what comes while the rest of us haven't done this in a long time. At the end of each day, we'll train…we'll fight each other. When we can't raise our sword arm because of exhaustion, we'll fight again. When we're in a deep tired sleep, we'll get up and fight. We need to get to the point where we will be in our top fighting form at all times, regardless of the situation or our state of physical exhaustion. We will cover our weaknesses and exploit our strengths."

"Thanks, Elrond," Tangus said. Looking at the expectant faces of all his friends, he reminded himself once again how important his leadership role was. It did not frighten him as it once did. Over the last few weeks of traveling, making decisions and plans, he felt he was starting to fully come into his own as a ranger. "This is what I've been working towards," he thought. Taking a deep breath, Tangus said, "We've all known the stakes for some time now. The training each of us are going to go through the next couple of weeks is going to be hard, but we already have all the skills and abilities we'll need to fight for Emmy. This is just going to be some additional last minute preparation. I hope it turns out that we're harder on you than our enemies will be. Does anyone have any questions? No? Well then, the barge is ready so let's load up."

The trip to Ordenskyr was an arduous seven day journey, not because of the terrain, but because of the constant training each person had to endure. Even Kristen received advanced training with her mace from Lester. It was required training for all paladins who belonged to his religious order because of its increased effectiveness against the undead, even more so than his two-handed great sword. Though generally tight-lipped about his past, during these one-on-one sessions Kristen gained his trust to the point that, as a priestess to the same goddess he followed, she became his confessor. It was not something she actively sought, but rather embraced as her responsibility. She learned that Lester was on a permanent leave of absence from his monastery. Though it required quite a bit of coaxing, he finally told Kristen the nature of his offense, insufficient tithing. He had donated his entire share of a small treasure won in battle to a poor family without tendering the required share to his monastery. The act itself was not what caused the trouble, it was the fact that, fearing the share would be taken from the impoverished family, he lied about it, for which he was chastised and permanently exiled. Though still a paladin, he no longer had a home. Kristen bristled with anger at what she considered such an injustice, but Lester had made his peace with the penance and probably was a better paladin because of it.

Stopping for only a few hours of rest in Ordenskyr, they took the Alpine out of the city heading north through the foothills of the

Olympus Mountains. To the east this imposing mountain range dwarfed everything. By mid-afternoon of the second day after leaving Ordenskyr, they rode into the small town of Fayette. From there they continued north on the Alpine until they reached the monastery of Mons Basilica. This would be the last civilized resting point on the Alpine until they reached the Hammer in Knight's Lament pass.

They traveled the Alpine into the foothills of the Olympus Mountains gradually moving up into higher elevations until, after seven days, they began the climb into the mountains. By evening of the following day, they reached the mountain pass that would allow them to go east through the mountains and on to Ascension, the last major city stop before the final long push to Elanesse.

"Why do they call the pass Knight's Lament?" Jennifer asked Azriel.

Azriel laughed. "If you have ever seen a fully armored knight on an armored battle horse climb the first part of this pass, you'd understand."

The attack came early morning of the following day. It was only by chance that Max saw the falling boulder, but no one had time to react to his cry of warning. The boulder hit the stone floor of the pass and shattered into hundreds of pieces, sending stone shrapnel in all directions. The two nearest the impact, Safire and Lester, both went down amidst cries of pain from their wounded horses. The two riders, however, were silent. Euranna and Christian, following several yards behind, took stone shards as well, though most were absorbed by Christian and his horse, Penny, as he quickly moved in front to screen Euranna.

Elrond, with Max at the end of the column, looked up to see a mountain giant, about one hundred feet above, looking down. As he watched, three gleaming magical tipped arrows streaked up the wall of the pass, striking the giant in the gut from three different angles. Tangus, Jennifer, and Euranna had already drawn their bows and were again releasing arrows before Elrond had the presence of mind to draw out his wizard's staff of power. Kristen, with Azriel following close behind, raced to Safire and Lester. The giant, with six arrows protruding out of his belly, lifted another boulder, until three magic missiles, comet-like balls of magical energy, suddenly exploded in his face, singeing eyebrows and causing his head to jerk back. The explosions caused the giant to drop the boulder at his feet and back away from the edge.

"We need to move fast!" Tangus yelled as he turned his horse and rode back to where Kristen was administering aid. "Go! Go! Go!" he screamed to everyone still on horseback. "Look up to both sides! There might be more!"

"Go, Max! You're not in a position to help!" Elrond shouted as he threw the reins of the packhorse he was leading to Max. "I'll cover Tangus and Kristen!"

Suddenly another boulder flew over the edge and dropped down, but it was thrown blindly and landed without harm. "Kristen, we don't have a lot of time," Tangus said.

Kristen already had the two horses healed and on their feet ready to run, having already determined Safire and Lester's wounds were not immediately life threatening. "Safire's head was grazed which knocked her unconscious," Kristen said. "Other than small cuts I think she'll be fine. Lester's been severely hurt and has lost a lot of blood. I've stopped the major bleeding, but I'll need to spend more time healing him."

Tangus looked at Elrond and Azriel. "Elrond, get Safire up with you. Then both of you get out of here."

Tangus and Azriel stood Safire up enough for Elrond to pull her up in front of him. Taking her horse's reins, he raced his horse forward. Azriel mounted and also kicked his horse into a gallop.

Each time the giant looked over the edge, Jennifer and Euranna sent it scurrying back for cover with arrows. Another boulder again did no damage, but was a little closer to Tangus, Kristen and Lester. "What can I do?" Tangus asked his wife.

"We need to get him away from here so I can inspect his injuries. Lester, can you hear me?" Kristen asked.

Lester opened his eyes, but they were disoriented. "What?" he said.

"We don't have time, sweetheart." Tangus took Lester's horse and had it to go down on its knees. Struggling with Lester's weight, Tangus was able to drag him onto his horse, holding him to the saddle as the horse got back on all fours. "Kristen, go!" Tangus said. "I'll get Lester back."

"But…"

"You're not expendable. Please go!" Tangus pleaded. "Do it for Emmy!"

Kristen nodded, got on Arbellason and took off toward the others. Tangus tied Lester's hands to the saddle horn and then mounted Smoke. While riding alongside Lester's horse, Tangus had a firm grip on the back of Lester's cloak collar. Another boulder came over the top and looked like it would land close behind Tangus. Suddenly a bolt of lightning exploded against it, taking several chunks out and knocking it off its trajectory, far enough away to do no damage to Tangus or Lester. The sound of the accompanying thunderclap reverberated up and down the mountain pass. Elrond held his staff, ready to release another lightning bolt should it be necessary. As Tangus reached the group, he didn't have to say a word. Each turned their horses and rode through the mountain pass away from the giant as quickly as they could.

"I could go up there and kill it," Elrond remarked to no one in particular.

"It is indeed an evil that should be removed from this earth, but we do not have the time, Elrond," Christian replied.

After they had ridden hard for a few minutes, Tangus held up his hand to stop the column and dismounted, carefully helping Lester down from his horse. Kristen was off hers quickly and knelt beside him. "I'm okay madam. Thank you, Tangus," Lester said as he sat up. "I'm just a little bit weary."

Tangus nodded, then got up and went over to Safire while Kristen stayed with Lester, who was also now conscious and had been helped off his horse.

"It's the blood loss, Lester. It'll take a day or two to get your full strength back." Kristen said as she checked his wounds. She was able to heal the worst. The rest would have to wait. She went over and joined her husband as he steadied Safire who was trying to sit up. "How are you feeling, Safire?" Kristen asked.

"I have one hell of a headache and I'm a bit dizzy. Oh and look, I have a hole in my cloak," Safire responded right before she vomited.

Tangus shook his head. "That matched the hole you had in your side before Kristen healed you." Turning to Kristen, he said, "I've seen concussions before and she definitely has one. Is there anything you can do?"

Kristen nodded. "I'll have to use my staff, I've used all my healing spells as well as my potions," Kristen sighed. "It's the ship all over again, Tangus, too many injuries for me to heal with magic. And that was only one giant. What happens when we go against vampyres or goddess knows what else? What if I can't save everyone?"

Tangus did not reply as Kristen stared at him. She finally turned away to heal Safire's concussion using her healing staff. After finishing, Kristen looked back at Tangus. Tangus took both hands and gripped Kristen's shoulders. "Sweetheart, there's never enough to help everybody. You and Emmy are the only two who must to be saved." Kristen bowed her head in reluctant agreement.

Tangus helped Kristen and Safire back onto their horses. Lester was able to manage by himself. Climbing on Smoke, Tangus looked at everyone. He thought a pep talk might be appropriate, but as he looked upon their faces he suddenly realized how much combined experience all his friends had. Suddenly feeling rather foolish, Tangus just said, "Let's go."

※

A few hours after the encounter with the mountain giant, the party came upon a great fortress, high walls curving outward with imposing towers. The fading sun at their back was hitting the citadel directly, outlining every detail. Everyone stared at its great size. The façade of the fortress revealed great age and some disrepair, but even still it compelled its will on the pass, as if it had a life of its own. It was a barrier that had never been breached and looked very much like it never would.

"That is the Hammer, my friends," Elrond said. "It stands a silent guard over the land below. Since being built several hundred years ago, no one has ever broken it though many have tried. No one tries anymore. Now it's more a way station for travelers than a true guardian. But it only slumbers. I would not want to awaken it once again. We'll be able to rest there for a few hours in safety."

One of the massive gates silently opened enough to allow a squad of twelve riders to come through and approach.

"Well-oiled gate," Max remarked.

"Let's wait here," Tangus said.

One rider broke away from the rest and came to within speaking distance while the others in the squad stopped and waited about fifty feet behind. The men looked rugged and well experienced. Each was sharply dressed in blue uniforms and red cloaks.

The leader stopped his horse, looking over each member of the party. As his eyes alighted on Elrond and Max, they widened and he smiled. "Elrond and Max! You two old dogs! What the devil brings you to the Hammer?"

Azriel grunted. "You haven't bedded anybody's daughter here, have you?"

"Every female is somebody's daughter," Elrond snickered as he and Max moved their horses past Azriel.

"Garston," Max called. "What'd you do to get this duty? Some dog houses just aren't worth it!"

Waiting for the two to reach him, Garston got off his horse and clasped arms with each. "I'm not in anybody's dog house, Max. It's just a normal six month assignment."

"Bet Chloe's not too happy about that!" Elrond said as he laughed.

Garston shook his head. "No, probably not," he said with a tinge of guilt in his voice. "But with five young ones running around, I was!"

"Five? You've been busy, old man. Here have a cigar," Max said as he drew out three from an inner pocket of his tunic and handed one to Elrond and Gaston. All three immediately lit them up and enjoyed a puff.

"Gentlemen," Tangus called out.

Elrond looked around. "Oh! Sorry. Garston, these are my friends. I'll make introductions later, but for now we need a place to stay the night. How much do you think it'll cost my friend Tangus here?"

"Since your friend Tangus is paying, no charge. I don't think my superiors will have a problem with that. We're not really in the business of making a profit anyway. You, on the other hand, would have been a different story, Mr. Goldpockets," Garston said with a laugh. "But all I can offer by way of food is standard military rations." Garston shrugged his shoulders. "They're hot and filling is about all I can say about them. We do draw the line at wine and anything stronger, however. We have it, but you'll have to pay for it yourself."

"Lead the way," Elrond said as he nodded. "By the way, we had a run in with a mountain giant a few miles back."

"We call him Mr. Personality," Garston said as he nodded. "We don't really care about that side of the Hammer, but every once in a while someone or something comes calling from there with the intention of bypassing our comfortable little abode. Mr. Personality has tried occasionally, but we've always managed to re-buff his attempts."

After going into the fortress, the mighty iron door shut behind them with a loud "gong". The finality of that sound reached everyone, touching each soul. It signaled the close of each person's old life, and signaled the beginning of a new one. Through the bond Kristen felt an elated Emmy. "You have come!" Emmy thought excitedly. "Yes. I am here, my darling," Kristen silently replied.

Through its tentative touch with the bond, the Purge took note of the contact. The time would soon be here. The release of the last empath was eminent.

The ghost of Angela Clearwater watched as Lukas slapped Luminista. "You have failed me once again!" he screamed.

"They are never alone, Lukas. Sometimes I smell men alone, but by the time I get there the scent leads away and back to the camp! What else do you want me to do? Their ten-man patrols are too much for Gyorgy and me to defeat on our own! I'm trying, Lukas, really I am!" Luminista replied aloud, but thinking someday soon she was going to shut him up forever.

Lukas stopped to consider. "We still have enough of the night left. I will go with you and Gyorgy. Surely between the three of us we can take one man."

"But what about the child," Luminista asked.

"Our little 'princess' will be just fine alone. No one will find this place," Lukas sneered.

After the three had left, Angela floated over to her daughter, still safely contained in the stasis field. The magic of the stasis would not let her touch it, so she placed her hand as close as possible. "He will not have you, my Emmy. I swear!"

Ester and her husband Milosh stayed in Elanesse longer than they had anticipated. Hoping to find treasure, they gave themselves thirty days of searching in the dead city before moving on to their next get rich quick scheme. But then Milosh inexplicably decided they had to stay. So they joined a band of mercenaries, along with other treasure hunters encamped nearby. When their supplies ran out, however, they were forced to scavenge for food because the mercenaries would not share. Now Ester had diarrhea and the constant cramping in her stomach made her cringe in pain, wishing she had not eaten that discarded piece of meat.

As Ester squatted behind some bushes with Milosh standing guard nearby, she heard a sound. Looking around, all she saw were bushes. Bushes moving without wind! "Milosh!" she cried. Ester looked back at Milosh as he came running through the bushes to answer his wife's call of distress. As Ester watched him run through the bushes towards her, she saw him stop suddenly and turn white. Without taking his eyes away from what he was seeing, he said, "Don't look, Ester. Just pull up your pants and run!"

"But..."

"Don't argue Ester, just do it," he shouted.

So she did.

Lukas, Luminista, and Gyorgy came upon the place hastily deserted by Ester and Milosh. "The scent is strong. Two I think. But we missed them," Lukas said angrily. "We must return. The dawn will be upon us soon. Tomorrow night is another opportunity."

As the three left, the ghost of Angela Clearwater took form. "Yes, tomorrow night will be another opportunity, Lukas...a missed opportunity. I will see to that."

The treasure hunters that had congregated around the mercenary company encampment were soon bored with simple camp life and, though unwilling to leave the city, they did not hesitate to continue their exploration, hoping the discovery of treasure might still be possible. As a consequence, some of Elanesse's secrets were eventually disclosed. One such secret was the brewery in what was once the Gypsy Quarter.

The treasure hunters of Elanesse came from all walks of life, cooks, carpenters, brick masons, and brew masters. They had the expertise to repair and bring the brewery back to life, which immediately became a priority. After resealing the large tanks, repairing and strengthening the main tank housings and rebuilding structural integrity, all that was needed was water, grain, and a fire. Relieving the mercenaries of grain turned out to be the only major difficulty. Determined men, however, will always find a way. Within a few days of the discovery, the brewery was functional in a limited capacity. On most nights ten to fifteen men were covertly getting drunk on freshly brewed alcohol.

Three figures, dressed entirely in black with large hooded cloaks, descended upon the drunken and unsuspecting men who barely had time to register what was happening before all but one were lying in pools of blood and guts…silent, grim sentinels to the holocaust just perpetrated. The one who had escaped ran out of the brewery as fast as he could, drawing his meager sword to defend himself. He did not know that he was already dead.

One of the three assassins started to go after the fleeing man, but was held back by another. "No, Ishiro. He belongs to Nightshade."

The fleeing man looked behind him and saw he was not being chased. A wave of relief flooded through every pore in his body. He did not notice the black mist lying close to the ground in front of him. He did not notice the black column fifteen feet high that had formed and now towered over him. Perceiving the evil, he suddenly stopped and looked forward. The black misty column solidified, out of each side four arms appeared, each with hundreds of inch long barbed spikes. Two fangs the size of a short sword sprang out of the head as gleaming blue eyes opened and looked down. The man could not move, he could not scream, nor could he even close his eyes. His bowels suddenly released. The eight arms engulfed him, forcing the barbed spikes into his body. They were not long enough to kill him, however. Though his voice would not work, his eyes shrieked with the pain.

THE SALVATION OF INNOCENCE

Nightshade let the fear and torment wash over her. The emotion emitting from the man revitalized her. His fear and pain were like a soothing balm to her eternally ravenous soul. She was satisfied. There was but one thing left to do. As the man watched, Nightshade's fangs descended and entered his chest. For just a few moments he felt his insides liquefy before he died. But death was not the end to his terror. His soul was eaten as well. Then the terror stopped, for one does not sense oblivion.

Nightshade let the dried husk drop to the ground. She and her three assassins left the brewery. As much as possible they needed keep a low profile. She was hired to take the empath and her bonded mother, not to kill all the mortals in Elanesse, something she truly wished to do. Nightshade always kept her end of a contract.

CHAPTER 14

The use of deception by a thief surprises no one. Why then should everyone be surprised when deception is used by a politician? Are they not thieves as well?

— *Book of the Unveiled*

Autumn had never been to the capital city of Taranthi. Unlike the buildings at Calmacil Clearing, which were principally constructed with granite and wood, most of the buildings of Taranthi were magically grown from the ground. Many roofs on the buildings were made from crystal or gems, spectacularly glittering as the sunlight hit them. Autumn had never seen anything like this before in her life.

"Pretty impressive, isn't it?" Father Goram said riding beside her.

"Oh Horatio, it's so beautiful!" Autumn replied as she kept looking around.

Father Goram laughed. "Please try to be a little less obvious, my dear. You're not a country bumpkin and I don't want the city folk to think of you as such. I would hate to have to defend your honor. That can get so messy sometimes."

Autumn smiled. "I will attempt to be more discrete."

Father Goram patted her hand. "I have a small place here that I keep for emergency meetings and…" Father Goram sighed, "…affairs of state."

"You say that as if it hurts," Autumn said.

"It does. Damn it, Autumn, I'm a priest, not a politician!"

Autumn looked over at Father Goram with a raised eyebrow. "I hate to break it to you Horatio, but most of what you do at the monastery IS politics, and you're actually pretty good at it."

"You're right of course. Sometimes I wish life could be simpler," Father Goram said sadly.

Autumn shook her head. "I'm afraid those days are long gone."

Father Goram's "small" place was the entire third floor of a magnificent three-story mansion. It was very elaborately furnished and impeccably maintained. The floors and walls were marble and the ceiling frosted crystal. Expensive throw rugs littered the floor of the main room. Besides a kitchen and formal dining room, there was a master suite and two guestrooms as well as two small rooms with magically enhanced plumbing. Autumn dropped her traveling pack on the floor and stared, again surprised by wonders she never knew existed. She looked at Father Goram.

Sheepishly, Father Goram looked at the floor before facing Autumn's stare. "Inheritance," he said. "It's kept in an independent trust fund that I have absolutely no control over. My parents were greatly distressed at my decision to become a cleric. The Goram name is well-known in the Queen's inner circle and they had other plans for me. When I announced my calling, father did not want to take the chance that I would sell off family belongings and give them to the poor."

"And would you have?" Autumn asked.

"No, I don't think so. Mostly out of respect for my parents who labored hard to build their 'empire' as father liked to say. But I also like to come here to getaway. It helps me to keep a healthy perspective on things," Father Goram replied. There was no hint of shame or regret in his voice.

Autumn looked around again. "I probably wouldn't have either. Althaya does not require poverty."

"You can put your belongings in the master bedroom, my dear," Father Goram said to Autumn. Turning to the two rangers who had accompanied them he said, "You've both been awfully quiet."

Both were unusually large elves, dressed in the typical ranger garb of greens and browns. Each carried a longbow and two scimitars. Considering everything that had recently transpired, Father Goram had gone to Magdalena and asked for a couple of rangers for escort duty. The two she decided to send, Arthon and Gunthor, were her best and completely loyal. Father Goram trusted Magdalena completely, but it helped the little doubt in the back of his mind that Arthon was her brother.

Arthon smiled. "My sister said to stay quiet and out of the way, but ever vigilant. She is most insistent that no evil shall befall either of you. She also has other rangers shadowing us here in Taranthi. We come from a large family of rangers, Father - nephews, nieces, cousins. You wear us like a blanket, a blanket that keeps you warm but yet you do not know it's there."

Father Goram just stared. Arthon continued, "My sister was extremely annoyed, Father, by the events that transpired with Vayl. Not just because she allowed herself to be tricked and kidnapped…"

"We were all tricked," Father Goram interrupted.

"Yes…anyway, according to Magdalena, all your new leadership hierarchy considers you indispensable. She told me if something were to happen to you I should, and I quote, 'Get my own damn self on the next boat to the mainland and don't bother to ever come back!' She was quite emotional at the time, Father. Sometimes she can be rather… intense. It really makes me quite proud."

Father Goram looked at Arthon, then at Gunthor. "If something were to happen to you, I'll be going with Arthon," Gunthor said. He seemed pretty adamant about that particular point. "Funny," Father Goram thought. "I always considered Magdalena to be such a sweet person." Shaking his head, Father Goram said, "Okay gentlemen, I think I understand the situation. It's late, so we're not going to the Royal Library until tomorrow after breakfast. Each of you help yourself to one of the guest rooms and…and just do whatever it is you do. Right now I could use some wine."

From the street the Royal Library looked like any other of the more elaborate single-story buildings in Taranthi, except it was circular with a domed top. At the front entrance were two elven warriors, members of the Queen's Contingent, the finest fighting force in all of InnisRos. The guards at the entrance recognized Father Goram and automatically waved him, Autumn, and the two rangers through. Inside the first door a twenty-foot wide corridor circled the entire building at ground level. Two more of the Queen's Contingent stood guard at another set of double doors across the corridor from the entrance. Arthon and Gunthor, however, were not allowed through the second set of doors. Both rangers bristled, but were reassured the library was under the Queen's personal protection and no harm could possibly come to Father Goram or Autumn.

It was not until a person went through the second entrance that the magnitude of the building was truly revealed. One hundred feet across and going down one hundred and fifty feet into the ground were five circular levels, each twenty-feet high with a ten-foot steel balcony and railing. A steel spiral staircase led down to the bottom floor. On the other side of the room an identical spiral staircase went up from the floor but stopped at the last level. Ramps reached out from that staircase and went to each balcony. The number of tomes, manuscripts, and books the library contained numbered in the hundreds of thousands.

"You're gawking again," Father Goram said as he lightly elbowed Autumn in the side.

"How can I not, Horatio?! I didn't know so much written knowledge existed in the world, let alone a single library," Autumn replied.

"I have to admit this library is quite special. A lot has been written during recorded history. Not just by our race, but also by the humans and dwarves, with theories of science and magic topping the list of researched articles. This library contains a good portion of those writings, all but the prophecies, however. Those are kept elsewhere," Father Goram said. "Very few are allowed to study them, and I'm not on that short list."

"Do they use a magical accounting system like we use in our library?" Autumn asked.

"Right you are, dear girl, but obviously on a more massive scale."

"Then it shouldn't be too difficult to locate what we're after," Autumn replied.

"We'll see," Father Goram said. "I've known the Librarian for a long time. He's pretty particular about his 'children' as he likes to call his books and scrolls. And even though I trust him, I do not want him to know the manuscript we seek. If the manuscript is here and if we get our hands on it, we will have to destroy it without him knowing and any of the library magic detecting its removal." Father Goram took Autumn's hand. "But let's deal with one problem at a time," he said. "Let's go down, shall we?"

As the two descended, the main station of the Librarian came into view. Father Goram didn't recognize the elf sitting behind it. "How may I help you?" the Librarian asked.

"Excuse me, but where's Judson? He's been at this desk since I was very young. Actually, I've never seen anyone else behind it," Father Goram replied.

A troubled look came across the Librarian's face. "I'm sorry sir, but I'm afraid Judson had an accident several weeks ago. He's dead."

Father Goram frowned. "When and how did it happen?"

"And you are, sir?" the Librarian asked.

"I'm sorry. I'm Father Horatio Goram, the chief priest at Althaya's monastery in Calmacil Clearing. This is one of my most trusted advisors, Autumn Vanerious."

"I am honored to make your acquaintance," the Librarian said. "Of course I've heard of you. I'm Flynn. I apprenticed under Judson. He was a good teacher and more importantly a good friend. In answer to your questions, he died several weeks ago, but I don't really know for sure what happened, Father. Supposedly he had a bad fall at his home and hit his head. He was very old after all. Even so, he wasn't frail by any stretch of the imagination, still very sure of foot. You have to be if you're going to climb around this library. I never quite understood it, but anything is possible I suppose." Flynn frowned. "Another strange thing now that

I think upon it. His formal funeral pyre happened very suddenly, like someone was trying to hide something. Some of his family on the other side of the island didn't have sufficient time to travel here to pay their last respects."

Father Goram started thinking about this unexpected turn of events, lost for a moment as the implications of this news confirmed what he had feared. Shaking his head to clear his reverie, he said, "I'm very sorry to hear about Judson. We've had many discussions over the course of my lifetime, particularly when I needed to inventory and establish an accounting system for the library at the monastery. But I'm sure everything was in order and Judson's death was accidental like it was reported. Why would anyone want to harm such a good fellow, right?" Father Goram said. "I'm also sure you're completely up to the task of running the library."

"I hope you're right, Father. The Royal Library is one of the Queen's pride and joys. I receive important people here all the time. It puts a lot of pressure on me and my staff," Flynn said. "But enough of that, how may I help?"

Father Goram had drifted away with his thoughts once again and did not answer. "Horatio, are you with us?" Autumn asked.

"Huh? Oh sorry. I'm afraid the news about Judson is very distressing and has completely caught me off guard. Why I'm here seems so trivial now." Pulling out a piece of vellum Father Goram had prepared earlier in the morning, he handed it to Flynn. "I need to reference this particular manuscript. I'm developing a new spell and we don't have this text in the monastery library."

Flynn took the vellum and went back to his desk. 'Let's see, *Five Observations of Clerical Magic as Applied to the Art of Healing*' by Tulane. We don't have much written by Tulane, Father. And with all due respect, what we do have is nothing but ramblings by what most researchers consider someone who was quite mad. But let me check." Flynn then whispered a command word that activated the magic in a flat crystal disk lying on his desk.

Autumn whispered, "What's going on?"

"I'll tell you when we return to my apartment," Father Goram whispered back.

"No Father, we don't have that particular manuscript. The magic never lies. Are you sure Tulane wrote such a work?" Flynn said from behind his desk.

"No, not really," Father Goram replied. "There's a vague reference to it in another source book I was using, but nothing really specific."

Flynn came back around from his desk. "Well, take heart. We don't have every manuscript ever written. I have no doubt it's out there somewhere. Sorry you've traveled such a long way though, Father. I'm sorry I couldn't help, but I can make inquiries if you're interested."

Father Goram sighed and then smiled. "No, that's okay, and it's never a waste of time to have a chance to visit Taranthi, Flynn. Making a trip like this often gives me a chance to get away from other problems. Anyway, thanks for your help and good luck with the library."

Back in the street, as the four of them were heading towards Father Goram's apartment, they were approached from behind.

"Goram! What a coincidence meeting you here in Taranthi!"

Father Goram knew that voice as soon as he heard it. Turning he said, "Mordecai. So wonderful to see you! And I see you brought your little harlot along."

Mordecai held back Amberley. "As did you," he replied, flashing a leering glare at Autumn.

Father Goram smiled, not rising to the bait. Autumn remained calm. "Excellent, Autumn! Don't allow Mordecai to play you," he thought. "What do you want?" Father Goram asked Mordecai.

"Nothing really," Mordecai said with a smirk on his face. "Since we just happened to meet here in the most unlikely of places I thought I should pay my compliments. I understand you had some problems at the monastery,"

"News travels quickly, doesn't it Mordecai? I sent a message to the Queen. She's aware," Father Goram replied.

"Of course she is," Mordecai said. "Did you know she called an emergency meeting of the council? She's quite concerned about the level of leadership at one of the largest monasteries on InnisRos. Her Highness, of course, wonders if maybe one younger might have prevented it. Perhaps someone who's not so blind to the treachery within your own midst? I myself speculated that maybe Vayl was set up to cover your own incompetence," Mordecai purred.

Autumn did not remain calm this time. "You damn whoreson!" she shouted. "Vayl is the lowest of elven garbage. His betrayal was very real and very cowardly! If I ever see him again I'll kill him. KILL HIM! DO YOU HEAR ME?!"

Other than holding firm to Autumn's arm, Father Goram let her shout, it would probably be cathartic and help speed the mental healing she needed.

Mordecai laughed and said, "What a little spitfire you've got there, Goram." He suddenly removed all pretense of humor and looked at Father Goram and Autumn with hard eyes. "Watch your back, priest."

Mordecai and Amberley turned and walked away. Father Goram watched their retreating figures as he put an arm around Autumn's shoulders, trying to calm her angry trembling.

Turning to Arthon and Gunthor, Father Goram said, "Don't even think about it. And call off any of your relatives that may be having the same thoughts. Mordecai expects it and probably has as many, if not more, allies watching over him. Let's just go."

~

As Mordecai and Amberley walked away, Amberley asked, "Why did you warn him?"

Mordecai shook his head. "Tsk! Tsk! My dear, there is much you still need to learn about manipulation. As long as Goram thinks someone is going to come for him, he's going to spend precious time looking over his shoulder and preparing to defend those he values over here. He has to, and that's time he won't have to help his daughter. If he is lost, she is even more exposed. Though Vayl failed, he succeeded. He showed Goram the threat was real."

"But why not just kill him and be done with it?" Amberley asked.

Mordecai shook his head, "Amberley, I can't just have him killed. He's too powerful and has too many connections with the royal house. If he dies, the Queen will surely launch an investigation, an investigation that could lead back to me. If that happens she'll learn about my plans. What do you think she would do with that information? I'm not strong enough to challenge the Queen yet."

"But you put yourself out in the open. He knows from whom the attack will come," Amberley replied.

"Does he now?" Mordecai laughed. "Think about it, Amberley. How do I neutralize him without the Queen getting too nosey about it?" he asked.

Amberley frowned, and then the pieces of Mordecai's plan fell into place. "That's brilliant! Use the Queen to bring down Goram. That way she won't start looking at your involvement. But the Queen's pretty smart. You must be wary playing such games with her," Amberley said. "I have one question. It's not a coincidence Goram's in Taranthi, so why was he here visiting the Library."

Mordecai abruptly let his smirk die. "Why indeed?" he thought.

"Let us go in first, Father," Arthon said when they reached the top of the stairs to Father Goram's Taranthi home. Autumn was still seething, but she seemed to have herself back under control, though she remained silent during the walk back from the Library.

"Not necessary gentlemen," Father Goram said as he unlocked the door and walked in. "There are certain security measures that have been in place for decades. My father did not coddle thieves. The first few who tried were found in the main room, their minds broken. They never regained their sanity. The reputation of the place is so horrifying that even the Queen herself would not attempt to enter without an invitation and escort."

Both rangers suddenly looked a bit unsure of themselves. Father Goram smiled. "Don't worry. My friends and allies will never come to mischief. You see, each person enters and is judged by their intent. I don't know what magic my father used, but someone entering to steal or otherwise do harm suffers a terrible fate, while a simple cleaning person could enter and be completely safe."

Once inside Father Goram started a fire and poured wine for everyone. Arthon and Gunthor went to the main room and made themselves comfortable while Father Goram and Autumn quickly put together a plate of sweetmeats, cheese, and bread for lunch.

"Father, Mordecai as much as said he was coming after you. You really need to get back to the monastery," Arthon said.

Father Goram, setting the tray of food down on a table and taking a seat on the sofa with Autumn, said, "Mordecai's coming after me, Arthon, but it won't be a direct attack. He's powerful, smart, and a survivor. What happened this morning was misdirection. He did it to force me away from the problem at hand which is making sure Emmy is not taken from Kristen and brought over here. Unfortunately he has the advantage. I have to defend myself for Kristen and Emmy's sake. And I don't know from which quarter Mordecai's attack will come when it does."

Autumn spoke for the first time since her words with Mordecai. "Is that the reason for your change of direction in the Library?"

Father Goram nodded. "When Flynn told me of poor Judson's death, everything fell in place. Vayl's treachery and Judson's death suddenly added up for me. I now know the Library did in fact have the manuscript and that it was stolen and Judson was killed to cover it up. Vayl was bought and his actions probably planned to keep me otherwise occupied while a more sinister plot was undertaken. The timeline fits. Although I suspected who was behind it as we left the Library, I didn't really know until Mordecai just 'happened' to meet us in the street. That was not a fluke."

Autumn grabbed Father Goram's hand. "What do you intend to do, Horatio?"

Father Goram had been thinking about that ever since Autumn and he left the Library. "I think Arthon is correct. We need to return to the monastery. But first there's someone I want to talk to."

"Who would that be?" Autumn asked.

"Erin Mirie," Father Goram replied. "She's Second Councilor and a close family friend. I need eyes and ears in the council and I think she will be more than happy to oblige since Mordecai's involved. They hate each other passionately." Turning his attention to the two rangers, Father Goram said, "Arthon, please tell your relatives I need eyes and ears on the streets of Taranthi as well."

"Not a problem, father. C'mon, Gunthor, we've got work to do."

"Don't get yourselves killed, gentlemen," Father Goram said as they went out the door.

CHAPTER 15

"A well traveled journey reveals many avenues of opportunity. It is the responsibility of the one making the voyage, however, to determine the correct path and to take the first step.

— *Book of the Unveiled*

THE JOURNEY FROM the Hammer to the City of Ascension took about a week of determined traveling. The party went through the foothills on the east side of the Olympus Mountains and had to ford several small rivers draining down from the mountains into the forest and grasslands below before arriving at the walled city of Ascension. Dirty, tired, and cold, everyone sat on their horses before the two western towers flanking the closed gate. Tangus wondered why the double gates to the city were closed and the portcullis lowered.

Jennifer, who was riding alongside Azriel, asked, "What are we waiting for?"

Azriel snorted. "Tangus just probably wants to see if someone is going to come riding out to either arrest or ban Elrond from the city."

Jennifer turned to look at Azriel. "Really?" she asked seriously.

Azriel laughed. "I don't know, my dear. But I wouldn't be surprised. Elrond and Max have gotten around. But more than likely it's because the gates are closed, which is very unusual." Azriel suddenly stood up in his stirrups. "Something's happening," he said. The portcullis slowly rose and one of the double gates opened just wide enough to allow several riders to come through and ride out to meet them.

Based upon their dress, the riders were obviously rangers. They stopped approximately fifty feet away from Tangus and Kristen. All the riders wore, on their left hand, the same style of ring Tangus, Jennifer, Safire, and Euranna wore, which identified them as followers of the goddess Aurora. They were carrying a black flag.

Unknown to the riders, a figure emerged from the opened gate with several others chasing behind. Tangus, in one smooth motion, grasped his bow, notched an arrow from his quiver, and let the arrow fly. The arrow struck the running figure in the side and it dropped to the ground instantly. From one hundred feet it was hard to tell if the figure was male or female, but the scream of pain that issued forth when the arrow hit was masculine. All the riders looked back and realized what had happened. "Thank you, sir," one of them called.

Tangus called back, "The gods be with you, gentlemen." Turning to Kristen, he grabbed Arbellason's reins and led them northeast. "We bypass this city," he said with a tone in his voice that did not allow for argument. He then kicked Smoke into a gallop. Everyone followed, soon leaving Ascension at their backs.

"What the hell just happened? Has Tangus gone mad?" Safire said to Lester as they rode away from the city.

"The plague has come to Ascension, Safire. And with it quarantine," Lester replied. "Anybody going in would not be allowed to leave. Anyone trying to leave must either be captured or killed. Unfortunate, I know, but I have seen the plague. It is very necessary to stop its spread. Maybe you had no experience with plague on InnisRos, but it is a far too common occurrence here. Tangus made the only choice he could."

Safire looked over at Lester. "I'm not done with this," she said angrily.

After about an hour they came to a small stream. Tangus stopped his horse, dismounted, and studied the water flow. It was flowing towards Ascension. Satisfied, he allowed Smoke to drink. Everyone else, taking their cue from Tangus, did the same. As Safire approached Tangus, she could see Kristen already talking to him. He had simply crossed his arms to listen as she spoke heatedly, waving her arms.

"Tangus, you murdered him!" Kristen said.

"He was probably going to die anyway, Kristen," Tangus calmly replied.

THE SALVATION OF INNOCENCE

About this time Safire joined the conversation as everyone else gathered around to watch. "If he was sick, Kristen could have saved him, Tangus. She's a healer! Lester mentioned a plague. By the goddess, there's no telling how many people Kristen could have saved from the disease! We all could have helped!"

"Tangus, it's my responsibility...we were going to spend the night there anyway. That's all I wanted! My husband, please explain this to me?" Kristen pleaded.

Tangus took a deep breath. "I understand your distress, my love, really I do, but you, Jennifer, Safire, and Euranna have had no experience with the plague. It's not just a sickness that can be instantly healed with magic or herbs. It overwhelms clerics with its intensity. Saving just one person can take all the magical energy a cleric normally uses in one day. I know that even one life is priceless, but yours is worth so much more. We've talked about this before. I know what your instincts tell you to do, that's why I love you so much, but there is too much at stake for us to take any chances. You know that."

"May I, Tangus?" Lester asked. At Tangus' nod, Lester continued, "I have experienced the plague personally. It is called the Black Death. Even clerics and paladins are not immune to this insidious disease. Heal a person one day, and the person can be re-infected the next. It appears to concentrate in populated areas such as cities. The only known cure is to allow it to run its course, to die out on its own. Very few people who get it survive. Very few people are immune to its deadly affects. One thing widely known, however, is that a person can be infected several days before he actually experiences symptoms. That is why it is so important to restrict travel into and out of infected areas. I know some of you are not native to this land, but how the plague is to be addressed is something all the civilized races over here have agreed to. Kristen, if you were to go in, you would not be allowed to leave, nor would you want to. The very same compassion you have for the people you want to help would prevent you from leaving lest you spread the disease to others. Tangus did a hard thing, but it was the ONLY thing he could do."

Kristen looked down at the ground. Tangus grimaced at the pain he saw in her eyes, but he knew it was a reality she must face.

They decided to spend the night where they had stopped to water the horses. It was a cold night, each person huddled around the campfire. Left to their own thoughts, no one got much sleep.

It was well past midnight when they reached the small town of Silverstone, approximately two hundred miles east of Ascension. Six days had passed. Silverstone was located at the junction of the northeastern leg of the Alpine and the Merchants Way, a well traveled road going southeast to the large city of Havendale. Though this part of the Alpine represented the last leg of their trip, Elanesse was still an eight day ride away.

Bypassing Ascension had put a strain on their supplies. With the exception of an occasional rabbit, wild game was not plentiful in the snow-covered grassland east of the Olympus Mountains. What grass that was available for grazing was buried under several inches of ice and snow. Consequently they were running uncomfortably low in food and feed.

All of the establishments in Silverstone were closed when they entered with the exception of a small tavern. As everyone dismounted in front of the pub, Tangus turned and said, "Please wait here. That means you too, Bitts."

"You stay as well, Romulus," Kristen said.

Tangus smiled his thanks at Kristen before addressing everyone else. "I don't want to give the barkeep a heart attack. From the looks of this place, they probably don't see travelers like us often. Kristen and I will see about food and a place to stay the night." Everyone nodded agreement. Both animals sat down. Bitts was used to this and accepted his master's orders, but Romulus looked at Kristen. She went to him and petted his neck while rubbing his side. "It's only because people fear big wolves, dear." She went over and took Tangus' hand as they entered the tavern.

THE SALVATION OF INNOCENCE

Inside, the fire in the huge stone fireplace, unattended, was slowly going out. A large woman was slumped over on a table near the fireplace, snoring loudly. There was no one else in the tavern. Tangus and Kristen walked over and studied her. She was a human, maybe thirty years old, with long red curly hair that covered her face. Her well worn leather top and trousers, which were stuffed into heavy boots, looked to be a little tight on her. Though she was large, it was not because she was plump, but rather because she was very muscular. At her feet lay a good-sized mace. The glow radiating from the metal head left no doubt that it was magical.

Tangus and Kristen both silently slid chairs out from the table and sat down. Kristen shrugged. "I don't know what to do? We're strangers. How do we gently wake her so she will not be alarmed?" she whispered.

Tangus reached down to move the mace out of the woman's reach. Suddenly a strong hand grasped his arm. "I wouldn't do that, sir," the woman warned as she sat up. Tangus could tell by looking at her that she was now fully awake and looking warily at them. He also saw a shield pinned to her shirt. *She is a law keeper.*

Upon seeing the holy symbol around Kristen's neck and the angel ring Tangus always wore, she visibly relaxed and released Tangus arm. "I've had a long day. What time is it?" she asked.

"About two hours past midnight," Kristen said.

"A bit late for you folks to be traveling, isn't it?" the woman asked.

"So then why is your tavern still open?" Tangus countered.

The woman smiled. "Indeed. This tavern isn't mine. I'm just temporarily watching it for old Bill. He's a bit under the weather. Damn, I should have closed up hours ago. I'm Agatha by the way," she said extending her hand.

Tangus and Kristen both shook it and introduced themselves. "We have eight others as well as horses and…other animals. Do you know where we can get something to eat and drink? Or where we can bed down for the night?" Tangus inquired.

"Bill's got an old barn out back I suppose you could use. I don't have a clue what's in it other than hay in a loft. There's also a well back there, if the water isn't frozen. I'm afraid Bill's tapped out in here. No beer or wine to speak of. The only food he has for customers are those pickled eggs on the bar. They're a copper each."

"Thank you for your kindness," Kristen said.

"It's my pleasure, madam. Where are you heading if I may ask?"

"Northeast on the Alpine," Tangus said guardedly.

Agatha's eyes narrowed. "From where?" she asked.

Tangus looked at Agatha. He knew why she wanted to know. "Ascension," he said.

Pain momentarily flashed in Agatha's eyes. "Are they still under quarantine?" she inquired.

Tangus nodded. Kristen said, "Yes, Agatha. Do you know someone living there?"

"This is a small community, everybody pretty much knows everybody else. Several of our merchants went down there several weeks ago to buy supplies and items to re-stock their shelves and bring back wine and kegs of ale. We've heard nothing from them since. We did get a messenger riding through telling us that the Black Death was there," Agatha said as she looked into the dying fire. "I don't think we're going to see any of them again."

Kristen grabbed Agatha's arm. "You must have hope!" she said.

Agatha put her callused hand over Kristen's. "Thank you. I gave up on hope many years ago."

"But you're so young," Kristen replied.

Sitting back down, Agatha said reflectively, "It seems like I've been on my own for an eternity. I've seen a lot. I finally find a place with good people who accepted me with open arms, a place where I could do some good, and now a quarter of the population, fathers and sons, are probably dead. This is going to be a very sad place when the list of dead gets to us. I guess I should have known." Shaking off her melancholy, Agatha stood up and said, "Take the pickled eggs free of charge. I don't think old Bill is going to mind. I need to close up."

"Are there any stores with supplies, particularly feed for our horses, that we can visit in the morning?" Tangus asked as he went over to the bar and took the pickles.

"No, not open for business anyway. What most people have they're saving to hold them through until the supplies get here. Now that we know that's probably not going to happen, we need to look to our own survival," Agatha replied. "Will I see you tomorrow?"

"I doubt it. We'll settle in the barn tonight and get some sleep, but we'll be on the road at first light," Tangus said as he put the pickles back down on the bar. "I suppose old Bill may need these more than us, though we appreciate your generosity."

"I suspect he will. Safe journey to you all," Agatha said as she escorted them out the door, her eyes widening with surprise and curiosity when she looked out to see the wide array of different travelers in this group, least of which was not the wolf. "What a story that must be," she thought as she closed the door behind Tangus and Kristen.

With dwindling food supplies still a concern, particularly for the horses, the trip was slowed as more time was needed for the horses to forage. And like the horses, the rangers were obliged to range farther away from the road to do their hunting.

As they moved into the Elderdale, a large clearing of farmland bracketed on the northwest by the Forest of the Fey and Lake Lorali to the southeast, their food concern for the horses eased considerably. Within the Forest of the Fey, further northeast, lay Elanesse. Hunting here was easier, and there was plenty of grass sticking up through a partially melted layer of snow for the horses to eat. In the early afternoon, on the seventh day after leaving Silverstone, they arrived at Saint Seton, the largest community in the Elderdale. From here it was only about a two day ride to Elanesse.

Though Saint Seton had little to offer by way of inns or taverns, the community was filled with honest, good, and caring country folk. The party was welcomed with open arms and homes were offered to accommodate everyone. Tangus thought it would be best not to separate and everyone agreed, so a large barn was soon appropriated for their use. Not long after settling in, warm food started arriving, cooked by mothers and daughters. A hastily thrown-together feast ensued. By dusk's falling, the barn was alive with laughter and the excited giggles of children. The celebrities of the evening turned out to be Bitts and Romulus, both of whom reveled in their newly found adoring fans. Kristen laughed as children climbed all over Romulus. It wasn't long before she was using Romulus to give the children rides on his back.

About midnight the gathering was over. All of the good people of Saint Seton had left, with many of the parents carrying sleeping children slumped over their shoulders. An abundance of food had been left behind for the road. As everyone sat around a large table, drinking wine, ale, or water, basking in the warm feeling they each had, Jennifer said, "Surprising people like this can be found so close to Elanesse."

"Elanesse is still at least a couple of days away by horseback, sweetie," Tangus said. "That's a good bit of separation."

"Aye," Azriel said. "I was talking to one old gentleman and there's also a strong military-type presence in the area. The 'Riders of Elderdale' he called them. The Elderdale seems safe enough."

Lester, normally quiet, spoke up. "Still, who knows what evils we will awaken or unleash rescuing Emmy?"

"There are always uncertainties in life, Lester. You know that," Max said.

Lester paused before answering. "Yes I do know that, Max. But sometimes a strong sword can remove some of that uncertainty. I spoke with a gentleman who is a member of the 'Riders of Elderdale'. He tells me they are always looking for warriors to help keep Elderdale citizens safe. They're only farmers, Max. There are some things they just can't defend themselves against." Lester looked at Elrond and Max. Safire, sitting beside him, took his hand. "I've been looking for a place to call home for a long time. The 'Company' was never that for me, just a way station along my journey. Saint Seton is that home, I can feel it. When we're done rescuing Emmy, I shall tender my resignation from the 'Company'. This is where I wish to live."

"Tangus," Safire said. "I want to stay with Lester."

There was silence all around. Elrond finally nodded. "You're a good companion, Lester. I wish you nothing but success."

"And you, Tangus?" Safire asked.

Tangus shook his head, not really understanding what Safire was asking. "I love you like a sister and I only wish you happiness, and it looks like you have found it. I have no hold over you. But if it is my blessing you want, I give it to you wholeheartedly."

Suddenly all the females squealed, got up and went over to Safire, hugging and congratulating her. All the males except Azriel stared. "What's that all about?" Tangus mused.

Azriel laughed. "You really don't know? As well as being like a brother, you're also the nearest thing Safire has to a father. You just gave her permission to marry the one she loves."

"Well I'll be damned," Tangus thought aloud.

As the sun peaked over the eastern horizon the following morning, they were back on the road, enjoying a breakfast from food provided by the farmers of Saint Seton the previous evening. At mid-day they entered the Forest of the Fey. By late afternoon Tangus, after consulting his map and talking with what had by now become his command council of Elrond, Max, and Christian, decided it was time to move deeper into the forest towards Elanesse. Tangus stopped his horse. He knew from studying his map that all the roads going into and out of Elanesse have long since been reclaimed by the forest, so there would be no roads to follow. From here, however, if they travelled northwesterly, they should reach Elanesse in about a day. Tangus looked out into the forest. After weeks of travel, it was finally time to begin the assault on Elanesse. But more importantly, it was time to save the last empath.

"Elrond," Max said. "What's wrong?"

Everyone turned their horses to look at the two. Max was reaching across and pulling on Elrond's arm, trying to get his attention, but Elrond didn't respond. He looked and acted like he was mentally elsewhere. Tangus and Kristen quickly rode to Elrond and Max's position at the end of their small column. Max was still talking to Elrond, trying to get him to focus on the here and now, trying to bring him out of the enchantment that had him so mesmerized. As Tangus and Kristen approached, Elrond looked at Max.

"Can you hear the music, Max?" he asked.

"No. What music, Elrond?" Max replied.

Tangus and Kristen had stopped their horses, but did not interfere. No one knew Elrond better than Max, and Elrond trusted no one more than he did Max.

"Elanesse's singing to me!" Elrond responded with a smile. There was not any hint of confusion or doubt in his voice or demeanor.

"You're being deceived," Max said.

"No Max, I'm not," Elrond said, nodding at Tangus and Kristen as if he just realized they were there. "I know you probably think I've lost my mind, but trust me, I am still quite sane. The city is alive. The city is asking for my help."

Tangus spoke for the first time. "Asking you for help? Against what, Elrond?" he asked.

"She does not know. There is a presence there, a cancer that has been killing her for thousands of years. Though feeling incredible pain, she rejoices that one finally has come who can hear her cry," Elrond said.

"And that person is you?" Max asked incredulously.

Elrond nodded. "It would appear so." Turning his attention to Kristen, Elrond said, "Elanesse knows about the last empath, Kristen. She deplored the magic that was used by her clerics to make it possible for rangers to murder the empaths. The population she so loved horrified and betrayed her. She feels shame. She has done what she can to help hide the empath's location from the power that seeks her out. She fears, however, that will soon no longer be possible."

Kristen nodded. "A couple of months ago I would never have considered the idea of an intelligent city, but now I find it impossible to deny. Please tell Elanesse that we come for the empath. But Elrond, Emmy is my only concern. We will try to help Elanesse if we can, however Emmy must be taken to safety as quickly as possible."

"The two are related, Kristen. In order to keep the last empath safe, this power of which Elanesse speaks must be destroyed," Elrond said.

Tangus nodded. "We'll deal with that when the time comes. It's getting late so I think we should stop for a few hours. I'll take Safire ahead a little way into the forest to find a suitable campsite. Tomorrow we should make it Elanesse. I don't need to tell anyone what that means." Calling out, he said, "Safire, on me!" as he walked his horse off the road and into the forest, followed by Safire with Lester trailing behind. This close to danger, Lester was not going to let Safire out of his sight.

Kristen smiled at Elrond and Max. "Whatever happens in Elanesse, I want you to know how much I appreciate the sacrifices you've made to come along."

"We would never let Tangus down, Kristen. He's our brother," Max said seriously.

As Kristen made her way forward, Max said quietly to Elrond, "Tangus couldn't have chosen a better wife."

"You're right about that," Elrond replied. Then, turning to look at Max, said, "Max, I'm not leaving Elanesse."

Max looked at Elrond confused. "What? You have some premonition of doom?"

"No, Max, it's nothing like that...although death is always a possibility in our line of work," Elrond replied.

Max laughed, "Yeah, we say that a lot."

"What I mean is that I'll not leave Elanesse by herself," Elrond said.

"C'mon, Elrond," Max responded. "Elanesse isn't a woman you can, you know, have a relationship with."

Elrond shook his head. "No, you don't understand. She needs someone to watch over her. She's been so alone all these years. When this is over, providing we survive, I want to move our base of operations here."

"That means breaking our ties with the Duke," Max replied. "And that means you have to end your on-again-off-again romance with his sister, the Lady Bronwyn."

"The Duke will understand. As for the Lady Bronwyn, maybe I can convince her to move to Elanesse as my wife," Elrond said with a smile.

Max was speechless.

The morning sun was just beginning its ascent into the eastern sky, though the forest still jealously guarded the last remnants of dark against the light. Jennifer and Azriel stood the last watch. They were sitting together on a moss-covered rock. Azriel was oiling and sharpening his huge battleaxe while Jennifer threw small sticks into the fire, thinking about Elanesse while listening to the constant sound of whetstone on metal.

"It'll be dawn in a bit, Azriel. Do you think we should wake everybody?" Jennifer asked.

"No lassie, let's give them another hour. We'll get the coffee brewing in a bit," Azriel replied without looking up. A constant stream of smoke rose from the pipe sticking out of his mouth.

"Azriel," Jennifer said.

Azriel stopped sharpening his battleaxe and looked up at Jennifer. There was something in the inflection of her voice that sounded urgent. "Yes Jennifer?" he said.

"I'm afraid," she said simply. Azriel could read the uncertainty in her voice. Aside from the dragon and the mountain giant, attacks which occurred suddenly and were over quickly, the upcoming battle for Emmy would be Jennifer's first real exposure to the mind games all soldiers experience before a battle. Azriel thought what Jennifer wasn't saying would probably fill a book.

"I know you are, lassie. And you should be," Azriel said as he put his rough hand on hers. "Let me ask you a question. When the dragon and later the mountain giant attacked, what were you thinking?"

"They were so sudden I didn't really have time to think. I just reacted," Jennifer said.

"You relied on your training, just as your father has taught you, and your warrior instinct. From what I have seen, his instruction has served you well. Trust in your abilities. Trust in your comrades." Azriel went back to sharpening his battleaxe. "You'll be fine."

"What do you trust in, Azriel?" Jennifer asked.

Azriel paused. "Mostly this," he said as he raised his weapon. The magic of its blade suddenly exploded brightly in the fleeting dark. "It likes to show off sometimes," Azriel commented as he smiled.

※

Breakfast was not sitting well with Kristen as she and the others made their way towards Elanesse. The bond with Emmy had been getting increasingly stronger the closer she got to the ruined city, but so was the corruption in the bond. With each step Arbellason took, her breath was becoming harder to draw in. She could feel her heart beating in her chest. Her mind was racing with questions for which she had no answer: "Can we win Emmy away from the evil that wishes to destroy her?", "What if the stasis field collapses before we get there?", "Who is going to die because I'm not a good enough priestess?", "Can I be the mother of an empath?", "How do I go on if Tangus is killed?" Looking around wide-eyed, Kristen suddenly found she couldn't take in any air at all. Her vision turned to gray and the world around her started to spin. She felt a strong hand grip her arm just as everything went black.

When Kristen awoke, her head was pillowed in the lap of a kneeling Tangus. Several concerned faces where looking down upon her. Romulus had his huge head lying across her legs. Kristen took an experimental breath and discovered she could breathe. Her world was no longer spinning. "I couldn't breathe," she said.

"You passed out, dear. Fortunately I was able to steady you as Arbellason stopped and went down on his front legs to get you closer to the ground. You've only been unconscious for a few seconds. How are you feeling?" Tangus asked.

"Embarrassed," Kristen replied sheepishly. "Panic attacks don't suit me. I'm better prepared than that. At least I thought I was." Sitting up, Kristen absentmindedly brushed a couple of tree leaves from her hair with her fingers.

"You didn't have a panic attack, Kristen," Elrond said. "I detected strong magic coming through your bond."

Kristen looked at Elrond. "You can detect the bond I have with Emmy?" she asked.

Elrond shook his head. "No, your bond is of a different kind of magic. In fact, I'm not even sure it is magic. It might be biological. But strong magic…REALLY strong magic…can affect it, stronger than anything I can do. You received a sudden 'burst' of magic. Some of the residual power was absorbed by my staff. That is what caused you to pass out."

"Why would this occur now and not sooner, Elrond?" Tangus asked. "Kristen's felt something foreign in the bond for some time now."

"There's only one explanation I can think of. The taint you felt in the bond was basically keeping track of your movements through magical tracing. But because you were so far away from the source of the magic, which I assume is in Elanesse, a tremendous amount of power was required to maintain it. Because of your close proximity, however, that power no longer had to travel as far in the bond, so you were hit with the full effect of the magic," Elrond explained.

Kristen, with Tangus' help, got to her feet. Using Arbellason to steady her further, she said, "If that's true then we're facing something of unbelievable power."

Elrond smiled. "Probably true," he said. "But another way to look at it is you took the full brunt of that power and yet you still survived."

Kristen nodded as she got back on Arbellason, thinking. "I also probably had a little help from Emmy." As she settled in the saddle she suddenly realized something. "Tangus, I no longer feel the corruption in the bond! It's as if it has been somehow purified," she exclaimed.

Tangus looked quizzically over at her from atop Smoke. "I think Emmy not only helped me survive the 'burst of magic' as Elrond described it, but also somehow managed to remove the taint from the bond," Kristen said with conviction. "She's is much stronger than anyone, possibly even Althaya, would have believed possible."

It was late afternoon when they came across the first ruined building on the outskirts of Elanesse. As they rode past it, the feeling of arrival became tangible. Before long many buildings came into view. Though the forest had mostly claimed these suburban homes as its own, there could be no mistake that the main part of the city was close. Finding a large, mostly intact building, they stopped for the night. Fearing that a fire would bring unwanted attention, they ate a cold supper and settled down to sleep after the night watch had been set.

The attack came a little after midnight. Azriel and Tangus were on watch. Azriel was silently complaining because he couldn't light his pipe for fear that he'd give away their position. Suddenly, from inside the building where the others were sleeping, Romulus growled a warning, closely followed by Bitts sitting at Tangus' side. Tangus shushed Bitts while he listened. He did not see the throwing stars until one had buried itself into his unprotected neck. Azriel grunted as he too was hit. Tangus lost consciousness as Romulus ran out the building and into the night. Bitts remained standing guard over Tangus. Behind him in the abandoned building everyone else was quickly getting up and drawing weapons.

Romulus charged a man dressed in black, crouched and ready for his attack. Romulus avoided the thrust of the leading katana, but the second scored his right shoulder deeply. Though feeling the pain, Romulus didn't stop, knocking the man down and ripping his throat out in one vicious bite. Leaving the mortally wounded man writhing on the ground and drowning in his own blood, Romulus raced to catch the second attacker. He did not notice the mist lying close to the earth. The scent of the other man faded and was replaced by something far stronger, something Romulus didn't understand. Realizing his error too late, Romulus ran into the waiting arms of Nightshade.

✼

The Purge was confused. It had lost track of the one bonded to the empath. It was now blind until the empath was released from the stasis field. Reaching out, it touched the minds of all those it had captured, giving them the ethereal scent of the empath. "Bring her to me when she has awakened! Kill the others!" the Purge commanded as it came fully awake, its power reverberating throughout the city.

✼

As Elrond rushed outside the building towards Tangus, he felt a sudden wave of pain, fear, and anxiety echo through his mind. Though it was gone as quickly as it had come, Elrond knew what it was. Elanesse had screamed in agony.

CHAPTER 16

The honest person can foresee the trickster's sleight of hand by practicing the trickster's skill himself. Once the cleverness of the trickster has been mastered, the honest person can then defeat the trickster by utilizing the lessons learned combined with the illusion of ignorance.

— Book of the Unveiled

Father Goram, Autumn, and their ranger bodyguards were a few miles away from the monastery on their return from Taranthi. Thinking back at what occurred before he left the InnisRos capital, Father Goram was still mentally chastising himself for not seeing Mordecai's latest stratagem in the battle for Emmy.

As he relived his conversation with Second Councilor Erin Mirie, he considered how productive it had been. There was nothing she wouldn't do to see Mordecai brought down. As far as she was concerned he was a power-hungry egomaniac who represented everything that went against the true elven way. The one major problem, however, was that he had the Queen's consideration as First Councilor. While Father Goram was meeting with Erin Mirie, him sitting in a chair while she sat behind an ornate desk, her valet brought in a message. She was to report to the council chamber for an emergency meeting.

"Horatio, it says here that you are to face a competency hearing!" Erin said as she looked up after reading the message, .

"Damn! But I'm not surprised. Mordecai as much as said he was going to recommend that. I imagine I'll be served a summons soon to appear and defend myself. It's only a formality of course, the Queen wouldn't actually remove me and Mordecai knows that. But these things can run several days. It's a ploy, Erin. A ploy to buy time," Father Goram replied.

"To buy time for what," Erin asked. Then she frowned. "What have you gotten yourself into, Horatio?"

Father Goram mentally kicked himself. For her own protection he didn't want to share with Erin all that had been happening. But as he thought about it, it would probably be smart to explain at least a little of what was going on. "I'm trying to prove Mordecai was behind Vayl's treachery. If I can bring something substantial in the form of evidence to the Queen, maybe I can get him removed from the Council, or even exiled from InnisRos."

"You'd certainly have my vote," Erin said. But she was an experienced politician and knew when someone was hiding something from her. She stared at Father Goram. "You're not telling me everything, are you?"

Father Goram stared back. Under no circumstances was he going to say anything about the tome to her. While it was true they each had the same goals and their friendship went back decades, she was still a major power-broker and couldn't be completely trusted with the virtually unlimited magic Emmy represented. "Plausible deniability if the Queen should ever take an active interest," he said.

Erin paused, thinking, than came to a decision. "I'm a politician so I understand the necessity. Very well, I'll do what I can to speed things along, Horatio. As Second Councilor, one of my responsibilities is to ensure meetings are run according to protocol. But that's about all I can do without exposing myself."

"I don't think there's any doubt about whose side you're on, Erin. But I agree. We shouldn't flaunt our common goal, particularly in the presence of the Queen." Getting up from the chair, Father Goram nodded to Erin. "I should probably take my leave lest we be found consorting and plotting; although I suspect Mordecai has people watching you and already knows."

"He did at one time. They've been neutralized," Erin said smiling as she too stood.

"Don't underestimate him," Father Goram cautioned.

Erin grew serious. "Never, Horatio, I know the face of evil when I see it."

Father Goram nodded. "Thank you, Erin."

"We've been friends for a long time, as were our parents. You would do the same," Erin replied.

The hearing took six days, and while the outcome was never in doubt, Mordecai skillfully used the very protocol Erin controlled to delay the proceedings as much as possible. By the time Father Goram left Taranthi he was furious for allowing himself to be maneuvered so easily.

Father Goram was brought back to the here and now by Autumn, who, riding beside him, laid a hand on his arm. "Riders approach," she said.

Father Goram halted his horse. He could now hear the gallop of several horses, and soon they came into sight as they rounded a curve in the tree-lined road. Magdalena, a couple of her rangers, and an armored knight, probably Landross, his security chief, drew near and stopped their horses.

"Horatio, it's good to see you back safe and sound. We heard about that mockery of a hearing but never really doubted you would prevail," Magdalena said as she nodded to her brother Arthon.

Father Goram could see worry on Magdalena's face. "We're only a few miles away. Surely you didn't round up this welcoming committee just to escort us the rest of the way. What's wrong, Magdalena?"

Magdalena looked at Father Goram. Her horse was anxiously moving around, clearly reflecting its rider's current nervousness. "A battalion of the Queen's Infantry has bivouacked in Calmacil Clearing. It would appear the Queen believes a stronger military presence is required in this portion of InnisRos."

The charade of the competency hearing suddenly made sense to Father Goram. As he suspected, it was nothing more than a maneuver to gain time…time Mordecai needed to place troops in Calmacil Clearing. As First Councilor, he had that discretion. Though Father Goram did not doubt the troops were fully loyal to the Queen, he knew Mordecai had spies embedded within the ranks, perhaps one or more of the several sorcerers or clerics each battalion employed. "We'll see if he has me as boxed in as he thinks he does," Father Goram thought.

"Landross," Father Goram said.

The knight moved his horse forward and saluted. "Sir!" he said.

"Have you talked to the garrison commander?" Father Goram asked.

"I have. He's as dumfounded about his mission as we are. Considering the strength of our forces protecting the monastery and surrounding area - our rangers, our clerics, my mounted knights, and our four-legged allies - he told me he'd probably need at least two or three brigades to defeat us in battle. Our strength makes his force seem, as he put it, 'a damn sight useless'," Landross said. "But he has his orders."

"Thank you, Landross," Father Goram replied, and then looked at Magdalena. "We have much to discuss. Please tell Cordelia I want all the department heads to join me in my quarters for a working supper."

"Very well, Horatio," Magdalena replied.

"Well folks, it is what it is. Let's go make the best of it," Father Goram said, kicking the sides of his horse and galloping to the monastery with everyone else following closely behind.

⁂

"You deployed a unit of my infantry to Calmacil Clearing?" Queen Lessien Arntuile asked Mordecai. It was not so much a question as a statement of fact. They were in the Queen's personal audience chamber. Behind her throne, six of her bodyguards stood at attention with an additional six placed at several strategic areas throughout the room. Very few received permission to be in the Queen's presence without her escort nearby.

"Yes, Your Highness. It is my right as First Councilor," Mordecai replied. He was not happy. Though he didn't expect the competence hearing to bear much fruit, only that it would buy him some time, he did, however, hope it would plant seeds of doubt in the Queen's mind. That would have made it easier to remove Goram without bringing unwanted attention to him or his plans. He couldn't have been more wrong. The Queen seemed to value Father Goram's guidance more than ever, and now the Queen wanted to talk about his decision to send a battalion of infantry to Calmacil Clearing.

"I'm not questioning your right to send them there, just your reasoning," the Queen said.

"I feel we needed a stronger military representation on that part of the island," Mordecai said. "All we have there is a monastery run by an incompetent…"

The Queen held up her hand and stopped Mordecai mid-sentence. "Please don't start that again. I know you and Father Goram hate each other, but let me make one thing perfectly clear. You are both MY subjects and as such I insist you work together for the good of the realm! Practice your skullduggery at your own risk. Do I make myself clear?"

"Perfectly so, My Queen," Mordecai replied with a slight bow.

"Good. Father Goram is not incompetent and you know it. Let's return to the subject of our original discussion, shall we? Tell me, First Councilor, have you ever been to the monastery?" the Queen asked.

"No, Your Highness," Mordecai said.

"Other than my Palace here in Taranthi, it's probably the most impenetrable place on the island. It's a fortress, First Councilor, a well defended fortress with a large enough fighting force to carry out offensive operations should that be called for. I think that part of the island is as well defended as just about anywhere else," the Queen stated.

"I am aware of its capabilities, Your Highness," Mordecai replied as he thought that Vayl's information regarding monastery strengths and weaknesses was the one thing he did right.

"That same fighting force is also very loyal to Father Goram, maybe more so than to me. As long as Father Goram leads that monastery, it will remain under my control because he has given me his loyalty. So you understand how important it is to keep the peace," the Queen said pointedly.

"Your Highness, they follow a heathen goddess. Remove Goram and exile the others. Put someone more pliable in control. It seems pretty straightforward to me," Mordecai replied.

The Queen sighed while tapping the arm of her throne with several fingers, her ring of office sparkling in the light of the late afternoon sun. "First Councilor, do you not see how that would be a most grievous error in judgment. Not only does Father Goram himself have many allies, but his family goes back generations on InnisRos. I do not wish to contemplate the number of friendships forged by them over the years. No, removing Father Goram would spark a civil war which I may not win, or, more to the point, survive."

Mordecai, however, understood perfectly what was at stake. He was not some snot-nosed little child that had to be lectured. He was convinced he could survive, and that was all he needed to do until he had the empath and the priestess. With them the Svartalfheim would be his. He did not care about InnisRos except he wanted to use the island as a jumping off point for the eventual conquering of Aster, after which, with the human armies at his command, he could launch operations against the Alfheim. "Do you wish me to recall the garrison, Your Majesty?" he asked.

Queen Arntuile thought about Mordecai's question for a few seconds. "No, now that the deed is done I don't suppose it will hurt. Rotate units through at six-month intervals."

"Of course, Your Majesty."

"Did you coordinate this with Father Goram?" the Queen asked.

"I did not," Mordecai said.

The Queen raised her eyebrow and frowned. "Not very accommodating, First Councilor, but so be it. I guess it was to be expected. Remember what I said about court intrigue, I don't like it. You are dismissed."

"I am dismissed....!" Mordecai started to sputter, but caught himself and bowed deeply, turned and walked out of the chamber. Twelve pairs of eyes followed his every movement until he was through the large double doors which silently closed behind him. Amberley was waiting outside the audience chamber.

"Well?" she asked as they walked away.

"Patience, my dear," Mordecai replied serenely, though inwardly he was seething and thinking to himself, "The Queen dares to dismiss me! ME! When this was over, I'm going to put her into a very deep hole! I will control every aspect of her life! She will wish to die! But that won't happen until I grant it and not a second sooner!"

When Mordecai and Amberley entered his mansion, Mordecai sent away his servant, preferring to see to his cloak and the fire himself. Sitting in a chair in front of the freshly stoked fire, he told Amberley to pour him a glass of wine. As he waited, he breathed deeply, forcing calm upon himself. Handing him a full crystal glass, Amberley sat down in the chair next to him. She started to say something but Mordecai held up his hand. She was wearing a very alluring dress, low-cut to expose her ample bosom, just as he liked. Her long blonde hair framed her pixy face. She was the most beautiful female he had ever seen. Most males only saw her exquisiteness, not seeing the extremely intelligent mind behind her sparkling blue eyes. Pity she's going to be Nightshade's payment, but it couldn't be helped. It was what Nightshade had demanded. Besides, Amberley knew too much of Mordecai's plans. Granted, it was his fault for letting her get so close...but her death had become a necessity nevertheless.

"So," Mordecai said, "the Queen has agreed to leave the infantry in place."

"Excellent! Now our spies can keep tabs on the priest," Amberley replied.

"Goram will have them ferreted out soon enough. I have no doubt he knows I have people planted in the battalion," Mordecai said. "But that'll keep him busy for a while. Vayl wasn't the only agent I have in the monastery. With him gone, I need to protect my other asset as long as possible."

Evening had fallen as Father Goram and Autumn sat down for a simple dinner of warm meat pies, cheese, bread, and wine. Joining them were Father Goram's command staff, Cordelia, Magdalena, Cameron, and Landross. Arthon and Gunthor stood watch at the entrance door to Father Goram's apartment. Autumn made sure each had a heaping plate of food. Father Goram had also called Ajax, who noisily ate a slab of venison. During dinner the friends only engaged in small talk, each knowing Father Goram preferred to reserve serious conversations for the main room with an after-dinner coffee.

Settling in comfortable chairs and sofas, coffee mugs in hand, everyone waited for Father Goram, as was his custom, to begin the round-robin discussions. Ajax, had taken his place stretched out in front of the crackling fire and dozed.

"Landross, what can you tell me about our new friends?" Father Goram asked.

Landross set his mug of coffee down on the table. "Their commander is named Balthoron. We had breakfast this morning…"

"Landross…breakfast? Already consorting with the enemy I see," Autumn said with a smile.

"I most certainly was not, madam!" Landross said with a bit of indignation.

Father Goram laughed. "Relax, Landross. Autumn was only joking with you." Turning his attention to Autumn, Father Goram said, "Honey, don't forget Landross is a paladin and a noble knight. They tend to take their duty very seriously."

Autumn apologized, but never lost her smile. Father Goram inwardly smiled as well. She was starting to get over Vayl's treatment of her, though she was still having nightmares almost every night.

"No need to apologize, madam. Father Goram is correct, but I am constantly striving to 'lighten up' as Cameron here advises," Landross said to Autumn.

"And he's making damn fine progress!" Cameron said. "A couple of weeks ago he probably would have fallen on his sword."

"I would not have…oh, you jest as well. It would appear I still have a long way to go," Landross said contritely.

Cameron turned to Father Goram. "Are you sure I can't charge him for our therapy sessions? I'd be wealthy!"

"Am I so broken?" Landross pleaded.

Cordelia patted a miserable Landross on the shoulder. "No more so than the rest of us, my friend."

"Please continue, Landross," Father Goram said, bringing the conversation back on point.

"Yes sir. Although I've never met Balthoron before this morning, I knew he had a reputation for being an extremely competent leader with a brilliant tactical mind. He chafes at this posting. As I mentioned earlier today when you first returned, he understands our strength and wonders at the logic of having his command sent here. He told me he almost wishes he could take his unit over to the mainland where he could do some real fighting," Landross said.

"And what is his unit strength?" Father Goram asked.

"Three-hundred with five sorcerers and the same number of clerics," Landross replied. "A third of his force is cavalry."

"Knights," Cordelia asked.

"No. Knights are brigade strength or higher. A battalion needs to move quickly on the battlefield. Armored knights require too much support," Landross replied.

"Cordelia, Balthoron's cavalry probably consists of rangers," Magdalena said.

"You are correct, Magdalena," Landross confirmed. "The make-up of a battalion is pretty typical in most armed forces."

"Horatio, if you're concerned about spies…" Cameron said.

"I am," Father Goram confirmed.

Cameron nodded. "They will probably be either sorcerers or clerics."

"Probably, but not necessarily," Cordelia said. "Who's spies, Horatio?" she asked.

Father Goram looked at his friends. "Folks, when we were in Taranthi I learned First Councilor Mordecai Lannian is behind an effort to capture Emmy. He is also no doubt the person who turned Vayl to treachery. As First Councilor, he has limited control of troop movements on InnisRos, and I think he's the one that gave the order to send them here. But, though he can control disposition of troops, it does not necessarily mean those troops are loyal to him."

"Indeed!" Landross said. "Balthoron's completely loyal to the Queen. And I believe if there were spies in his command, he would know it."

"There are ways of hiding in plain sight, Landross, which someone, even as good as Balthoron is purported to be, might not discover if spells or enchanted items are used," Father Goram said. "But I'm out of my element when it comes to sorcery. I really should employ a wizard."

"There is one making his home in Calmacil Clearing, Horatio," Magdalena said. "He calls himself 'Eric the Black'. He's rather young, but he's very good. I've seen him perform magic shows for children."

Father Goram dismissed the notion. "He's probably just a con artist good at sleight of hand."

Magdalena shook her head. "No, I've seen him do a lightning spell, Horatio, multiple bolts the colors of the rainbow. That's powerful magic. I don't know what his story is, but I think he's the real deal."

Father Goram consented. "Very well, Magdalena, go see if you can put him under contract to us. Cameron, go with her and see if you can get some background information on him. I don't want one of Mordecai's allies in our own house…again. And Cameron, do it delicately. I'd prefer him to be for us and not against us."

"Understood," Cameron replied.

"And while I'm on the subject of recruitment, Landross," Father Goram said, "I'd like you to spend some time with Balthoron, you know, soldier to soldier. If we can get him to be favorably disposed towards us, I'd feel a lot more comfortable about his presence."

"I will try, Father, but he will not be dissuaded from his loyalty to the Queen," Landross answered.

Father Gorman shook his head. "That's not how I meant it, Landross. I want him to understand that we hold no threat to the Queen. The gods only know what rumors Mordecai's spread about us."

"Aye, Father," Landross agreed.

Cordelia looked at Father Goram. "Horatio, you've told us of Emmy's importance and why Kristen and Tangus need to rescue her, but what does Mordecai want with her? Does he want to control her magic?"

"Good question. Do I tell them all of it?" Father Goram wondered to himself. He then looked over at Autumn, who squeezed his hand and nodded slightly. "Alright," he said. "But what I'm about to tell you does not get discussed outside this group. Is that perfectly understood?" Everyone nodded. Father Goram went on, "A few weeks ago Autumn brought to my attention an ancient tome. She found it quite by accident in an old wing to our library that had been hidden for thousands of years."

"I didn't know the monastery was that old?" Cordelia said.

Father Goram nodded. "It is. What history I've been able to turn up seems to indicate this was at one time the fortress of a warlord back before InnisRos was consolidated under one rule. Anyway, we already know that if Emmy were to die, with her would also die all the healing magic in the world. There is nothing Althaya can do about that. Emmy, as the last empath, is the only bridge between Althaya's healing magic and Aster. But it gets even more complicated. If the tome is to be believed, when an empath is taken to the Svartalfheim, the resulting explosion of magic will make the one controlling the empath unbelievably powerful, enough to gain complete control of all the magic of the Svartalfheim. Furthermore this release of magical energy will destroy not only the empath, but the entire empath bloodline."

"That means Kristen would also be destroyed?" Landross said.

"Yes Landross. And I'm afraid it doesn't stop there. You see, Kristen and Emmy are of the same bloodline as Althaya," Father Goram paused to allow that piece of information to sink in. "We would lose our goddess."

"Horatio, how much credence to you give this tome?" Magdalena asked.

"At first not much, but I didn't really want to sit around and hope it to be the ravings of a lunatic," Father Goram replied. "Knowing the tome I had might not be the original, Autumn and I made the trip to Taranthi to visit the Royal Library to see if it contained either the original or another copy. Based upon what I learned during that trip, I believe the original, or a copy, was indeed there, and that somehow Mordecai has taken possession of it. I also believe he intends to kidnap Emmy and take her to the Svartalfheim. It goes without saying that stopping Mordecai from doing this is now our number one priority."

"I should say so!" Cameron said.

"I'll take my knights and…" Landross began.

"You'll do no such thing!" Father Goram said. "Landross, there's no way we can get to him with a direct assault. He's too strong and I don't really think the Crown would appreciate it."

"Why not just go to the Queen?" Cameron said.

Cordelia snorted. "I can tell you why. She'd want Emmy for herself."

"I'm afraid Cordelia's correct. The Queen's not corrupt like Mordecai, but don't ever misjudge her desire for power," Father Goram replied.

"My contacts in Taranthi are already keeping track of Mordecai," Magdalena said.

Father Goram looked over at Magdalena. "Tell your people to be careful. Mordecai knows I'll try to keep him under surveillance and will be taking steps to minimize it," Father Goram said. "I've talked to Erin Mirie and she's agreed to do what she can as Second Councilor. I'm also in contact with Kristen, so we're not totally in the dark with regards to her and Tangus' progress."

"Is there anything else?" Cordelia asked.

This time it was Autumn who answered solemnly. "We remain vigilant. We try to counter any move Mordecai makes that threatens either Kristen or Emmy. We keep Tangus and Kristen aware of the dangers coming at them from Mordecai. We gather our strength and our allies so we can directly confront Mordecai and, if necessary, the Queen."

Landross shook his head. "Autumn, you're talking treason!"

"No one says it's going to come to that, Landross," Father Goram said. "My loyalty to the Queen is as strong as yours, but my loyalty to the ideal of right and wrong, good and evil, must take precedence. Tens of thousands of lives are at stake, including Kristen, Emmy and Althaya's. I'm not going to stand by and let them be murdered. You can understand that, right? Can all of you understand that?"

There was a general consensus all around the room with the exception of Landross. He remained silent. "I'm a paladin! My oath is my bond!" he said as he stared into his half empty mug of cold coffee. No one said a word as he weighed the contradicting impulses between the oath he had given his Queen and the oath he swore to combat evil. Finally he sighed and said, "There can be no other answer, Horatio. I am with you to the death."

Father Goram reached over and clasped him on the shoulder. He then looked at every person in the room. "Very well," he said. "The safety of Emmy is paramount. To that end we must prepare for what might come as best we can. My friends, I task each of you to 'man your post and stand your watch.' Dangerous and hard days lie before us."

Mordecai sent Amberley away to her own apartment instead of allowing her to spend the night with him. She resisted, but he was adamant, telling her that he didn't feel well and wanted to be alone. She finally relented only after being assured that he still loved her and would see her first thing in the morning.

Not long after she left he was sipping his third glass of wine, thinking about his conversation with the Queen. "She has to be dealt with," he thought angrily. A course of action soon started to take shape in his mind. It was dangerous, but the reward would be great. Getting up, he folded back a large fur covering the floor in front of the fireplace. Underneath was marble floor, no different from the floor in the rest of his mansion. He whispered a command and a section of the floor slid open revealing a metal spiral staircase going down.

The room Mordecai descended into had as much floor space as the entire first floor of the mansion above. Light from stones spelled with magical light were embedded in the walls and kept the room brightly illuminated. In the center of the room was a large circle of red rubies with glowing magical runes around the circumference. To one side his work desk and a library of demon summoning tomes and scrolls. The other side of the room contained a blood-stained altar. Instruments of torture such as knives, picks, and tongs lay on a table nearby. An empty cage sat in front of a large fireplace. Branding irons were scattered on the hearth.

Mordecai went to his desk and sat down on a large fur-cushioned chair. Reaching inside his belt pouch he brought out the communications crystal he used to speak with Nightshade and laid it on his desk. She had the matching crystal with her. Speaking the command word, the crystal glowed red. The eerie, seductive voice of Nightshade answered almost instantaneously.

"*Yes, Mordecai,*" Nightshade said.

"Report," Mordecai commanded.

"*I have found them and made contact,*" Nightshade replied.

"They have the empath?" Mordecai asked.

"*They do not. It was just a small excursion to gage their strength and throw them off-balance. I also wished to put fear into them. I love fear, Mordecai.*"

"You must not put the empath and the priestess in jeopardy, Nightshade. Do you understand?" Mordecai said.

"*I understand you need them for your plans for the Svartalfheim. I will bring them to you,*" Nightshade replied. "*Trust me.*"

"Out of curiosity, how did the attack fare?" Mordecai inquired.

"*I lost one of my mortal assassins to a large, savage dire wolf. It was not afraid, but instead defiant and fearless. In the moment I had it within my grasp I came to respect its savage efficiency and loyalty to the priestess. I chose to let it live,*" Nightshade purred in a soft tone.

"I told you they are very dangerous. As for the wolf, no matter, it can die another day. Nightshade, I want you to help the priestess get to the empath without them knowing," Mordecai ordered.

"And after," she asked.

"Return to me alone," Mordecai said. He could almost feel the anger directed at him from thousands of leagues away coming through the crystal.

"We have an agreement, Mordecai! I do not wish to be returned back to the Abyss," Nightshade said chillingly.

"I am the one who summoned you! You do as I command!" Mordecai replied back just as frighteningly.

"I have no choice but to obey you. But remember you could one day die by my hand. It will not be a death you will relish," Nightshade replied.

Mordecai breathed deeply. "Calm down. You will receive your payment soon."

"What do you mean? I have not yet fulfilled my part of the bargain," Nightshade said.

Mordecai smiled. "It is not yet time, and I have others plans for now. If you do your part, you will have your reward and rule with me." Mordecai paused to let his words sink in. He continued after a moment, "No plan is perfect, Nightshade, and I have realized mine has a flaw. For too long I have been working in the shadows from a position of weakness."

Mordecai could tell from the pause that he had not only thrown Nightshade off guard, but also managed to intrigue her. *"What is the new plan, my mortal master?"* Nightshade asked seductively.

"Good, I have her," Mordecai thought. Speaking out loud, "After you have helped the priestess to retrieve the empath, leave your two assassins as shadow guards to help in the protection of the empath and the priestess. We have time on our side. You can bring them to me later."

"You are taking a great risk, Mordecai. The empath is a valuable commodity. If her importance should ever become widely known, there will most certainly be further attempts on her life or her freedom. My assassins may not be able to keep her safe," Nightshade said.

"Then hire more!" Mordecai screamed. After taking a deep breath to control himself, he continued much more composed. "Nightshade, my plans to dominate the Svartalfheim would go much smoother if first I ruled InnisRos. I need you here for that. We shall talk more about my plans after you have helped to rescue the empath and returned to InnisRos," Mordecai said into the communications crystal as he laughed. From Elanesse, Nightshade nodded her approval and surprised her two assassins with laughter of her own.

Vayl stood at the railing of the ship looking out at the night sky. He listened to the sound of the waves as they struck the ship's side and were brushed aside as she made her headway in the water. They were only about two days from docking at the large port city of Palisade Crest. The passage from InnisRos to the mainland had thus far gone without incident. Vayl had plenty of time to soul search during the voyage. He remembered all the occasions he, Autumn, and Horatio had spent as comrades, working together for the common good, a time when he followed Althaya and was a devout priest. He remembered the day when Kristen and Mary McKenna came into his life. He thought about Kristen's exuberance when she was a child, always asking questions and seeking answers to satisfy her curious mind. He remembered how painful it was when he trained her for the quest she now risked her life to achieve. His lessons had been hard and necessarily cruel to prepare her for the world she would someday travel. He did not relish the harsh steps he had taken in her training, however, for he loved her like a daughter. But one day she would have to rely on that training to make the difficult decisions necessary to keep her and Emmy safe.

Then he had been approached by Mordecai. His whole life changed. The promises Mordecai made had fueled Vayl's dark need for power. Vayl had allowed the mellifluous words of Mordecai to turn him traitor to the beliefs he, at one time, held so dear. Most horrifying, he had turned traitor to all those he truly loved, losing that which was most important - his heart, his soul, his identity. Now he traveled to hire and lead an army against Kristen and Emmy, the last empath, and probably the one person the world held most dear. He now understood his mistake, and there was only one penalty for what he had done. Without further hesitation Vayl quietly climbed over the rail and dropped into the water. No one raised an alarm and soon the ship was well past him. As he treaded water, he looked up into the star filled sky. "It's so beautiful!" he thought.

Soon he no longer had the strength to stay afloat. Sinking, his body started thrashing as he breathed in water, drowning. Just before Vayl lost consciousness, a blue light appeared in his waning vision. Althaya appeared before him smiling. "Welcome back, my priest."

CHAPTER 17

Underestimate the power of love at the expense of your own destruction.

— *Book of the Unveiled*

Kristen awoke to Romulus' warning growl. Before she had a chance to wipe the sleep from her eyes, Romulus had darted from her side. Bitts barked once from outside, than all became silent until she heard Jennifer's panicked voice call out to her father.

Hurrying out of the dilapidated building, Kristen saw Safire and Euranna helping Azriel sit up. He was shaking his head as if to clear it from a mind fog. Elrond, Max, and Jennifer were kneeling next to Tangus as Bitts worriedly whined. Christian and Lester had established a perimeter and were staring out into the night's blackness. Of Romulus there was no sign. Rushing over to where Tangus lay, she saw he was convulsing violently, his eyes had rolled back into his head and frothy blood-filled foam came out of his mouth. A silver throwing star was imbedded in his neck. Poison! Quickly looking over at Azriel she knew he would probably be fine, a dwarf's constitution makes them immune to most poisons.

By the time she knelt down beside her husband, his convulsions had quieted, but Kristen knew he would die if she did not act quickly. Whispering a prayer to her goddess Althaya, Kristen laid her hands on Tangus' chest. Blue light emanated from them as the healing magic she called forth sank into his body. The magic didn't neutralize the poison, but that did not concern her. At this point the most critical thing she needed to do was to stabilize his bodily functions, making the heart beat stronger and faster, slowing the spread of the poison, and repairing body organs already damaged.

She then turned her attention to the throwing star. This was undoubtedly the source of the poison. She turned and said to Elrond, "Remove the throwing star without touching it." Without thinking, Elrond silently whispered a command word. The staff that was forever in his hand suddenly glowed and the throwing star exited the point of penetration and rose into the air. Elrond made a slight movement with his hand and the star suddenly flew into a nearby tree, burying itself completely in the trunk. Drawing upon her will for a second time, Kristen laid her glowing hands on the bleeding wound and closed the underlying blood vessels, muscles, and skin. As soon as that was accomplished, she clapped her hands together as if praying and brought them up to her forehead. Closing her eyes, she bowed her head slightly. This time her hands glowed red, healing through destruction. Placing her hands over Tangus heart, the magic jumped into Tangus body and sought out the poison, destroying it wherever it was found, until no traces of the offending toxin remained. By the time Kristen came out of her spell trance, Tangus' eyes were already open and he was trying to get up.

"Please, my husband, rest for a few moments while I check on Azriel," Kristen said as she got up and went over to Azriel. "How are you?" she asked.

"I'm fine, lassie. Don't you worry about me, it'll take more than a little poison to bring me down," Azriel said as he brought out his pipe. "Guess they know where we're here. I reckon there's no harm done lighting my pipe up now. Elrond, do you mind?" Elrond looked over and smiled as he cast a cantrip to light Azriel's pipe. Inhaling deeply, Azriel got up. With his pipe sticking out of his mouth and his brilliantly glowing battleaxe held in both hands, he said, "I'm going to split someone in two!"

Kristen turned and looked out into the night. She looked over to see Tangus standing at her side. "Romulus is out there," she said.

Tangus nodded. "I know. Elrond, Max, and I are going to look for him."

"I'm coming too," Kristen said.

Tangus paused. "Yes, I know." Taking her hand, he said, "Thank you for saving my life, Kristen."

This time it was Kristen's turn to pause. "How could it be any other way, my love?" she asked.

"I just wanted you to know that I appreciate it," Tangus said. "Do you need to take anything before we leave?" he asked.

Kristen turned to go to her bedroll. "Let me get my staff of healing," she said.

Bitts picked up Romulus' scent approximately a quarter mile from the campsite and they found him soon after. He was alive and conscious, but lay still on the ground. He had eight open wounds, four on each side, which were bleeding slowly. Most of the blood Romulus had already lost had soaked into the thick grass covering the rich black dirt of the forest floor. Kristen and Tangus knelt down next to him while Elrond, Max, and Bitts stood ready.

Quickly inspecting Romulus' wounds, Kristen said, "They're not too deep. The wounds look to have been opened outwards, which means the tip of whatever stabbed him was barbed. I think he's been injected by some type of paralytic agent which is already starting to wear off. He's also got a deep gash in his shoulder. It looks like it came from a sword."

"So he's going to be okay?" Tangus asked.

"His wounds are not life threatening. Give me a moment," Kristen said as she closed her eyes and concentrated. Soon the familiar blue light was transferred from her hands into Romulus. He got up, completely healed, and licked Kristen's cheek. Kristen laughed and buried her face into his fur while wrapping both arms around his huge neck. Bitts walked up and they touched noses.

"Over here!" Max suddenly called out from about fifty feet away.

"What you got, little buddy?" Elrond asked.

Max was kneeling down and inspecting the ground. Turning up to look at Elrond, he said, "Stop calling me that!" Pointing to the ground in front of him, Max said, "There's been a struggle here. Look at the blood. There's too much for whatever lost it to have survived."

Tangus studied the pool of blood and then started looking around at the tracks that manifested before his trained ranger's eye. "Someone was killed here. That part is obvious." Kneeling down to get a closer look, he shook his head. "But this doesn't make sense." Pointing to a spot before the blood pool he said, "Two sets of prints, barely noticeable, head from our campsite in this direction. These, no doubt, belonged to our attackers. Then Romulus' footprints can be clearly seen following. One of the attackers must have turned to face Romulus and was quickly taken down by our big boy. The second set of tracks, however, continued on. Romulus, after killing one attacker, went after the second." Getting up, Tangus followed the twin set of tracks to where Romulus had been found. "The second attacker kept running, but Romulus' tracks suddenly stopped. Romulus' paw prints end here, but there are no signs of a struggle or anything else for that matter."

"What happened boy?" Kristen asked Romulus. He just stared at her and then issued a growl from deep within his body.

"Can't you, you know, talk to him? As a ranger, that is," Elrond asked Tangus.

"I may try later, but animals, even ones as smart as Romulus or Bitts, don't think in the same terms we do. His body language and warning growl however does tell me that he has never before seen or experienced whatever attacked him. Look back down at the ground. Whatever it was he faced left no visible signs of its passing. And the body of the one Romulus killed disappeared without a trace being left behind." Turning to look at Elrond and Max, Tangus said, "I think we're dealing with something supernatural. We already know about the vampyres, but I don't think this was them."

Kristen nodded. "We also know there's something else in Elanesse that wants Emmy, the same thing that was tainting my bond with her. Maybe it was that?"

"The cancer Elanesse speaks of," Elrond said, "the Purge."

"I don't know," Tangus said absentmindedly as he walked a few paces away, studying the ground as he did.

"What has you so distracted," Max asked Tangus.

Kristen answered for Tangus. "He sees something else. What is it, Tangus?"

"A third pair of footprints," Tangus said as he bent down to inspect the new set of tracks. "This set is lighter. It has the look of being even more graceful than the other two. This one is a female." Standing, he faced everyone. "These are highly skilled assassins, probably led by a demon of some sort, because I don't know of anything else that can physically manifest itself and attack without leaving a trace."

"There are clerical spells that will allow you to do that," Elrond said.

"To pass without trace, perhaps, but to bring Romulus down and leave nothing behind?" Tangus shook head. "I don't think this was the work of any magician or cleric."

As they headed back to the campsite, Tangus kept shaking his head. "The only thing I can't figure is why Romulus was left alive," he said.

※

Lukas was not happy. When he accidently discovered the means of draining the stasis field's power, he felt he would soon have the innocent for his own. He could sense the power radiating from her. Though its presence frightened him somewhat, he salivated every time he thought about draining the blood from the girl and the feeling it would give him as her power washed over him. The anticipation was intoxicating. But recently he, Luminista, and Gyorgy had not been able to find the prey they needed to overcome the defenses of the stasis spell. Long ago the prey started congregating in groups too powerful for the vampyres to overcome. This forced them to take stragglers, prey, who for one reason or another, were alone. Several times over the last few weeks they were close to succeeding, but then always seemed to miss the prey by heartbeats. It was as if some unknown guardian was warning them away at just the last moment.

Lukas had considered using Gyorgy, but quickly dismissed that thought. Though the stasis field didn't outright kill him as it did Drina,

THE SALVATION OF INNOCENCE

Lukas didn't want to take a chance with another attempt. He was too important to the vampyre because he could endure sunlight, making Gyorgy a valuable commodity. Then there was Luminista? At first she was useless, a very weak and timid vampyre, the exact opposite of Drina. How Lukas regretted the ill-fated moment when Drina carelessly touched the stasis field! But Luminista was now beginning to come into her own. The parasite within her, within all vampyres, took control soon after she was infected, but it did not make her the vicious killing instrument of evil he expected. Though she still killed to survive, there was almost a gentleness or compassion in her demeanor whenever she took prey. Perhaps more disconcerting, however, was the fact that there were now times when Lukas gave her orders, though she always complied, he saw a look of disobedience and hate in her eyes that frightened him. It was a look that seemed to be reserved for only him. It was as if he were prey. More than ever he now needed the power of the innocent to maintain control over what was left of his coven.

Luminista broke Lukas out of his reverie. "Do we go out again tonight, Lukas?" she asked.

Lukas looked at the stasis field. It was getting weaker even without manipulation, but at a very slow rate. He estimated it wouldn't end for another couple of months at its current pace, and the small army coming together on the surface kept expanding. Sooner or later they would discover this chamber. If that happened, what chance did he have of taking the innocent?

"Yes, we go out tonight, and tomorrow night, and the night after that. We must succeed in this venture!" Lukas replied.

"I will give you one more week, Lukas, after which I will leave," Luminista replied. "I am tired of your obsession with this innocent child."

"I am you master!" Lukas shouted.

"I was turned by Polina and she is dead. I am my own master. I control the parasite within. The child makes you weak. Your desire to drink her blood and acquire her power has also made you stupid. I will not accompany you down the road to perdition much longer," Luminista said.

"I will destroy you, Luminista! Don't think I won't!" Lukas shrieked, spit coming out of his mouth.

Luminista did not back away, but instead calmly said, "You can try." In Lukas' eyes she saw a momentary flash of fear. "Good," she thought, "it is I who shall soon be HIS master, and then I will exterminate him like the vermin he is!"

Lukas looked at Luminista. For the first time since Polina he saw a vampyre more powerful than himself. In a very short period of time, by vampyre standards, the parasite within her had grown to be more dominant than the one inside of him. He did not have much time.

Angela's spirit, standing in a dark corner, witnessed this turn of events. Though the presence of Luminista had become more menacing, she was inwardly satisfied. Lukas was still the primary threat to her daughter and she hated him with a passion. Any disruption of his plans, be it from the work she did to keep souls away from his ambition, or from Luminista, was welcomed. As the vampyres left, she followed close behind, ready to frighten away the next foolish person she found alone in the night.

Tangus, with Kristen at his side, led the approach to the city of Elanesse from the southeast. Elrond and Max were riding behind Tangus and Kristen, instead of their customary place in the rear of the column of friends. Coming out of the surrounding forest, the city suddenly stood before them. As Tangus stopped, everyone moved their horses up so that they were all in a line, each desiring to study the city that, until now, had been only a place on a map.

The journey through the forest from the Alpine had taken a day of grueling travel through thick brush and tall trees, all the while being constantly on guard for dangers that might suddenly materialize. Many in the party were rangers trained for the forest, but none of them felt at home in THIS forest. Even though everything appeared normal, each ranger felt a great affliction had befallen the forest and its heart was struggling to beat. It was an affront the rangers hoped to end.

They were now looking upon the old Gypsy Quarter, which was on the very southeast end of the city. By the time they arrived, the sun had begun its daily descent into the western sky. As the night started to prevail over the day, the shadows of the tall trees darkened, while the thick brush became more secretive. Before them were one and two story buildings, some of which had been destroyed. For whatever reason, the forest did not approach these areas, preferring instead to leave them to their own decay. Those buildings that stood were made from sturdy wood and, though dilapidated, looked to still be functional if one were to make some minor repairs. Curiously, here and there, hovels had been erected. But it was apparent from the original structures these were built by squatters and not by the original inhabitants of the city. As with Elanesse's own buildings, these hovels had also been abandoned long ago.

"This is an eerie place, Jennifer. This city has not felt the warmth of good in a long, long time. Evil prevails here," Azriel said.

Jennifer looked over at Azriel. "The Purge?" she asked.

Taking a puff from his pipe, its smoke drifting lazily upwards, he nodded, "Yes, child, the Purge. People did terrible, wicked things in this city because of it. The ghosts of the ones murdered here still roam the buildings, seeking justice. That's why you see indications people trying to live here did not do so in any of the existing buildings, but instead built shacks. The buildings of Elanesse are haunted."

"You don't really believe that, do you?" Safire asked.

Azriel hit the bowl of his pipe with the heel of his hand, discharging the burnt tobacco. As he put the pipe back in its pouch, he smiled and said, "Ask me that question again in a few hours."

A few yards away Tangus turned to Kristen. "Does the bond let you know where Emmy is?" he asked.

Kristen continued looking over the city. "I feel the bond stronger than ever, but it does not tell me exactly where she is. The bond is designed to be a support system between the an adult and the child empath, a means by which I can protect her from strong emotions of hate until she reaches maturity. The closer I get the stronger the bond becomes, but even still it will only give me her general location." Looking over at Tangus, Kristen said, "She's in this part of the city but underground. In my vision she was in a chamber of some type. The glow of the stasis field magic served as a good light source, but other than Emmy, the bones of her mother Angela, and a fireplace, there was nothing to distinguish it from any other underground chamber."

Tangus nodded and moved Smoke over to Elrond. "You claim the city speaks to you. Can she give us any idea where to look?" he asked.

Elrond shook his head. "No. Elanesse is aware of Emmy's presence and the vulnerability of the stasis field, but other than a general idea of the location, she can't help more than she already has. Tangus, Elanesse has been helping to support the stasis field with her own life-force. If not for that, Emmy would already be lost to us. Soon however she will be forced to stop in order to save herself. The Purge is no longer dormant and hurts her greatly."

"Do you have any other suggestions, Elrond?" Tangus asked. "You're the sorcerer here, is there anything you can do magically like detect magic or something similar that will allow you to find the magic of the stasis field? Althaya worked the spell and it's lasted over three-thousand years, so we know it's very powerful magic."

"Maybe," Elrond replied. "But since the chamber is underground, I'd still probably need to get almost on top of it to detect it. The detection spell also has time limitations. Any magical detection from either a spell or my staff won't last all night."

"I know," Tangus said. "I've traveled with you enough to understand that." Sighing, Tangus continued, "I don't really want to search each building for a basement. I need answers. Anybody have any ideas?" Tangus called out to everyone else.

"I'm not sure there are any better alternatives, Tangus," Max said. "We need to do a systematic search. We can begin by searching taverns, inns, and shops, places that more logically will have underground chambers for storage of wine, goods or supplies needed for everyday operations. If we don't have any luck with that, then we can start looking into the bigger houses, the ones that look like the previous owner was a person of substance."

Kristen shook her head. "No, that doesn't sound right, Max. I know you have worlds of experience, but this chamber was used by vampyres. It's not going to be a place routinely used. It's going to be a place that's secretive or abandoned."

"You're right of course, Kristen, unless the vampyres impersonated normal people and lived within their midst. Then we're looking for a place that doesn't need to be open during the day, maybe a tavern or specialty shop. We can probably rule out inns, at least for the initial search," Max replied.

"Max, vampyres use slaves…thralls…to do their bidding during daylight hours," Kristen said. "That being said, however, I really don't have any better idea where they might have Emmy than anyone else. I think your premise is well reasoned and I agree inns can probably be ruled out for the time being."

"It's dark so do we start in the morning?" Elrond asked.

Both Tangus and Kristen said "No!" at the same time. "Elrond, we are so close! We need to start now. I need to get to her!" Kristen said.

"You understand the vampyres will probably be out, right?" Elrond replied.

"We're aware, Elrond. I'm looking forward to meeting them," Tangus said. Perhaps it was best the darkness covered the smile on his face as he thought about their death. No one would have recognized him. Reaching over he gave Kristen a quick kiss on the cheek, then spurred Smoke to move forward. The rest of the party took Tangus' lead and followed, keeping an alert eye out for any movement.

"Beware the mist!" Azriel called.

As Angela came up from the underground chamber and into the open night, she immediately felt a change in the atmosphere of the city. It was almost as if there was an enormous expectation of release or…freedom. Something important was starting to happen. Angela stopped suddenly as she realized what it all meant. Kristen was here! Finally, Emmy was going to be shielded from all those wishing her harm!

As Angela glided between buildings to find Kristen, Emmy's salvation, no longer caring about Lukas, Luminista or any success they might have this night finding prey, ghostly tears started to form in her eyes and drop to the ground. They had no substance just as Angela did not. But they were real, nevertheless, because the emotion that brought them to life was real. Angela realized that soon she would no longer be needed to protect Emmy. Kristen would now take this responsibility. The happiness Angela felt about the impending rescue of Emmy was tempered with a great sadness. It would soon be time for her to move on and leave her little girl in the care of another.

Of the first few buildings checked, several did indeed have basements, but each was empty and showed no signs of habitation for hundreds or perhaps thousands of years. During the course of their investigations, Safire recommended checking jails which might contain underground cells. Everyone agreed it was a fine suggestion but as they continued their investigation of the Gypsy Quarter, they found no buildings even remotely appearing to be a jail or an office of a law keeper.

"How can that be?" Jennifer asked her father.

Tangus shook his head. "I don't know."

"It's because the elven rulers of Elanesse refused to expend the necessary resources to keep the law in the Gypsy Quarter," Kristen said. "That's what is written in the history of Elanesse and the Purge. The people in this part of the city were pretty much left on their own."

Jennifer shook her head. "Those poor people!" she said. "How could Elanesse's rulers treat their citizens that way?"

"It's always been that way, lassie," Azriel said. "All races are guilty of class distinctions and prejudice. As individuals most of us do not condone it, but outside our personal sphere of influence we are powerless to stop it. Hate will always be in the world with us, as will the need by some to feel superior to other people or races."

"But surely there is something we can do?" Jennifer asked. Her distress was clear to everyone.

"There is. Just be you, Jennifer," Azriel replied as he laid a hand on Jennifer's arm. "The goodness in your heart will always find a way to make the lives of those around you a little less harsh. Sometimes I think good and evil are in the world to provide each of us the opportunity to discover our true character. I constantly hear clerics preach free will and balance, and I agree to a limited degree with that philosophy. But I also know that it's easy to be good when surrounded by good. The challenge each of us must face is our response to evil when surrounded by evil. Can we stay the path when everything around us is in chaos?"

"Pretty high and mighty," Max commented.

Azriel looked over at Max. "Always the pragmatist, aren't you, Max," Azriel said before returning to his conversation with Jennifer. "But he's right, lassie. Most ordinary people are mostly just trying to survive the best they can. Putting supper on the table for hungry children usually takes precedence over the intricacies of right and wrong. Perhaps our paladin friend has a different slant on the subject."

"Miss Jennifer, it's not quite that simple…" Lester began but didn't have a chance to finish his thought.

Tangus and Elrond came out of the building they were checking. Everyone else looked at them expectedly. Both shook their heads "no" as they mounted their horses. Max again questioned why they didn't split up to cover more ground. Neither Tangus nor Kristen, however, felt it was a good idea to separate. Elrond surprisingly agreed. "No Max.

I feel what Elanesse feels. We're sitting on immense evil just waiting to explode. It's far too dangerous," he said.

Elrond, as he turned back from looking at Max, had to pull on the reins sharply to stop his horse from moving ahead of Tangus and Kristen, both of whom were staring into the darkness of a side alley. A luminescent blue light was materializing just a few feet away. Soon the entire party was watching.

"See Jennifer…haunted," Azriel said.

The blue phantom light materialized into the distinct shape of a woman. Both Romulus and Bitts remained calm, sensing no danger. As the seconds went by, her form steadily took a more familiar shape. "I recognize her," Kristen suddenly said.

Tangus turned to look at his wife. She looked back. "That's Angela, Tangus. She's Emmy's mother."

"The vision you told me about? Are you sure that's her?" Tangus asked.

"Yes," Kristen said as she dismounted.

Tangus did the same. From behind he heard Azriel whisper loudly, *"Elrond!"* Not long after Tangus heard Elrond cast a fire cantrip spell and saw the night briefly light up behind him. Smelling the pungent fragrance of cherry wood pipe tobacco, Tangus smiled. Some things never change. Azriel was smoking his pipe.

Kristen walked up to the ghost of Angela. "I wish I could hug you. You've suffered so much!" she said.

Angela smiled. She showed Kristen her neck to reveal the vampyre bite marks she carried into eternity. Kristen nodded her understanding. Angela then turned and started to glide away, looking over her shoulder to ensure Kristen and the others were following. They were.

※

Lukas, Luminista, and Gyorgy were finally having a bit of long overdue success. They had found a young couple who decided their carnal needs outweighed the dangers of being alone in the night. Lukas and Luminista stealthily approached. This hunt was going to be effortless. Suddenly Luminista grabbed Lukas' hand. "What!" a surprised Lukas blurted out without thinking. The couple, prompted by the unexpected voice, got up, grabbed their clothes and ran back to the safety of their campsite and sleeping comrades.

"Are you crazy?" Lukas shouted.

"No time to explain! Wards I set to warn of intrusion at the mansion have been triggered. We must hurry back!" Luminista said.

"I don't take…" Lukas started to scream but was interrupted by a slap on the face from Luminista which was strong enough to knock him off his feet and onto his back.

Pointing at the prone Lukas, Luminista said, "Do you want the girl or not?"

Lukas stared. The danger in her voice could not be ignored. He got up and followed her.

Angela led them to a large three-story mansion. During its prime it no doubt stood out in the Gypsy Quarter as a place of wealth and power, something very rare in old Elanesse for one of the non-elf races. Angela waited on the large front porch as everyone dismounted.

"Elrond, Max, Jennifer and Azriel come with Kristen and me. Christian, take command out here. Keep the horses ready to go at a moment's notice. When we get Emmy we'll be coming out in a hurry. Post a guard and remain vigilant!" Tangus said.

Christian nodded. Both he and Lester were imposing warriors who had faced many an enemy in battle before. They knew what needed to be done.

Angela led Tangus, Kristen and the others down a hallway, through an open door and down stone stairs to a naturally occurring subterranean vault. As they reached the bottom of the stairs, a soft, silvery glow could be seen coming from a hole in a wall on the opposite end of the room. The room was otherwise empty.

"Kristen, do you detect any evil?" Tangus asked.

"No. Wait, I take that back, this whole room is tainted with evil in both deed and intent. This is a vampyre lair, but I do not think they are here at the present moment," Kristen replied.

"Good. Let's get Emmy and leave before they come back," Elrond said.

Carefully approaching the hole and looking inside, Tangus and Kristen saw Emmy surrounded by the stasis field, bones lying against one wall and a fireplace. The room, like the room before it, was empty. Stepping aside, they let Max stick his head into the room. Though Kristen had said she did not think the vampyres were in the area, he felt caution was still called for. He looked up at the ceiling, knowing from experience a favored attack by the vampyre is to wait on the ceiling of large rooms and drop down on unsuspecting victims. Satisfied no ambush was imminent, he next studied the floor for any type of trip wires, pressure plates, or other indication the floor was trapped. Finding none, he nodded and stepped aside so Tangus and Kristen could make their way to Emmy.

Emmy peacefully slept within the protective embrace of the stasis field created by Althaya thousands of years ago. She was a beautiful little girl with long blond hair and perfectly symmetrical features. All her fingernails and toenails were royal blue, the color favored by Althaya, but Kristen could not tell if they had been painted or if it was natural. She was dressed in a simple blue dress with a wide leather belt circling her waist…the type of clothing favored by gypsies. A blue headband was wrapped around her forehead with multi-colored beads which hung down from the back and intermingled with her hair. A blue hooded cloak, glowing with magic, was wrapped around Emmy, held together at her neck by a similarly glowing amulet of the same design as the one worn by Kristen and all other clerics of Althaya. Angela moved beside Kristen and smiled down upon her daughter. As they took a few moments to look at the child they both loved, Emmy opened her deep blue eyes and smiled. Kristen felt the bond between them flair up in joy and greeting. Glancing over at Angela, she wished there was some way she could share the bond with her if only for a few seconds. But that couldn't be.

Looking back at Emmy, Kristen reached toward the stasis field and touched it. An outburst of multi-colored light filled the room as the magic of the stasis spell succumbed to Kristen's contact. Emmy stood up and wrapped her arms around Kristen, clutching her as if she would never let go again. Angela stepped back, smiling. Emmy will be safe now.

Then everything changed as Emmy cried out in horror and pain. Kristen, too surprised and inexperienced with the bond to deal with the onslaught of what Emmy felt, was crippled with that same pain as it came from Emmy to her. Tangus rushed over and caught both in his strong arms before they had a chance to collapse onto the cold stone floor. Jennifer went over to help her father. Romulus and Bitts, standing guard over the four of them, both started to growl. Elrond and Max drew swords while Azriel spit on his hands and raised his axe. Looking contritely at Jennifer, he said, "Such a nasty habit, but it actually helps me to grip the handle." Two explosions suddenly rocked the house from above.

In a prior life, before he became a slave to the will of Lukas, Gyorgy was a master swordsman and a lieutenant in the Guards of the Dark Shrine, the temple complex in Madeira dedicated to Tartarus, the primeval god of the dark, stormy pit which lay beneath the foundations of the earth and beneath even the realm of Hades. Gyorgy relished every opportunity to destroy living creatures, his thirst for blood only held in abeyance by his master, Lukas. Now, however, he had his Lord's permission to kill as many of the interlopers as possible. The only exception was the innocent, she belonged to Lukas.

Gyorgy made his attack as soon as Luminista discharged fireballs from her magical wand. A large male half elf and smaller female elf were outside of the building standing next to their horses when the fireballs exploded. Both horses were immediately turned to unrecognizable charred forms, but their sacrifice saved the lives of their riders. Gyorgy charged in past the smoking remains of the horses and caught both temporarily disoriented by the explosions.

The female was the first one of the pair he came to, still on the ground shaking her head to clear it. Gyorgy quickly stabbed through her with his sword, but his thrust was off-center as he turned to defend himself against the male. This opponent was an experienced warrior and very good with his sword, perhaps as well trained as he. But Gyorgy knew he had the advantage because he wasn't recovering from the effects of two fireballs. Gyorgy successfully parried the first and second attacks, then sidestepped, began a thrust to the suddenly exposed side underneath the armpit, and then changed direction and went low, slicing the leg off. The magic of his sword allowed him to cut through both flesh and bone with little effort.

As blood rushed out of the severed leg, his victim's face went white and he toppled over. Gyorgy rushed into the house knowing he had dealt a killing blow. As he entered the door, however, he saw an armored figure - a knight - rushing towards him. Behind the knight was still another adversary pulling back on a bow. Preparing to dodge both the massive two-handed sword being wielded by the knight and the arrow about to be shot, Gyorgy felt an explosion of pain in the center of his back. Instinctively turning around, he saw the female he thought he had killed sitting up, blood running from the side he had stabbed, already pulling back on another arrow. As that arrow buried itself in his chest, he felt a second arrow strike his back. His sword clattered to the ground as he dropped to his knees. Gyorgy was already dead when Lester severed his head from his neck.

Two misty forms, unnoticed as Gyorgy made his attack, descended the stairs to the chamber below.

THE SALVATION OF INNOCENCE

The battle above could be clearly heard in the chamber. As much as Elrond and Max wanted to rush to help, they, as well as everyone else, understood that what was happening above was mostly a diversion. The real battle for Emmy's freedom was to be fought in the chamber and adjoining room.

Elrond cast light spells using his staff on several items discarded around the room. He knew when defending against vampyres, the darkness was not your ally. Emmy and Kristen had quieted as Kristen learned how to use the bond to help Emmy ward off the hate directed at all living creatures by vampyres. She was sitting next to Emmy, holding her close as she stroked her hair. Tangus and Jennifer got up and, along with Elrond, Max, and Azriel, faced the opened hole, drawing weapons and providing a barrier of protection around Emmy and Kristen.

Suddenly a harsh voice called from outside the chamber. "Leave me the innocent and you shall be allowed to live."

No one within the chamber made a sound. Tangus quietly said to Kristen, "Now would be a good time to cast that new spell your father developed. The one you've been practicing."

"You mean *Bladebarrier Sanctuary*? I'll only be able to maintain that spell for about ten minutes," Kristen replied. "Be careful, my love."

Azriel barked a laugh. "Don't worry about us, lassie. This is not going to be a good night for the undead."

Kristen concentrated, calling upon her goddess to grant her the power to bring forth magic. A blue glowing cage sprang into existence surrounding Emmy, Kristen, Romulus, and Bitts, an impenetrable barricade of hundreds of spinning knives. Inside the barrier on each side but separate from the spinning knives, was a solid blue glowing wall of magic. The magic of the *Bladebarrier Sanctuary* spell worked on two levels, the spinning knives served as protection against physical attacks while the second magical barrier cancelled magic used to teleport or otherwise gain entrance with magic, exposing any attempt to breach the barrier of the blades. Its chief drawback was anyone inside the perimeter of the spell could not cast magic outwards.

Elrond looked over at Max. "We're trapped in here. And Elanesse tells me other men move in our direction – men sent by the Purge. I don't think they're a welcoming committee."

"You think maybe we should run out there into a dark room and fight a vampyre?" Max asked incredulously. Elrond nodded his head.

"He be right, lad," Azriel said to Max. "I'm in. But before we go, Elrond, if you wouldn't mind?"

Elrond looked over at Azriel and saw he had his pipe in his mouth. Waving his hand, a flame appeared above the bowl of the pipe to light the freshly packed tobacco.

"Watch it, Elrond! You burnt my nose!" Azriel complained.

"Are you with me, Max?" Elrond asked, disregarding Azriel's grumbling.

Max sighed, then straightened up. "Hell yeah I'm with you!" He raced out of the chamber into the darkness, closely followed by Elrond and Azriel. Tangus started to follow, but stopped short. "Stand ready, Jennifer!" he said, clearly uncomfortable letting his friends lead the charge without him.

Suddenly there were two fireball explosions outside the room. A large tongue of flame supported by the concussion deposited Azriel through the hole and back into the chamber. He landed on his backside and slide across the floor, coming to rest at the feet of Tangus. With smoke coming off him and his face red from the searing heat of the spell, Azriel got up, looked over at Jennifer and winked. "We got 'em right where we want 'em, lassie." When he noticed his mangled pipe lying on the floor, however, his annoyance boiled up into a crescendo of verbal insults, all of which were directed at the mother of the vampyre who was the instrument of his discontent. But as he suddenly remembered Emmy, he quickly stopped his rant, calmed, sighed, and whispered, "That was my best pipe," before he ran screaming back into the outer room.

THE SALVATION OF INNOCENCE

The room Elrond, Max, and Azriel rushed into was dark, but as trained warriors they had learned over the course of their careers to rely on their other senses as much as they relied on their sight. They had caught the two vampyres waiting outside by surprise, though the female was able to release two fireballs from a wand she was carrying before Elrond and Max were upon them. Azriel was blown back into the chamber by the force of the blasts, but he returned to the fray quickly enough, little the worse for wear but minus his pipe.

The ensuing battle did not go well for Elrond, Max, or Azriel. Vampyres are extremely powerful adversaries equipped with the ability to turn into a mist at will, to move very quickly, almost unlimited endurance, and they are masters of illusion. But their most effective advantage is their experience, some having hundreds if not thousands of years of perfecting their fighting and weapons-use skills. Both vampyres were now using these qualities to the extreme detriment of Elrond, Max, and Azriel. Though Elrond was able to wound the female with a volley of magic missiles from his staff at the beginning of the melee, the next few seconds of parry, thrust, riposte, attack and counter-attack left the two elves and the dwarf with multiple cuts of various depths and lengths from the magical swords each vampyre used with great effectiveness. The magical spell of protection Elrond had cast on Max, Azriel, and himself was quickly exhausted by the sheer speed and number of successful attacks each vampyre made. As the fight progressed, the floor soon became slippery with blood. It became harder to grip weapons as blood ran down arms and hands. Exhaustion was also taking its toll. An experienced and well-trained warrior can fight for hours, but vampyres can fight for days, and the extra energy it took to defend against the speed of the vampyre attacks would quickly wear down even the most seasoned warrior if the battle became a prolonged affair. For every strike made on a vampyre, several were made on Elrond, Max, and Azriel in return.

Both vampyres suddenly disengaged and stepped back. The male was smiling. "I repeat, you do not need to die. Just give me the child," he said.

"You will not get away from us that easily," Azriel said with a grin, but he was deadly serious.

"So be it," the male vampyre replied.

Before the battle resumed, however, the female flicked her sword and an arrow, cleanly cut in two, dropped to the ground. Two other arrows hit the male in quick succession. Screaming in pain, he suddenly rushed forward between Elrond and Max, slicing Elrond's hamstring as he passed, and was standing in front of Tangus and Jennifer, both of whom were standing outside the chamber and had arrows pointed at his chest. Before they had a chance to fire, however, he was through the hole in the chamber, but not before slicing the bowstrings of each bow with his sword as he passed.

Both Tangus and Jennifer dropped their bows, pulled their swords, turned and followed the male vampyre back into the room. The female vampyre did not follow the male, but simply stood in the place where she had been fighting Elrond, Max, and Azriel, effectively preventing them from turning to support Tangus and Jennifer. Not that Elrond could. His cut hamstring made it impossible for him to walk without assistance.

Lukas stood against the wall, placing the magical *Bladebarrier Sanctuary* spell that enveloped Kristen, Emmy, Romulus and Bitts between him, Tangus, and Jennifer. Tentatively reaching forward with a hand, he touched the magic, wincing in agony as a finger was lost to the blades as a consequence. Tangus and Jennifer each approached from a different side of the chamber, being careful to be in a position to block both sides of the barrier, though neither knew how they could defend against his frightening speed if the vampyre should decide to engage either of them.

Emmy stood and looked at Lukas. His obvious hate for her was plainly visible on his face. She shook off this emotion, however, letting her bond with Kristen absorb the impact. Kristen, her balance restored, also stood, but did not place herself in front of Emmy, ignoring every fiber in her being telling her to do so. Emmy had a purpose for confronting this evil.

"You killed my mother!" Emmy said angrily.

Tangus and Jennifer stopped their approach. Like Kristen, they felt something was about to transpire which should not be interrupted.

Lukas smiled. "I did not, girl. Polina struck the blow that killed your mother. I only made it possible. You were there. You know this," he said. "Polina is dead and no longer has a claim to you. That claim is now mine. Of that there can be no doubt. I will drink your sweet innocent blood and rip the tender flesh from your throat and dine off of it. First, however, I will kill the priestess standing with you and all her friends. No one here can stop me. I am too fast and have over three-thousand years experience with prey. I am immortal."

Suddenly Lukas' eyes widened in surprise and pain as a wooden stake flew into his chest. It was the very same stake Polina used to kill Angela. Lukas stared into a dark corner on the other side of the chamber. Unnoticed until now, he saw the source of the power that drove the stake into his black heart. The spirit of Angela looked upon him. Her eyes did not reflect the empty triumph of revenge, but rather sorrow for the circumstances that forced her to be his executioner. The last voice Lukas heard as he dropped to the floor was Emmy's. "My mother appreciates irony," she said. Like Angela, there was no joy in her voice or in her expression.

Tangus walked over to the body of Lukas and swiftly decapitated it. Grabbing the head by the hair, he threw it to one side. "Keep your magic up for as long as you can, sweetheart, while I go see what's happening in the other room. Jennifer, stay ready," he said as he turned to leave. Standing in the chamber and blocking his way, however, was Luminista. She had entered unnoticed. Her posture, though, was non-threatening. She held in her hands a strongly glowing long sword and Elrond's magical staff.

Azriel, bleeding from several wounds, rushed into the chamber and stopped. Breathing heavily, he said, "We tried to stop her, Tangus, but she's too damn fast!" Elrond, being helped by Max, limped into the chamber as well. They did not approach any closer than the door, however, preferring to wait until they saw which direction the standoff was going.

Tangus quickly studied the situation. Elrond, Max, and Azriel were blood-soaked messes and looked to be about half-dead. Attacking the vampyre in their current state would probably be tantamount to suicide. Their best weapon, the magic of the cleric, was essentially cancelled out by the magical protective barrier surrounding Kristen, Emmy, Romulus, and Bitts. Tangus and Jennifer could probably do some damage and might even get lucky enough to kill it, but the risks for disaster were high and their deaths, should the vampyre be victorious, would eventually expose Kristen and Emmy to the vampyre without any type of support. And even if they were successful, the battle would be so costly they might not be able to escape the dangers they still faced from the Purge in Elanesse.

All the while Tangus had been weighing his options, the vampyre had been studying Tangus. "I see you understand the situation," Luminista said when she had seen that Tangus had come to completely understand her tactical advantage.

"Yes I do," Tangus said.

"Then you know that if we do battle, it will go very badly for you," Luminista replied.

Tangus nodded in agreement. "Maybe, but what choice do I have? You can't have Emmy."

Surprising everyone, Luminista said, "I don't want the child."

"I don't understand," Kristen said.

Directing her gaze to Kristen, Luminista said, "When I was taken by Polina I had a family - a husband, children, mother and father, aunts and uncles. I was a normal, happy woman. They of course have been dead for centuries now. That's what was taken from me by Polina, Lukas, and their kind. All the evil I have done since my conversion has been contrary to everything I believed in when my heart was still beating."

Luminista paused then shook her head. "Lukas' obsession with this innocent child over the last few months has been foolhardy, and I am glad it was a path that led to his destruction. I do regret the harm I have caused you and your friends leading that idiot to his doom. I owe you a debt for that." Luminista pointed to the headless body of Lukas. "Destroy his head or put it in a place that will never be found. The blight of Lukas should never again touch this world."

Kristen shook her head. "Vampyres are well known as great deceivers. How can we trust you?"

Sensing the innocent could detect deception, Luminista looked at Emmy. "Child?" she said.

"She speaks the truth," Emmy said calmly, but there was sadness in her voice.

Luminista smiled at Emmy. "You have gained much wisdom and power while you slept. Perhaps Lukas would not have been able to destroy you after all."

Emmy shook her head. "I would not have survived without both my mothers. I have much to learn. I am still a little girl."

Luminista smiled. "I suspect there is more to it than that."

"What will you do now?" Kristen asked.

"Return to my home in Palisade Crest. I never wanted to leave there in the first place. Without the influence of Lukas' or the coven maybe I can find some way to atone for my past evil deeds. I like to think that just maybe a small part of my soul remains within." Luminista turned to mist and swiftly exited the room. Elrond's staff dropped to the floor.

"She will never find peace in this life, I fear," Kristen said as she banished the *Bladebarrier Sanctuary* spell. "But perhaps in the next."

Emmy rushed over to the corner where her mother had appeared, but the ghost of Angela was now gone. Looking up, Emmy said, "You can rest in peace now, mother. I love you."

Kristen had already started mending the wounds Elrond, Max, and Azriel had sustained in their battle with the vampyres. Emmy turned and went to help, her hands glowing blue as she drew forth the healing magic of the last empath.

Above, unknown to anyone below, Christian and Euranna were in a fight for their lives. After dispatching the vampyre slave, Lester and Safire quickly rushed to help their two wounded friends. Lester took rope and tied a tourniquet around Christian's amputated leg a few inches above the stump. Though that slowed the bleeding somewhat, so much blood had been lost that Christian was already in shock. Euranna, after she had fired her arrows into their attacker, crawled over to Christian…but she was far too weak from the devastating sword wound she had received to do any more than hold Christian's hand. Their blood mingled in a pool on the floor.

"We don't have much time, Lester." Safire said calmly as she worked to staunch the blood flow from Euranna's side and back with bandages.

Lester tightened the tourniquet on Christian's leg. "Do you have any healing ointment?" he asked Safire.

"In my backpack lying next to me," she said. "Give me a second. Euranna, wake up dear."

Euranna's eyes flickered and then opened. "Christian?" she asked.

"We're trying to save him, honey," Safire replied. "Focus on me, Euranna. I need you to hold this tightly. It's going to hurt, but we need to stop the bleeding. Can you do that for me?"

"I'll try," Euranna whispered.

Safire took Euranna's hands, first one then the other, and placed them on the bandage covering the wound on her side. She then gently rolled Euranna a little to expose the exit wound and stuffed fresh bandages into it. Euranna cried out. "I know, honey," Safire said. "Stay with me." Safire then took a roll of cloth and wrapped it completely around Euranna to secure the bandages in both wounds. When she was done, Euranna was unconscious but the bleeding had stopped. Her breathing, however, was labored and she was making gurgling sounds.

"Damn," Safire exclaimed. "I think a lung's been punctured. She's drowning in her own blood." Safire quickly opened her backpack and pulled out a jar of magical healing balm. Crawling over to Christian, she applied about one-half of the jar's contents to the severed stump.

THE SALVATION OF INNOCENCE

Immediately the blood flow stopped as the magic closed the arteries and veins opened by Gyorgy's sword. Without hesitation, Safire went back to Euranna and untied the cloth holding the bandages to Euranna's wounds. She applied the ointment to each wound, stopping the bleeding. But the damage done to Euranna's lung would not be healed so easily.

"She needs Kristen or she's going to die. One of us has to go and get her!" Safire said.

"We're too exposed out here and I don't think we should take the time to move them inside," Lester replied. "Since we can't leave them alone, you go, Safire. You run faster."

Safire silently nodded and immediately ran for the stairs.

Kristen and Emmy were just finishing the healing of Elrond, Max, and Azriel when Safire suddenly ran into the room past a startled Jennifer who was keeping watch at the opening to the chamber. "Kristen!" Safire said. "You need to get upstairs quickly. I think we may lose Euranna!"

Kristen rose and grabbed Emmy's hand. "Not again!" she said as she started to run, following Tangus and Jennifer, who were already in motion.

Mariko and Ishuro, Nightshade's two remaining assassins, had just finished killing the thirteen men racing to attack those Nightshade ordered to be protected. They paid no attention to the two explosions heard a few buildings away as they efficiently dispatched the last man.

"These fought like crazy men, Mariko. I almost had to break a sweat," Ishiro said.

"Indeed. It is odd. It's almost as if something else was controlling their minds," Mariko said as she kicked the one at her feet. "This one here kept fighting even after I took an arm."

"They were berserk. Do you think Nightshade will pay extra?" Ishiro asked.

Mariko shook her head. "No. You know how she feels about honoring an agreement. We do what we were hired to do regardless, and right now that's to protect those we once hunted, unless you're interested in asking her to renegotiate our contract. But if you do, warn me so I can travel to another continent."

Ishiro laughed. "I don't think even being on another continent would protect you, but don't worry. I don't ever want to cross that particular demon."

"Good," Mariko said as the two blended into the night.

On InnisRos, Autumn was in the process of healing a young boy whose legs had been tragically crushed when his horse stumbled and fell. Unexpectedly the magic she called forth flashed brilliantly. This astonishing flair quickly settled to the familiar blue glow of the magic, but it was brighter and stronger. Autumn smiled. She would have to tell Horatio if he didn't already know. Kristen and Tangus must have succeeded in rescuing the last empath. Autumn's smile, however, soon turned to worry, for she knew only part of the battle for Emmy had been won.

All across Aster good clerics of all disciplines experienced the same energized magic with their healing spells as Autumn. Though they did not understand or even care why they received this gift, they knew the world in which they lived had for some reason been subtly changed.

EPILOGUE

AT LAST THE location of the empath was finally revealed to the Purge. For several days those whom the Purge controlled with the strength of its will had been searching blindly. Now it could direct its seekers to a specific location. Though the men it sent earlier were lost, that did not matter, the Purge had many more men to send. Soon the empath would be before the Purge. Soon the empath would suffer the same fate as all those who had come before, only this time, the Purge would destroy the empath itself. The Purge could not know joy, but it could experience completion.

Mordecai and Amberley waited in a small forest clearing in a remote section of land owned by Mordecai's family outside the city of Taranthi. It was a cold night, the arrival of warmer spring weather still several weeks away.

"Why are we here?" Amberley asked once again. She had been puzzled by Mordecai's recent withdrawal from her as well as the secrecy surrounding this meeting which exposed both of them to the cold in the middle of the night. She longed for the comfort of Mordecai's bed and the blazing fireplace in his bedroom.

Mordecai turned to her. "My dear, I have a meeting with someone whom I wish to remain anonymous, hence the reason for the secrecy. Normally I wouldn't inconvenience you with such matters, particularly when it puts you at the mercy of the harsh elements, but I might have need of your negotiation skills." Reaching over with a gloved hand and stroking her cheek, he said, "You are such a delicate flower."

Amberley smiled, grabbed his gloved hand and kissed the back of it. "I'm just curious. You know I would do anything for you."

Mordecai reached into his cloak and produced a metal flask. "Here, have a drink of this. It'll warm you up while we wait."

Amberley took the flask and sipped from it. She felt the warmth of the whiskey as it went down her throat and started spreading throughout her body. As she started to take another sip, Mordecai took the flask from her. "Not too much, I need you clearheaded," he said.

Amberley nodded that she understood, but already she was starting to feel lightheaded. One drink should not have that much of an effect on her. She felt detached from her body as she watched Mordecai take the flask and dump its remaining contents onto the ground and then throw it into some nearby bushes. She tried to ask what he was doing, but the words wouldn't come out. The last thing she remembered was Mordecai putting his arms around her to keep her from falling.

Nightshade appeared in the small clearing, stepping out of a swirling vortex which quickly closed behind her, to find Mordecai and the girl. The girl had clearly been drugged. Mordecai looked at Nightshade. "I wish I could travel the world like that," he remarked wistfully.

Nightshade glanced at Mordecai. "The vortex my kind use to travel would kill a mortal. The girl?" she asked.

"She merely sleeps," Mordecai said.

Nightshade looked down at him. She saw no fear in his eyes which was good. If she was going to have a mortal companion it must be as fearless as she. Demons did not tolerate weakness. "What makes you think I will not kill you once my indenture to you is concluded?"

Mordecai smiled. He did not fear the demoness because knew she would accept his proposed modification to their current agreement. "I offer you a new contract and a chance to stay in the mortal realm. Like most demons, that is something you greatly desire. And unlike the Abyss where you answer to many masters and have little influence, here at my side you will have real power. I do not wish to hold dominion over you, but to rule with you. That is my new promise. Do we have an accord?"

Nightshade looked long at the mortal, considering. He had offered her much. "Very well," she decided. "I will have your blood on it."

"Yes, I expected that," he said as he slowly lowered the sleeping Amberley to the ground. Taking a knife from a sheaf on his hip, he motioned with it. Nightshade extended one of her arms. Mordecai cut it without hesitation. He then extended his. Nightshade did the same to him with a razor sharp talon. Holding out their bleeding arms, they let the blood drop, mingling on the ground in a reddish-black pool.

"Done," they each said.

Mordecai held up his hand. "Nightshade, there is no need to consume her soul. She has served me well. Let it be free to go wherever souls go," he requested.

Nightshade wondered if this request meant Mordecai was weak after all, but decided it was only consideration for a loyal ally. "Very well, Mordecai," she said."It will be a show of good faith."

Turning her physical form into a blackish mist, she entered Amberley through the nose and mouth. Amberley's soul did not put up resistance and quickly left the body. Nightshade rejoiced. It had been a very long time since she had worn a mortal's physical body. Mordecai stepped back and smiled as Nightshade made several transitions between her demon and mortal manifestations, testing the conversion and ensuring she had complete control over the process.

Settling into her Amberley form she turned to Mordecai. "It is good," she said. "Let us go and consummate our arrangement, after which we will start making plans to bring InnisRos under our control."

"And after InnisRos, the Svartalfheim," Mordecai replied.

Made in the USA
Middletown, DE
24 October 2016